A Green and Pleasant Land

By

Chris Davie

First edition, published in the UK 2016 by Spider, Meet Fly.

ISBN 978-0-9935397-0-1

Ebook ISBN 978-0-9935397-1-8

Printed by Amazon Createspace.

For Mum and Dad

Chapter 1

Up, up and up it flew. The emerald projectile span as it rose into a scarless, blue sky. It twinkled as it reflected sun-flakes in a shower of sparks as it reached the zenith of its gentle curve. It gathered speed as it adhered to that oldest of laws. Down and down, quicker and quicker. Black smoke billowed from the blazing rag someone had hurriedly stuffed in the top.

Joshua barely registered the faint reflection of himself in the window he was looking through, mouth gaping open, eyes as wide and expansive as the blue beyond. The bottle neared the end of its arc. The line of riot police it was aimed at dropped to one knee and shoved their thick plastic shields towards the sky as if they were defiantly showing the heavens the company emblem emblazoned upon them. The bottle smashed against the phalanx, showering the policeman cowering below with flaming liquid. Where it had hit, the much maligned emblem had puckered and blistered black. Behind it he thought he could just about glimpse a helmet and a face. A split second after the explosion the blast rocked the bus on its suspension. Suddenly he felt like more than a spectator.

'Did you see that?' Anthony whirled around to look at Joshua then whirled back to look out of the window. Excitement lit up his face with a childlike glee that was at odds with the shirt and tie he was dressed in. 'Those bug munchers are throwing petrol bombs at the plastys!'

The police pulled in closely together, nervously watching the sky. A second petrol bomb seemed to signal a new stage in the violence, an escalatory gauntlet, thrown by one side but reacted to by both. The bus driver needed no prompting, the engine revved and the bus inched forwards, nervously crossing into the no-man's land between police and protestors.

On the top floor there was an even mix of impeccably dressed school children who nervously peered out; mothers who held soft young faces away from glass windows; smartly dressed commuters, like them, who watched with interest as though their attire was somehow a shield of civility that the mob below couldn't tear through.

'What is it those idiots are kicking off about this time?' Anthony said. Joshua began to reply but he spoke over him. 'Ah, who cares anyway? Fucking bug munchers.'

Joshua grinned and shook his head emphatically. He undid the top button of his shirt and relaxed his tie a little.

'This isn't on.' Anthony continued. 'You can't tear up the country every time there's legislation passed that you don't agree with.' The police line was on Joshua and Anthony's side of the bus. Even as they passed slowly by, more blue and red vans arrived, their sides bearing the G4ITAS logo. The back doors opened the moment they stopped, more and more policemen fell out and ran to bolster the line. A steady, menacing rhythm vibrated the bus as they beat their shields.

'I thought you didn't know what it was about?' Joshua said.

'This lot are going to get their arses whipped!' Anthony gleefully nodded his head towards the opposite side of the bus. Joshua stood up to look. On the other side was the furious crowd who snarled and chanted and waved placards that read 'Resist Rebuild', or 'Freetopia for power'. One stood out to Joshua, it said: 'Who will feed my child when I can't?' A lot of people in the crowd had covered their faces with bandanas and grotesque Halloween masks. Some were dismantling their placards to reveal sharpened poles.

'G4ITAS will find these lot after today.' Anthony said. His voice had lost its power as if it had spent its venom. Joshua glanced at his friend. Anthony stared intently at the crowd, examining each face as if he would find those he was looking for; lost in a fantasy of unsated rage.

'How are you feeling about the dinner?' Joshua asked.

Anthony shrugged. 'Same shit, different year, I do it for Beth really. If we didn't all meet up for these anniversary dinners then I'd never see her.' He didn't take his eyes off the crowd as he spoke.

An old woman sat on the seat opposite. She wore a threadbare jacket and clutched a handbag on her lap with hands which trembled as though she were cold. She saw Joshua looking over and shook her head sadly. 'Those poor people down there.' She softly sighed the words as though their passing hurt her.

Joshua started to reply as he sat down but Anthony spoke first. 'They're gonna get what they deserve love, a bloody good pasting, just like they did at the election last year.' He cackled nastily.

'Come on, Anthony. Leave her alone.' Joshua frowned.

The woman shook her head again. 'It was like this for your people once, laddie. I remember when I was a girl in the 1980's and the riots in Brixton…' Outside, the tempo of the banging increased. Joshua found himself nervously tapping his foot in time.

Anthony stood up, the low roof of the bus made him hunch over, making him look bigger than he was. The old lady shrank in her seat as if he had physically threatened her. 'My fucking people, lady? I'm as English as you are. Are you trying to say that I'm not welcome here? Why don't you just call me a darkie and get it over with? Old cunt.' The woman looked away, out of the window, refusing to turn back towards them. A middle aged man wearing a suit nervously looked at Anthony and licked his lips. 'What?' Anthony spat at him. He too looked away. Anthony sat back in his seat and looked around the bus defiantly, daring someone to challenge him.

'What did you have to do that for? She was only talking to us.' Joshua said.

'Ah come on Josh, don't get all pissy on me. You've got to play the race card every now and then. It's the only way to keep you white folk in check.' Anthony winked at him.

Joshua laughed. 'You're real dick.' He looked out of the window again. The banging had grown louder and the police had been joined by what looked like a militarised fire engine. 'Here we go. The plastic police have brought in the reinforcements: water cannon.' He said with interest.

'Ah, I'm tempted to get off so I can stay and watch.' Anthony sounded almost wistful.

'It could be arranged, baldy. Those Freetopia people would rip you to shreds.'

'Nah, I'm a minority, the lefties love a good minority.'

'Not one as privileged as you.' Joshua laughed. Finally the bus reached the far side of the no-man's land between the warring factions. They stood so that they could follow the action. Necks craned and people pushed towards the back of the bus to get a better view. The two sides, now facing one another properly, held still as if unsure of the etiquette that governed such a situation.

'Privilege is in the eye of the beholder.' Anthony replied loftily. 'My parents worked hard to leave me an inheritance, you bug muncher.'

Joshua's face reddened, he went to retort but the battle cries behind the bus silenced him.

Chapter 2

'Mum and Dad.' Beth's voice slurred ever so slightly as she raised what was left of her glass of wine. Some of the red liquid splashed up the side and dripped on the table cloth, the stain spreading purple. Her hand trembled as it hung in the air, waiting for the others to join her.

Anthony lifted his glass and gave Joshua a look. 'Mum and Dad.' He rolled his eyes.

Beth noticed and started to speak but Joshua and Tamsin both raised their glasses. 'Devon and Carina,' they both said quickly.

Beth put her glass down and lowered her eyes for a moment. When she looked up she looked directly at her brother. Anthony sat back and coolly returned her gaze. Beth shook her head and looked away, her large, frizzy afro moving independently of her head.

Although it wasn't even ten o'clock the restaurant was all but deserted. One couple sat in a corner, talking intently in hushed tones, eyes never rising from one another. Several waiters gathered around the bar, looking at their watches and yawning. The news had said that the curfew would be in effect until the troubles had died down again, they looked eager to get home to safety.

'I can't believe it's been five years.' Tamsin said. Her voice was sad and distant. She played with a napkin, folding it into small segments and then tearing along the creases.

Beth reached out, took her hand and squeezed it. 'Thanks for coming tonight, Tam.'

Tamsin smiled, her delicate, oval face lighting up. Her hazel eyes shined with un-spilt tears. Joshua noticed how dark the rings beneath them were. 'How could I not come? It was such a shock. I'll never get over it. Devon and Carina were like parents to us.' She looked at

Joshua who looked down. 'I mean…obviously our parents are still alive, but…well, you know.' She shrugged and smiled brightly. The truth of the statement hid behind a veil of pauses.

'Are you coming for a cigarette, Tam?' Beth asked. Tamsin nodded and they both left the table.

Anthony watched them cross the restaurant. 'Is she still shacked up with that loser? He said.

'Mario's alright. Obviously I would've preferred her to marry someone who didn't live on the estate but they seem happy enough.'

'Mm.' Anthony replied.

'Don't.'

'Don't what?'

'You know what. Just don't. She's happy, leave her be. You did enough damage when she was younger.' Joshua said.

'Ah, I never meant her any harm. She's like my little sister too you know.'

'And you'd do that to your sister?'

'Yeah ok. Not to Beth anyway.' Anthony pulled a face. Joshua laughed and took a sip of his pint. They chatted in the pigeon language of private jokes and insults that had sustained them since childhood until the door to the restaurant opened and Beth and Tamsin came back in. The group of waiters followed their progress, commenting to one another in low voices. Tamsin blushed and pretended not to notice, Beth looked indifferent. She was as tall as Anthony and her frizzy hair, which exploded from her head in a blond-highlighted afro, added several inches. Her large frame made her seem bigger than she was and would have made her look unfeminine were it not for her face, as pretty and exquisite as her mother's had been, if not more so. Although it was clearly Tamsin the waiters were talking about, to Joshua, Beth had always fizzed and crackled with a vital energy that people naturally gravitated towards. Tamsin walked behind her, delicate and pretty in a classic way that had always made men fall at her feet, but her timid demeanour meant that once people had seen past her initial beauty she didn't command the same attention as her vivacious best friend.

Beth and Tamsin sat down. Anthony drained his pint and wordlessly held it in the air until a waiter came and took it from him. 'Another.' He said curtly without looking at him.

'Tony, do you have to be such a rude bastard?' Beth said, shaking her head.

'What? He's one up from a fucking bug muncher. Why should I be polite?' Anthony looked genuinely perplexed. Joshua could have told her that it was easier to ignore him but she knew. This was part of the tradition; older than the meal itself.

'Oh, don't start with all that bug muncher shit. Do you know how offensive that is? Tamsin works in a ready meal factory, does that make her one your bug munchers?'

'So what? I'm not picking on Tam, am I, Tam?' Anthony said. Tamsin shook her head without looking up. 'Anyway, wasn't it your newspaper that coined the phrase "bug munchers"?' Anthony grinned, knowing he had won the point.

Beth's caramel cheeks coloured slightly. 'I don't necessarily agree with everything that the paper prints.'

'Ah, but what about journalistic integrity? And there was me thinking that my little sister was going to change the world!' He laughed sarcastically.

'Come on you two, don't start. You do this every time we all get together.' Joshua said. He looked at Tamsin for support but she looked down at the table and picked up the torn serviette again.

Beth didn't look at him. Her green eyes were fixed on Anthony. 'You want to talk about integrity? Really, Tony? You two work for NASRA.' Her top lip curled slightly as she awaited his return salvo.

'See, this is what I never understand about you lefties. You want the world to be a better place and you want the rich to look after the poor but when that happens you get your knickers in a twist. Have you forgotten why we're here? What the bug munchers took from us?' The waiter arrived with Anthony's pint and placed it next to him as unobtrusively as he could.

'Thank you.' Beth said, giving the waiter a bright smile. Her eyes were full of tears. 'As I've argued many times, Tony, our parents' murder was a symptom of everything that is broken in this country.'

Joshua could see that Anthony was getting agitated but he kept his face calm, not wanting to give his sister the pleasure. 'Don't call me Tony.' His jaw tensed, his teeth hardly separating as he spoke. 'That's a leftie cop out. They were murdered by thieving scum. Surely you're not still banging on about bringing back the welfare state? All it ever did was encourage slags to breed and wasters to drink and take drugs.'

Joshua decided to weigh in. 'A lot of people were screwed after they took away the welfare system. It wasn't all about dole money, there were pensions, the NHS…and state education, of course.' He looked at Tamsin, the one whose life had been the most affected after Day X, although she had just been a baby at the time. She had shredded one serviette and moved on to another. He wondered how much of this she was paying attention to.

'Exactly, Josh.' Beth said. 'At least someone understands, but then doesn't that make you worse than him?' She smiled to show that she was joking but Joshua knew when he was being called a hypocrite. She turned back to Anthony and her smile withered. 'The Rebuild Britain party might yet prove to be the nastiest government in our history but at least the Freetopia Movement has their hearts in the right place…' She said sitting back, knowing the reaction she would provoke.

'Come off it, Beth, what are you talking about?' Anthony spat. 'They're attacking our cyber infra-structure, causing riots and they've admitted to assassinating someone. How can you defend that?'

'It seems to me that they've only targeted the guilty.'

'Guilty of what? Banking? Fracking for gas? Opening coal mines in Sheffield? We need commerce and resources, Beth. The country can't operate without them.' Anthony held his hands up in a gesture of exasperation.

'If we invested in green energy…'

'You and your fucking green energy.'

'Why do you have to dismiss anything that doesn't fit your agenda?' Beth leant forward interested, as if she expected him to answer.

'Let's look at an example.' Anthony said as if he hadn't heard her. 'People are complaining because they were moved out of Sheffield to clear the way for the mines, but what right had they to be there anyway? They're all squatters.'

'Well, *Tony*, that's a matter of opinion.' Beth replied acidly. 'Another opinion would be that tens of thousands of people were forcibly evicted.'

'Don't call me Tony.' He said. 'The housing association charges the bug munchers rent, they don't pay it but they stay in their filthy hovels spreading disease and committing crime. They're fucking squatters.'

'Let's look at that shall we, *Tony*? Why are their homes filthy? Because the utilities companies switch their services off. Surely water is a basic requirement for life? Do you think that they want to live in filth?'

'Why do they switch their services off? Because they can't pay their bills!' Anthony snapped back, his lips spreading in a victorious grin.

'Why can't they pay their bills? Because there are no jobs for them. The government has sold or out-sourced anything that belonged to us as a country. The multi-nationals who own everything have squeezed the labour market to a bare minimum to maximise profits. What are they supposed to do?'

The waiter who was hovering nearby chose this moment to interject. Joshua was relieved. 'Sir, your taxi is waiting outside.' He said, talking to Anthony although there was nothing to state it was specifically his. He nodded curtly. 'Josh, why don't you and Beth share this one, you're both going to have to get on the train back to London before the curfew. I'm going to stay in Reading and go and see someone. He lives near Tam so we'll share one in a bit.'

Joshua looked at Tamsin who smiled at him and nodded quickly. Joshua sighed inwardly and reminded himself that they were both adults and it was none of his business. However, a dull flare of anger warmed his belly. They all gave each other kisses, even Beth and Anthony. As they were leaving he looked back and saw Anthony whispering into Tamsin's ear. Tamsin giggled at whatever he had said and whispered something back.

'What does she see in him?' Beth muttered. 'For that matter, what do you see in him?'

Right at that moment Joshua found it difficult to answer.

Chapter 3

'If I'd just been just twenty minutes late this morning that could've been me.' Nigel Warner said to no-one and everyone, from the desk opposite Joshua's. His self-important whine was like driving a crystal nail deep into his already aching head.

'I'm sorry, what?' He snapped, more testily than he had intended. He looked up from the report he was scanning through. Nigel arched his thin, groomed eyebrows with innocent surprise. Although nothing would be said, Joshua knew he would be left out of the coffee run for the next week if he didn't show at least half an interest. He sat back to show Nigel that he had his full attention but it was too late, Lara swept in like a protective hawk.

'Nigel's upset, Josh. For God's sake.' She got up from her desk, next to Joshua's, and made a show of going around to Nigel so that she could put a defensive arm around his slight shoulders. Nigel's lip quivered and crocodile tears filled his pale blue eyes. Joshua mentally groaned while he tried his hardest to look sympathetic.

'I'm sorry, Nigel, I didn't mean to snap.' It was all he could do to not grit his teeth. 'What's the matter?'

'That could have been me this morning.' He sniffed and rested his head against Lara's chest.

Joshua's temper flared. 'You're the most punctual person I've ever met. How could it possibly have been you? Think about Ricky and Francesca and all the others.'

'Oh and I only saw Francesca yesterday… Those Freetapioca people or whatever they call themselves, they're bastards.' Nigel sniffled again as Lara patted his head and looked at Joshua as though he were the devil incarnate.

Joshua thought about Beth's comments at the anniversary dinner, six months ago. He wondered if she still thought so well of the Freetopia Movement. 'We all saw her yesterday. She was at work. We all were. Besides, you barely knew her.' He replied with irritation.

Lara leapt to his defence. 'They used to say hello at the coffee machine…sometimes.' Her voice trailed away. She leant down and whispered to Nigel who sniffled some more and nodded his head. Lara returned to her seat, kicking Joshua's chair on the way. He wasn't sure if it was supposed to be an admonishment or if she was just ill co-ordinated. Either way he didn't care. He shook his head as he buried it back in to the job quota spreadsheet that he was working on.

He had nothing specifically against Nigel, he just found him to be hard work. He was a pathetic man-boy who thrived on drama and had a deep compulsion to make every issue about himself, regardless of whether it was or not. Joshua concentrated on the spreadsheet. The promotion to admin officer in the allocations team of NASRA had given him renewed vigour in a job that had already begun to stagnate. His previous role as a corporate liaison officer to the criminal discard project had been easy but it hadn't challenged him or given him any sense of real purpose. He had felt as if he were responsible for shuttling nonsensical electronic information around a futile labyrinth. The work that he was doing now as an admin officer was more demanding but it also it gave him a lot of personal satisfaction to be working for NASRA, the National Agency of Social Re-Alignment, still a part of the Home Office but a semi-autonomous entity that, to Joshua, was one of the few parts of government that actually meant something for where he was from.

Winning the Wal-Tesc scholarship hadn't just made him feel separated from Tamsin and his family, it had made him stand out from the other boys on an estate where it didn't pay to stand out. While they had all been left to fight each other, and thousands more, for poorly paid jobs labouring or cleaning or any of the other menial tasks that didn't require a person to read or write or think, he had been given the opportunity to rise above them, to transcend his roots. And the other boys had reminded him of it every time he had seen them. For some people that might have given them the resolve to escape the horrors of the estate and never look back, Joshua had been left with a profound sense of guilt. Working for NASRA helped assuage that empty feeling, it was as if he were paying his dues.

The job quota spreadsheet was a weekly set of guidance notes compiled by NASRA. It was Joshua's job to liaise with the human resource departments from the six employment partners in the country who, along with Vircorp News who didn't employ from the Transport Scheme, effectively employed almost eighty five percent of the population. These were the powerhouses behind the industrial revival; mining, agriculture, manufacturing – all the activities that had once been out-sourced to the third world, until the third-world became the new world and began to charge accordingly. The report was used by NASRA to provide targeted labour from the Transport Scheme which was helping to clear the estates, the hostels, the gutters. Joshua was proud of his part.

*

The six o'clock desertion was a sombre affair that evening. Many people knew someone who had lost their lives but even those who didn't were keenly aware that their numbers were short. People had to take tubes, buses, trains, where they would eye each other with suspicion, looking fearfully at any bag or suitcase. Even those who could avoid public transport still had to walk down crowded streets where any common-place box or bin could explode into a thousand fragments that tore, ripped, maimed, killed. A dull fear lurked in the shadows of eyes.

Outside in the colourless street the sky steadily cried grey tears for the fallen whose ranks had swollen as the day had drawn on. Whispers sighed through the office of another twisted bundle found within the torn belly of the tube train that had arrived at Embankment but never left and never would. On social media websites, vacuous prayers were sent as messages to friends and acquaintances of acquaintances. Prayers for the fallen whose fragile flame had been extinguished under the force of a fire that burned much brighter; prayers for the heroes who crept on bellies through gnarled blossoms of torn metal to reach those who hadn't made it to work; prayers for the injured whose blood ran in the veins of the saints, Thomas and Bartholomew; prayers for the brave politicians who refused to negotiate with terrorists.

The streets were a swarm of jostling umbrellas that seemed to deliberately seek eyes to poke and necks to drip down. Electric buses hummed as they surged past carrying grey suits and nervous grey faces. Wheels met puddles and left shocked indignation in their wake as feeble fists were raised and futile threats were threatened.

 Joshua turned left on to Horseferry Road. Usually he took the tube from St James' Park to Whitechapel and then walked from there to Bethnal Green where he rented a pokey box room for an inflated price. Today he thought he'd brave the rain. He reached the river and followed Millbank past Thames House where armed plastys guarded the arched entrance and serious looking men in suits scuttled in and out murmuring urgently into their phones. He passed by Victoria Tower Gardens where shocked figures smoked cigarettes and stared at the sluggish river, and then the dilapidated Houses of Parliament that seemed more serious and dour than ever.

He swerved and thrust his way through the faceless tide of the un-dead. Animation and zest were long gone for most of these lined faces: a soul exchanged for numbers on the sealed scrap of paper that landed on desks every month. The daily tide that would go out, drawn by the gravitational pull of high definition televisions, digital downloads and searching for gadgets, garments and games. Families united by one roof, separated by a cyber void.

He could have crossed the river at Lambeth Bridge and then at Westminster but grim curiosity kept him going towards Hungerford Bridge. He didn't know if it would be open, given its proximity to Embankment tube station, but he had to see. It was the compulsion that slows traffic past an accident, that makes passers-by stop and watch a fight, that presses the play icon on the video that you know will sear itself onto your eyeballs for a long time to come.

Victoria Embankment was closed at the junction with Northumberland Avenue. Beyond the cordon were rows of ambulances, fire engines and police vehicles. All bore the same logo that was on the uniforms of the bloodied, dirty and shocked men and women who rushed past bearing the myriad items that were so vitally needed deep beneath the street: bright yellow oxygen tanks, green boxes of medical supplies, trays of tea. Some shuffled up into the gloom, blinking to clear their eyes, burdened with stretchers carrying tattered, bleeding, blackened rags. Some just stood and watched, their eyes seeing a different scene. The crowd that followed the diversion up Northumberland towards Embankment Place slowed as it passed, each soul secretly relishing every breath its body took.

Suddenly through the forest of black, shiny rain coats, he saw a face that he knew. It flashed for a moment between a tall man in a black suit who held his soggy paper over his head as he loudly told his mobile phone that he wanted sausages for dinner tonight, and an aged but stocky nun who preferred to hold her umbrella tilted to use as a battering ram rather than as protection from the elements. The glimpse was so brief that he wasn't even sure if it was her. The kinky black hair was wild in the rain, her face scrunched and shrugged into a dark jacket against the heavy drops. He pushed past the black suit, ignoring the loud tut and dirty look, the nun charged him with her weapon but he made it through. A bulky, tall figure that matched her shape walked with her back to him. Her hair dripped over the back of her jacket, its uncontrollable frizz sagging under the weight of the water that it held like a sponge. He put his hand on her shoulder still unsure if he was inviting embarrassment. The figure whirled around in surprise, her piercing green eyes crackled with suspicion as they met his and a defensive scowl curled her lip. But then her face softened in recognition, the lips spread in a tired, wan smile, her expressive eyes dilated almost imperceptibly and her cheeks coloured slightly.

'Well, if it isn't Joshua Baker.' Beth said through her smile. 'I hope you're going to buy me a coffee on this rainy afternoon. I could use one.'

Joshua smiled back. 'I might Ms Thomas. It depends if you play your cards right.'

'I know just the place.'

Beth silently led the way. Conversation wasn't possible as they pushed against the human flow towards Villiers Street. They passed the back entrance to the station. Just inside the open door, two armed and nervous plastys guarded a heap of carefully stacked black bags; Joshua's stomach suddenly felt hot and hollow. Beth saw him looking, 'I know.' She said quietly and took his hand and squeezed it for a moment before letting go. The crowd thinned and they huddled together under a small umbrella that she produced from her handbag. A man sat with his shoulders hunched in a doorway, covered in a filthy, tattered sleeping bag. He wordlessly held his hand out, Joshua only saw him when Beth stopped and gave him some change from her pocket along with a smile that shamed the grey sky.

'Poor guy. The police will move him along soon.' She said as they hurried on.

'Where will they move him on to?'

'That's just it. There is nowhere to move him on to. He's got nowhere to go.' Beth replied.

'Things must be getting better though. Haven't you noticed that there seem to be a lot less of them these days?'

'Why do you suppose that is?' She asked.

'Well, it's part of NASRA's work to resettle them with jobs and housing.'

'Hm.' She replied.

They came to a café and Beth indicated towards the door. 'I swear this place does the best coffee in London.' She said as they walked in. The small café was crammed with people trying to escape the rain. Luckily one table was free near the back. They sat down and ordered coffee from a pale, stick thin girl with a pinched, worried face.

'Are you ok?' Beth asked after the waitress left.

'Yeah… it's just…seeing it all laid out like that, the firemen and the ambulances…and the bodies.'

'Yeah I know, it's shocking.' Beth studied the table intently and spoke without looking up. 'I've spent the day down there, not underground of course, I'm only a junior. I was supposed to get interviews with the emergency services, survivors, you know… I felt like a parasite.'

'You were just doing your job.' Joshua replied. 'Freetopia…what are they doing? I mean, I used to agree with a lot of what they did, you know? The assassination of that guy from REW Coal and Gas, the time that they sabotaged the gas power station at West Burton; I thought they had the right idea. But now, bombing a tube train? That's just not on. I think they'll lose a lot of support for this.'

'Hm.' Beth looked up at last. Joshua felt something like a minor jolt in his chest. Before he could interpret the feeling their coffee arrived, steaming and inviting. She waited until the waitress had left to continue. 'You know, several of the paper's more senior journalists and an army of photographers were invited to the scene almost immediately. I heard on the office grapevine that a plastic police escort arrived at Fleet Street within the hour to make sure the press had no trouble getting through the traffic.' They both mused in silence for a moment before Beth continued. 'They will lose a lot of support won't they? It just doesn't seem like them, something seems wrong with the whole modus operandi.'

'The what?'

'The way they did it. Freetopia don't usually use bombs because they're too indiscriminate. They've clearly stated that again and again. Innocent civilian targets as well? That's more like something the IRA or Al Qaeda did; again, not Freetopia's style. Have you heard that they've come out denying any involvement?' She added casually. Her eyes betrayed her words' urgency.

'And that's not like them either is it?' Joshua replied.

'No. They like people to know what they've done and why they've done it. It's kind of the point. I've actually got a friend who's involved with them…'

'Jesus, Beth. Really?' Joshua instinctively lowered his voice and darted his eyes around them to see if anyone had heard her nonchalant statement. 'Be careful, the plastic police are cracking down hard on them and I've heard all sorts of stories and rumours about MI5 detaining people…'

Beth leaned forward on her elbows, her frizzy hair dripped on to the table. 'Go on, I'm listening.'

Joshua laughed. 'There's nothing that I would go on record as saying.'

'You're off record. Come on Josh, let's say I've got an interest in these kind of stories that's beyond the professional. Besides, I wouldn't get that kind of story into print.'

'Of course you would. Everyone loves a bit of corrupt power, that's the kind of stuff that shifts newspapers.'

'Not with this administration.' She laughed easily. 'Did you know that when the old red tops reported the Eye-for-Eye Act vote rigging scandal their sales actually dropped while that story was front page? People don't want to know. Contrast that with the impact that the Kensingate Scandal had for King William; people couldn't get enough of it and the tabloids fed the fire until they got their referendum and we got the Republic of England and Wales. Rebuild could do no wrong in opposition and they can do no wrong in government. This country is peopled by narrow minded idiots who follow the populist banner. We're not trained to think for ourselves anymore.'

'We're not trained to think for ourselves anymore? Come on Beth that sounds like the kind of conspiracy theory that you see splashed all over social media.'

'Maybe.' She replied. 'So have you been to any of these Resettlement Estates that NASRA keep talking about?' She asked.

The turn in conversation caught Joshua off guard. 'Wait, this isn't for your paper is it? I'm not going to find myself quoted by name in the Vircorp Journal am I?'

Beth laughed easily. 'Come on Josh, I know it's been awhile but you should know me better than that. Besides, I'm just a junior, remember? I don't get to write stories for the paper just yet.'

'Yeah ok.' Joshua replied sarcastically.

'Come on, you can trust me. I'd never string you up like that.' Beth gazed directly into his eyes.

'Between you and me, I've heard that the Resets are off limits to everyone except G4ITAS personnel.'

'Resets?' Beth's brow wrinkled.

'Resets – Resettlement estates. Come on Ms Thomas, you're supposed to be the intelligent one.'

Beth pulled a face and stuck her tongue out. 'I have heard that once the Transports go there they aren't allowed out.'

'Really? I'm not so sure I'd believe that, it sounds like a prison.' He replied.

'Exactly.'

'How would they get away with it? No, I don't believe that. NASRA are always going to be criticised for how they are sorting things out.'

'Anyway, you've avoided answering my question.' Beth said.

'What question was that?'

'I believe you were going to tell me about the rumours you've heard.' Beth grinned mischievously.

'Ah I see.' Joshua smiled back. He decided to relent. 'It's not much. I just heard on the grapevine that Freetopia suspects are being…detained under the National Defence Amendments Act.'

'That fascist piece of legislation is the equivalent of an English Guantanamo Bay.'

'Yeah I suppose it is...' Joshua said. 'But if it's going to keep us safe from terrorists…'

Beth snorted and shook her head. 'I don't mean this cruelly, Josh, but I think that you've got a lot to learn.' He went to reply, his heckles up, but Beth smiled sweetly disarming him. 'What are you doing this weekend?' She asked.

'Why?'

'Want to come to a demonstration?'

Chapter 4

The more Tamsin tried to focus on the endless plastic trays of plastic food slowly passing her by, the more she found she couldn't. Her mechanical hand, a rebel against the flesh, robotically scooped a lump of grey protein paste from the chilled unit in front of her and placed it in the appropriate indentation on a tray before the conveyor belt lined up another, and another, and another. The grey pulp had the consistency of lumpy mashed potato but it smelt musty like old, damp books. Away from the conveyor belt a team of cooks, who had the spurious job title of 'chefs', loaded steamer cupboards with trays of writhing meal worms and hopping crickets that sometimes escaped and made a bold bid for freedom across the kitchen floor. Such endeavours were usually ended swiftly by a chef's boot but every now and then one got away. Tamsin wished them all the luck in the world. Bug munchers – that was the slang term for those who lived on the estates, beyond the means to eat real meat. It was a name she hated almost as much as the rancid grey slop she served all day and then went home to eat.

Further down the line, robots like her, wearing matching blue hair nets and blank expressions, scooped up lumps of green vegetable puree and a white substance that had little to do with the potatoes it was supposed to represent. Other robots placed sealed packages of plastic cutlery and sealed rolls of plastic bread. They would be sealed again, packaged and sent out to be sold to the poorest at an exorbitant profit that was still vastly cheaper when compared to the soaring price of 'real food'. It was hard to believe she had been working here since she was sixteen, five years had passed in a flash. She had started in the numb, shocked weeks after Devon and Carina's murders.

'Pssst…hey…girly…' A subtle whisper made her look up. Jenny kept her eyes on the trays and placed a bread roll on each. 'Did you get your wages ok this week?'

Tamsin looked back down at the belt and kept scooping and placing. Her face remained bored and impassive. 'I don't know, I've not had a chance to get to the cash-point yet. They'll probably be short again. Are you ok? How did it go with Bobby's work yesterday?' She spoke in a low voice that was barely perceptible over the mechanical murmur of the belt.

'It's not good. He's only got another week, then...' The sentence finished itself.

'I'm so sorry, Jen. Will you be ok?' Scoop place, scoop place.

'Yeah, we'll survive until he finds something else. Don't worry, girly, I'll be fine.'

Tamsin snuck a look and Jenny beamed back at her. 'Anyway, that's enough about me, you smell the man this morning? My days, I aint never smelt nothing like that.'

Tamsin struggled not to smile and draw attention to herself. 'I haven't noticed. I try not to get too close.' She scooped she placed, she scooped she placed.

Mr Brown swooped on them as if aware by some means of extra sensory perception that he was being spoken about. 'Something amusing, girls?' His tone was amiable enough but Tamsin didn't look up, she carried on mechanically scooping and placing, scooping and placing.

'No sir.' Jenny said. She picked at her earlobe with her free hand.

'Lunchtime is for talking, girls. Alright?' He adjusted his tie and walked on pausing occasionally to glance at the smartphone he constantly carried in his hand. He stopped by one of the refrigerators and leaned casually without looking up.

'Fucking pencil dick shit-head cock sucking twat.' Jenny muttered, quieter this time. Tamsin bit her lip.

Simon Brown was a ridiculous caricature of a man. Tamsin thought that it would be difficult to find someone else who was his equal in physical and mental unpleasantness. He was short, his blond hair was greasy and lank and, although he was in his late twenties, his round face was liberally coated with red and white acne, making him resemble a toadstool. A stale miasma hung around him, a combination of sweat and sour coffee breath that almost made the eyes water. Rumour had it that his father was part of the management team which was the only possible explanation as to how he had acquired such an easy job. He was too physically weak to labour, his mental agility was as lethargic as his body and, as the icing on a particularly sour cake, he was argumentative and given to petty displays of power and childish feuds.

As he saw her looking his eyelid drooped in a foul wink and he blew a lecherous kiss that made her skin crawl. She scooped she placed, she scooped she placed.

Tamsin longed for lunchtime so she could go outside and breathe some fresh air and feel free, if only for half an hour. At least it was Friday, only one more day until she had her day off. Spring was turning into late spring and this February morning had been one of those tantalising tastes of the summer to come. The ready-meal factory wasn't far from the estate so she walked to and from work every day. In the winter this was a terrible hardship, her body quivering as a lubricious Arctic wind tore at her thin coat, threatening to rip it away so that it could cruelly explore the flesh beneath. Now that they were on the cusp of summer she could enjoy the journey again, at least until August's biting winds cut through her once more.

Mr Brown walked away from the belt in the direction of the pot wash, scratching his head then inspecting his fingers as though he expected to find something there. Tamsin shuddered.

'So how are you feeling now?' Jenny whispered. 'You better?'

'Yes, thank you. I wasn't as bad this morning, I'm hoping it's passing.'

'Any word from *him?*' Her voice carried the grimace that her face was sure to.

'No, not since…I realised. It doesn't matter, he doesn't matter.' Tamsin shook her head.

'Are you sure? I mean, could it not be his?'

'It's not, alright? Drop it Jen.' She snapped. Scoop place, scoop place.

'Ok, ok, sorry. It's only because I care. Do you know how far along you are?'

'I'm not sure. I've missed two periods now.'

'No doctor, I'm assuming?

Tamsin smiled at the thought of such a luxury. 'No doctor, no pregnancy test. We can't afford all that. It's just me, my man and my baby.'

'Speaking of who, how is Mario?'

'He's ok.'

'Old Brown will send you down the road as soon as he sees your bump, you know that don't you? It don't matter how many years' service you got, girly. When he works out that you've been doing the do with someone who aint him he's gonna fire your arse quick as he can. Get me?'

Tamsin laughed out loud. 'I've got more to worry about than Simon Brown.' She had laughed a little too freely.

'I HEARD THAT!' A voice screeched from across the kitchen. Tamsin felt a small, hard knot twist in her stomach. The belt juddered to a halt as Mr Brown hit the emergency stop button. He stalked over to the bay where Tamsin and Jenny stared meekly at their hands. It wasn't unusual for him to lose his temper spectacularly. It was a case of weathering the storm.

'I've warned you enough times.' He wagged a fat, sausage-like finger as he stared at Tamsin's chest. He lightly put his hand around her forearm and began squeezing gently and rubbing her with his thumb. 'I won't have distractions on my belt.' His voice sounded strained as if he was struggling to talk and breathe. Suddenly he let go and barked Jenny's name.

'Yes sir.' She replied without looking up.

'Go and tell Anoushka to take over from you. You're leaving us.'

Tamsin looked up in shock. 'But Mr Brown, you can't, it was me…'

'Sir, please. My Bobby's lost his job and this is all we're going to have coming in. Please. I need this.' Jenny's voice choked with tears.

Tamsin's eyes felt hot and heavy. 'Mr Brown, sir…'

'THAT'S ENOUGH!' He roared. 'I make the decisions around here and I will not be dictated to by my staff. Jenny, get out. And someone restart this fucking belt.' He swaggered away, clearly pleased with the assertive manner with which he had dealt with the issue.

Jenny reached over the belt and squeezed Tamsin's hand. 'It's not your fault.' She whispered before a sob escaped. She hurried away, out through the kitchen door. Tamsin stole a look around to see if anyone else was looking, if they'd been affected. No-one had looked up from their work station. Each drone was devoid of emotion. The machine started again.

*

The bang of the front door slamming shut awoke Tamsin from her doze. If she was this tired now how would she be when she was six months gone, or eight? How would she be when the baby was here? She got up, feeling guilty that Mario was only just home. He burst into the front room while she was still trying to extract herself from the ancient, but incredibly comfortable, sofa. He grinned as he saw her struggling. 'Don't get up on my account, it looks like hard work.'

Tamsin smiled back, Mario's huge grin touched every part of his face and was as infectious as it was genuine. When he smiled his warm brown eyes positively glowed and his face wrinkled like a raisin. She felt the familiar stab of guilt. 'How was your day?' She asked as she groggily pulled herself upright.

He crouched to kiss her forehead. 'The usual.' Mario hated his job as a cleaner at the hospital and refused to talk about it beyond the vaguest of generalities. He sat down heavily on the flat cardboard boxes that were spread all over the floor and immediately began picking at a hole. This was a habit that drove Tamsin to distraction. She slapped him lightly around the head then tousled his sweaty, black hair.

'Do you have to do that? You'll be the one who has to go and find more boxes when these fall apart. Or are you going to buy us a carpet?' She grumbled.

'Sorry dear.' His smile spread even wider, which was no mean feat. Tamsin sighed, it was impossible to get angry with him. It had been three years since he had first asked her to go out for a walk with him and one since they had married. Finally she felt that she had worth beyond satisfying Anthony's needs whenever he wanted her or cooking meals for an ungrateful, hating father who berated her at every opportunity. Tamsin understood though. It must be hard for him to be stuck at home in a wheelchair all day, he must get frustrated. She knew his reasons for his unmasked hatred of her and that only made her empathise with him more. The poor man, he doesn't work downstairs and someone else gets his wife pregnant? He must have been furious, livid. Tamsin couldn't even begin to understand how badly he must have been affected and so she didn't blame him for taking it out on her. Nor did she blame her mother; after all, a woman has needs. Sometimes she wondered how much longer her soul would have survived living under the same roof as him. Technically they still lived under the same roof, in fact he was her roof, but that didn't matter. They still lived in the same flats but they hadn't seen one another since the wedding, even then he'd gotten too drunk, too early and had wet himself. Joshua and Anthony had to carry him back up to his flat to sleep it off. She flushed with shame at the memory.

The little flat was exactly the same lay out as the one she had grown up in which was in a way comforting, Tamsin didn't like a lot of change. She saw the place where she was as a happier version of the safe place she had grown up, but instead of the tyrannical father she had dopey, smiling Mario. She pushed away *those* feelings; vestigial flutters for the addiction she struggled to quit. Tamsin put her arms out for a cuddle and he crouched awkwardly down so he could oblige. 'I love you so much you know.' She whispered in his ear. His perpetual grin spread so wide she worried his face would crack under the strain.

'I love you too baby. What did I do to deserve that?'

'Nothing, you're just you and that's enough.'

Mario leapt up, turned around, crouched again and kissed Tamsin's stomach through her t-shirt.

'Your mummy is the most beautiful mummy in the world little one. You are very, very lucky...You're dad aint bad either.' He added as an afterthought. Tamsin squirmed inside and forced her smile wider. 'You chill out here, Mum to be. Put the TV on. I'll do dinner.' Tamsin protested but he was insistent. 'It's ok, your Mum's popping down this evening isn't she?'

'Oh my days, I'd forgotten, I'd better get in the bath.' Tamsin started to get up.

'No you just rest, I'll run it for you while dinners on. Relax, for Christ's sake, woman.' With that Mario smiled and walked out leaving Tamsin to wonder what on earth she had ever done to deserve such a man.

*

An hour later Irene knocked on the door. Mario knew his place and after saying a quick hello he disappeared into the bedroom, ostensibly to listen to the football on the radio but really he was drinking home distilled tatty-water that he'd bought from someone downstairs and smoking some home grown weed that he had lovingly cultivated in the spare room.

'So how are you, love?' Irene asked making herself comfortable. 'Dad says hello...'

Tamsin understood why her mother was always tried to make him sound like a normal parent but she refused to play along with the lie. 'He wouldn't like to hear you call him that, Mum.'

'I know. It's hard for him, Tam, being stuck in that wheelchair all the time. And...well, you know...he always took it out on you.'

Tamsin shrugged uncomfortably. 'I didn't put him in the chair and I didn't make you have an affair.' She blushed violently. It had been a long time since they had spoken about these things. Tamsin decided it was safer to steer the conversation to more neutral waters. 'How's Josh? Have you heard from him?'

'Not in a few days. You know what he's like.' Irene looked relieved to take on the concerned look she always had when she spoke about Joshua. She hated that his life had separated him from them, that she couldn't even imagine him going about his daily business.

'Don't worry about him Mum, I'm sure he's fine.' Tamsin tried to be as reassuring as she could.

'I know, dear, I know. I just worry about him living up there in London on his own. He seems to work such long hours since he's transferred to this job with NASA.'

'It's NASRA Mum.' Tamsin replied. She tried to hide her smirk.

'Well, whatever it is. Don't laugh at me young lady you're not too old for a clip around the ear you know.' Irene gave a small smile to show she was joking. Tamsin was suddenly struck by how rare it was to see.

'How's work?'

'It's ok; there are a lot of rumours going around though. People are saying we might close down. More of these bloody robotics that people keep talking about, they want to automate the whole process. Are they looking for anyone at your place? Or Mario's?'

The concern in her mother's eyes and the desperation in her voice took Tamsin by surprise. 'They definitely aren't looking at my place. They just took two new girls on. I can ask Mario, shall I call him?'

'No, not now love, it's not important. Maybe you can later.'

A knock at the front door interrupted them. Doors out in the hallway banged as Mario went to answer it. Tamsin rolled her eyes at her mother – they both knew how much noise he made. Jenny burst into the room, her face was pale and worried. She sat down and sank into the threadbare sofa with a theatrical sigh.

'I suppose Tam's told you Irene.' She didn't wait for a response. 'Can you believe he actually said that? The bastard... Sorry Irene. So we're both out of a job, no savings, nothing.'

'Jen, I'm so sorry...' Tamsin began but Jenny silenced her with a hand.

'It's not your fault, girly. He's just a bastard. Now look, don't cry, you'll start me off.' Jenny patted Tamsin's leg and squeezed herself up close. 'I wanted to ask you something. I picked up this leaflet, it's for this Transport Scheme that they've been talking about on the news. Basically, right, if you agree to go they pay off any rent arrears, they give you packing boxes for your stuff, pay for all your travel and they ship all your stuff up for you separately. All you do is pack and go to the station and they do everything else. Aint that great? No hassle at all. Then when you get there you get your own flat, the rent's cheaper on it, I did ask about that when I called 'em up, I said "why's the rent cheaper?" They aint pulling the wool over my eyes, but they said that the rent's cheaper 'cos what they do is they block purchase the flats so they can afford to give them to us at a lower rate! You don't have any say over which site you go to so it could be up North somewhere or even Devon...wherever really. They reckon that with my Bobby's experience he can get something on the mines up North no problem and I could go into one of these new factories that they're building. Work, cheap flat, I reckon we should all do it before everyone else gets wind of it. What do you think?'

Tamsin was silent for a moment. Jenny's verbal onslaught was a lot to take in at once. She went to say something in reply but instead burst into tears.

Jenny exchanged a glance with Irene and moved to sit next to her. 'Oh my dear, what's wrong? I'm sorry have I upset you? I didn't mean to it's just me putting my foot in it as always.'

'No it's ok Jen, I'm feeling a bit emotional that's all. I just don't want you to go. It does sound like a good idea if things are that bad. Just make sure you look into it properly.' She tried to smile as she wiped the tears from her face. She knew that her friend had a habit of rushing into things without thinking them through and Bobby wasn't much better.

'*Anyway*, guess who *I* saw today...I'll give you a clue. She's pregnant and it might not come out the colour of her husband!' Jenny squealed delightedly. No-one noticed Tamsin blanch. The conversation descended into gossip about the people who lived in the flats. Jenny's opinionated rants had Irene and Tamsin in hysterics. But however hard they laughed a black cloud hung over them, somehow the laughter seemed a little forced and Tamsin felt an immense sadness growing inside of her.

Chapter 5

The train hit a poorly maintained joint in the track, the jolt shook Anthony awake and he wobbled on his feet. He still couldn't get used to these early mornings, working for a living was a bitch. He tried to peer out the window but he couldn't see past the dense crowd of sombre faced commuters whose heat fogged the windows. An electronic advertisement board above the door to the next carriage scrolled from a high end sports car to holiday villas in the south of France to a designer tailor on Saville Row. It helped to have reminders of what it all meant.

 A flash of something went past that he vaguely thought might have been Highbury and Islington. He'd be at St Pancras soon and then it was a quick hop on the tube to the Home Office and another day of mundane drudgery. He understood that these days you needed a steady job and he even understood that a job with the government was pretty secure; it was just unbelievably boring. He hated every second he spent there. He hated his dour faced, devoid of personality, jumped up manager. He even hated the plastic tasting tea that came out of the machines in the lift lobby on his floor. This was the reward for all those years of hard work. You spent your youth working, studying, sitting tests and exams so that you could earn yourself the right to subjugation that lasted until the merciful release of retirement or death.

Anthony studied the grey faces of the other suits and saw in them the silent desperation that filled him with a kind of dull terror. At what point did you die inside? Was it after you were passed over for that promotion, again? Was it when you realised that you had risen as high as you were ever going to and that now you were just marking time until you got your thirty pieces of silver and a carriage clock? Or was it when you realised with a sick falling sensation in the pit of your stomach that you'd sold cheaply the gift of life and the most fulfilling thing you had achieved was the wank that you had in the shower that morning. By the time he arrived at St Pancras he was thoroughly depressed.

The tube journey wasn't much better. If anything the dourness of grey, living dead faces was accentuated by the glaring artificial light that allowed each wrinkle to tell its individual story of disenchantment and apathy. There had to be something better than this. Something more than this cheerful arsehole who wants me to mind the gap, these tired, worn out people sluggishly pushing and shoving through the crowds to get to a place that they detest to support a life they've given up on; the hideous pollution that sears the lungs when you get to the street or the piercing beeps and horns from the endless torrent of courier riders, delivery trucks and mopaxis. Then there it is, work: louring over you, hungry to eat your hopes and desires. Your ambition and your youth.

The Home Office building was a sad remnant of another time. Garish coloured glass had faded, a once stylish angular façade over the entrance was grimy and broken, one lone and sickly silver birch tree shed blossom tears for his soul. By the time he was in the elevator, Anthony could have cried himself. He knew that he should be grateful, of course he should. He worked then went home and ate dinner. One led to the other, many did neither.

The elevator doors opened and the stifling oppression hit him. Stale air and cheap aftershave that by the end of the day would be replaced by stale air and stale sweat. Helena from admin favoured him with one of her beautiful smiles as she passed him by. 'Good morning, Anthony.' He knew that she did it compulsively just for that hit of self-respect, they all did. Even armed with that knowledge he still felt a stirring in his trousers, better hurry to the desk before the fantasy he had about her last night came flooding back and semi grew to full erection. He made it to his desk in time to avoid embarrassing himself or any of the sweet old ladies with dead eyes who worked on his floor. He opened his emails to descend into his own personal hell of servile banality and obsequious nonsense. The first email he opened dragged his mood down further than he could have thought was possible: a surprise meeting with Jimmy Francis. Twenty minutes ago.

Sometimes he cursed his meteoric rise at the Home Office: four grades in as many years. It was almost unheard of for someone of twenty-four. It meant more money, respect and power, all things that Anthony held dear, but sometimes he missed the days when he could spend half the night drinking, snorting and shagging then come to work in the morning and cower behind his desk in peace. Now he had section leader training sessions, one-on-ones, management workshops and ridiculous early morning meetings with a superior whom he regarded as inferior. *Christ, I need a fag.*

He knocked on the door to Jimmy's office. 'Come!' Jimmy barked. Anthony opened the door and walked in, he had perfected his greeting smile and he unleashed its full radiance on Jimmy who scowled a reply. Jimmy was the principal officer of the logistics division of NASRA – his immediate manager.

'Good afternoon Mr Thomas.' Jimmy rumbled sarcastically in his thick Welsh accent.

Just fuck off. 'Er…sorry, my train was delayed this morning.

'Do you not live in Hackney? Trainline.com didn't report any delays.' Jimmy's gaze was un-wavering. Anthony inwardly cursed his hurried, ill thought out excuse.

'I meant the tube.' He replied, wishing that his fogged-in brain had come up with something a little better thought out that showed Jimmy who was in charge of this particular conversation.

'Hm. Anyway, you're not here to discuss the short-comings of Transport for London. Please have a seat.'

Anthony sat down opposite Jimmy. Cruel artificial light glared off the reflective surface of his large desk which, coupled with the stuffy air in the office, increased his hangover by a factor of at least ten. He resisted the temptation to wipe the sweat that gathered around his eyes.

'An opening has come up under Rick Benson at the Manchester Clearing Station and I need to recommend someone from our team, I think you are right for it.' Jimmy let that sink in for a moment and busied himself looking through a file for some paperwork.

'Well I can't say I'm particularly interested in relocating. What is it you want me to do up there?'

Jimmy closed the file and took off his glasses. He blinked twice, his heavy grey eyebrows falling deliberately, owlishly. 'You'll be overseeing the new Transports as they arrive, making sure they are sent to the right area, evaluating skills, that kind of thing. They need a Senior Executive to oversee things.'

'But I'm only an Executive Officer.' Anthony replied feigning innocence.

'The promotion is part of the deal and it will stand when this post is no longer necessary.'

'Is it a temporary post?'

'Of course it is, Anthony.' Jimmy snapped impatiently. 'The National Agency of Social Realignment can't exist forever because at some point society will be realigned, won't it?'

'Of course.' He replied through gritted teeth. *He wants to watch his tone.*

'If I can be frank, Anthony, I need some eyes and ears on the ground. I'm sure you're aware that between Rick Benson and I, there is some...conflict. I'd like to keep on the ball with what he's up to.' Jimmy's face spread into a large smile, his short temper of only moments before gone.

Anthony understood the terms of this transaction. He'd find some dirt on this guy alright, to cover his own arse. Which of the two section heads was left standing would come down to which one was most likely to further his career. He had enough on Jimmy Francis to cover his back. 'Ok, I think we can come to an arrangement.' Anthony smiled at Jimmy and Jimmy smiled back. As much as he hated his job he loved all this manoeuvring; he should have been a politician.

'Ok, you're going to need to go through some extra security procedures for this role and I'm instructed to get you to fill out some psychological profiling forms that will need to be evaluated, but, all being well, you should be in your job within the month. Any costs you incur from moving will be covered by the Home Office, obviously. Any questions?'

'None that can't wait.' Anthony had a million questions but something told him that Jimmy Francis wasn't the man to answer them.

'Excellent stuff. Shall we go and have a smoke? I don't know about you but I'm dying for one.'

They made their way down in the lift and made banal conversation. Anthony wasn't present though; his mind was drifting through the stratosphere that his career was rising into. His parents would have been proud.

*

Even though it was only Joshua that he was expecting, Anthony liked to make an effort. He got out of the shower and stood appreciating the surroundings in his steamy bathroom wearing a thick, white, fluffy towel and dripping water on to the slate tile floor. He had chosen the fixtures in this room before he'd moved in; the Roman pedestal basin, the antique roll-top bath. He loved the elegant ambiance of this inner sanctum where only he was allowed – guests had their own bathroom. He flicked a chrome switch set into the wall and the opaque window turned clear in an instant, revealing the city that had been hidden. He squeezed the old fashioned diffuser bulb that hung limply from the bottle of specially prepared room fragrance on top of the toilet; a light citrus perfume wed itself to the steam and settled on his damp skin. He frowned then adjusted a slightly crooked charcoal grey towel that hung on the heated chrome towel rail. He smiled at the resulting order.

He studied his freshly washed face in the mirror, squinting to see through the mist. There was a slight suggestion of shadow on his naked scalp, he'd have to shave. First he washed with a scruffing lotion to slough off dead skin and deeply cleanse. Using a rosewood and badger hair shaving brush he lathered thick, creamy soap from a boutique perfumery in Covent Garden, on to his head. He'd found out about this stuff from a men's magazine and now nothing else would do. Only then did he fetch his antique straight razor; stainless steel with a black marble handle, made by a German craftsman. He slowly scraped the sharp blade across his scalp as he had been shown at the lesson he had at the Pall Mall barber shop where rumour had it King William had often gone before his laughable abdication and retreat into luxurious ignominy.

Twenty minutes later, he stepped out into his immaculate front room feeling fresh and good. The wall opposite was largely glass which made the room light and open. The dramatic backdrop of tower blocks, offices, steeples, chimneys and roofs sprawled for as far as he could see. Somewhere beyond, the somnolent river was oblivious to the bustle and rage around her. His black leather sofas formed a U shape around a steel and glass table, handmade by a Parisian designer, he had bought on the internet. On the wall was a huge flat screen television, its dark face perpetually watching back. Anthony loved his home. He felt a lump in his stomach at the thought of renting this place out; someone else loving his things, his space.

A loud buzz told him that Joshua was downstairs. He pressed a button on his remote control and the television flashed into life. Joshua's wide grin and extended middle finger greeted him, taking up most of the screen. Behind him the lobby's understated opulence was pleasing on the eye.

'Stop being a dick. Let me up.' He said tapping on the glass as if he were stuck in the television. The concierge hovered disapprovingly behind him.

'Yeah ok. Have you got Rizla?' He suddenly remembered he had run out.

'Fuck you man, I have to drag my arse all the way over to your swanky bachelor pad *and* supply the Rizla?' Joshua walked away sullenly, shaking his head. Anthony grinned and went to open the door.

*

'What a weak week man. I am tiiiired!' Joshua said collapsing with theatrical weariness into Anthony's sofa. His lips thinned, he hated it when Joshua did that, it left tiny scratches. Joshua knew that he hated it and he knew that Anthony knew that he knew that he hated it, but he still did it; and that wound him up even more. However, to criticise would be to open himself to abuse for the slight obsessive compulsive disorder that he had displayed since childhood and hand Joshua the opportunity to call him "Little Bitch." When they were kids Joshua would come around to play and Anthony would follow him around his bedroom, putting away the toys that he had got out and cast aside.

'How's work? Settling into the new section?' Anthony asked.

'Yeah it's ok, I guess. You know me, Tony, I hate working.' Joshua replied as he kicked off his trainers and pulled his feet up. He studied Anthony's face for signs that he was getting to him but he kept it impassive. 'Skin up.'

'You skin up.' Anthony said grinning as he reached down into the cupboard under a coffee table next to him. In here he kept his leather-cased snorting kit and his mahogany smoking box. He pulled out the reddish wooden box and handed it to Joshua.

'Come on, man, it's your flat. You're supposed to be the hostess with the mostest.'

'Shut your whining and roll one. I'll get some beers… And take your bloody feet off my sofa.' It slipped out, he couldn't help it.

Joshua grinned. 'Little bitch.' However he took his feet down as asked and began rolling a joint.

He was quick in his craft and the end of the joint was already glowing orange and crackling comfortingly by the time that Anthony had returned. He carefully placed Italian leather coasters on the coffee table followed by misty glasses fresh from the freezer and two opened bottles of an imported Russian beer that had been chilled to a fussily correct three degrees centigrade. He had read somewhere this was the optimum drinking temperature for lager and he had purchased a digital fridge for that purpose.

'Smells good. What is it?' Anthony said taking a seat on the sofa opposite. 'Will you please use a bloody ashtray? I'm going to ban you from smoking in here.'

'Little bitch.' Joshua's grin was wide, carefree and stoned already. He leaned over and got an ashtray. As he did a few crumbs of ash dropped onto the sofa, he looked guiltily at Anthony who raised an eyebrow. Joshua gently wiped and studied the surface.

'Sorry mate.' He looked genuinely contrite. 'It's called Bluecheese Haze.' He passed the joint and the ashtray carefully.

Anthony took a few pulls, inhaling deeply. 'Ah, Bluecheese Haze. A pleasant Satvia with cheeky undertones of citrus, blueberry and…my word, is it that mulberry?'

'Indeed my good fellow, how astute of you to notice, truly you are a connoisseur.' Joshua replied. They both burst out laughing. They finished passing the joint to and fro in silence.

'I've got a bit of news.' Anthony said when he had ground out the sticky roach. He'd been building himself up to it.

'Really? Sounds important. Spit it out.' Joshua's brow wrinkled, he had picked up the tension in Anthony's voice straight away.

'I've had a job offer.'

'Ooh, check you out, Mr-High-Flying-Government-Official. Still in the civil service I assume?'

'Of course. You know I'll never leave.'

'Outside of NASRA?'

'No, still within NASRA. It's in Manchester, working for Rick Benson.'

'And you turned it down I'm assuming?' Anthony studied Joshua's face trying to work out if he was joking or not.

'No mate, I'm taking it.' He said quietly. He looked down. Suddenly he couldn't meet his friend's gaze. 'It's a good opportunity…' He knew how lame he sounded, he cursed that Joshua was able to make him feel this way.

'Well, congratulations, I guess. I can't say I'm not going to miss you but if this is what you need to do I understand. I know your career is important to you.' Joshua reached out for the box and started rolling another joint.

Anthony felt his heckles going up. 'Am I supposed to feel bad that I take my career seriously? Maybe you could do with taking a leaf out of my book.'

Joshua laughed. 'I work to survive, mate. I'll leave the career stuff to you.'

'Do you think that because you didn't have to work hard at school it's affected your ambition?' Anthony asked.

Joshua thought about the question while he drained his beer. 'Is that what you think?' He asked eventually. 'You're right, I'm not very ambitious at NASRA but I think that's because I have no interest in the work beyond collecting my pay packet.'

'But don't you think that's sad? Surely there's more to life than just marking your time by your wage slips.' Anthony leaned forward.

Joshua shook his head. 'You, my friend, come from a more privileged place than me. I've never forgotten that I got my education through sheer luck. Without Wal-Tesc and their Social Outreach Scholarships I would've been chasing labouring jobs with the rest of the wankers from the estate, just like my dad before me. For me ambition is getting back through the estate to visit my parents without getting mugged.'

'And when did you last bother to do that?' Anthony asked, enjoying watching the colour creep into his friend's face. 'I've got ambition. I wouldn't settle for being some lowly admin officer. I'm going places.'

Joshua laughed loudly. He caught sight of Anthony's serious face and stopped, then started again. 'Sorry mate, I can't take you seriously.'

'You could never take anything seriously, Josh, and that's always been your problem.'

'Maybe it is and maybe it isn't.' Joshua shrugged. 'But maybe I take the right things seriously.'

'What's that supposed to mean?'

'I take your feelings seriously. I wouldn't mug you off.' Joshua lit the joint and stared directly at him.

'So when have I mugged you off?' He replied. He felt a delicious chill settling over him. He knew what was coming.

'I know you were fucking Tamsin again. You're a selfish bastard, Tony. You do exactly what you want.' Joshua's words stayed in the air as though he had written them in the dense atmosphere.

In a strange way Anthony felt better. He liked lying and ducking around a subject, particularly with Josh, it made him feel in control. But what was the point of a lie if it didn't come out at some point? What was the motivation to behave like a bastard only to have your best work slip by un-appreciated? He thought carefully about how he would answer. Contrition? Defiance? This wasn't about whose turn it was to buy the beers, this could determine how their relationship would fare through the years. That's why it was important to have the upper-hand. Always. 'So what?' His lip curled with an insolent sneer. He wondered dimly how the conversation had soured so quickly.

'Look I'd better be going.' Joshua said abruptly as he grabbed his things and got up to leave. 'Give me a call mate, yeah.' He mumbled as he quickly left. The front door slammed leaving hollowness behind. Anthony sat back and took an angry swig of his beer. *He's always got to make everything about him. He didn't even congratulate me.* He bitterly shook his head and began to roll a joint from the small bud that Joshua had left behind for him.

Chapter 6

Beth hurried over Hungerford Bridge cursing the drizzle that would surely make her hair go frizzy. *This will be the second time in a row that Josh will see me looking a state.* She realised she was smiling shyly and mentally chastised herself. She stuttered down the steps at the far end of the bridge and thought of the horror that must still lie beneath her feet. Usually Beth would have taken the short cut through the station and on to Villiers St but that was still closed off. She turned on to Victoria Embankment and then right on to Northumberland Avenue. Spring's blossoms had given way to fresh buds of green in the spindly street trees that coloured the drab road and made the rain worthwhile.

As she drew near to The Sherlock Holmes pub, her eyes were drawn to a man on the other side of the road. He was wearing a long, tatty winter coat, he was so engrossed in picking through a bin, his head was actually inside it. It was unusual to see a bin at all, they had disappeared from the streets of London when the terrorist threat was from the IRA and they'd stayed away through the years of religious extremism and now The Freetopia Movement. There was always a threat; every generation had their cross to bear. The man pulled himself out of the black hole holding a half empty paper bag of chips. Beth's heart ached for him. She checked her watch, she still had half an hour before she had to meet Josh at Horseguards'. As she crossed the road he stiffly lowered himself to the floor and leaned against the wall of an expensive hotel. His meagre possessions were strewn before him: a dirty flat cap, a tattered grey blanket, a walking stick that had once been part of a fence and an impeccably hand written cardboard sign that said "Victim of progress, please help." His beard was ragged and gnarled and his hair, grey in patches, stuck up at crazy, damp angles. His lined face, grey and worn, played host to soft brown eyes that were wide and vital. He studied his meal of cold chips with a half-smile. The prick of her gaze caught his attention and he looked up. Beth felt uncomfortable, she wanted to shrink away, feeling that she had disturbed his moment of shame but then he smiled; a smile so bright it shone in his eyes, unfurling there a joy and lightness. Even his dirty, pale skin flushed with a healthy pallor and Beth realised that he was far younger than she had first thought. His lips spread to reveal gaps between his teeth. She was impelled to smile radiantly back at him.

'Good afternoon, Miss, can I help you?' He said in a soft Welsh accent that gave the simple phrase a poetic cadence.

His words struck Beth as odd. She reached in her bag for her purse and found a few bancor coins. 'No, I thought I might help *you.*'

'Very generous of you, Miss, very generous indeed, There aren't too many of you left, you know.' The man said as a trembling hand held out the filthy cap to gratefully receive alms. 'It's a tough life on the streets, Miss, 'specially these days.'

'I can imagine it is,' Beth replied softly. 'But why 'especially these days'?'

'Dark days these are, Miss. But nothing a nice young lady would want to know.'

'Maybe I would. You could say I've an interest in dark stories. What's your name?'

'Everyone calls me Happy, Miss. May I ask what yours is?'

'Of course they do.' She grinned. 'My name's Beth.' She felt instantly at ease with this man. There was something safe and comforting in his light. 'Listen, I'm going to get some lunch from the burger stand down the road, can I get you something?'

'That would be very kind of you Miss Beth. I'll have whatever you're having please.' He flashed his beaming smile again. Beth was struck that some faces are made to be sad no matter how happy their owner; others are the opposite.

Five minutes later Beth came back, laden with two greasy burgers with chips and cans of coke. 'Is there room for another down there?' She asked.

'Oh, there's always room for another down here Miss Beth, *always* room for another.' Happy smiled sadly. Beth went to sit down on the cold wet floor but he hurriedly gave her the box that he sat on. They ate in silence for a while, Happy seemed surprised to see Beth tucking into her burger with the same voracious zeal as he did.

'Hungry?' He asked with a grin. Beth shyly nodded as she finished her mouthful and wiped the grease from her lips.

'I love this crap but I don't usually allow myself to eat it. My arse doesn't need any help getting bigger!'

'You're a beautiful size Miss Beth and don't let no-one tell you otherwise. It's been some years since I had lunch with a lady of your beauty. To what do I owe the pleasure? You strike me as a kind lady but you're not having lunch with old Happy just to be nice are you?'

'No, you're right I'm not.' She admitted. 'I'm a journalist and I want to know about your dark stories.'

'I don't really know that a nice newspaper would want to go printing the sorts of dark stories I got.' He smiled slyly, seeming to size her up now that she had stated her purpose.

'Maybe not, but I've heard a few different dark stories lately, maybe too many. You could say I've got an interest in them.'

'That being so, you have to play carefully with the dark stories. Dark stories can have a habit of doing dark things you know. Sometimes when you hear too many they can infect you, like a disease. Make *your* story dark.'

'My story is already quite dark.'

Happy slowly nodded and resumed work on his burger; he seemed to chew Beth's words along with the hot, fatty meat.

'You'll want your notebook.' He said as he finished his burger and daintily wiped his chin with a paper napkin. Finishing her own food she delved in her bag and pulled out her notebook. As she did her copy of Walden nearly fell out.

'When we are unhurried and wise, we perceive that only great and worthy things have any permanent and absolute existence, that petty fears and petty pleasures are but the shadow of the reality.'

Beth smiled broadly. 'This is always exhilarating and sublime.' She replied.

'A very clever man was Mr Thoreau.' Happy said with a conspiratorial wink. 'Did you know that he cheated and would go and stay with his sister when it got too cold out at the pond?'

'No I didn't.' Beth replied with some considerable surprise. 'What do you think he would make of today's world?'

'I wouldn't like to think. However I could hardly be accused of materialism myself, could I?'

Beth cast her eyes sadly down. 'No I guess not…What…put you here?'

'Fate put me here, Miss Beth, and don't you misunderstand, there's no wheres else that I'd rather be. When you got nothing there's not a thing can be taken from you. I get enough of what I need to live by and that does me fine…If life would leave me alone, a happier man you would not find…' His eyes darted furtively around them.

'Who doesn't leave you alone?' Beth slowly opened her notebook as unobtrusively as possible. She didn't want to break the spell.

'Have you noticed that there are a lot fewer of us alls a sudden Miss Beth? Street people I mean.'

'My friend works for NASRA, he thinks it's because they are helping to house people but I'm not so sure. What do you think?'

'There were more of us than ever last winter. Eight years I've been on the streets and I've never seen it that bad. Some nights you'd get to your favourite digs and there'd already be twenty people laid out in boxes. It was getting beyond a joke, y'know? Then, alls a sudden, maybe six month ago, people starts going. Less and less of them anywhere. It was a nice change at first, queues were shorter at the Sally Army and you could find space in the usual digs. Then the rumours started, plain white vans going around offering cups of tea then chucking people in the back. Not those Plastic Police though.'

'Have you seen anything yourself?' Beth asked trying to sound amazed rather than incredulous.

'I have, Miss Beth. Saw it with my own eyes. I was on my way to a building site over near Smithfields, some offices they're doing up. There's a loose bit of fence and some shelter between all the cabins. The security boys knows we do it but they don't mind so long as we're gone by morning when the old foreman comes in and starts bellowing at everyone. Anyways I get near to the site and there's a white van round the side, back door is open and some bloke's handing out the teas. Now, I've been hearing rumours for a while, whispers and black gossip, so I hangs back round the corner to see what's going on. There's about ten street people all standing around, having a cuppa and chatting to two big blokes in tracksuits. I starts thinking to meself that I should go and join them. We gets people coming round with tea and food, helping us out. You can't mistrust everyone and you can't turn down a freebie. I was just about to then I saw someone fall down. It was weird cos for a moment everyone stands there gawping, like they didn't know what to do. Then another goes and another. There's a big old commotion and a few try to run but they didn't get far. These two blokes, they chase them down and just hit them. Knock them clean out. Then they chuck everyone in the back of the van and speed off. It can't have taken more than a few minutes. I tell you, they'd practised that. Anyway I ran off, no way was I going to sleep there. So what do you make of that Miss Beth? Someone's rounding us up like dogs.' A tear sparkled in the corner of Happy's eye. Beth felt an overwhelming desire to take him home with her and let him stay. No person should be left vulnerable on the streets to fend for themselves. She reminded herself to be professional.

'Were there any markings on the van? Did you see the license plate?'

'No I didn't see and it was just a plain old white van. What do you make of all this Miss Beth?'

'I don't know. If you asked my friend he'd say they were taken off to be housed and given jobs.' Beth replied evenly.

 Happy smiled sadly. 'I think your friend might be a little naïve Miss Beth.'

'I think so too.' She put her hand on his arm and squeezed gently, she was shocked at how little flesh clung to the bone. 'I have to go Happy. Do you have any way of getting out of the city? Going somewhere else?'

'There's no where I can go to. Nowhere I'd want to either. London's my home. Once in a house, now on a street but it's still my home.'

Beth fumbled in her pocket and produced a twenty bancor note. 'It's not much but…' She mumbled uncomfortably. Suddenly her throat felt clogged with emotion. Happy patted her hand that still held his arm.

'Thank you Miss Beth. You go and meet your friend now. Is this the friend who works for those NASRA people?'

'Yes it is.'

'Then it's up to you to make him see, Miss Beth. Be his eyes for him.'

'I will, Happy.' Beth got to her feet and walked away. As she did her eyes misted over and she swallowed what felt like a huge, dry lump.

Chapter 7

The green, leafy avenue of Constitution Hill plinked with drips of rain that trickled from the young leaves above to the old, gnarled branches below. The drizzle had ceased for a short break but all knew that it waited on high for its moment to come once more.

Excited conversation bubbled along the busy pavement, drowning out the buzz of the tireless traffic. A river of excited colour flowed uphill. Wide eyed toddlers, swaddled in rain coats, sat aloft on shoulders, bemused at the passing pageant below; homemade banners were tentatively unfurled to proclaim felt-tipped rage. Hurried footsteps from expensive hiking shoes and designer wellies were indistinguishable from those of scruffy work boots and tattered trainers. All feet, however shod, tramped in the same direction.

The urgent excitement of the crowd was rubbing off on Joshua. He looked around, drinking in the carnival atmosphere, a smile fixed on his face.

'So tell me again what this protest is about?' He said, being deliberately flippant. Beth narrowed her eyes as she tried to establish if he was trying to wind her up or not.

'I told you already.' She replied with strained patience. 'It's about the forced transports of protesters after the riots last month.'

'That's it. After the riots last month? So basically we're protesting about a protest?' Joshua grinned inanely, glad to have been able to reduce it to the banal. The scowl on Beth's face soured him.

'It's not funny, Josh. It's bad enough that they're moving around those who are in need of food and work but at least that's understandable. They're forcing people into the same system as a form of punishment for protesting.'

'Maybe those people needed transporting? Do we know what their situations are?'

'It's not really the point. This government is already using slave labour as a way to fix our economic problems, now they're using it as a way to subdue protest.'

'Who said anything about slave labour?'

Beth shook her head. 'What else do you call what they're doing? You've got to stop being so naïve, that's why I asked you to come today. It's about time you and Tony saw what it is that NASRA are doing.' She lowered her voice. 'What you're involved in.'

'So that's why, then. I'm supposed to convert, am I?' Joshua snapped. The crowd around them had become denser as they approached the outer fence of Hyde Park and other tributaries joined the river. He tried to turn away from her but she pushed in so she was at his side.

'Why did you think I asked you, Josh? And if you're not interested then why did you say yes?' She flared, her eyes flashing with temper briefly before softening. 'Look I care about this stuff and I care about you. I know that Tony doesn't really look beyond the end of his own nose but you're better than that.' Her green eyes had darkened to hazel under the shadow of her frown.

'I've always got an open mind.' He said holding his hands up in a placating gesture. The crowd had carried them into Hyde Park which hummed with latent energy. They soon joined a large gathering that spread out from Speakers Corner, filling the paths and spilling onto the grass where people sat on flattened boxes and waterproof jackets to protect them from the sodden ground. People were so densely packed in that it was impossible to see the low black railings that separated the paths from the grass. Beth stood on tip toes trying to scan the crowd.

'I had no idea it would be this busy. I said to my friend, Kane, I'd meet him further on but we can't get there.' Beth's words were all but lost in the urgent babble all around them.

Under a large oak that grew not far from the site of the old Tyburn Tree, a man wearing a black bin bag over his clothes got onto a step ladder and began taking advantage of the crowd that hadn't gathered to hear his quasi-religious, polemical rant. His disjointed voice yelled hoarsely, vying for attention until someone thrust a microphone into his hand. Immediately his unhinged garble sprang from a jumble of different speakers, eliciting grimaces of distaste and cat-calls from the crowd.

'That's his first mistake. Bloody amateur.' Said a voice at Joshua's elbow. He turned to look and found a short, wiry teenager staring at the man with obvious disgust.

'What's his mistake?' Joshua asked loudly trying to drown out the crowd along with the speaker.

'Religion, The crowd never takes the religious nut-jobs seriously. The plastys don't mind them though. It's when people talk politics that they pull the plug and give them a round of batons in the back of a meat wagon.'

'Do you think that's how we should deal with people whose ideas we don't condone?' Joshua replied conversationally with a smile that was only meant for himself.

'Do you?' The boy's eyes were hewn granite and his lip curled in a derisive sneer. Joshua regretted his attempt at play. He tried responding flippantly but the words were snared, foundering on barbs those eyes implied.

To his relief Beth turned back to them. 'Oh, hi.' She said, seeing the boy. 'What's your name?'

'They call me Ky.' He replied. His dark hair and low eyebrows almost met before pinching into an angular nose making him look alert, present. His clothes were shabby: a faded, torn army jacket and dirty jeans. Only his black, military style boots were brand new. His eyes blazed with an intelligent fury that stopped a joke dead in Joshua's throat.

'Well, I'm Beth and this is Joshua.' She said smiling brightly. Joshua automatically put out his hand to shake. Ky returned the gesture with a dirty hand that felt rough and solid.

'I'm pleased to meet you both. Even you.' The boy replied, strangely formal on the one hand yet barely able to contain his scorn. 'Do you have any food?'

'Are you on the streets, mate?' Joshua asked.

'Does it matter if I am?'

'Not at all, I'm just asking.'

'Yeah I am. I come here most days to see what's going on. There's quite a buzz about this guy. I read in the paper that he's the closest The Freetopia Movement has had to a leader since the political wing was excluded from parliament.'

'Is he really?' Joshua replied with interest. 'What have Freetopia got to do with this?'

Ky looked incredulously at Beth who was still looking around for her friend. 'Where did you find him?' He asked sarcastically nodding towards Joshua to emphasise his point. 'Who else would have the balls to stand up to this government?'

Joshua flushed with an anger that ill hid his embarrassment. 'Maybe the majority don't feel there's a problem. Rebuild are an elected government, they're not some third world dictatorship.'

'Well you can tell what side of the tracks *you* were born on.'

Joshua was about to snap a reply when Beth interrupted with an amused smile on her face. A tall, pale man, whose receding hairline held in check a wild, ginger mop, had pushed through the crowd behind her.

'Play nicely you two. Joshua this is my friend, Kane Singfield. Kane this is Joshua…and his new friend, Ky.' She smirked. Joshua returned with a sarcastic smile before fluidly moving into one more genuine for her friend. Kane pushed forward to speak properly to him and Beth started talking to Ky. Kane spoke but it was difficult to hear above the crowd. He tried to focus his attention, not wishing to appear rude but his mind and eyes kept wandering towards Beth and what was turning into an animated discussion with the boy.

'She has that effect doesn't she?' Kane said with a warm smile that dragged Joshua's attention back.

'What?' He said, more sharply than he meant to.

'The young lady is of infinite more interest than this aging reactionary.' Kane retorted with his grin unchanged.

Joshua smiled a reply and looked away to where the religious nut was still being heckled by the crowd.

'Does she know how you feel?' Kane said.

'That's a bit presumptuous isn't it? I haven't said I feel anything.'

'It's written all over your face, mate. I wouldn't worry, knowing her she'd never figure it out; far too self-deprecating for her own good. Not an attractive quality in a young lady you know, they should shout their beauty loud and proud. The world loves a coquette.' Kane drooped one eyelid in a pronounced wink.

'So how well do you know her?' Joshua asked frowning.

'Not as well as you'd like to.' Kane laughed emphatically, throwing back his head. 'Relax my friend, she's not my type. He is.' Kane gestured his head towards a heavy set skin head to their left who held a solemn baby. He caught them both looking and turned away, studying the clouds which had started to release their burden again. The baby watched them for a moment longer before the man pushed away through the crowd.

'Ah I see.' It was only as he relaxed that he realised that he had felt threatened by Kane.

'Do you?' He replied. Joshua was unsure of how to answer.

Just then something seemed to ripple through the crowd, a buzz of excitement. The speaker stopped talking abruptly as he was pulled down from the ladder. An uneasy stillness descended punctuated only by the occasional cough. An ageless man got up on the ladder to a deafening cheer and a round of applause. At first glance his wizened face spoke of a ripe age and a life of hardship, yet his eyes glowed youthfully and he bounced with ill-disguised glee. Silence fell again. The rain increased its intensity, sympathetic to the moment. He turned his head deliberately, surveying the crowd. The only sound was the phlat of heavy rain drops on taut umbrella fabric.

'SPEAKER'S CORNER, CITIZENS OF THE REPUBLIC OF ENGLAND AND WALES; FREETOPIA BROTHERS AND SISTERS. I AM STICKLES.' His strong, firm voice rolled across a crowd that roared its approval. 'WE COME TOGETHER TODAY

THAT YOU MIGHT LEND ME YOUR KIND ATTENTION. THE DARK SPECTRE OF TYRANNICAL TYRANNY HAS RISEN OVER THIS LAND ONCE MORE. THIS TIME, MY CHILDREN, IT IS YOU WHO MUST BEAR THE YOKE OF OPPRESSION AND TOIL UNDER ITS CRUEL MASTERY.' He paused. The crowd stopped breathing. With a flourishing bow he launched breathlessly again. 'THE SIGNS HAVE BEEN THERE FOR MANY YEARS NOW. STEALTHILY, CROOKEDLY, SUCCESSIVE HOUSES HAVE ALIGNED THE STARS AGAINST US. THE RELIGIOUS DIVIDES, THE ECONOMIC APOCALYPSE; ALL PROVIDED THE ELITE WITH EXCUSES TO ENERVATE THE RIGHTS FOR WHICH OUR FOREBEARS FOUGHT. IMPRISONMENT WITHOUT TRIAL; CLANDESTINE COURTS; STATE-SPONSORED MURDER OF THE ORGANS OF OPPOSITION, THE INVESTIGATIONS CARRIED OUT BY THE SAME CORRUPT ORGANISATION THAT COMMITTED THE CRIME. THEY BLINDED YOU WITH THE LIGHT THAT SHONE FROM THE SCREENS OF YOUR TELEVISIONS, YOUR LAPTOPS, YOUR SMARTPHONES. THEY MADE YOU BELIEVE *THAT* WAS WHAT FREEDOM WAS WHILE THEY TOOK AWAY THAT WHICH FREEDOM *IS*.

AS YOU STAND WITH THE TEARS OF THE SKY WEEPING ON YOUR NECKS YOU MUST REMEMBER YOUR BROTHERS AND SISTERS WHO, AS I SPEAK, LANGUISH IN PRISON CELLS, CHARGED WITH NOTHING, GUILTY OF NOTHING THAT THE LAWS OF THIS ONCE GREAT COUNTRY DO NOT ALLOW. THEIR ONLY CRIME WAS TO MARCH PEACEFULLY ON THIS VERY SPOT A MONTH AGO TO THIS DAY. THEIR CAUSE? THE END OF BARBARISM; MODERN SLAVERY THEY CALL THE TRANSPORT SCHEME.' He let that sink in as he raised an accusatory finger and swept the crowd as if looking for the very perpetrators. 'TAKEN. ARRESTED. BUT NOT ARRAIGNED IN ANY COURT THAT I KNOW OF. OUR GOVERNMENT, HANDMAIDENS TO THE GLOBAL CONGLOMERATES, HAS MADE ITS RESPONSE:

THAT OUR BROTHERS AND SISTERS ARE TO BE TRANSPORTED TO THE ENGLISH GULAGS.' Stickles paused his thunderous rant letting his last statement sink into the still air. When he spoke again his voice had dropped to a theatrical whisper. 'WHAT CRIME IS IT THAT OUR LESS FORTUNATE BROTHERS AND SISTERS ARE GUILTY OF? PENURY. IN THESE TURBULENT TIMES ARE WE NOT ALL AT RISK OF OUR LUCK RUNNING OUT? ARE THESE THE TENDER MERCIES WE CAN EXPECT FROM WHITEHALL? TO BE *TRANSPORTED?*' The crowd erupted again apoplectic, thirsty. 'AND WHAT SHALL WE DO?' Stickles cried. Veins stood out on his forehead, spittle joined the rain. 'WE SHALL MARCH. WE SHALL MARCH. WE SHALL MARCH THROUGH THE STREETS AND REVEAL UNTO THEM OUR REDOUBTABLE RAGE. WHO'S WITH ME?'

The air split with a tumultuous bellow, loud enough to be heard in Downing Street. Chants filled the damp air. Stickles started to say something else when suddenly his voice was reduced to an angry whisper that rasped across the crowd. Heads turned in confusion, a buzz flitted from person to person. The very air crackled. The absence of Stickles' fervent rant was as palpable as its presence.

'Technical problems?' Joshua said turning to Beth. Her eyes like everyone else's were glued to the screaming man who seemed somehow physically diminished, as though his aura relied on the means to reach out to the ear.

'I think the police might have killed the sound.' Beth said. Her face was troubled. She attempted a sickly smile. A far off rhythmic drumming made heads crane to see what was going on. Some, sensing danger, were already slipping away across the open park.

Dum dum dumdum, dum dum dumdum, dum dum dumdum.

The portentous beat grew louder. Timid eyes flashed unsure warnings to one another. Panic leapt from face to face, feet shuffled uneasily in puddles and mud. The one drum became many, clattering their rhythm. Joshua found his foot tapping to the sinister beat. Jeers mingled with cries of fear from the edges of the crowd as the columns of police came into view, marching up the broad avenues of the park, penning them in. Some pushed their way out, spoiling for trouble, other pressed inwards seeking safety in the anonymous pack. The crush became uncomfortable as fear, dread and fury wove between the rhythm of batons beating against riot shields.

Dum dum dumdum, dum dum dumdum, dum dum dumdum.

Through the crush of bodies, Joshua caught a sickening sight of the approaching tribe, barely human in their black armour, snarling behind the plastic shields that they menacingly beat as one snorting, growling beast. Black war-paint was streaked beneath equally black eyes, rain ran down helmets and across Perspex visors that separated man from warrior. Each was identical in appearance and thirst. The crowd pushed together obscuring the war party from his view. Dozens of hands holding mobile phones and cameras shot into the air, determined to capture it all.

Unseen hands passed a megaphone through the crowd from person to person, hand to hand until it reached the one it was meant for. Stickles' roar rose again; Lazarus threw off his grave cloths. 'AND HERE THEY ARE MY CHILDREN; THE PRAETORIAN GUARD, THE PLASTIC POLICE. TELL ME, PLASTIC POLICE, ON WHOSE AUTHORITY DO YOU WEAR THAT UNIFORM OF OPPRESSION? YOU ARE THE SYMBOL OF RAPACIOUS CAPITALISM, THE COMPANY WHO DEEM TO OPPRESS UNDER LICENSE FROM A GOVERNMENT SO CORRUPT THEY BARELY DESERVE THE NAME.'

The crowd started chanting meaningless platitudes about not being moved. The police advance halted just shy of the line. Bottles sailed over the divide, encouraging the police to surge forward swinging truncheons, breaking noses before withdrawing to screaming distance where shields were beaten. All the while the crowd were pushed together tighter and tighter.

'MEDIA OF THE WORLD, WITNESS THIS NOW!' Stickles screamed hysterically, his voice cracking. Beth grabbed Joshua and pulled him close to her.

'They'll charge soon, when they do it'll be chaos and we'll lose each other. Get out of the crowd and then walk away, don't run.'

'I'm not leaving you, stay close.' Joshua had to almost shout to be heard above Stickles whose rants had descended into semi-coherent appeals to an online world who would silently watch after the day was lost. Suddenly screams cleaved the air. The loud hissing of a mechanical leviathan pierced the cacophony. The air around them clogged with a chemical cloud that choked Joshua's throat and made his eyes stream. He gasped for air but all he could breathe was the bitter gas which burnt his throat. He clawed at his chest grabbing impotent handfuls of jacket. He heard and felt the sickening crunch as the crowd splintered when the charge came. Bodies fell back on one another. Batons hacked, searching for soft flesh. A teenager staggered into Joshua nearly making him fall, her blond hair was matted with bright blood that pumped freely from a jagged, crimson rent in her scalp; a man in a green jacket clutched a sodden beret while his shattered nose bubbled red mucus as he fought to breathe; an old woman was bent double, clutching her ribs and wheezing silently.

The pressure of the crush was relieved and he found space around him. He tried to grab Beth's hand but he found nothing but corrupt air. He swung his head around but all he could see through his tears was gas, blood and confusion. A hand roughly grabbed his arm.Ky was shouting something at him but he couldn't hear over the cries of the battle. He saw the skin-head who Kane had pointed out, he was sprawled on the floor, his head beaten into an unnatural shape. The baby he had held was still nestled in the crook of his arm. He seemed calm and unafraid of the violence and panic around him, he merely watched with wide eyes that were red and inflamed. Joshua managed to point at him and shout something unintelligible. Ky seemed to understand and dashed to grab the infant. He caught a glimpse of Kane ducking through a break in the line, they hacked and tore at him but he bolted through. Joshua grabbed Ky and ushered him and the baby towards the gap. They made it, but it closed before Joshua could break out. A savage baton blow smashed into his hip making him stagger, a second swiped at his head. He saw the eyes of the beast, wild and rabid behind its mask, before a nebula of purple and mauve stars burst before him. Dimly, he felt his knees give way and another blow smash into the back of his head as he fell. In the darkness he felt the rough pavement scrape his face as the battle wore on above him, away from him. The roar receded as he rolled and floated on a black sea under a starless sky.

Chapter 8

The doorbell woke Tamsin from her doze on the sofa. In her confusion its piercing ring was almost indiscernible from her mother's voice, shrill and panicked as Mario opened the door.

'Mum?' She said opening the doorway to the hall. 'Is everything ok?' Irene Baker's face was blotchy, her eyes puffy and damp. Mario's expression was ashen.

'Tam, why don't you go and lie down again…' He started to say.

'Don't you bloody dare.' She flashed with an anger that made her husband recoil as if she had struck him.

'Tamsin.' Irene said, her voice quavered. 'There are some people from the housing association upstairs in the flat. They say we're behind with our rent and that they have to Transport us. What do they mean? I've been paying it, you know I have. You came with me to the post office to pay last week. I mean, I know we were behind when I was out of work but I paid. Tamsin, please come and tell them I've paid.' The hysteria in her mother's voice was alien to her.

'Of course I will, Mum. Mario, you come too. Let's go and sort this out.'

Although only twelve steps separated them, it had been a long time since Tamsin had climbed them. She fancied she could feel Paul Baker's presence before Mum opened the door. He sat in his usual wheelchair, in his usual place; unshaved, grizzled, gaunt. He slurped loudly from a can of beer without taking his eyes off the visitors who sat calmly watching him back. Foam smattered his grey stubble and an un-suppressed belch bubbled through his chest. An unfamiliar anger rose in her chest at seeing him. When she had grown old enough to understand him, her fear had been replaced by a sense of pity, but tonight she wasn't sure if she was angrier with him or the officious looking trio who regarded her with curious contempt.

'What's the meaning of coming here and upsetting my mother?' She demanded angrily. Paul sneered and growled something indecipherable. Tamsin gritted her teeth against the acerbic comment that she nearly hurled at him. Her fury was new, uncomfortable and cathartic. The three visitors stood to receive her. A large built man wearing a suit that was too small for him; a timid, pale boy who looked like a young girl but wore a man's suit; a steel faced woman whose lip seemed stuck in a curl of disgust as if the wind had changed while she was putting out the rubbish. The big man pulled himself up to his full height and puffed his chest out like an angry bull frog. He eyeballed Mario as if he expected him to leap at him at any moment.

'Well?' Tamsin flashed again while the woman fussed through some papers,

'You must be Tamsin Baker?' The woman said, barely looking up from the rows and columns of figures that quantified human existence into an easy table.

'Tamsin Budzak. My mother isn't going anywhere.' She stated, hoping she sounded defiant. The big man snorted. The woman smiled indulgently as one would to an angry child who refuses to go to bed.

'Mrs Budzak, as I'm sure that you are aware, your parents have fallen behind and accrued a certain amount of debt with the housing association. Now we could evict but the government is trying to avoid moving problem tenants from one place to another…'

'My parents aren't problem tenants. They always paid their rent on time until recently. They've caught up on anything they owed.'

'Yes, it's true that your parents have an exemplary record and that they have now paid what was owed in terms of rent, but I'm afraid that for the six months that they were behind they accrued a sum of some eight hundred bancor in charges that needs to be paid. Do you have eight hundred bancor that you could pay for them?' The woman's voice dripped with sickly sweet sarcasm. Tamsin resisted the almost ungovernable urge to look at the floor but she couldn't stop the shame from reddening her cheeks. 'I thought not.'

'You can't just add a fortune on to the debts. Surely that's illegal?' Tamsin said.

'The housing association guidelines stipulate that we are allowed to charge whatever we see as a reasonable and fair punitive charge, that means punishment dear, and we are also at liberty to withdraw housing assistance at any time, provided we have given fair warning.'

'We've not received warnings.' Irene spoke shyly from the back of the room. Her colour had faded like the wall paper. It seemed to Tamsin that all brightness and life had slowly drained out of this flat over the years, she prayed silently that she would never live in such a sad, joyless place.

'Well we sent four by post. Did you not receive them?' The woman smiled. Tamsin had to crush an overwhelming desire to punch her in the face. That would result in the plastic police being called and who knew what would happen then.

'You know damn well that the postmen won't deliver here anymore.' She snarled, feeling more and more impotent with each second that dripped past.

'All your mother had to do was visit the post office in town. If she had, she would have received our warnings, now wouldn't she?'

'As I'm sure you know the post office keeps office hours which fall when Mum is working. How is she meant to pick her post up?'

'I'm afraid that's just not our problem, Tamsin. Now as I was trying to say, the government don't want to move the problem tenants from one place to another. If we evict them from here they'll end up down at the Grazely estate with the rest of the bug munchers. This is why NASRA are implementing the Transport Scheme.'

'Look, my brother works at NASRA, can't you talk to him?'

'I'm sure he does.' The woman stared, unflinching in her disbelief. The pale boy smirked.

'He does.' Irene piped up uselessly.

'Even if he does, I don't work for NASRA. I work for REW Development who, as your legal landlord, has the right to evict. Downstairs are G4ITAS operatives, contracted by NASRA, who are waiting to Transport all the people from this block who are being evicted. You have one hour to gather what belongings you need. Here is an advice sheet which tells you more about what you can expect from the Transport Scheme. I'd advise you to read carefully the "What will I need?" section. The G4ITAS boys like you to be punctual and they'll be quite insistent that you leave within the hour. That section will explain what possessions and clothes it would be prudent to take.'

'But what about the rest of our stuff?' Irene said forlornly. Her voice was as colourless as the flat. It occurred to Tamsin that there wasn't much stuff here.

'Well your daughter is here. Might I suggest you give it to her? Now, I have fourteen more families besides you to see and every conversation that takes this long means the rest get less time to pack. At this rate G4ITAS will be finishing the job for us. Dean.' She summoned her guard dog with one shrill syllable and stormed out of the small flat leaving a stunned, empty silence. The younger man lingered behind. He pulled a sheet of paper from his jacket pocket and handed it to Tamsin.

'This might interest your man after…you know…' He uncomfortably gestured at her swollen belly as his face reddened before he flitted away after the others. Tamsin stared in disbelief at the flyer he had given her; it offered a one off payment of one hundred bancor to each man who presented himself at the health clinic in town for a vasectomy.

Tamsin's defences crumbled. Heavy, round tears rolled quickly down her face one after another after another. Mario's olive skin had blanched.

'What are we…?' He started to say but there seemed to be nothing behind it; un-planned words that had no purpose other than to uncoil in the void and provoke someone else to fill the stale air.

'What are we what, Mario?' Tamsin screeched rounding on her husband. 'What are we what? Where were you? Why didn't you say a fucking word? You could've…' Sobs tore through her throat and she crumpled against the wall of the dingy hallway. Mario put his arms around her shoulders and whispered gently in her ear. She fought against him briefly then melted against his body. Un-noticed, Irene went into the bedroom, still holding the advice sheet the woman had thrust in her hand as she left. She began packing some clothes. Only Paul remained un-touched. He stared pensively at his hysterical step-daughter, whom he hadn't seen in years, watching her pain with interest.

'When you're done with your fucking banshee-wailing get me a beer.' He said lightly.

*

Tamsin knocked softly on the door to her parent's bedroom as she pushed it open. Being here, in this flat, made her feel small again, she half expected Joshua to burst through the door from their old bedroom, his smile lighting the dingy hallway. *Why aren't you here Josh?* Irene sat on the side of her bed staring at the advice sheet.

'What does it say, Mum?'

'It says we'll be given work according to our abilities. That's good isn't it? They say we'll get our own flat and we'll be given food and everything we need. It says that people of our age won't be expected to work too many hours and there'll be doctors and dentists we can see and it's all free, just like it used to be. Maybe this is a good thing, you know?' Tears spilled from her tired eyes, flooding the deep creases beneath them and making the purple skin sparkle. 'But I don't know where we'll be sent to, it could be anywhere in the country. They say you can come and visit us but how will you afford to? And the baby…' Heavy tears ran over onto her cheeks as sobs choked her voice. 'When am I going to see the baby, Tamsin? My first grandchild, I've been so looking forward…I just…if I could…just hold him…her…just once.' Tamsin knew no words that fitted the moment. She pulled her mother to her, stroking her hair.

*

They heard the escort before they thundered on the door. Urgent shouting and the fall of heavy boots echoed through the stairwells of Beechfield Road. Irene looked fearfully to her daughter across the sitting room. Tamsin tried to smile reassuringly back.

'No need to be sad. It's a new start for us. We'll get out of these flats. I might even stop drinking.' Paul said chirpily as he straightened the tie he had insisted that Mario tied under the collar of his tatty, grey polo shirt. 'How do I look?' He said brightly. Tamsin's mouth dropped open. It was the most cheerful she had ever seen him. She had to resist the urge to slap him.

The door shook as it was thudded again. 'Come on. It's time.' A voice hollered impatiently. Irene stood up. Taking a deep breath she smoothed down her jumper and held her arms out to her daughter. Mario opened the front door and said something quietly to the men in black uniforms who snorted their replies but waited. Tamsin tried not to look at them, their rifles slung casually over their shoulders, their faintly amused sneers; the hated G4ITAS badge. Paul rolled himself out without a word. Tamsin and Irene held each other for as long as possible, whispering words of love and care into each other hair, words that later neither would remember although both would try. Words whose content doesn't matter but whose meaning are worth the world.

Chapter 9

Anthony stood to join the impatient, identical suits who waited in the aisle of the crowded train carriage as it pulled into Manchester Piccadilly Station. The final jerk as it stopped nearly tipped his early evening hangover over the edge and he had to swallow a mouthful of bitter, acidic vomit before it pushed its way out onto someone's shoes. Bodies buffeted his, making him nudge into the next person and the next, like a bleary-eyed pinball, until he half fell through the turnstile at the end of the platform. A frowning policeman with blond hair whispered into his radio with one hand while the other played nervously with the trigger guard of his rifle.

'Excuse me, sir. Could you stop there a moment?' A polite voice spoke behind him taking him by surprise. Another policeman, this one escorted by a hungry looking Alsatian, had snuck up behind him. He turned back and found that Nervous Blondie had silently crossed the distance that had stood between them.

'Where the fuck did you come from?' Anthony slurred with half-drunk bewilderment.

'Papers please sir.' Doggie Copper said, trying to be stern. *These kids look barely out of school.* Anthony fumbled in his pocket for a second then handed over his wallet.

'ID card is in there.' He pulled his posting documents from the inside pocket of his suit jacket and handed them over as well. They pored over his documents while the dog investigated his bag. Anthony turned slightly and let out a silent fart. *Take that, pooch.* He smirked to himself. 'Something funny is it, sir?' Nervous Blondie asked insolently. He didn't look quite as nervous now that his colleague had arrived.

'Yes, I just farted on your dog. Now have you finished with my fucking documents or do I need to have a word with your CO?'

'No need to be like that, sir...to us or the dog...here we are.' Doggie Copper handed the documents back with a smile. 'Have a pleasant evening.'

He liked this guy, he seemed to have a sense of humour, a character trait missing in policemen since privatisation. If it was up to him they'd all be injected with a humour gene when thcy crawled from under their rock and signed up.

'And to you my friend... Sorry dog.' He said as an afterthought. Well, it wasn't the dogs fault.

Manchester Piccadilly Station was like a ghost town. All the retail units that had once lined the terminal were closed down and boarded over except for the ubiquitous fast food shop where policemen leaned on tables outside drinking cokes and eating burgers, their rifles leaned against tables as casually as umbrellas. He was hungry but he couldn't stand the thought of the same old plastic tasting crap that you got up and down the country. McShitTesc, Joshua always called it. He thought briefly about the worrying phone call he'd had from Beth before leaving. He pushed it from his mind; he loved Josh and always would but if he'd shit the bed he would have to sleep in it. He wasn't going to get his hands dirty by bailing him out again. He felt a twist of guilt in his stomach that he hadn't at least dropped by to make sure he was alright and say goodbye.

Walking helped the dense fog to clear from his mind. The station was nearly empty now, the people who had shared the train north from London had all hurried on their way to catch connections, meet drivers, get taxis, beers, whores, drugs. Since the election the Transport Scheme had vastly expanded beyond its relatively humble beginnings as a knee-jerk-policy designed to do little more than gain the popular vote. As the vocal minority opposition, no-one in the party had ever really thought about implementation and the headache that this wild policy making had caused had been dumped on the newly formed NASRA to turn into reality. Slowly, from this embryonic idea, the roots of massive social re-ordering were sunk into society, one frail idea and one tentative suggestion at a time. It had started with burgeoning prison populations being relocated to industrial areas, then the more desperate, lawless areas of the country; now it was being rolled out nationwide as an elective program that complemented the mandatory elements already in place. The real progress had come with the corporations' eagerness to co-operate and fund the project. The gargantuan wheels of change had slowly screamed into life.

Lower land prices and the distribution of resources meant that the industry of the revival was based in the north, making Manchester the main national hub for the sorting, categorising and distribution of the new product - Transports. The corporations, along with NASRA, had set up offices here to over-see the trade and little by little, as the old business' left and the urban poor were re-distributed for their own good, Manchester had turned into a city that served a new market place. "Going to Manchester" had become a euphemism in the civil service for indulging oneself in all the transient pleasures that money could buy and the flesh could withstand. It was simple economics; there were dealers here and dealers south, whores here, whores south, beer here, beer south. But no-one up here had any money so if you wanted to sell vice you could only charge half of what you would in London, which meant that he could have double the fun. A simple calculation that had been instrumental in his decision to take this posting.

He hurried across the concourse in the direction of the main doors, as he did he checked his phone for the email which had his new address. He stepped out into the cool evening and savoured the fresh air; the savage headache that had been gnawing on his brain was temporarily assuaged. He glanced around him and quickly saw what he was looking for, a line of mopaxis waiting in front of a line of plasty trucks. He wandered over to the first one and a teenage boy came running over from a crowd who stood talking and smoking. 'Evening, chief. Where to?' Anthony showed him the address without a word. 'That'll be a fiver, Chief, ok?' Anthony nodded his agreement and climbed onto the back of his moped. The boy handed him a battered black and yellow helmet, started the engine and pulled away.

Anthony tried to take the opportunity to drink in his new surroundings but there were no streetlights lit and the weak moped headlight showed little more than ten feet in front of them. The streets were quiet and dark but in the background Anthony could hear the faint hum and bubble of the city, an almost primordial sound that was independent of the people who lived here. He wondered in an abstract way if a deserted city would still make that low key rumble from force of habit, the metal and concrete structures thrumming as though all the energy and life that had been poured into them had somehow rubbed off. The moped turned a corner and the hubbub grew perceptibly louder. He could start to discern a beat and hear individuals shouting and laughing.

'Oi. What's that noise? Where's it coming from?' He said, leaning forward and speaking to the boy.

'Aytoun Street Night Market, sir.' He shouted back. 'You can get pretty much anything you want down there.'

'Anything?'

'Except for guns sir. Don't get no guns down there.'

'Take me there I want to see.' He demanded. 'You can wait for me and finish the journey.'

The boy pulled over and stopped the moped at the end of the street. Although the music was tantalisingly close and his stomach growled at the enticing aromas of barbequed meat that floated on a warm current of smoke, the street was still empty.

'Do you want me to come with you, sir? It can be a bit much first time round, like…'

Anthony climbed nimbly off the back of the moped. 'I think I can take a walk down a fucking street.' He snapped. 'Look, wait here for me. I'm going to need transport around this place for a while yet, we'll come to an arrangement.' He walked around the corner wondering what floating fairy had made him feel something approaching guilt for snapping at the low life kid. That thought and any others died un-mourned as he turned onto Aytoun Street and saw for himself.

The old, austere, Victorian court house rose bleakly against the cloudless, charcoal sky. Laid at the feet of this grand, yet tatty, old lady was the equally tatty, but not so grand, night market. The stalls spilled over on to Aytoun Street proper but mostly they were crammed together on disused tramlines and what had once been manicured gardens. Barbeques threw blue smoke billowing into the night carrying delicious aromas. On the whole the meat looked of rather questionable provenance but it didn't stop Anthony's stomach from gurgling in case he'd forgotten it existed.

Ephemeral alleys and thoroughfares, formed fleetingly by rows and rows of white tarpaulin stalls, were thronged with people in as many flavours as the food. Men in suits prowled in packs drinking beer from chipped brown bottles, plastic police in their black uniforms swaggered by with rifles slung over their shoulders; prostitutes wearing tiny skirts and boob-tubes picked their way through the crowds looking for work; harrowed teenagers ran with boxes balanced on their heads. A sound system pumped reggae through homemade speakers that made the ground shake, an old, black DJ with twisted, grey dreadlocks nodded his head smoothly as the comically large splif he smoked crackled and glowed. A small group danced before him, swinging their hips and gyrating to the lubricious bass line. Mopaxis ambled through the crowds wobbling as they tried to stay upright at such low speeds, one car nudged its way gently through the throng drawing whispers and a certain distrust that could be felt emanating from all who cast a troubled eye in its direction. The stalls that made streets of the chaos sold everything from engine parts to clothes pegs, bicycles to brillo pads; vegetables to virginities. Everywhere was alive with people selling, eating, haggling, smoking, drinking, buying, laughing, crying, singing, shouting. Existing.

Anthony was smitten. This place fired energy around his body like his blood was incendiary. Its disorganised chaos, its colour, its vibrant energy, he suddenly felt like this was what he'd been looking for. It felt dangerous but more alive than anywhere he'd been before; it thrummed with a latent power that he couldn't describe. He didn't feel like he was in England, it felt like London was far away in another land. This was some other place where staid Englishness had vanished and the people drank beer and danced on the streets. He liked it, no wonder there were so many rumours about people in the service losing themselves up here. He was suddenly hit with a pang of homesickness, but it wasn't home he missed, it was Josh. *He'd love this place.*

He saw a mopaxi meandering through the crowd. It was his ride. He whistled and got the boy's attention. Five minutes later he was sitting on the back and suspiciously picking at some charred bones as they wobbled away.

'Are you sure this is chicken?' He shouted to the driver.

'Oh yes, sir, sure it is.' He couldn't see the boy's grin but he could hear it in his voice. Distrusting, he threw the food away and just had time to see several ragged youths fall on it and each other before they turned a corner and suddenly everything was gone. The light, the smells, the heat; all vanished leaving only the whisper of smoke, the distant beat and chatter of people to remind him it was real.

Anthony held on to the handle behind him and leaned back. He rested his eyes preferring the bright tapestry of his mind to the bleak, empty buildings they passed by. This was going to be an interesting place to get to know. He loved figuring out new places and new situations to see how they could work for him. It was like the first day at a new job. You showed up and you were at the bottom of the pile, the new boy. It was an upward struggle to attain social standing and respect. You had to be strong and clever, you had to undermine people and sneak into the boss' affections but at the same time make allies who would watch your back and, if it was beneficial, you would watch theirs. It was all a game, a battle, and he was a fucking winner. Working out a new area was exactly the same. Who were the dealers you could mess with, who were the ones you showed a bit of respect; where could you get drunk and piss in the pocket of the pool table, where would you get your head kicked in for doing the same; where did you find the whores, how much did you pay them... It was all a matter of understanding one's parameters.

They buzzed through shadowy streets where the street lights hadn't been lit in a decade. It was as though the un-banished night was taking hold with each becoming imperceptibly blacker than the last. After a short time they creaked around a corner into light. The road was lined on both sides by brightly lit buildings of exposed steel, glass and red brick. Signs were outside each offering rooms for the night or long term apartments. They stopped outside a block of apartments called Berkley House.

'This is Trafford Gardens. Hotel Row.' Said the driver. 'Your new home?'

Anthony ignored the question. He took five bancor out of his pocket. 'Come here in the morning, eight thirty sharp. You can be my pet driver.' He said sharply as he got off the moped.

'Thank you, sir. Here.' He rummaged in his jeans pocket and produced a grubby slip of paper with a long number on it. 'My mobile number, sir, night or day. I know the best places if you know what I mean.' He tipped Anthony a wink that could be interpreted in many ways and nodded as if agreeing with himself before driving away. Anthony shook his head with a bemused smile. He picked up his holdall and walked towards the main entrance. A doorman opened the door for him and stood respectfully by as Anthony strutted importantly to the reception desk.

'Anthony Thomas. I believe you're expecting me?'

'Good evening Mr Thomas.' The pretty, young receptionist replied with a smile. 'Your flat is waiting. Your luggage was delivered earlier and has been placed upstairs for you. Is there anything else I can do for you, sir?'

Anthony took the key she handed to him and considered saying something inappropriate but he was too tired to bother. 'No that will be all, thank you.' He slouched off towards the lift; he was going to feel at home here.

Chapter 10

If he clicks that pen just one more time... Joshua seethed. Although if he were to be asked the question 'one more time, what?' he doubted he would have an answer. The air in the small office was oppressively hot. He could feel sweat dribbling down his rib cage across purple and yellow skin. James Francis, Jimmy to his friends, sat on the opposite side of the desk clicking his pen thoughtfully. His chest was prominent like a strangely formal penguin and his chin was slightly raised, possibly so that he could look down his nose at the sorry sight before him.

A week off work had allowed the worst of the injuries to die down, he could now at least walk and he no longer had to stare with dull panic at brownish tinctured urine every time he went to the toilet. However, he was far from healed. An angry, purple scrape across his forehead was still flaky with yellow scabs; his scalp was covered in various hard, knotty lumps that had yet to fully retreat; his left eye was open but only just, a pregnant bulge of bad blood still pushed down on the eye-lid making it an effort to keep open; his torso resembled a patchy sunrise on a cloudy morning.

The aftermath of the riot was still a blur. He remembered being thrown in the back of a van where he had bled on to the lap of a woman who had cradled his head whilst she screamed incoherently. The G4ITAS headquarters had been a fragmented nightmare which his injuries had partially spared him. He had drifted near to the edge of consciousness in a tiny cell with ten other bloodied men who moaned and railed and screamed and shouted. Too tightly packed in to be able to sit down properly, the others had taken turns to stand but his injuries had exempted him, he had needed to lie flat but he had to make do with his knees pushed up to his chest. He didn't know how long they were held for until they were taken out and processed one by one in quick succession by a bored duty manager who looked like he was ticking boxes without paying any attention to the dishevelled procession that passed before him. Several of the men with Joshua were unemployed, they were taken away to be Transported. It was only by virtue of his employment that he was sent away with a caution. He had barely understood when they had told him he was free to go, although even in the state he was in he'd realised that he was far from free. He gratefully left the police station and stumbled around the corner to St James' Park tube but the guard on duty wouldn't let him through the turnstile. He had no money for a mopaxi, his only option was the long limp back to Bethnal Green.

His phone had been taken from him by the police, leaving him stranded in his lonely bedsit. When he eventually found the energy to log on to his emails he found a string of worried messages from Beth. His initial joy that she cared was quickly soured by a sense that she had gotten him involved in a protest that he had no place in being at – a feeling that was magnified now that he was sitting facing Jimmy Francis.

They hadn't even allowed him to sit down at his desk when he had walked in, his line manager ushered him silently through the office past the gawpers and starers. Laura had been at the printer, she stared at him with a curious mix of pity, loathing and glee. He had kept his chin high, made no eye contact and walked with what he hoped was a certain amount of dignity. Or as much dignity as he could muster while still limping. And now Jimmy sat clicking the lid of his pen as if he had to think about what to do with him. A printed out email lay precisely positioned on the blotter in front of him. The Human Resource manager's name was in bold black letters at the top, the subject line read: JOSHUA BAKER ARREST. He didn't need to read what it said below.

'Now then, Joshua, do you understand that membership to these Freetopia people is tantamount to terrorism?' Jimmy said.

'I'm not a member, Jimmy…'

'Today I think I'll be "Mr Francis" to you, Joshua.'

He bowed his head. 'I'm not a member, Mr Francis. As I explained to the police, a friend and I found ourselves at Speaker's Corner by mistake. The pla… The police arrived so quickly and attacked straight away, we didn't have time to get away.'

'Well the police report on your actions is very different, young man. The arresting officer said in his report that you attacked two of his colleagues.' He arched his bushy eyebrows quizzically.

'That's a lie, Mr Francis. I did nothing wrong and nor did anyone else there, since when was it a crime to protest?' The words fell out before he could stop them. They tumbled one after another, effortlessly, as if their weight would have no bearing. Jimmy's frown deepened, wrinkling his brow further.

'Well, Joshua, you are very right, to protest is not illegal. However, the Freetopia Movement were some years ago added to the Home Office list of proscribed terrorist organisations making membership illegal under the Terrorism Act 2000. As you're in the employ of the government, clearly we cannot take any risks whatsoever. The police may have released you under condition of random surveillance but we cannot be so lenient. Joshua I am afraid you are to be dismissed for gross misconduct, taking effect immediately.'

The words hung in the stifling air. Joshua closed his eyes for a moment. He saw himself studying at university, collecting his diploma, starting work. Then Mum and Dad having to go without the money he sent each month and him queuing up for labouring jobs with the rest of the hopeless from the estate. A job is for life. Protect it; so the old advert said. They weren't kidding. He wouldn't get another at this level with a gross misconduct reference following him around, the job market was too tough. His hands felt sweaty and clammy, suddenly his tie was tied too tightly.

'Would you like a glass of water?' Jimmy said nervously. He looked as though the second to last thing he wanted was for Joshua to stay any longer but the last was for him to pass out. He shook his head slowly.

'Jimmy…Mr Francis, I didn't do anything wrong I was just in the wrong place. Please help me, I'll never get another job, you know I won't. Please, I'll take a pay cut, I'll drop a grade, do the filing…anything.' He stared at the man, imploring with his heart and mind long after his mouth had finished.

Jimmy squirmed uncomfortably. 'A job is for life, so they say.' Clearly he'd seen the same adverts. He looked sad, unsure of himself as if he believed Joshua's version of what was essentially the truth but couldn't bring himself to risk his career on his honesty. Somehow that was even more heart breaking. He shook his head slowly. 'There really is nothing I can do, Joshua. You'll be escorted off the premises by security.'

He rose to his feet, his body felt as heavy as a marble statue. The chair behind him fell away making a large clatter. Instantly a G4ITAS guard was in the room grabbing him and dragging him towards the door. The very sight of the emblem on the guard's uniform made his chest quicken with fear. One more guard arrived and they escorted him, wedged limply between them. He tried to avoid the eyes and not hear the whispers. He imagined emails being sent, whispered conversations at the water cooler, gossip about him flying around NASRA at the speed of light. In the lift the guards relaxed their grip.

'So what did you do?' One of them asked as casually as if he wanted to know the time. Joshua looked at him incredulously. He wanted to cry, he wanted to scream in this man's face that he was a victim of injustice, that it wasn't his fault.

'I didn't do anything wrong.' He replied with a shocked whisper. 'Nothing at all.'

Chapter 11

Anthony grunted something unintelligible as he climbed on the back of the moped.

'Good morning to you sir, where will we be going?' The driver said in return.

'NASRA. Go slowly. I've got a fucking hangover.' He growled.

The moped pulled away into the still morning. A heavy gauze cloaked the street and made the air feel chilly and damp. High behind the grey muslin a fierce amber jewel glowed hazily, its heat not yet apparent but waiting in the wings. They picked up speed and rattled through the eerily empty streets. By daylight he could see that his new local area seemed to consist solely of hotels and expensive apartment blocks; accommodation for the business clients who came from all over the country, and indeed the world, to trade with NASRA for Transports. Anthony had heard that similar projects were taking off globally and that a lot of interested eyes were on the Republic of England and Wales as one of the more advanced schemes.

'It's quiet around here.' He said, more to himself than the driver.

'It is, sir. Thems from the companies aren't up yet and thems that work are already gone from round here.'

'What's your name?' Anthony shouted to be heard.

'Browny... sir.'

'Browny, call me Mr Thomas.'

'Thank you, sir.' He shouted back over his shoulder. *There is no helping some of these people.*

A question occurred to Anthony. 'Where is the local Reset?'

'What's a Reset' Browny replied as the moped wobbled alarmingly. Anthony was glad they had the road to themselves.

'Resettlement Estate.'

'Oh I see. South of the city, place called Shadow Moss. You don't want to go there do you Mr Thomas?' The moped swerved as Browny turned to answer.

'No, just curious.' Anthony muttered. He decided to leave his questions about the city until they weren't driving.

The hotel district soon gave way to street after street of mean, grubby looking hovels which eventually gave way to a labyrinthine industrial estate of boarded up shops and empty units with hopeful signs saying "TO LET." Some places had been broken into, the boards covering the entrances ripped off and the inside plundered for whatever the thieves could get. Outside what was once a furniture outlet stood the burned out remnants of a delivery van; an electrical wholesaler spilled its burned out innards onto the car park; a branch of a long dead logistics company had the words "THIEVING BASTARDS" graffitied on the roller shutter doors in four foot high letters. The industrial revival seemed to be something that was happening far, far from this desolate place.

They pulled up outside a shabby two storey building that was bigger than anything else on the estate. Its discoloured walls and yellow plastic trim seemed suited to a past incarnation as a third rate firm selling office supplies, he wondered briefly if the driver had brought him to the right place. A hastily constructed barbed wire fence separated the building from the estate. It bisected the cracked tarmac of the car park giving it an ephemeral feeling, like this was a dream that could only ever be a brief interlude. He got off the moped and stretched his legs. The early morning mist was lifting quicker than the fog inside his head, he'd had too many whiskies lying on his new bed and going over the notes Jimmy Francis had given him before he'd left London. He'd felt lonely and small, the early evening hangover making him emotionally frail. The whisky had helped.

He crossed the car park and approached a gatehouse built from scaffolding and a patchwork sheet of tarpaulin. A teenaged G4ITAS guard checked his ID and papers before sending him to be searched by a guard who held a sniffer dog on a lead. After he was satisfied that Anthony carried nothing that offended, he wordlessly pointed at a door marked reception.

The reception area smelt musty and damp. The carpets were stained, the furniture sparse and the walls were bare of the kind of soulless art that organisations used to brighten their spaces. Anthony felt uncomfortable surrounded as he was by all this ugliness. Already he missed the aesthetic charm of London. This end of the country was an uncivilised backwater, a neglected place that had been mauled by the economic nose dive of the last two decades. A woman sitting at the reception desk unenthusiastically greeted him and waved him towards the only sofa with a careless flip of her hand. Her dull eyes peered suspiciously from behind thick lensed glasses. She whispered into a phone and went back to whatever mundane task he had disturbed her from without looking at him again.

Finally a harassed looking man hurried down the main stairs and went over to the desk. The chatty woman pointed in Anthony's direction. *Who else could I be? Idiot.*

The man hurried over to him. 'Good morning Anthony. I'm Rick Benson.' He put out his hand to shake as Anthony rose to greet him. 'First things first, we start work early up here, seven am, ok?'

He raised his eyebrows in surprise. If this was Jimmy's problematic counterpart he was going to have fun stringing this fucker up.

'Really? Jimmy didn't tell me that, I apologise.'

The man smiled pleasantly enough. 'I can imagine there's a lot Jimmy didn't tell you, there's a lot Jimmy doesn't know. Come with me, I'll show you around.'

They walked up the stairs and into a busy office that was partitioned to create dozens of tiny, cell-like cubicles. Ants that wore suits scurried busily past without looking at him. Each cubicle click-clacked with tapped keyboards, printers buzzed and jittered, conversation hummed as if the power lines above hung too low. The contrast with the lifeless reception jarred Anthony's senses. This place vibrated with a pervading sense of urgency and barely controlled chaos. This was somewhere that felt important.

'Let's go and have a talk first, you need orientating.' Rick Benson said as they walked through. 'Things work very differently up here. You've a lot to learn.'

The far end of the room was sectioned off into individual offices. Benson opened the door to one and they went in. As soon as the door was shut there was an eerie silence and Anthony realised how unobtrusively clamorous the office actually was. The small room was over-taken by a large, but empty, desk behind which Benson sat. Apart from a blank computer screen and a keyboard there were no personal items at all, no photos of a wife or children, nothing to betray a life beyond this operation.

'Sit. Would you like coffee?'

'Yes please.' He answered. Benson called his order through to an unseen minion.

'Ok, Anthony, so what have you been doing down in London for us?' Benson asked leaning back and cocking his head attentively.

'I've been leading a four person team handling name lists for transport, providing the accompanying paperwork, that kind of thing.'

'Ok, so mainly the administration behind the transport lists?'

'Yeah, pretty much.' There was a knock at the door and both men fell silent as a sallow faced teenage girl brought in a tray of coffee. *She'd be worth one if you left the light off.* He favoured her with a smile to which she didn't respond. *Frigid bitch.*

Benson waited until the girl had left. 'Pretty much? What does that mean? Does it mean yes?'

'Yes it does.' Anthony replied. This arsehole was getting to him.

'Good. Did Jimmy tell you much about what your role would be here?'

'Not a lot. He said that I would be over-seeing new arrivals and evaluating their skills, other than that I don't know a lot.' Anthony tried to keep an insolent tone from creeping into his voice but he was struggling.

'Ok, well, essentially that's it. Once a day at around twelve noon you will meet the arriving transport train along with the two other members of your team and the doctors. The Transports come to you individually and you check their names against the list that your replacement in London will have prepared. We ask for specific skills such as manual trades, any qualifications, that kind of thing. You make an evaluation based on that and a certain set of criteria. We don't need anyone older than fifty five, no physical disabilities or the mentally disabled, no non-English speakers, no-one with a history of drug addiction or alcoholism, no-one temporarily ill or hurt. There are special rules for babies and expectant mothers. Don't worry about remembering all of this, it's all outlined in an information pack that I will give to you.'

'Ok, so what happens to the Transports after that?'

'The Valids are taken to the Rainbow Market.'

'The Rainbow Market? What is that?' The cheerful sounding name took Anthony by surprise.

Benson smiled as though this was a reaction he had seen before. 'It's named after the building it's housed in: Rainbow House. It's where representatives from the companies bid on the valid Transports as individuals or blocks, depending on their skills, fitness etc. From there they'll go to the Resets. Some will go to farming camps in the countryside, others to the deep pit collieries or factories. They go all over the place and they are looked after, fed and housed. Wherever possible we attempt to retain family units, it tends to make a happier work force.'

'What about those who don't fit the criteria?'

Benson straightened himself and adjusted his tie. He smiled a grim smile that had nothing to do with amusement. 'The corporations won't touch those who don't fit the criteria so they are humanely discarded.' He paused there, aware that his words needed space to breathe. He studied Anthony's face with interest. He kept his face impassive. Benson let the silence hang, poisoning the air in the office. Anthony could feel tiny pearls of sweat pushing their way to the surface of the skin on his scalp. Fury and impassioned outrage pounded against his ribs, threatening to tear their way out. A coherent thought would have done no justice to the feelings he had; feral emotions that defied attempts to confine them to words. Eventually, mercifully, Benson moved on. 'Unfortunately, Anthony, we no longer live in a society that can afford to support its surplus. The government, in its wisdom, is using one of this nation's weaknesses to fix one of its other weaknesses. We are using our burgeoning poverty to rebuild the industries that were given away to foreign markets in the name of short-sighted globalisation. In that model there can be no space for crippling compassion. I take it from the look on your face this is the first you have heard of the Discard Program?'

'Yes. I mean, there were rumours but no-one took them seriously...' Anthony felt like he was replying through a thick cloud. His words felt soft and unreal, as though this conversation were a strange dream.

'How do you feel about it?' Benson replied. 'I need people who are onside for the exciting changes that we are bringing to this country. It's not easy I know, I realise that it takes a little getting used to, but understand this: people are starving to death up and down the country, is it more humane to just let them die? Or if we open our dilapidated coffers and feed everyone, what happens then? The fragile economic recovery collapses and everyone is in the same boat. There are too many to feed and by not acting we condemn ourselves to the same fate. Anthony we are on a precarious life boat of economic recovery, if we allow ourselves to be swamped by the infirm and morally corrupt we shall all drown.'

He took a deep breath to say something, to berate him for his lack of humanity and scream his revulsion but something rang true. Something in this monstrous revelation, and the part he was expected to take in it, made sense. He felt giddy and sick but something felt right; something felt right.

'Think about it Anthony.' Benson purred soothingly. He opened a drawer and produced a bottle of twenty year old single malt whisky along with two glasses. As he spoke he carefully poured a couple of fingers into each. 'When I was first told what was going to happen I wanted to punch the minister who had told me, I'm guessing that's how you feel about me. Its ok, don't answer, I understand. It's an entirely human response to feel that way, to want to protect your fellow man in whatever gesture you can, however futile. I've read your file Anthony, I know about your parents. They weren't victims of poverty they were victims of murder, right? Of course that's how you feel and anyone would. But the reality is that they were direct victims of the disease of want that has settled over this once green and pleasant land. Their death was symptomatic of the state of play. We need to clean up and realign society in such a way that tragedies like yours are no longer common place, where people don't have wants that can't be filled. The economist Thomas Malthus said: "The power of population is so superior to the power in the earth to produce subsistence for man that premature death must in some shape or other visit the human race." Society can't operate along the lines that it previously has, there are too many of us, in the country, in the world.'

'So would you describe yourself as a social-Malthusian?' Anthony asked.

'Not at all. The social-Malthusian ideology is one of non-intervention. Their strategy would be to let poverty's sick theatre play out to its inevitable conclusion. No, what we're doing is pragmatically embracing what the Malthusian catastrophe means and dealing with it accordingly. We're acting for nature in removing the weakness from our species. As part of a globalised system we could support the numbers we had, we could provide employment and we could even provide for those who couldn't, or wouldn't, work. But we no longer live in that same globalised world, we can't afford to. For too long we have been trying to play catch up with economies such as America and China when in reality we are a tiny country with a fraction of the resources. We're chasing the ghosts of a colonial past. It's the same with all the European powers. Europe is desolate, we priced ourselves out of the race too early and now we're paying for it. The death of the Euro, the second global economic breakdown and Day X; it stretched too many budgets too far and we haven't got a pot to piss in. The surplus needs to be taken out of our society, governance leaves no space for compassion. So, how do we achieve that from a sober, pragmatic perspective? If part of society needs to be taken out of the equation which part should we take? The educated part that works hard for our economy, spends and obeys the law? Or the group that leeches from the state provides nothing and murders law abiding citizen such as your parents in cold blood?'

Anthony took a sip from his drink and relished the burning sensation, it tethered him to reality. He felt confused and troubled yet deliciously cold and vital. Finally he spoke. 'Can I just get a few things straight here? First: you want me to decide who lives and who is... discarded based on some arbitrary set of rules that you've come up with. Second: this is a process that has already been happening for some time and third: this is for the good of the country, including those who we are *discarding*. Have I got it about right?'

Rick Benson took his time before answering. He held his whisky and swirled it around before smelling it and making a show of revelling in its aroma. Anthony guessed that this was a tactic designed to let his mouth run away from his mind and talk himself into a corner. He kept quiet, waiting for the older man to finish his dramatic rigmarole and answer him. 'I guess that's it. You've summed it up well, but you've over-simplified. You're missing the point that these people are ultimately doomed. We don't live in a society of plenty where they can be looked after. There is a place for a labour force and that labour force will be self-replacing. We shall take steps to ensure that levels are kept at a constant, but we cannot have a surplus. What we do now may seem monstrous but posterity will teach those who come after us that it was a necessary, and even humane, thing to do. We have to craft our society into a shape from where it can grow to strength, like a tree that has been pruned in the right way. We need to learn lessons from nature and accept that we are still very much a part of it; the fittest, leanest, most adaptable species will survive – not the species that tends to its diseased, rotten elements like those were desirable traits.'

Benson stopped as if controlling the fervency this cause so obviously raised in him. It gave Anthony a moment to think. As brutal and distasteful as it was, Rick Benson was right. There *were* too many people, that much was undeniable. People *did* routinely starve to death on the streets of London, Reading, Birmingham, any major city. The homeless patrolled the streets in droves searching for their next meal or some shelter for the night. As much as Anthony thought these people were scum, the dregs of society, he also recognised that they were no happier than the populations they terrorised. Maybe it was for the best if those elements were taken out so that England could move forward? Maybe this was what they had needed all along?

'Ok, Rick, so how does this play from a legal perspective? There can be no way that this is legal under English or international law, so as a perpetrator where would this leave me?'

'Come, Anthony. The Eye-for-Eye Act showed that the REW appetite for soft governance had come to an end. The public had long clamoured for the death sentence to return and now they wouldn't have it any other way. As a government employee you are exonerated from responsibility, you followed orders that were given to you. Anthony, we live in a different world to the one that held countries responsible for its wrong doings. Look at America and their Immigrant Control Bill, it's little more than an excuse to round up anyone who's not been naturalised. South Africa and the formation of the United Southern African States, they're systematically ridding the continent of anyone white. Israel and their push to end hostilities in the Palestinian enclaves, it amounts to ridding their land of Palestinians for good. It's happening everywhere. We are just being practical about our weaknesses and acting on them. The UN is an ineffective, anachronistic entity that was conceived to make the world a better place when it was a better place. Its finger of blame is pointing in too many directions now to make it settle anywhere. Today we live in a time of geo-political Darwinism; the strong survive and the UN is little more than a puppet in the hands of the superpowers that use it to perpetuate the kind of oppression that it was supposed to stop. You show me a country that is playing fair these days and I'll show you one who can afford to support the work-shy and those incapable. In nature if you can't feed yourself you die and so it will be here.'

Anthony took a few seconds to let this last diatribe sink in. The warmth of a logic he could understand gently gripped his heart. 'Ok then Mr Benson, but you're going to have to look at what you're paying me.' He said with a smile. 'I might have some ideas that could be of use to you.'

Rick Benson smiled; it was the first genuine emotion he had shown since meeting Anthony. 'Good man, that's what I need; ideas people. Jimmy said you'd be good for this role, I rarely listen to the idiot but it seems that on this occasion he was spot on.' He held his glass up to Anthony, he returned the gesture.

Chapter 12

The hot sun, making its first real appearance of the summer, acted as a magnet on the middle class population of London. Drones left their hives and swarmed in Green Park to eat sandwiches in the sun. Dowdy office women shed their suit jackets and undid a blouse button to become ephemerally transformed. Skin glowed with a healthy flush; shoulders un-hunched from the dual dreariness of work and winter; hair was shaken loose of its shackles to let the sunshine caress it and tease out tones that hid in the dark winter months. Smiles lit sad faces and made wrinkles into laughter lines. The loose-tie brigade was in attendance; the young men who unashamedly gawped, the old who guiltily stole glimpses of women half their age, the single whose eagerness was repellent, the married who hid their rings. For the first time since yesterday's meeting with Jimmy, Joshua smiled.

It felt good to sit on the grass, mildly damp though it still was from the morning dew. He had managed to get a good spot before the lunchtime hoards had descended brandishing cups of coffee in gaudy paper cups and plastic sandwiches in plastic packaging. Almost all available space was taken now, with the exception of the small private rings that surrounded each enclave, big or small. These inviolable spaces between were secured against invasion by side-ways glares or even a sharp sucking of the teeth. Joshua chuckled. *You can take away the name Britain but we're all still so very British.*

His eyes were drawn to a woman who looked at him over her book. She sat with her knees up to her chest, her bare feet sunk into the luxuriant grass. One hand held a copy of Moby Dick, the other held her flowing white skirt to her thighs, protecting her modesty. Raven curls tumbled over her pale, slight shoulders and her bright orange top. Her rich, coffee eyes met his, she responded in kind to the smile she'd correctly assumed was for her.

'Spare any change?' A sharp voice broke the connection. She looked away, as if scanning the park, then back at her book. Joshua turned to the voice's owner with slight irritation.

'What? Oh...It's you...' His surprise came out as disdain.

'Don't sound too enthusiastic.' Ky replied sarcastically. 'You can sit here and enjoy the sights if you like but you need to do as I say.' His eyes darted around settling on the curly haired woman. He still wore the same army jacket, shiny boots and scowl that he had the day of the protest.

'I don't *need* to do anything.' Joshua replied sharply. He disliked looking up at the boy. 'The last time we met wasn't the happiest of occasions. Whatever it is you think I need, I can assure you I probably don't.'

The boy smiled, it was the first time Joshua had seen him do so. It was a pitiful affair that looked uncomfortable on his pinched face. The scowl suited him better. 'What about if I told you that it was a message from Beth and Kane?'

'Is it?'

'Would it make a difference?'

'The last time Beth asked me to meet her I got beaten up by a pack of mercenaries and I lost my job. You could say she's not on my list of favourite people right now.' Joshua said.

'It wasn't her fault was it? Jesus, why is she bothering with you? The longer you argue the worse it is. They're following you.'

'Who are?'

'Santa and his fucking elves.' Ky shook his head. 'NASRA, you fool.'

'Why would NASRA follow me?'

The boy's eyes flitted suspiciously around again. 'You need to give me a few coins and wait until I leave. Then get up and walk to the corner of Caxton St and Broadway, near the tube. Can you manage that?' Joshua went to rise to his feet in anger. 'Sit your arse down and do as I say, you idiot.' Ky growled. Fury flashed in his grey eyes. Each red blood vessel stood out, burning itself into the incandescent background. He reached into his pocket, took out a few coins and dropped them into Ky's outstretched hand.

'Ignore your dick and stay away from curly locks, she's your trail.' He said casually before putting the money in his pocket and doffing an imaginary cap. 'Much obliged.' He sauntered away across the park. Joshua followed him with his eyes as he stopped now and then to ply his trade. Some ignored him, some passed him a few bancor without looking in his direction. None noticed his eyes, recording and filing every detail; scanning, searching, seeing so much more than was there.

Why the hell should I do what some kid says? But he knew that the kid was just the messenger. When he was out of sight he got to his feet and stretched, as he did he watched the curly haired woman out of the corner of his eye; she didn't look up from her book. *It's paranoia, he's lived on the streets for too long.*

He ambled through the park, stepping carefully around people. It was close to two o'clock and the lunchtime sun worshippers were starting to miserably drag their feet back to gloomy offices which would look all the more dull for the fleeting escape. Joshua felt a twinge of jealousy. He walked against the growing crowd, out of the park and towards the old palace. He passed by the long queue of tourists that snaked out of the old parade ground, waiting for a glimpse at the fabulously opulent remnant of another era, a different world. Outside the tall black gates stood the timeless guardsmen in bearskin hats that looked so plush that he longed to run his fingers through it in a shock of kinaesthetic delight. These guardsmen were as synthetic as their bearskin hats. At the end of a shift spent looking dead ahead with unwavering eyes, they changed out of their uniforms and into civilian clothes. The Household Division, whose job it had been to guard the monarch, had been disbanded years ago along with the monarchy itself. At the time Joshua had been among a minority who were sad to see them go. To him the monarchy, no matter how parasitic, had represented a national identity that had been irretrievably lost. The endless stream of traffic roared past him as he ambled down Buckingham Gate. A thousand purposes and missions tied up in the rushing and roaring mopeds, the delivery vans, the cars, the bicycles. Fumes and soot poured into the air and mingled with the cloying stench of blat; the illicit, backstreet fuel made from cooking fat and used engine oil that coughed from the back of most mopeds. The government knew all about blat's existence and its toxic effects on air quality but it was seen as a necessary evil, a release of some of the economic pressure caused by skyrocketing petrol costs. Sometimes he hated this city. He looked about to see if he could see the kid but he was nowhere around. Someone caught his eye as he looked behind him, it was the curly haired woman from the park. *Coincidence.*

'That's a beautiful smile for a man with a black eye like that.' A voice said from beside him. 'Carry on walking. Don't look at me. It's Kane.'

'Why did you want to meet me?' He said keeping his eyes fixed on the back of a man in a suit who walked in front of him.

'Beth said she doubted you'd listen to the boy. I can't be seen with you in public so someone's going to bring you to me separately, after we take care of your trail.' Kane replied.

'The boy said someone was following me. The woman with dark hair, behind?'

'Yeah. They've been following you since you were sacked.'

'How do you know I was sacked?' Joshua said.

'Because I've had someone following you too.'

'What the hell?' He exclaimed. 'Why have you had someone following me? Why has someone else? What does everyone want with me?'

'You were a NASRA employee who was arrested at a Freetopia protest; believe me, they've got a keen interest in you as have we. Besides… your Ms Thomas insisted we look after you.' Although he didn't look, the grin in Kane's voice was unmistakeable.

'*My* Ms Thomas?'

'*Your* Ms Thomas. The lady wanted me to use my…influence to make sure you were ok, we knew that your job was over when you were arrested so I had our mutual friend check up on you.'

'Our mutual friend? Do you mean Ky?' Joshua said.

'Yeah. It turns out that the boy has an ability to be invisible that comes in useful to me. In return I'm looking after him and his new companion.' Kane laughed.

'He has a companion?'

'Of sorts. All this would be better discussed elsewhere, Josh. Can I call you Josh?'

'Yeah, why not. Where shall we go?'

'As I said, you can't come with me. Wait here while I walk on, a mopaxi will stop in a sec and pick you up. The rider will take you to meet me.'

Joshua stopped walking. Kane's figure, dressed all in black, walked on without missing a beat or looking in his direction. He watched him walk away and turn down a side alley. He looked to his right as casually as was possible, the curly haired woman had stopped to look in a shop window. The human flow passed around her as a river does a rock. She stood, twiddling her hair between her thumb and forefinger like an absent minded child. *Surely not her? She's beautiful.*

Suddenly a hand thrust from the crowd and grabbed at her bag. She span around, her teeth barred in a snarl, the crowd cleared around a ragged teenager wearing a tattered grey t-shirt and black shorts. He let go of the bag, something glinted in the sun as he hit out, catching her in the chest. She fell down, red instantly staining her top, clashing with the orange, as she stared at the wound in subdued dismay as though all she was concerned about was that the colours clashed. The crowd rushed to her, the boy snarled and jabbed at them with his knife keeping them away. He ran and jumped on the back of a moped that had just pulled into the kerb; timed perfectly, executed in moments. Joshua stood in stunned shock as people began to scream and shout. Suddenly he felt vulnerable and guilty. The confusion was watched by interested passers-by, London street theatre that the river of mopeds slowed to see. One pulled into the kerb, the driver pushed up his black visor. It was a dark skinned, older man with a missing front tooth.

'Josh? You need to get on.' The man hissed urgently.

Without thinking about it he jumped on the back, grabbing at the handle behind his seat. The moped sped away weaving in and out of the traffic, weight swinging from one side to the other as the rider threw the bike aggressively around the other road users. Soon they were clear of the snarl and heading away towards Victoria.

They pulled into a side road and the rider stopped at the kerb. 'Put this on.' The man said passing Joshua an eye mask.

'What? I don't need a blindfold.'

'Rules is rules, mate. Put it on. Kane's orders.' *Kane's orders? Who is he?* He put the mask on.

'Here.' The rider handed him a spare crash helmet that was hooked over one handle bar. He put the helmet on over the mask, it felt like his head was cocooned. The man pulled away quickly taking Joshua by surprise. He slipped backwards and had to throw his arms around his waist to stay on.

'For fuck's sake, take it easy.'

'Yeah man, whatever…' The rider chuckled as he crunched a gear change. Joshua didn't share his amusement.

Deprivation of one sense serves to hone those that remain to a knife edge, heightening every sound and every smell, every twist and every turn. A thousand pin pricks of dust were driven into his face. Horns blared, their sound elongating as they passed him by. The rushing air from passing vehicles made it feel as if they missed him by a fraction of space; unexpected corners made his body bend like a sapling in the wind. Eventually the bike slowed to a stop.

'We're here. Keep the mask on.' The rider said. Joshua did as he was told but gingerly lowered his feet to the unseen road. Delicious relief shivered through him. Hands and a soft voice guided him across a path, up one slight step then more steps, in through a door, catching his foot on the frame, then down more steps into what had to be a cellar. Finally he was guided to a seat and the helmet and mask were removed.

Light flooded in, stinging his eyes and making him blink. He scrunched them shut, balling his hands and jamming them into the sockets involuntarily. Slowly he let the offender in, opening cracks and testing the brightness.

'Better?' Asked Kane. Joshua opened his eyes fully. His mind's eye had formulated a dusty industrial unit, warm and grimy. This was a tastefully decorated, middle-class kitchen in a basement flat. He let his surroundings sink in for a moment. Kane gave him a moment, seeming to understand that he needed to settle. They sat opposite one another at a large, glass table. The cupboards and work-tops were trimmed with a brushed aluminium finish that was fashionable at the moment. Subtle down-lights flooded the basement with a warm, almost natural light.

'Nice place.' Joshua said at last. 'Yours?'

'No. Cuppa?' Kane's eyebrows arched with the question. Joshua was struck by the expressiveness of his face. He asked with all his features.

'Er…yeah. White, two sugars.' He replied. Kane nodded emphatically as if this most mundane of questions was as he had expected. He turned away and busied himself filling the kettle. 'Was it you?' Joshua asked.

'Not me personally. Nor was it I who ordered it. Those decisions aren't down to a mere minion such as myself…thank the Gods. Is it an act that you disagree with?'

'Yes of course I do. She was a young, pretty girl…she was stabbed in broad daylight.'

'And what part of it bothers you Josh? That she was young and pretty? Or that it was broad daylight?' Kane poured water in the cups he had prepared and stirred the tea. Joshua watched transfixed. The commonplace task seemed absurd next to the ghoulish conversation. He felt uncomfortable, angry; he felt complicit.

'That she was hurt at all. Just because she was following me.'

'All I can say is that is not how I like things done. However, she is…was, the enemy and we are at war.' Kane handed Joshua a hot cup of tea and sat down opposite him.

'She quite probably worked for NASRA, so did I, So does Beth's brother. Does that make us the enemy too? It was her job. She was doing as she was told.'

'Does the fact that a person has been told to do something remove their responsibility for their actions? A person's level of involvement determines where they stand on this particular battlefield, Josh. Yours was never very high reflecting your ambition. Others become collateral damage.'

'So does that make Anthony an enemy? Someone who it's fair game to stab in the street? He's Beth's brother and my best friend.'

'Josh, in this dirty war nothing is as it seems. Beth understands that, as will you. But these are details we'll get to. Tell me, what did you see as your job at NASRA?'

'Hang on. Are we just going to brush that girl away? For fuck's sake, Kane, she might die. Don't you care?'

'Of course I care about someone getting hurt but I'm just an actor in this play, as are you.' Kane's voice remained even and calm. 'Now, please, Josh. What did see your job to be?'

'Admin, compiling lists, names, addresses, financial histories…that sort of thing.' He replied defensively.

'No, no. What I mean is how did you see your role in the wider picture? In the context of the country in its entirety.'

'I guess I saw myself as helping. I came from an estate and I was lucky enough to get a scholarship and escape, but that was pure luck.' Joshua said.

'It wasn't pure luck. Surely it was your intellect that got you the scholarship? You had to work for it.' Kane leaned forward, his eyes searching. They were powder blue, almost grey, but warm and animated. His genuine curiosity was inviting, Joshua had to remind himself to be guarded.

'Of course. But I could've just as easily been over-looked, someone else could have got it in my place. My point is that I got out but others didn't. NASRA are helping those without work.'

'Ok. So it's safe to say that at heart you felt it was the right thing. Now, what do you think of the Freetopia Movement's position that the Transports are in fact slaves?'

'I can't agree with that, Kane.' Joshua shuffled uncomfortably in his chair. 'Of course they're not. They're given work and are repaid with food and shelter. How does that differ from earning a wage to spend on what you need to survive?' Joshua was irritated, he had to remind himself that it was no longer his responsibility to defend NASRA against these petty charges of exploitation.

'A slave is defined as someone who is owned by and has to serve another. It's that ownership, that lack of freedom that makes the difference. If you're paid money you have the choice to shop where you want, to spend your money on what you want.'

'The entire country is owned by a handful of corporations. How much choice do any of us really have?' Joshua replied.

'That's a fair point. It could be argued that we are all enslaved to a certain degree and I think I would agree. However, what I'm referring to is a little more direct.' Kane replied calmly, taking a sip of his tea. 'Have you heard of the Rainbow Market?'

'The Rainbow Market? Sounds like a colourful place.'

'Very funny Josh.' Kane seemed annoyed for the first time. 'The Rainbow Market is where Human Resource representatives from the corporations bid on Transports as if they were cattle.'

'No I've never heard of that place but I knew that the corporations were expected to pay NASRA a resettlement fee for each unit... I mean person.' He corrected himself.

'Exactly Josh. These are people, not units.'

'Of course, it's just office speak, it doesn't mean anything…'

'Of course…' Kane took another sip of tea and let his words brew before continuing. 'People, are being bought and sold as commodities. They're made to work for no benefit other than the vitals they need to survive.'

'But survival costs money, it's right that people should work.'

'Of course, this is the way our society is set up. But who should receive the money that the vitals of life cost?'

'Well…the company who produces the goods consumed.'

'Like water? How can such a vital resource be sold?'

'But it needs purifying, processing…that all costs money.'

'Ok, so we pay for a service. But are we paying a fair representation of what that service costs or are we in fact exorbitantly billed for that which nature has provided? What about food?'

'What about it?'

'Is it right that someone owns and sells something that grows wild in nature? A self- replicating animal or plant. Are these goods to be bought and sold?'

'Of course. Animals cost money to feed and produce.'

'Tell me, how did they do before man came along to feed and produce them? What about grain?'

'Well someone has to grow it and harvest it.'

'Does that not happen as part of natural process? If you wanted to could you go and purchase some seed and sprinkle it on the ground and grow it to eat?'

'Well, no because I don't own any land.'

'Should land be owned by anyone? What about the seed that you would have had to buy? Should that be owned?'

'But the grains have had to be modified and selected to produce a genetically superior product. That cost someone money.'

'Does that give the people who carried out those processes the right to own a grain? To patent a type of grass so that no farmer on the face of the planet is allowed to plant their seed without paying them? These grains feed the livestock as well as us. Effectively one company owns the entire food chain. Do you think that's right? That life itself is a commodity?'

'I don't know...I...'

'Joshua, we're getting off the subject. What I am trying to say is that, yes, to a certain degree we all live in a cycle of slavery. Property is theft by the strong and the weak are made to pay. But these people, these *Transports,* are being held in physical bondage purely because they couldn't pay the bills.' Kane grimaced. 'One of the reasons Beth wanted my help is that there is something that you need to know. Your parents have entered the Transport Scheme. It only happened a couple of nights ago. Your sister managed to get a message to her. She's very upset.'

'What? My parents? But how? Mum works…'

'I know. Apparently they had some late payment charges from a period when she was out of work. I'm sorry. So how do you feel about the Transport Scheme now?'

Joshua felt like he was going to throw up, a sharp pain stabbed him in his stomach. The whole conversation seemed now to have been a protracted ensnarement, a moral tangle designed to hog-tie him. Tears made his eyes throb.   'That's not fair Kane. That's not fair at all.' He felt faint. The tears started to fall now.

'Josh, I don't want to upset you but you have been working to these ends, giving yourself the moral loophole that you're doing a good deed but you've been helping to rip families apart and send them to the four corners of the British Isles to be incarcerated on estates.'

'Incarcerated? But they're allowed to leave…' A hot rock sat in the pit of his stomach. He swallowed hard, hoping he wouldn't vomit.

'Don't be naïve Josh. They've been purchased; do you really think they're free to wander? They've been sold. Their purchaser, if they have one, is not going to want to risk his investment.'

'What do you mean 'if they have one?' Everyone is given work.'

'I hope so Joshua, I really hope so.'

'What's that supposed to mean.'

'Nothing. Look, we're getting off the point.'

'What exactly is the point?' He snapped.

'The point is that you have been sold a half truth. As I said, nothing is as it seems.' Kane leaned forward, his eyes pleading. 'Joshua we need help, so do your parents and so do you.'

'Why do I need help?'

'You've lost your job. Without help what will you do?'

'Get another one I suppose.'

'Get real Josh, you're not a stupid man. Jobs don't grow on trees. You'll be dragging a gross misconduct dismissal around on your E-CV forever. There's no getting away from it. Without help you'll end up either chasing labouring jobs or on a Resettlement Estate.'

'So what are you saying?'

'I can offer you room and board at my place. Freetopia will cover a little pocket money and expenses. In return you'll be expected to help us…gather information. We have a plan to free the Transports and still provide work, but we need help. Your help.'

'Why me?'

'Because you understand how NASRA works. You're in a unique position to help us and help the country. Everything they've told you, Josh, everything they've told everyone: it's all lies. The masses are lobotomised with plastic goods, plastic media, plastic ideals. We've become plastic people. There's no political awareness, no social conscience. We don't see past the ends of our own noses. We've let a succession of right-wing governments ride roughshod over rights that were earned in blood over the course of many generations. And what did we throw them away for? Ipods, laptops, four by fours, cheap energy, dirty fuels, plastic fucking reindeer that crap jellybeans when you wiggle their tail, devices that tell you if your beer is cold enough, USB pen-drives shaped like dicks; life has become vacuous and we have with it. We consume at a rapid pace with no thought for the consequences, the Freetopia Movement intend to change all that.'

Joshua's head was fuzzy with the clutter of half remembered conversations with Anthony; things that he had read and seen; questions he had asked. He wasn't sure about what this man was saying, or if he could even trust him. One thing did ring true, he had next to no money, no job and he wasn't going to get one in the near future. Whatever this was it might be his only option other than going back to the estate. 'What if I said no? What then?'

'Are you going to? You need to understand that the girl, she died.'

'What's that got to do with me?'

'I'm afraid that NASRA will already be looking for you. Joshua, I'm sorry. I just follow orders.' For the first time in their conversation Kane looked uncomfortable.

Joshua took a moment to compose himself, to breathe and settle before his reflexive scream of rage could fly from his throat and attack. 'I've been set up, haven't I?'

'Yes.' Kane replied quietly. 'But for what it's worth it's for your own good as well as the greater. I didn't know that was what they were going to do.' Joshua shook his head. Bitter rage coursed through his veins, he tried to speak but he couldn't. Kane spoke for him. 'You'll stay with me. It really is your only option.'

'Could I leave if I wanted to?' Joshua finally found his voice.

'You'd be arrested in the hour. Stickles likes to stack the odds in his favour.'

'And this had nothing to do with you?'

'As far as I knew we were bringing you in to persuade you to stay. I had nothing to do with the attack on the NASRA woman.'

Joshua studied Kane's earnest face. 'Ok then.' He replied with a sigh. 'But you might want to keep me away from that old bastard Stickles.'

Chapter 13

Anthony wondered what it would be like to sleep next to a woman. It was something he had rarely done in all his twenty six years. This was a fact that he would brag about in the pub, usually when someone had to leave early because of a troublesome wife or girlfriend. He would laugh and say that he never had those problems; hc always left before it dried on the sheets. Tonight though, he wondered what it would be like to share the night with her. As was his habit, he threw stones in the mill-pond of his imagination, but tonight she refused to break apart into disparate reflections. What secrets would he share in their dark, warm cocoon? What parts of his labyrinth would she find by deconstructing the walls he had built brick by brick? Would she like what she found? Would he? He shoved the thought away. This was reality, right here. There was no point in imagining anything other than this empty, sweat-soaked bed in a soulless hotel.

His relationship with Tamsin had smouldered slowly for so long that it was a part of each of them; something as intrinsic as the colour of their hair or their skin. Her making cow's eyes at him as he played with Joshua, him speaking louder when she walked into a room, becoming conscious of how he might look to her. Their early forays into the world of sex had of course been with each other and much earlier than was probably appropriate. Sleep-overs where they'd giggle under the covers, showing each other what they had to show while Beth and Joshua slept innocently on his bedroom floor, stolen fumbles avoiding their mothers' suspicions and then, of course, the first time for both of them. Eventually she'd wanted more of course, and then what had always been their special secret, their forbidden fruit, had rotted and turned sour. But then that was the beauty of a secret liaison, wasn't it? When it's a secret no-one has to know that you're a shit. She was better off with that Lithuanian ponce Mario, he was welcome to her. But habits can be difficult to break and they had both struggled to forget.

His resolve broke. He had promised himself that he wouldn't drink tonight, he needed to be fresh for the morning. It was all too much. *Just a drop.* He sat up and turned on the bedside light, the soft glow brought disorientation and a pang of homesickness. He blew on his sweaty forehead to cool himself and got up. He padded to the kitchen in his boxer shorts where he poured whisky over chunks of ice that steamed and fractured like a glacial crust. He plumped up the damp pillows on his bed and lit a cigarette. The smoke filled his lungs in its familiar and comforting way, he didn't care about the dull pain he felt there. He savoured its presence before slowly voiding them. A drink and a smoke reminded him he was a man and not some scared little boy whose mum would come running if he screamed loudly enough. *There wasn't enough air in the world to scream that loudly.*

He coughed smoke like a dragon; it felt like it was tearing his throat apart. He swallowed a large gulp of whisky to anaesthetise. He grimaced as if swigging medicine. *It is medicine. My medicine.* It anaesthetised more than his throat. Tomorrow was the first day on the platform. Only with the familiar and comforting warmth in his belly could he admit to himself that he was terrified. He wondered what would happen if he refused, if he just didn't show up and headed back down South. For a start he would lose his job and never work for the service again, that was for sure. His E-CV would register a gross misconduct. He'd never work at anything worthwhile again. All that education, wasted. He wouldn't be able to keep up the mortgage payments on his flat and within a year he would probably be on the platform anyway, just on the other side of the clipboard. And there was the adapted version of the official secrets act that he had signed in Rick Benson's office earlier. Underneath the usual guff was a new line that wasn't in the paperwork he'd signed when he had initially joined NASRA: THE ACT OF ABANDONING VITAL POSTS OR PASSING SECRETS OR INTELLIGENCE TO ANY ENTITY OUTSIDE OF OR NOT AUTHORISED BY THE GOVERNMENT OF THE REPUBLIC OF ENGLAND AND WALES CONSTITUES A TREASONOUS ACT. And that was that. What it didn't need to state was that treason was one of the offences that came under the Eye-for-Eye Act.

You couldn't argue with the underpinning logic, something needed to be done. There were simply too many people to support, numbers needed to be reduced. The fragile economy couldn't support all the bastard's that the feral under-belly kept spawning. There was no getting around it, if they didn't reduce numbers then nature would. Besides, if it came down to that then who knew what would happen, those Freetopia idiots might actually get enough support to fuck up the system and that couldn't happen. *Christ, we could wind up with some egalitarian communist state where everyone was called comrade and fed a bowl of fucking rice a day.* No-one wanted that. The corporations would leave overnight and the entire country would be unemployed. England would eat itself within six months. It would be like a return to the Stone Age, a savage, undeveloped brave new dawn. As a government employee he had to do his duty how he saw fit, no matter how repugnant he might find it.

His first week had been interesting and challenging. He felt for the first time in his life truly out of his comfort zone. He felt alive. A lot of his time had been spent getting to know his colleagues at the Manchester Satellite Office. They mostly seemed alright, there were a few boys who seemed up for a laugh, a few jobsworths who he would find time to crush and a couple of women who he would inevitably sleep with. Fortunately everyone seemed to like a drink so his social success could be assured. Two nights ago he had gone out drinking with the two men he would be working directly with, Paul Rice and Raj Bueller. Paul was from Taunton and had been in the North for a couple of months; Raj was from Camberwell in London and had been there since the project began testing a year ago. They'd had a good laugh and gotten riotously drunk, which always endeared anyone to Anthony. They had given him the low down on the office: who was a twat, who was a grass, who was easy, who was uptight. They finished the night by sealing their new bond at Selina Petrov's, a brothel legendary throughout Manchester and beyond; Paul and Raj were regulars. They'd been treated deferentially from the moment they walked in the door. Paul had explained that a source of unofficial income was commission from the eponymous Selina on the prettier Transports who they sent to her instead of the Rainbow Market. This was the closest they came to talking about the job. Now, as he lay awake, he wished he'd asked the real questions. How did you cope with a woman going mad at you because she was sent one way and her husband another? How did it feel when you looked someone in the eyes and stamped their paperwork with a D for discard? He understood that you called the plastys to deal with the physical threat but what about the threat to your sanity? What did you say when someone asked what D stood for? How did you sleep at night knowing that the people you had discarded…the thought was open ended, refracted into its elemental emotions through the exquisite prism. Anthony shuddered, sleep was far away over a black horizon. He took a deep drink of his whisky and lit a cigarette from the previous one. As he did he noticed how badly his hand shook.

*

Paul and Raj were waiting outside Manchester Piccadilly station as they had agreed. 'How are you feeling this morning?' Raj asked cheerfully. His wide smile reached his bloodshot eyes. Raj was a bulky man, broad and tall with a considerable paunch. His light brown skin and soft eyes had maybe given him an appeal when he was younger that he still tried to play on wherever possible.

'Yeah, I'm ok thanks mate.' Anthony lied.

'Are you feeling alright about all of this?' Paul asked. He was wiry and short but his face was angular and attractive. 'Don't worry about it, it feels strange at first but then after a while you just get used to it. Just keep reminding yourself that it's a shit job but someone's got to do it.' Anthony said nothing.

The cavernous main concourse was eerily still, even the fast food place was quiet today. Somehow it made him feel better. Disused retail units, boarded up sentinels, lined the sides of the station. One had the boards taken off. A dark sign above told that it had been a tie shop, once a common part of any train station, now it lay empty. Anthony wondered if Stephenson had selling ties in mind when he had invented the Rocket.

They walked over to the former tie shop. Raj unlocked the door and opened it. Inside was a small waiting area in front of three small cubicles, partitioned with rough, unpainted plywood. Mildew stained hospital curtains hung as makeshift doors.

'Ok, here's how it works.' Said Raj pushing his chest out. 'The Transports are lined up outside on the concourse, the plastys take care of all that, it's not our problem. They are called forward in groups of nine, six wait in here and three come into the cubicles. He moved over to the left hand curtain and pulled it back to reveal a desk with a chair on both sides and another curtain at the rear. On the desk was a computer monitor, keyboard, mouse and a tray for paperwork; other than that the room was stark. 'They come in and sit down. You check their name off against the list that is updated daily in the shared folder. Just make sure you mark them with either a D or a V. If it's a V you write any relevant work experience in the comments box to pass on to the boys at the Rainbow Market.'

'Discard or valid?' Anthony asked; partly to double check, partly to show he wasn't completely green.

'Yep, spot on.' Raj replied. 'I'm sure Benson went through all this but I'll say it again, no-one over fifty-five no matter what, the companies won't take them. They took everyone in the early days, just like the public were told, but soon they realised it wasn't profitable, that's when the discard process was introduced. No-one with any disabilities, either physical or mental and no single mothers or their children; we can't take people who can't look after their offspring. If Dad's there and he can go to work great we'll take them, if not, discard.'

'What about unaccompanied kids?'

'Hm, most of the time you would discard them but keep an eye on the quota counter on your desktop. Each time you mark a Transport as valid the quota counter for the day goes down by one. When it reaches zero we can't take any more. After that everyone is discarded, regardless of skills. They can only deal with so many Transports at the Rainbow Market, we found that if it was flooded safety became an issue. You don't want too many of them kept in one place for too long, they get itchy and then they have to be controlled. They're given a questionnaire to fill out on the train; place of birth, previous experience, qualifications, disabilities, family; that kind of thing. If they're valid the stamped paperwork is passed on to the Rainbow Market, if they're discarded we keep it for our records. With regards to the computer system all you have to do is mark the Transports presence and the outcome.

'So what happens to them at the Rainbow Market?'

'I wouldn't have a clue, mate.' Raj said. 'Look, what happens to them when they leave here is not our fault, our problem nor our business. Our job is to decide if they can be of use and that's it. Where they go, what they do…not our problem. Moving on, the doctor will give the valids a quick examination which will ultimately determine what stamp they get. After that they send them out back.'

Raj moved through the cubicle and opened the curtain on the other side; here were three more cubicles and two doors in the back of the shop; one painted blue and one painted green. 'The valids get sent to your doctor's cubicle for checking, discards go straight out through the blue door. There, a plasty will tell them where to go. If they're valid you give the paperwork to your doc, if they are discards you keep it on your desk. Questions?'

'Yeah, where can I get a coffee and where can I smoke a fag?'

Paul and Raj both grinned, 'You're going to fit in well here, son.' Paul remarked. Behind the doctor's cubicles was a small kitchen area, Raj made six cups, three for them and three for the doctors.

'They're always bloody late.' He explained. 'They all live in the same apartment block and they're bloody animals. You can guarantee that one of them will have to nip off and throw up, every day.' He chuckled and shook his head indulgently. 'Right.' Raj checked his watch. 'Train'll be here in ten, let's smoke a couple of fags.' They traipsed out of the blue door and into a sectioned-off walkway that had been made using tall metal panels. Above this narrow pen the humid grey sky was a thin strip of light. Anthony lit a cigarette and offered his around. Paul poured a generous dash of brandy into their coffees from a hip flask that he produced.

'You'll soon get the hang of this, it's not hard.' He said as he poured. 'It is a bit weird at first but you just have to keep reminding yourself that they aren't any use to anyone and you're probably doing them a favour. After a while you see them for what they are and it gets easier.'

'What do you mean, "What they are."?' Anthony asked.

Paul and Raj exchanged a look. 'They're basically cunts.' Raj replied. 'They come in here with an attitude and think they can speak to us like shit because they've been moved up here. If they had anything to offer they'd have jobs already and they wouldn't be shipped around the country for work. They do my fucking head in, if it was up to me I'd discard the lot of 'em. You'll see, mate, you learn a lot about people doing this job.'

'Fair enough.' Anthony replied. They finished their cigarettes and went back in. By now the three doctors had arrived: Ben, Tintin and Sam. As Raj and Paul had said, all three looked as though they had been up all night and their combined smell was enough to make anyone want to never drink again. Introductions were made and Anthony relaxed a little. They swapped stories about the local bars and brothels, Anthony was a keen pupil. He hardly noticed the rumbling noise outside of a human wave poised to sweep through. The front door swung open and Anthony could see through the middle cubicle that a young man, hardly more than a teenager, had come in wearing the black G4ITAS uniform.

'NASRA boys!' He shouted. 'They're lined up and ready.' Several policemen walked in carrying rifles and wearing full combat gear. They walked through to the back, muttered good mornings and walked straight out through the rear doors.

'We call them the bell boys.' Tintin explained. 'Partly because they're only function is to hold the door open and say: "Keep moving along to the coach." Partly because they're fucking bellends.'

'Ok boys, to your stations, please. Said Raj. 'Anthony, you're in the middle where we can help you. If you need something just shout, ok?'

The group dispersed to their separate positions like soldiers before a battle. Anthony went into the middle cubicle and sat down. He turned on his computer and opened the relevant spreadsheet. He took a large sip of coffee and thanked the Gods there was something strong in there.

'FIRST THREE FROM EACH ROW STEP FORWARD AND INTO THE OFFICE.' A deep voice bawled, distorted by a loudhailer. Now that he was alone Anthony could hear the subtle mumble of a thousand confused voices who wanted to know what was happening. He could feel his heart thumping in his chest. He wiped the palms of his hands on his suit trousers, feeling the quality of the material settled him. His curtain pulled back and a nervous looking woman with fiery red hair came in and sat down.

'Hello, have a seat please. I'm 'Anthony and I'll be helping you. Can I see your paperwork please?' She meekly handed it to him without a word. Anthony looked at what was there. 'Ok, I see that you've got some experience in factories. I'll mark that on your notes. Step through to the back and see Doctor Walsh in the middle cubicle please.' He stamped her paperwork with a V and handed it back to her with a false smile. She stared frostily back at him. *Fucking slag, what have I done?* She left and he waited for the next. He heard Raj shout "Next" and realised that was what he had to do.

'Next.'

A big man, with a neck like a tree trunk, came in wearing a Chelsea shirt. He was middle aged, maybe forty-five Anthony guessed. He smiled his greeting and asked for the paperwork. The man grunted in return and rudely thrust the papers into his hand. Some construction and security experience.

'What fucking work are you lot gonna make me do?'

Anthony was caught off guard, he opened his mouth but no words came at first.

'Cat got your tongue? Tell me where I'm fucking going.' The man leaned forward placing huge fists on the table. Anthony felt a sheen of perspiration creep to his brow.

'I'm not sure. You'll be taken to the selection area where you'll be selected by an employer for work and…'

'What work? What do these employers do?'

'Well there are manufacturers, farms, mining…'

'I aint going down a mine. I've got a bad back and claustrophobia. I'm not doing it.' Tree Trunk Neck sat back in his chair and folded his arms.

Anthony wanted to punch him. 'Well it's not up to me to assign your work. Maybe if you speak to the doctor he can make a note...'

'I don't want to speak to a fucking doctor, I'm speaking to you and I'm not going down a fucking mine.'

'I appreciate that. As I've said, it's not up to me where you go but if you ask the doctor...'

The man shot forward and slammed his hand on the desk. 'I'M NOT TALKING TO THE FUCKING DOCTOR I'M TALKING TO YOU!' He roared.

Every sinew in his body tautened with rage. *How dare this cunt?* However, he was nothing if not professional. 'Give me just one second please, I'll consult with my colleague.' He forced a smile.

'You do that.' Tree Trunk Neck returned as he sat back and folded his arms. Anthony walked out of the back of his cubicle, and put his head around to Raj's. An old lady sat on the other side of the desk. She looked up in surprise at the intrusion. 'Sorry Raj. Have you got a sec?'

'Yep, one mo. Ok, that's you done, out through the blue door please.' He said, smiling at the old lady who shakily got up from the chair. She thanked Raj enthusiastically and smiled at Anthony as she passed him by.

'Raj, I've got a guy that's being an arsehole. He says he won't go to the mines because he's got a bad back but he won't speak to the doctor and I don't know what to do.'

'Fuck him, send him away.' Raj retorted with ill-disguised impatience. Anthony started to feel a bit stupid.

'I don't know, he looks like he's going to be trouble…'

'Look, there are two ways of dealing with this, you can either call the plastys to deal with him or a trick I use is to tell them that D stands for disabled so they'll be looked after and won't have to work; that usually sorts them out. The companies don't like troublemakers; it upsets the labour force.

'I can just discard him with no real reason?'

'Yeah, too bloody right you can. If they start being twats I discard them as a matter of fucking principle. It works better if you don't tell them too much and don't bother to get into a conversation. If you tell them what to do they generally just go with it. Ok?' Raj smiled and gestured Anthony to go back, the discussion was over. Anthony took a deep breath and confidently marched back into his cubicle. Raj called 'NEXT.' Tree Trunk Neck now had his feet up on the desk.

'Ok, I've spoken to my colleague and he says that's fine we can send you somewhere else.' Anthony picked up his rubber stamp and rolled it to D.

'Where?'

'It's a convalescence hospital here in Manchester. For your back.' Anthony smiled genuinely.

'That's better. Why didn't you just say that from the start?' Tree Trunk Neck smiled the insolent grin of a man who feels he has won this particular battle, another in the long line of battles that have marked out his life.

'My apologies.' He stamped the form D. 'Blue door *sir*, enjoy your day.' Anthony smiled at the man as he left. All of a sudden his face crumpled and tears sprung into the corners of his eyes. His heart pounded and his stomach rolled over. He sat still, breathing heavily as cold sweat prickled his body. It took him a few moments to regain his composure.

'Next.'

A woman walked in who was somewhere near Beth's age. She carried a new born baby and led by the hand a tiny blonde girl with her hair in bunches. She smiled sweetly but nervously at Anthony as she handed over her paperwork. 'Hi there, I'm Gaynor.' She gushed and put her hand out to shake.

Anthony accepted. 'Hi...Anthony.' He looked down at her paperwork. She was quite pretty, he prayed she had a husband. He scanned through the answers she had scribbled hurriedly on the train, maybe while trying to watch the toddler and hold the baby. They all used the same treacherous, black ball point pens; handed out and taken back in so that they could seal people fates again, again and again. Marital status: single.

Anthony's chest constricted until he felt like he couldn't breathe. His throat was dry, he tried to swallow but couldn't. The toddler smiled up at him revealing the gap in her teeth of which she was obviously proud. Her mother smiled down at her with pride of her own as she shuffled the sleeping baby into a more comfortable position. As he was moved, the baby frowned in his sleep as if troubled by a nightmare. Foul bitterness rose in his throat and he had to repeatedly swallow to keep it down. He stopped looking at them and tried to clear his thoughts. The hand he lifted to stamp the form felt like it was made of granite. 'Blue door.' He mumbled almost inaudibly, still he couldn't look.

'Ok, thanks then Anthony. See you around. Say thank you to Anthony, Cara.'

'Fanks Ant'ny.' Cara lisped. Anthony forced himself to look at them, he forced himself to see and feel what he was doing. They left. As the curtain swept shut behind them he felt something in him change, a candle in his heart flickered out. He couldn't hold it anymore, he grabbed the wastepaper bin from under his desk and vomited into it. Hot tears seared his eyes, bitter sobs that tasted of vomit caught in his throat. Finally he controlled himself.

'Next.' He finally called in a shaky voice. An androgynous wreck shuffled in wrapped in a filthy sleeping bag. It's hollowed out eyes, cadaverous face and the beads of perspiration on its forehead screamed of drug abuse. It handed over the paperwork and scabs that ran up its arms confirmed his suspicions. He stamped a D without bothering to read anything and sent it on its way. This time he felt nothing.

Faces came and faces went; a seemingly endless flood. Most were valid and sent to the Rainbow Market and ultimately on to work, to be productive in a way that Anthony thought they maybe hadn't been before. Some were discarded. Some of the discards were easy, like the drug addict he-she. Some he would see again that night when he couldn't sleep and he stared at the ceiling chain smoking and drinking whisky. He got through four bottles in the first week and the second. The third week he was down to three and by week six it was two. But never less than two.

Chapter 14

Diet starts today. Got my new Smartphone, at last – thanks dad. Happy Birthday, hope your well. Like this picture to send love to victims of hurricane rebecca. Joshua could feel his soul drowning in grammatically poor, vacuous mire. The social media feed, a backdoor innovation by Freetopia's IT unit, gave a cross-platform cross-section of the nation's information diarrhoea.

In Joshua's opinion it would have been a more clever trick if they'd managed to get rid of the advertisements as well. 'Earn 2000b a month without leaving your home. Third Gen Antibiotics, as recommended by PhiZen-JohnKline, now only 299b a course! Wal-Tesc Premium Brands – guaranteed 100% bug free.' The long list shivered shamefully as it automatically updated. Frustration threatened to boil over as it had done repeatedly over the past three months.

Kane's living-room was dominated by over-stuffed book shelves and an expensive corner sofa that you sank into rather than sat upon. The high-ceilings, typical of the Victorian townhouses of Kilburn, kept the room cool despite the hot summer outside. The trees, whose blossoms were unfurling expectantly when he had begun his incarceration, were clad in proud green feathers that rippled under a breeze. The sun was riding a lone cloud, high above the city and more than over the yard arm; he decided it was time for a joint. He had promised Beth that he would try not to smoke so much but it was difficult, boredom was crippling his mind. He understood that he had a good deal. He had a place to live and a job. It was more than he could have expected after losing his previous employment in the way he had.

 He put down his laptop and hauled himself out of the grey, corduroy sofa. He picked up his rolling box and crossed to the large bay window and sat down on a cushioned seat that matched the sofa. He waited a moment, cocking his head to listen to the house, making sure he was alone, before opening the window and breathing a deep, satisfying gulp of what passed for fresh air in London.

Ky was his only real problem. Fortunately the boy did his own thing a lot of the time which made living with him just about tolerable. The truth was that he scared him. He would dress it up in his mind in different ways in an attempt to make it palatable but the boy's intensity and knowledge made him uncomfortable. Although young, he had a ferocious capacity for learning and devoured book after book. He would quiz Kane, making sure that he absorbed every last drop of information. Despite his age he made Joshua feel physically intimidated. Although he was young and skinny he was wiry and solid, carved out of granite from a life of sleeping on the streets. He and Joshua had developed a relationship built on shared mistrust and animosity. Joshua knew that he spoke to Kane about himself but Kane wouldn't say anything other than that he had led an interesting, if hard, life. His only soft spot was the baby – Meditant, he had named him, although Joshua had been able to find no trace of what that name might mean. Initially he and Kane had done all they could to find the baby's family but they had nothing to go on, other than the vague recollections that they had of the man they assumed was his father. Ky had begun to care for him under instruction from Beth and the baby had taken to him with a trust that can only be displayed by the truly dependent.

Joshua finished rolling his joint and lit it. After three pulls his conscience pricked him into closing the window and sitting back on the sofa. He might not like Kane's rules but they were there for a reason. The consequences of some concerned citizen smelling weed and reporting it to the police were too far reaching to contemplate.

He was stubbing out the joint when he heard a key in the front door. He tensed as he always did but stayed where he was, if it was the plastys running would do him no good. Kane threw open the living-room door making the windows rattle. 'Good afternoon Joshua. How is my favourite prisoner today?'

Joshua tried his best to scowl. At first it had been easy but as the weeks had worn on it had become harder. 'Alright. You?'

'That was almost a smile today you sweet boy. That's not so hard is it?' Kane sighed as he sank into the sofa.

Joshua ignored the dig. 'Are Ky and the baby not with you?'

'Master Ky is out working on a little something just for me. Beth's got the baby. Should anyone from Freetopia come here and ask, he was here all day. I hope you've been reading that properly.' He nodded towards the laptop that was still open on the social media feed.

'For what it's worth.' Joshua grunted. He reached for his box and began to roll another joint. The freedom that Ky had rankled him.

Kane gave him a disapproving look. 'The lady will be here soon. Do you really want to be all stoned and mono-syllabic?'

'I've been captive for months, what else do you expect me to do?'

'Keep following the live feed, that's what you're paid to do.'

'Some pay.'

'How much rent are you paying? And what about food? Or your precious weed?' Kane asked feigning innocence.

'Yeah ok…'

'I know it's not the most interesting thing in the world but it's important. We need to monitor social media.'

'I've been stuck in here looking at this shit for three months. When am I going to be allowed out? This wasn't what I had in mind when I joined the so-called revolution.' Joshua scowled as he rummaged through his box before abruptly throwing it back on the floor.

'May I remind you that you joined because you had no other choice?' Kane's voice remained mild and unconcerned. He had grown used to dealing with Joshua's tantrums.

'Yeah but that was before I'd processed everything, you know? I was still confused after the riotand my parents...' Joshua's voice trailed off. Kane discreetly looked away as he composed himself. 'Anyway, this social media crap is pointless.'

'Why is that?' Kane said.

'Because the people who are in the Transport Scheme can't afford a device to update their social media account. That's kind of why they're being transported.'

'There are such things as internet cafés you know.'

'Right, so people are being whisked away, supposedly at gunpoint - '

'We don't know that. Don't spread libellous rumours against our benevolent government.' Kane interupted.

'Whatever. People are being whisked away to work in some sweatshop in Manchester soldering circuit boards or digging coal under Sheffield and they turn to the plastys and say: Hang about mate, I've just got to change my status to 'in government sponsored slavery.'? Come on...'

'I don't make the rules Josh. This is what we've been assigned to do. Look, all it takes is someone with a smartphone and we've got evidence.'

'Do you really think the plastys are letting the Transports take *phones* with them?'

'We have to cover all angles.'

'I don't understand why we don't just send someone into one of the Resets, that's the only way to find out what's happening there.'

'We've not found a way to beat the retinal scanners yet, I've heard the boys in the tech division are on to it though.'

'Where did you hear that?'

'A little bird.'

'Did that little bird happen to be a six foot skinhead called Craig Tollbar?' Joshua grinned. Craig was in the Freetopia IT unit, he frequently came to the house to carry out maintenance on the un-addressed servers hidden in the attic that powered the Movement.

'Maybe.' Kane replied tartily.

'I knew you were shagging him.' Joshua crowed triumphantly.

'Jealous honey? Just because I'm getting some. So when are you going to put Beth out of her misery?'

'Not again...' Joshua could feel his cheeks colouring which irritated him.

'Oh come on Josh, we all know she wants it. She's been here almost every evening since you moved in. Although I've no idea why, you stroppy shit.'

'What do you expect?'

'We've kept you alive. You wouldn't have lasted five minutes without us.'

'Well if you lot hadn't killed the NASRA woman...'

Kane rolled his eyes. 'Don't start. They were following you for a reason, they'd have had you on something eventually. Come on, Josh, let's not do this again. I get that you're angry with Stickles but don't take it out on me. I've only ever tried to help, and so has Beth.'

'Fuck Stickles.'

'I wouldn't touch that insane old bastard with yours.' Kane replied. They both started giggling, dispelling the tension.

Joshua knew all that was being said to him. He almost felt it his duty to himself to raise the argument again and again to prove that he hadn't rolled over and allowed himself to be manipulated. 'How did he get to be the mouthpiece of Freetopia?' Joshua asked more conversational now.

'He was with the committee when they started. He was the only one crazy enough to be visible. The Movement needed a face.'

'He's still a bloody nutter.'

'Oh I know, but he's a brilliant nutter; never forget that.' The front door-bell rang in a certain sequence. Kane went to answer it and came back followed by Ky who scowled at Joshua who smiled in return.

'Big man wants to see you.' Ky muttered as he sat down.

'Ok, I'll get going.' Kane replied.

'Not you. Him.' He jerked a thumb in Joshua's direction.

'Me? What does he want with me?' Joshua asked. His belly did a back flip at the thought of being able to leave the house. His excitement was quickly quelled by a flash of anger. *So I get to meet Stickles at last.*

'Since when does he tell me anything? There's a mopaxi out front.' Ky snapped his fingers sarcastically while he held out the helmet with the other hand. 'Quickly.' Joshua grabbed it and put it on as he rushed past. He didn't need telling that his face couldn't be seen in public.

Outside in the quiet street the air smelt fresher than anything that Joshua had ever smelt before. He felt hot and stifled by the motorcycle helmet. He longed to rip it off and feel his hair tousled by the gentle breeze. Waiting at the curb was a beaten up moped that he recognised. The rider flipped up his visor and grinned toothily – it was the same man who had bought him here.

'You again.' Joshua stated, not without pleasure. He was outside, nothing could ruin his mood.

'Me again.' He laughed. 'You coming for another little ride with old Vinnie?'

'I guess I am. I need to go to…'

'I know where you're going, boy. Get on.'

'Do I need a mask?'

'No mask this time boy. Stickles has his own mask for you. He has one for everyone.' He said, cackling as Joshua got on.

This time the ride was infinitely less scary. He could see the oncoming traffic as the moped weaved in and out of the traffic and prepare himself for sharp corners and sudden braking. They weaved in and out of the heavy traffic of Maida Vale before turning left at Edgeware Road tube and heading along Marylebone Road. It felt perverse that the city had changed so little in his absence. While he had been smoking and reading and researching, life had carried on just as it always had. They passed Angel, Old Street and Shoreditch before passing the turning on to Whitechapel Road where he and Anthony had staggered back to his so many times. They shot past Lahore Kebab House where they used to giggle while they queued up for sweaty hunks of meat that he would inevitably throw up in someone's garden on the way home. The sun went behind a cloud and the street suddenly looked grey and morose. He smiled sadly behind his visor and wondered where Anthony was. He wondered when they would speak again.

They passed by old tower blocks, recently emptied of their impoverished inhabitants, standing proudly as teams of high-vis tailors clad them in new suits for their new, more affluent residents. Old, tatty high streets were being ripped apart to make way for new branches of Wal-Tesc, restaurants, expensive bars. Everywhere seemed to buzz with drills and saws and sanders as London cast off the rags of depression and prepared itself for a brighter future.

As far as Joshua could tell they were heading east towards the old docks that were rumoured to be experiencing a renaissance since fuel prices had spelled the demise of air freight. He found it funny that years ago those with money had moved out of London and into these former slums with the decline in shipping. Now, opulent apartment blocks, that had once over-looked marinas and views of the river, stood empty as the cranes, noise and ships had returned. Flats, which had been sold for numbers with too many zeroes after them, were rented cheaply to the dockers, stevedores and tradesmen who had returned.

Finally they pulled up in a street that appeared to have escaped the cycle of gentrification and the inevitable slip back to ignominy. On one side of the road was the back of an old gas works. The huge drum had long sunk to its lowest level leaving only a rusted frame like a stage, above. On the other side a huge, crumbling, brick monolith loured over the street and blotted out the sun. High, arched windows with smashed glass were boarded up from the inside. Weeds and moss grew in the dusty joints between bricks. Above a large door that might once have allowed lorries access, white letters had fallen away. Only their ghosts remained to spell out the word 'Brewery'. The doors were clasped shut with a suitably huge chain that had bled rust down the peeled green paint. This was a corner of London forgotten by Rebuild's industrial revival.

'Off ya get.' Vinnie said. 'Go around the side and knock on the green rusty door. Just follow your nose man.'

Joshua walked down an alleyway choked with undergrowth. A beaten track led through the tall weeds to a solid metal door. He rapped firmly, the sound reverberated deep into the bowels of the building; it didn't seem possible that anyone could answer. The fury he had felt towards Stickles in the early days of his incarceration had matured, mellowing with age but growing deeper and fuller. He looked at his hand and saw it was trembling. *Am I going to have to argue with him?* Better to play it down: aloof, but not confrontational. No, it wouldn't pay to be arrogant. In fact friendly might work; you caught more flies with honey. *Pussy.* The voice in his head sounded like Anthony's.

He nearly turned around to go back the way he had come but he heard Vinnie's moped buzz away down the street. Just then he heard a faint muttering and the swish of slippers against the floor. The door swung quietly open on well-oiled hinges, Stickles stood before him at the top of a stairwell that descended into the ground. Now he was close, Joshua could see that his eyes were dazzling, a purplish shade of blue that approached violet. They flashed intensely as he thrust out his leathery talons to grasp his hand and pump it like he was a dear old friend. His sallow skin hung off his thin jowls, a sneer made it look as if he were kissing his teeth. Even now the man swayed ever so slightly as if trying to contain an energy that threatened to explode, destroying the vessel and all who stood before it. 'Now, you must be Joshua.' He said, his nasally voice booming in the small passage. Joshua nodded his reply. 'Well then come in, boy. Come and see the circus.' He half dragged Joshua through the door-way and swung the heavy metal door shut behind them.

With the door shut a solid black blanket covered his eyes. 'Follow me, follow me.' The old man's voice was already halfway down the stairs. He opened a door at the bottom and a pure light flooded into the stairwell, crisp and blue. Now he was able to see, Joshua followed him down. His nose confirmed what the light hinted at.

The humidity hit him instantly, making his breath catch in his chest before it settled into the thicker air. He followed Stickles through the door where a large man blocked his way. 'Frisk.' The man's deep voice rumbled like a train. Joshua put his arms up, his hands trembling. The man patted him down roughly before grunting something and moving out of his way. Now that his view was no longer obscured he could see the cellar was wide and long with a low, filthy roof. From halfway down, the walls and ceiling were coated with reflective foil and row after row of intense bulbs hung low over a green sea which undulated and twitched as cooling fans swept its surface. As far as Joshua could tell each row was at a different stage of development. The first row was approaching maturity with open, fist sized buds that yawned towards the light, the last were spindly weeds that struggled to reach out of the root basket that hung over a hydroponics reservoir. The air was heavy and cloying, it tickled his nose and made him want to sneeze. Underneath the verdant, polleny stench, ghosts of yeast and malt still haunted the air. As his eyes adjusted he could see figures dressed in black moving amongst the rows, busying themselves with their tasks while they looked up at him with hostile interest.

The bright lights and charismatic plants had caught his immediate attention, now he looked around the front of the cellar. There was a small kitchen area where a group of four men, including the man who had frisked him, were playing cards with wedges of obselete twenty pound notes, their machine guns leant against the table. Joshua nodded as casually as he could. Cold gazes returned his civility. Stickles gestured at a pair of armchairs that faced each other near to a trestle table where three teenaged boys, stripped to the waist, thin and grimy, were stripping and cleaning rifles. They sat down facing one another,

Stickles studied Joshua's face, his heart, his mind, not seeming to need him to speak.

'So that's why they call this place The Greenhouse.' Joshua said when he could stand the examination no longer.

'Revolutions don't fund themselves, my boy.' Stickles replied. A sarcastic half-smile turned up the corners of his lips. 'The irony has always made me chuckle. Our embryonic uprising is funded by the teenage children of the bourgeois overlords whose world we shall tear asunder. They fund us through pocket money, hand-outs, trust funds; Daddy's sweat. It's beautiful isn't it?' He picked up a battered smoking tin from the floor and began to roll a joint.

'It has a certain eloquence.' Joshua said as his eyes settled on padlocked, metal cages that lined the walls. Standing to attention, like a prison roll call, were rows and rows of machine guns stacked on top of each other. At the bottom of the cages were sealed wooden boxes with numbers painted on the sides.

Stickles followed his gaze. 'Part of our arsenal; but not the best part.' It was clear that he was trying to keep the excitement from his voice. He sprang to his feet and beckoned Joshua to follow. Next to the cages was a door that he opened. Inside was a further chamber full of wooden crates and shelves full of what looked like children's toy guns. On one shelf was a row of machines that looked like large, transparent microwaves.

'What're they?' Joshua asked.

'Three dimensional printers my boy. Guns for everybody. The quality is poor but they only need to work for long enough to take better ones from the oppressors.' Stickles closed the door carefully as though children slept inside.

'So you're going to flood the country with cheap guns. Is that a good idea?' Joshua said as they sat back down.

'Revolutions aren't fought with sticks and stones, boy. They're fought by men with guns.' He barked. 'Violence is the only language that will be understood.' He rolled the joint he had been working on and licked the side to stick it down.

'And what happens to the guns when your oppressors are chased away? What happens to everything? Will you redesign the system from the bottom up, or will it be from the top down. Surely that's what usually happens after a revolution.'

The expression on Stickles' face stayed calm although red spots had appeared high on the folds of skin that rested on his cheek bones. 'Once the people are free from the yoke of consumerist culture they'll have no need to take anything from anyone else. Violence is a symptom of a diseased system, we shall cure the root disease. However, the Freetopia Movement is not on trial here.' His gnarled fingers finished tapping down the joint. He twisted the end and threw it to Joshua who lit it, keeping his gaze on the old man.

'And the implication is that I am? Surely it's a bit late for that?' It was impossible to keep a shrill quake from his voice.

'You've been watched most closely. Believe me, if your loyalty was questionable you would have gone the way of your unfortunate NASRA colleague.' Stickles tittered into his hand. 'No, I wanted to make the acquaintance of our own little turncoat, NASRA's boy who's become our own. The boy from the estates with a university degree. Why did you switch sides?' A joking smile turned the corners of Stickles' mouth up but his eyes, now vibrant violet behind the veil of smoke, bored into him.

Joshua passed the joint without breaking eye contact. 'I'm not sure you gave me a choice. I was sacked from NASRA after the riot at Speakers Corner and I've been a prisoner ever since.'

Stickles took a pull, making the orange cherry glow. He inhaled deeply and slowly let the smoke out. A foolish grin spread across his face. 'Come now. Of course you've not been a prisoner, it was for your own protection. We took you in at your weakest moment. But that doesn't mean you should be trusted, oh no. How do we know that you're not a traitor? A rat, an impostor, a spy? Hm?' The grin didn't leave his face; his eyes widened so that the whites were more prominent than their iris'. Joshua was sure they were bleeding already.

'How do you know if any of your people are spies? However, Kane Singfield approached me, on recommendation of Beth Thomas. I didn't approach the Movement.'

'Ah sweet Bethany. Sweet, sweet Bethany. I understand that you have a warm place for her, hm? Is this so? She makes you sticky?'

'I…well…not exactly…we...we were childhood friends.' Joshua stuttered. Only now did he break eye contact.

Stickles shot forward and clasped Joshua's hands in his. The joint stuck out from his mouth at a crazy angle, lazy smoke was shocked into an angry swirl. 'There it is! There's the lie that I needed. I have a certain nack, a nack for seeing people's lies. You're all the same. Your eyes dart around, your pupils dilate. You all have some outward sign. You lied to me then. Maybe you lied to yourself too, I don't know. But now I've seen it I'll always know.' The quick change in his temperament confused Joshua but he battered on. 'No need for the old insurance policy but never mind, this is how we does it anyway. We like to ensure our loyal operatives remain loyal to us, boy.' As he spoke he reached down to the haphazard pile of papers. He carefully and deliberately fingered through the sheaf, one at a time as if counting, before seizing a large photo. With a flourish he handed it to Joshua along with the joint. It was already in his mouth when he realised what he was looking at. He stopped mid smoke and let the bitter acridity drift out. 'What is it, hm? What do you see Joshua?'

'You know exactly what I see. It's a photo of my sister.' He said coldly. Behind him he heard the soft scrape of chairs being pushed back and the whisper and click of guns as they were raised into shoulders.

'Yes Josh. Yes it is. My assurance of your loyalty.'

'You can't…'

'I can but I won't. Not as long as you're a good boy Joshua, hm? Now I have a job for you. You and the boy.' Stickles waved a placating hand at the unseen gunmen.

'No, I want to talk about my sister.' He snapped. 'Just leave her out of this.'

'And I will Joshua, and I will. You behave and pretty Tamsin stays well.' Stickles let out a high pitched, excited snigger. 'To the mission. Now, the boy.'

'Ky?'

'Yes, he. A sprat of un-questionable loyalty but his foundling baby is my insurance of the fact. You and he are to do a little look-see-looksing. Now smoke, young Joshua, smoke. We have a mission to discuss.'

Stickles prattled away as Joshua smoked, occasionally nodding to show he was listening. With each inhalation the old man's voice drifted further away and bitter fury churned in his stomach.

Chapter 15

'Next…Next…NEXT!' Anthony held his breath. He heard nothing. He let out the captured air slowly and deliberately. Another shift at the coal face was done. He loved the silence that pervaded after the scum had been dispensed with. He put his face in his hands and indulged his exhaustion by closing his eyes, relishing the disorientation as his mind tried to snatch stolen scraps of sleep. A metallic jangling jolted him as the curtain at the rear of his cubicle was hurriedly dragged back.

'Come on, Thomas. The day is done and the night is young. Get your arse in gear.' Paul shouted in.

'I'll have to meet you boys at The Prince tonight, mate.' He replied as he shuffled together hundreds of innocuous pieces of paper, all stamped with identical, innocuous D's.

'What description of poofery is this, I hear?' Raj boomed, unseen from his cubicle.

Anthony grinned. 'I'll only be an hour or so, you pair of withered cunts. I've got to go to the office, Benson wants to see me.'

'Oooh!' The pair mocked in a falsetto duet.

'Has someone got to polish the old man's plonker?' Paul said grinning.

'Sod off you pair of arseholes. I'll see you at the pub; you can buy me one and leave it in the pump.' It was imperative not to get behind on the rounds.

*

The moped slowed down and stopped outside the NASRA office. The six o'clock exodus had begun and the building was rapidly emptying.

'Wait here.' He muttered to Browny. 'I've got to see the boss and then I want to go back to The Prince.'

He nodded to acquaintances and fielded various jokes about working overtime as he swam upstream against the warm current of happy people. He sauntered through the nearly empty office, smiling at a secretary who he caught spaying herself hurriedly with perfume and checking her face in a handbag mirror. *Someone's getting laid tonight.* He felt a warm surge of his own and decided that tonight was a Selina's night. He walked through to the back of the office and knocked on Rick Benson's door. 'Come,' said a deep voice from within.

Anthony had developed a certain amount of respect for Benson, which was an unusual thing for him. He was neither friendly nor personable, rather he had a direct, brusque manner that bordered on being rude, but Anthony found in that a refreshing honesty; you knew where you stood.

Anthony walked in and sat down without being invited. 'Nice to see you, Anthony.

How goes it down at the station?' Benson said without looking up from his paperwork.

'Everything is fine thanks. The usual problems with the plastys but nothing we haven't got in hand. You wanted to see me?' He replied, keeping it brief. Benson hated to be told anything that he didn't need to know.

'Yes I did. I've got a special task for you, if you're up to it?' Benson didn't wait for an answer. 'I have been asked by the Home Secretary's office to visit our attached DPC to check that those goons who have the contract are running it to our standards. I need you to visit DPC04 and run through a series of checks, ok?'

Anthony felt a chill tickle his spine. *I'll get to see the process.* The doomed black cat of macabre curiosity unfurled itself and began to purr seductively. 'Ok Rick, no problem. When do you want me to go?'

'Tomorrow, I've arranged a driver for you. Be here at eight am sharp.'

'Will someone be taking my place on the platform? It's just that the trains are busier than ever and now we're doing two a day...'

'Yes ok, I'll send Gareth over there in the morning. Have Raj and Paul meet him outside. I'm assuming you'll be seeing them tonight?' Benson levelled his gaze at Anthony who squirmed like a naughty school boy.

'Er...yeah I would have thought I'll see them.' He replied. He hated that he had been caught off guard.

'Just make sure you're able to function. Take an overnight bag in case you need to stay.'

'Ok, Rick. I'll see you in the morning.'

'Good night.'

Anthony closed the door behind him and thoughtfully walked through the deserted office. So he was finally going to get to see the Discard Processing Centre. After these months of standing at the fringe he would watch the process, see it, smell it. Would it bring about some development of conscience? He doubted it, he had dealt with his conscience on this matter a long time ago now. Once you took that petty humanity out of the equation all you were left with was a deep curiosity. Curiosity about the process of course, but more so its effect on him. After all, he was the faceless bureaucrat, the person that made these life and death judgements from afar. Would he have the balls to stand up close while it happened? This would be a test of his mettle. But it was also an opportunity. Everything was.

*

The bell had rung at some point. The warm, close atmosphere of The Prince swapped for the chill of the August night. A scuffle, nothing too dramatic. Some pushy-pushy posturing that descended quickly into raucous laughter that was so close to snarls. The three of them stumbling as they attempted to walk with arms around each other's shoulders. The direction they fell in was fixed, no-one questioned it, no-one needed to. Falling through the night, falling through a dark door in a dark alley in the dark city.

The bouncer who opened the door glowered menacingly, his dark purple face softened to a friendly grin as he recognised them. 'Good evening, gentlemen. Selina was expecting you earlier tonight.'

'Got engaged in the crusade at The Princey, Monk. You know how it is…' Raj slurred, winking at Monk. He stepped to one side allowing them to pass into the stairwell uncomfortably close to him. They climbed the stairs calling down, asking him when he was going to join them for a session. Monk replied that he would be honoured to be invited, as he always did. A rush of warm air greeted them as the door at the top of the stairs opened into what was once the reception of a design company, or a record label, or maybe an art gallery. The scuffed wooden floor was almost hidden by a sumptuous red rug and several over-sized beanbags which they sank into, reclining lazily like latter day lords. Selina waited patiently as they made themselves comfortable and shouted at one another. She clapped her hands and a red curtain swished to one side. A naked girl appeared carrying a tray; two whiskies, one with ice, one without and a rum and coke. She tottered self-consciously across the room, unused to the high heels that elevated her to the height that she might still grow to. She bent over to place down the drinks, the ice in the glass tinkled cheerfully as she trembled. Raj ran an appraising hand up her leg, giggling as she twitched nervously. She shrank away behind the curtain under their watchful eye. Selina stepped forward, only now choosing the appropriate moment to make her presence known.

At five and a half feet, Selina's physical presence was hardly imposing. Her once stunning, innocent looks had soured and shrivelled as the corners of her mouth had turned down and her eyes had grown colder. Selina Petrov was a veteran; a seasoned professional who had cut her teeth meeting the needs of business men and military officers in the Russian city of Warsaw, where she had grown up. She had come to England as a middle-aged business woman and had clawed herself an empire from the desperate years that followed Day X. Now she owned brothels throughout the country, her operation thriving like a bloated tick on the side of the Transport Scheme. She fed and clothed those women, girls and boys who caught the eye of the selections teams. She even employed those who found their way to her door themselves. There was always work to be done.

'A good evening to you, gentlemen. How was your day today?' She purred in her thick accent. She continued speaking over the slurred responses, skilfully silencing them without appearing ill-mannered. 'I was much impressed by the girls who you sent today. They seem good, sturdy. They will last well, I think.' Selina raised her hand in the air and theatrically clicked her fingers three times. The curtain pulled back and one by one a procession walked into the room, all wearing nothing but the cheap black lingerie and hold-up stockings that Selina insisted her girls wear. The old hands came first, three girls who they had all had at one point or another. These girls were professionals; upstanding citizens who paid their rent and earned their wages. They smiled and waved coy hellos, playing the game the way they had learnt. They were met by catcalls and jibes which they volleyed back, holding their own. Selina laughed with them and took a few good-natured comments that flew her way. Behind them came three new girls whose posture differed from the old hands. Their scared eyes flitted around the room, they moved slowly, hanging back. They turned their shoulders away and hunched their bodies up as though that would shield them from lubricious eyes that crawled over their soft flesh. Two had dark hair, one was a redhead. The redhead came last. She had an angry bruise on her cheek that looked fresh. Anthony recognised her; he had interviewed her and sent her here, just today. *I saved her.*

'Have you seen the fucking cellulite on that one? Shit…her thighs look like fucking orange peel. Oi you…you, Ginger. Turn around.' Raj shouted. The redhead looked mournfully at Selina who shot her a look which made her flinch. Her hand instinctively went to the red and purple welt on her cheek. She stepped forward, her right leg turned ever so slightly inward, her back hunched. She looked at the floor. A single tear fell from the tip of her nose as her shoulders trembled. Anthony was suddenly incandescent with desire. That potent thought seared his mind again: *I saved her.*

'I said turn around you fucking slag. Show my boys your dirty arse.' Raj shouted belligerently. The girl looked at Selina again before slowly shuffling around. Raj tried to get to his feet but fell back into the beanbag making Paul and Anthony laugh hysterically. Eventually he shakily got to his feet and grabbed at the girls thighs. 'Look. Look at this cunt. I fucking hate it when a slut doesn't look after herself.' He laughed as he shouted. Paul rolled around howling as though he were in pain. Anthony had fallen silent.

'Leave her alone.' He said in a quiet voice that made Paul abruptly stop laughing and look at him.

Only Raj laughed on, unaware that the joke had passed. 'What? You're not interested in this piece of shit are you?' He shoved the girl dismissively and she lost her balance and stumbled against one of the old hands who tutted and shoved her away, clearly peeved to be bereft of attention and the tip that she could have made. The redhead girl sobbed openly now, her chest rising and falling, her alabaster skin stained as crimson as her blotched face.

Anthony shot to his feet. 'I said fucking leave her alone. She's mine.' He snarled at Raj. Out of the corner of his eye he saw Monk tense.

Raj held up his hands in a placating gesture and fell back into the beanbag laughing. 'All yours, Anthony my boy.' His brown skin flushed a furious red. The friendly words belied his tremulous voice.

Anthony smiled down at him and grabbed the girl by the arm. She looked fearfully at him with round green eyes that streamed tears. 'Usual rates?' He called to Selina who demurely nodded her head and moved to the back of the room. She opened the red curtain gracefully with one hand while the other invited him to take what was his to where he knew to go.

Behind the red curtain was a small warren of thin partitions and doorways covered with other red curtains. Some nights Anthony liked to peer in at other people, to watch their faces as they concentrated, closing their eyes while they imagined themselves in some parallel fantasy where the old trout they slept next to would let them do what these girls had to. He liked to watch the girls too, woodenly grinding their hips against fat flesh and grey pubic hair. He liked to watch their faces; the resignation, the pain. Tonight he strode with purpose, not stopping to peep, dragging his prize after him as she tripped and stumbled to keep up. Her sobs increased in pitch, promising to become wails, her breath hitched in her chest as if caught on something. The hot metal that threatened to burst his trousers hurt him now, aching deep into the pit of his stomach. He came to a doorway where the red curtain was pulled back, inside was a flimsy wooden bed covered in a black sheet. He noted with pleasure that this was the room with the mirrored ceiling as he threw the girl in. She hit the bed and fell onto it, sprawling as she let out a cry of pain and fear. He yanked the curtain shut, not caring if it was open a crack where some other voyeur could stand and peer; he almost wanted someone to see this.

*

Later. He left the room, gently closing the curtain behind him. He'd left a tip on the bed, a generous one. He wondered briefly if she'd be able to find it or if someone else would when they cleared up. It didn't matter, he'd left it and that was the important thing. He walked back into the reception room stretching his tired shoulders. He caught Selina sitting on a bar stool with her head leant against the wall, soft snores escaped her lips. She sat upright looking wary and sly like a trapped animal. It took only a moment for her to regain her composure, Anthony looked away and busied himself deliberately taking out his wallet and counting out crisp bancor notes.

'Mr Bueller and Mr Rice…they left some time ago.' She sounded confused and tired. Anthony wondered how long the old girl could keep this up for.

'That's ok. I fancy a walk home on my own.' He smiled, he hoped, charmingly, and handed over the money. As he did a girl, one of the old hands, appeared at the curtain frantically gesturing at Selina. She nodded at him politely to excuse herself and went to the girl who jabbered a garbled whisper that he couldn't decipher.

Selina nodded thoughtfully and came back over to him. 'Mr Thomas…I'm afraid I may have to charge you a little extra tonight. You understand?' Her eyebrows rose slightly.

He understood when he was being chided. 'Of course.' He looked down, feeling uncomfortable, even a little ashamed. But a quiet voice spoke deep within, it chattered incessantly as he handed over a thick roll of bancor notes; it told him he had nothing to be ashamed of, that what he had saved was his to take.

Chapter 16

As far as socialist guerrilla fighters went, Graham Mackey was quite far from Joshua's preconceptions. He was tall and willowy, it looked like a stiff breeze could knock him off of his feet. His eyes rarely stayed still for more than a moment at a time and his lined face had laboured under the same expression of distrust since he had met Joshua and Ky at Manchester Piccadilly yesterday. As they had walked through the station, Joshua had noticed a long queue of people snaking out of a closed branch of Tie Rack with white-washed windows. Armed police watched them suspiciously and whispered periodically into radios clipped to their chests. Joshua had asked Mackey what it was. 'Selections,' was his brusque reply. Tired, after the long journey north, Joshua made a frustrated gesture with his hand for elaboration. Mackey had furtively looked around him, which Joshua thought probably brought them more attention than just speaking.

'That's where NASRA decide who goes to the Rainbow Market and who gets light duties.'

'What's the Rainbow Market and what do you mean by light duties?'

Mackey had rolled his eyes to the high roof of the station. 'I thought the idea of Stickles sending you was that you were supposed to be an expert. Jesus Christ… Those fit for work go to the Rainbow Market to be sold, those unfit go elsewhere for light duties.' Joshua went to speak again but Ky's hand on his arm had stayed him.

*

In the city the summer still felt cruel and oppressive, even after the sun had drooped lazily below the skyline and the clouds of smog. However, out on the moor, long past the witching hour, autumn's breath hung vaporously in the air and the mossy grass underfoot felt brittle, as if the water that flowed through thread veins and capillaries had slowed to a sluggish slush. Although he was wearing a thick jacket, Joshua had been shivering uncontrollably for what felt like hours.

Mackey whispered that it was time to stop again. Joshua passed the message back to Ky who grunted, the sound was shockingly loud in the cold, empty night. Joshua crouched down leaning his back against a large rock. He closed his eyes for a second but forced them open again, refusing to give in to the overwhelming fatigue that threatened to shut his body down. When he did he found Ky staring at him with a look that was halfway between sympathy and disgust. He nodded but got no response.

They had stopped in a hollow between a large rocky outcrop and the debris that had fallen off of it over the eons. Grey boulders, almost white in the fading moonlight, sheltered them from a cold breeze that whipped across the tops of the heather and gorse on the open moor beyond. Ground up chunks of gritstone which had crumbled from the rocks above, peppered the ground around them reflecting tiny chinks of light. The moon was falling away, losing its crispness. The coming sun greyed the sky with angular lines, ghosts of rays to come, but its time was, as yet, an un-kept promise.

Their long walk had begun with jumping unceremoniously out the back of a delivery lorry whose driver had been paid to see nothing. His instructions were only to pull over, in a certain layby along the A635, high on Saddleworth Moor. The clandestine travel and the twilight over the moor had given Joshua a feeling of adventure. Even Ky had managed to not look like he wanted to kill someone. But as the last purple streaks had faded from the clear sky and the stars had one by one appeared, the temperature had dropped sharply. The terrain got harder as they left established dirt paths, Joshua had found himself struggling to walk faster than a slow stroll. He cursed every cigarette he had ever smoked. Mackey led the way, he seemed nervous about the clear sky above them. He frequently stopped to listen for patrols and look for the tell-tale signs of flashlights from across the vast, empty landscape.

'It won't be long now, we're really close.' Mackey whispered theatrically.

'So why don't you tell us a little more about this place?' Joshua whispered, partly to stall for time. His feet and legs throbbed in protest at the alien exercise.

Ky tutted loudly. 'Has anyone else noticed that it's starting to get lighter?'

'Don't worry, lad. I'll get you there in plenty of time. It's me getting away that I've got to worry about.' Mackey replied. He clapped a hand on the boy's shoulder who shrugged it violently away.

'Do you mean you're not staying with us?' Joshua asked. It dawned on him, as the sun would soon, that he would be spending the next twenty hours stuck alone in a hole in the ground with this strange boy who hated him.

'Sorry boys, my job's just to show you where the place is. I've got another place to get to over the other side of the valley. I'll be spending the day there before I pick you up in the evening.'

'What are you doing there?' Ky asked.

'Asks some questions your boy does, don't he?' Mackey whispered. He clapped his hands together and blew on them for warmth. 'I'll tell you all I know. This place has been here for decades, bloody decades. We've got a contact inside NASRA up here, nothing high level unfortunately. He heard about this place being rented to G4ITAS by the Home Office so I was sent up here to look into it…'

'How long ago was that?' Ky interrupted.

Mackey gave him a long, cool look. 'You get a bit above your place don't you, boy?'

Joshua snapped. 'He's putting his arse on the line just like the rest of us.'

'Whatever…fucking Londoners.' Mackey muttered. 'It was about a fortnight ago that we got the heads up. We tried watching it on skyeye.com but it was blocked. So we did what research we could and then I came up to recce the place and see what I could find out.'

'And what have you found out?' Asked Joshua.

'Not a lot, NASRA man, that's why they've sent you up from London.

'I'm not with NASRA.' Joshua said quietly.

'Whatever. The place started life as the Saddleworth Foreign Combatant Detention Centre. It was built in 1939 when the Allies felt optimistic. It didn't see much in the way of foreign combatants for the first few years, then when the tide turned in Europe it became a popular destination for captured German and Italian troops.' He laughed at his own humour, quickly moving on as he realised he was on his own. 'After the last poor buggers were returned to their respective mothers and motherlands, it lay empty for years and years. When the Cold War came along it was re-opened as a Missile Command Centre until some bright spark realised that a Missile Command Centre would probably be better placed under ground where someone else's commanded missiles couldn't get at them. After that the army used the place as an urban combat training centre until Day X when the government of the day closed anything non-essential in an attempt to stay on top of the interest payments. We think it's a work camp operated by G4ITAS.'

Joshua frowned. 'That doesn't make sense, G4ITAS don't manufacture anything, the only facilities they own are prisons.'

'So the NASRA man does know something.' Mackey shuffled uncomfortably on his haunches. 'That's why we think it's where those unsuitable for the Rainbow Market are sent. They have a couple of bus-loads of people arrive a day. Mostly the old and infirm from what we can see. NASRA have made a big deal about their jobs for everyone shit, we think this is where the crumblys come for light duties.'

'If that's the case what work are they doing?' Joshua said.

'You're the NASRA bloke you tell me. We've not been observing the place long enough to tell.' Even in the gloom Joshua could see Mackey's sarcastic grin.

'He told you he's not NASRA. Are you slow? Is that why you're just the messenger boy?' Ky said.

Mackey went to retort but Joshua cut him off. 'We need to get moving on, it's getting lighter by the minute.'

Mackey mumbled something about it being "about bloody time." Joshua was too tired to respond.

They trudged on in silence. Joshua could barely lift his eye from the floor before him, looking up only occasionally to check that he still followed Mackey. Colour seeped into the ground he trudged over, the shades of grey turning green then growing lighter, changing with the coming day.

'How long do you think? I'm starting to worry, it's nearly dawn.' Joshua whispered to Mackey after they had been walking for half an hour.

'Soon. Don't get your knickers in a twist, NASRA bloke. Their night patrol will get back to the camp soon and they won't send out another one for a few hours yet.'

Joshua smiled, the cold made his skin feel as though it would crack. 'That's pretty efficient intelligence, mate, are you sure you're not the NASRA bloke?' He heard an alien noise from behind him, a small, throaty chuckle. He wanted to look back but resisted.

'I've been up here off and on for a week. We started off considering it as an industrial target. You know, to take it out of operation.' Mackey replied.

'You mean bomb it? What about the people who work in there?'

'There's always a certain amount of collateral damage when we carry out these operations.' Mackey stopped walking. He looked around while he took out his water bottle and drank deeply.

'Collateral damage? That's what always bothered me about you Freetopia bastards, all you care about is your bloody cause. Fuck whoever gets in the way. You're no better than the bastard government.' Joshua spat.

'Oh, so it's *you* Freetopia bastards. Not on the same side are we, Joshua?' Mackey crowed quietly. 'Maybe I need to put in a call to the old man down in London. I'm sure he's got a picture. Wife? Kiddies? He'll order it as well, he's done it before. Skinned some bird alive, they did. Her bloke got caught on an operation, stalking one of G4ITAS's top boys for a kidnapping. Grassed up his handler. They videoed it and put it up on the internet as a warning. Very messy. You want that to happen to your special someone do you, Joshua? I can make it happen, I'm connected.'

Joshua's hand bunched at his side and he started to shake uncontrollably. He opened his mouth to retort but he didn't trust his shaking lips not to stutter or his tensed arm not to lash out. Ky pushed past him.

'Where is this observation post, Mackey? He might not have the old man's ear but I do and if you don't sort yourself out I'll see to it that you're sent to the crew trying to find a way onto the Reset in Sheffield. I hear they're expecting to spend fifteen hours a day underground at the coal face. Fancy that?'

'You're just a kid, what can do?'

'Do you want to gamble on that?' Ky glared furiously at him.

Eventually Mackey snorted derisively, shrugged his shoulders and looked away. 'We're here anyway.'

Joshua looked around them. They were on a narrow path that cut into a hillside, below them the ground fell lazily away to a barren expanse of gorse, cut only by a small stream. Above them the hill rose to a rocky summit. 'Call me stupid, mate, but where's the bloody camp?' He hissed. He glanced at the horizon where the first sliver of the sun's corona peeped over the far away hills.

'It's here.' He gestured towards a pile of boulders. 'This is the entrance to the observation post.' Mackey dropped to his knees and busied himself moving a rock. As he shook it and pushed a sliver of black opened and grew with each push.

Joshua and Ky looked at each other in surprise. 'I hope you're not claustrophobic.' Joshua mumbled.

'Are you?' Ky replied.

'We'll find out won't we?' Joshua smiled weakly, to his surprise the boy reciprocated.

Soon Mackey had exposed a jagged black hole just wide enough for a man to crawl through. On the back of the rock were handles for pulling it back after they were in.

'This is where I leave you. I'm spending the day over the other side of the valley. I reckon there's a spot where I can get a better view, maybe shed a bit of light on this place. I'm sorry things got a bit heated boys, bit tired. No hard feelings eh?' He awkwardly stuck out his hand to shake; he proffered it to Ky first. 'If I'm not back to you by midnight something's happened. Have you still got the map I gave you?' Joshua felt his pocket and nodded. Mackey nodded grimly in reply. 'Get yourselves back to the road. The same driver will be back for you, wait off the road though. I'll see you boys later.' He trudged off down the path, confidently sauntering as if he was out for a country ramble. Joshua shook his head. *Bloody idiot.*

Chapter 17

Selina's must have gone upmarket. The room seemed the same but somehow grander, larger; more sumptuous. Heavy, woven cushions, upon which he reclined alone, had replaced the tatty bean-bags. The floor was covered in a strange, dark rug that seemed to undulate as the pattern moved like an optical illusion. The cheap partitions had gone, replaced by thick walls and a low ceiling. It felt like an eastern souk, although the wares sold at this particular market were very specific. The redhead thrust aside the curtain as she confidently sashayed towards him. Her hair trapped the low light making it glow like an old ember. It hung over her face obscuring her eyes from him. Her pale, naked body was smooth and free from blemishes; the only pigment was in the pink nubs on her chest and the thatch of hair between her legs. He felt heat surge through him, molten longing pumping with sluggish power through his veins. As she neared him she shook her head, throwing her hair away. Her eyes were black and purple, one was swollen shut. Her lips were puffy and split, dried blood stained her chin. It was only then that he realised it was Tamsin.

'Nearly there, Mr Thomas.' The kid's voice awoke Anthony. He opened his eyes and reluctantly let fluid dream become solid reality. He squirmed around to try and hide the bulge in his suit trousers. Out of the car window hedgerows blurred as they sped by. He felt sick, last night's fun was catching up on him. The car slowed down and ahead he could see a discreet farm track leading off from the main road.

'Is that it?' He asked, pointing.

'Yep, we turn down there and it's just a little further.' By the time the words were spoken they had skidded off of the main road, through an open gate and plunged into a sunken lane that cut through the moor. 'Sorry about that. They don't let me out very often. Petrol shortages.' The kid said bashfully. His grin twisted a puckered scar on his cheek. He looked like he was anything but sorry.

The lane was wider than seemed necessary. Anthony guessed it had been dug out to allow the passage of large coaches. The road was rough and dusty from months of drought. Spoil from the recent excavations was banked loosely at the sides of the track, covered in stubble of sickly, parched weeds. The kid had slowed down, but only a little and Anthony was thrown around like a rag doll. Eventually the lane broke to one side and the car slowed to nearly a stop before turning right and climbing the dug-out bank onto the open moor. Anthony turned to the kid to tell him to slow down but the view stayed his tongue.

The camp sat in a depression between two ridges. Behind it the landscape climbed dramatically to a craggy out-crop, littered with disordered boulders. Something flashed high up in the rocks. Anthony guessed it was a patrol, sat out of sight, radioing in his arrival. The car bounced over the pitted track, exacerbating his hangover. He wondered how they got coaches up here. As they got closer he could see guards in the two watchtowers following his approach, their guns clearly visible. The double layered security fence bristled with rolls of barbed wire along the top, making any attempt to scale it impossible. Between them, excited Alsatians, taunted by the sound of the engine, howled and leapt, throwing their weight at the outer fence which bowed alarmingly. The tarmac road curved around to the left and they stopped outside of a large double gate that loomed fifteen feet over them. To the side was a small shed that was used as a guardhouse. In the middle of the freshly painted gate, set in wrought iron was the emblem of G4ITAS. Two guards cautiously approached the car while another stayed in the shed and whispered into his radio. They wore combat uniform and hi-vis jackets, which to Anthony seemed mutually defeating. They both held their rifles tensely as if they expected to have to use them. Neither looked a day older than twenty and the one using the radio didn't look old enough to shave.

He opened his window and signalled to the men. 'Speak to the organ grinder, not the monkey, boys.' He shouted. One came to his side and one to the driver's.

'Good morning, sir. Papers and IDs please.'

Anthony fumbled and got out the paperwork he had been given by Benson. 'He's not

got clearance, is there an unclassified area he can wait in?' He nodded his head towards the driver. The kid's face showed petulant disappointment.

The guard poured over their ID's and paperwork. 'I'm afraid not, sir. He'll have to wait down the hill.'

'Down the hill? Can he not even sit outside, here in the car?'

'No.' The other replied curtly. 'Your governor should have sent someone with clearance, my boss won't be happy.'

He turned to the disgruntled looking kid. 'Sorry mate, you're going to have to wait in that last lay-by all day.' After the little shit's racing car performance this morning, Anthony took a lot of pleasure in his words.

'For fuck's sake. Benson said you might have to stay over-night, what will I do then?'

'Sleep in the fucking car.' He snapped. 'If you're not down there when I get out, be that tomorrow or three fucking days' time, your arse will be taken to the cleaners.' Anthony got out and slammed the door. The kid would be there if it took a week, no-one could afford to lose a comfortable job.

'Can I at least turn around inside the gates?' The kid snarled through the window as he started the car and revved the engine.

'No. Fuck off back down the hill, there's a good lad.' Sneered the closest one. The kid wound up the window. Anthony smiled as he caught sight of his red face as he started to reverse.

He lifted his rucksack on to his shoulder and sauntered towards the opening gate. He looked up at the hill and saw the same flash of light again, he opened his mouth to ask the guards about it but they had already walked on. The imposing gates loomed over him as he stepped over the threshold and onto an empty tarmac car park. He walked through, relishing the long, slow icy trickle that caressed his spine. The two older guards watched him carefully as the younger spoke whispers into his radio. He straightened himself and glared insolently back at them. They looked away disinterestedly. There was a click and a buzz as the mechanism began to shut the gate behind him. 'You're to follow me.' Barked the first guard self-importantly, he winked to his friends outside the gate before swaggering away across the tarmac. Anthony hurried after him, disliking being made to run.

The car park was dominated by the two storey main building. It had a carved, ornate doorway and window frames that were more befitting of a stately home than the detention centre it had been built to be. It seemed oddly grand and out of place against the stark moor behind it and the fresh, black tarmac in front. Behind the buildings a new chimney jutted into the sky, spewing black filth into the clean morning air. As Anthony studied it he registered the smell that clung heavily to the air, a sweet, cloying odour that was hard to place. Realisation bit hard with savage teeth and his stomach flipped over. He coughed, wanting to void his body of the noxious fumes that clung to his throat. Hot tears of sweat scalded his forehead.

The guard turned to him, 'Come along, sir. I've not got all day.' The kid had a bout of late acne that erupted from his face, Anthony grinned despite his nausea.

'Ok princess, I'm coming. You realise that it's my job to examine this place, don't you?'

'I don't know anything, sir. It's my job to take you to the boss quickly.'

Anthony noticed a slight Cornish lilt to his voice. A path took them behind the first block and he saw it had a twin, just as grand and imposing.

They carried on walking towards three clean, white buildings that lined up at the back of the camp. 'Where are you from, mate?' Anthony asked, trying to force the guard to turn back and walk with him.

'Do you need to know for your report?'

'Nope, just asking. Why the hostility?'

'I'm not being hostile, sir. I just don't see what it's got to do with you.' The young guard replied.

'You're right. It's got nothing to do with me.' Anthony replied lightly. 'However, if you don't start showing me some fucking manners you'll be mentioned by name in the report, you jumped up plastic, rent-a-squaddie cunt.'

'Well...I...I'm sorry.' He finally got out through gritted teeth as his face changed from shock to seething anger.

'I'm on your side mate, there's no need to be a twat. Let's start again. I'm Anthony, what's your name?'

'Private Collins.' He answered shortly. The path forked to go off to the separate blocks. They headed towards the farthest building.

'Get real Collins, you're a rent-a-squaddie plasty, you ain't a fucking private any more than I'm a bloody teddy bear. What's your name?'

'Colin...*sir*.' Gritted teeth again. Anthony was having fun now.

'Cornish Colin Collins? Fucking hell, flower, your parents didn't like you, did they?' Anthony giggled loudly, a little too loudly and a little shriller than he would have liked. Colin Collins had nothing more to say and that was fine.

The morning sun was shaded by the opposite building leaving the deserted lobby cool. Goosebumps textured Anthony's arms. The inside of the building was as stark and soulless as the outside. Clean, white corridors branched off from either side of the lobby, broken only by non-descript grey doors bearing nothing more than a plastic plate which told the room number. The smell of fresh paint hung in the air, replacing the stench of smoke outside. The building's sterility was heightened by an eerie silence that felt like a tangible presence. Immediately in front of the main entrance was a flight of stairs which Collins started climbing without waiting to see if his charge followed.

The second floor was identical to the first. They walked in silence past silent doors until Collins stopped outside one, distinguishable only by its number. He rapped loudly and waited a moment. A short, fat man wearing round spectacles that complimented his body opened it. He looked at the guard with ill-disguised contempt but a false smile lit his face as he saw Anthony. 'Ah Mr Thomas I presume? Collins, you are dismissed.' His tone when addressing them matched the expressions he favoured them both.

'You must be Craig Masterton. I'm pleased to meet you.' Anthony moved forward past the soldier. 'Thanks for your help *Private* Collins. I hope to see you later.' Anthony gushed. He was rewarded with a sidelong, poisonous glare that made him smile. Masterton frowned as he ushered him in.

The office gave the impression of barely controlled chaos. A pin board, heavy with scraps of paper, dangled from the wall. Paperwork was piled high on the desk and spilled out of a filing cabinet that was too full to close. Bookcases groaned under the yoke of a hundred files.

'Please excuse my office Mr Thomas; we've been exceptionally busy since NASRA upped our work-load.' He quickly changed tack. 'Of course, we don't mind. Business is business after all. It's nothing we can't cope with.' Masterton laughed jovially but his dark eyes and grey skin betrayed him.

'Please, call me Anthony. I don't know what you have been told about my visit but it's merely a formality. We just want to check that things are running as we would wish them to be. Obviously your numbers speak for themselves.' Anthony gave Masterton what he hoped was a winning smile. He wanted to instil confidence, for the man to open up to him, to let slip something, anything, which could be used as leverage.

Anthony's official brief was to observe their practises and report back. However, Benson had told him, unofficially of course, that the Home Secretary wanted the discarding operation speeded up. It was his job to find out if inefficiency was an issue at this particular installation, and he was determined to. That morning Benson had made a passing comment that hinted a promotion might not be far away. Finding dirt on Craig Masterton and DPC04 could be the key. He liked working on the platform with the boys but he aspired to loftier heights.

Masterton seemed to relax a little, 'Of course, Anthony. I'm glad that the agency is pleased with our figures. We are working flat out at the moment. In fact we have just introduced a night shift to speed up turnover.'

'Excellent. Maybe you can explain the process to me in detail as we tour the installation?'

'Of course, how long are you with us for?'

'Until I've seen what I need to. However, I have a driver outside who wasn't allowed on site so I'd rather we could finish today.'

'That shouldn't be a problem. My apologies that we couldn't let him in, security clearance. I hope you understand.'

'Of course, Mr Masterton. I'm pleased to see such vigilance. It will go in my report. Shall we walk and talk?'

They made small talk about the weather and mutual acquaintances as they walked through the building and out of the main doors, into the autumn sunshine. The camp had a feeling of understated solemnity. No-one walked on the paths, no chatter of conversation could be over-heard anywhere and yet he had the sense that beneath this still façade was a toiling heartbeat, thumping violently against the ribs that caged it.

'So how long have you been with G4ITAS, Mr Masterton?'

'Career man. I've been with the firm since I left university.'

'Oh really? That long? You must have seen some changes.'

Masterton threw him a sidelong frown. Anthony noted that his barb had caught flesh. 'Yes. I started out with the oil and gas team in the Middle East. Back then we were securing key installations against the Islamist threat, keeping the pipeline flowing and all that.' He laughed to himself. 'I came back to England after the peak oil crash and went into correction facilities. When the Eye-for-Eye Act was being legally tested, before the referendum, I was drafted in to head up the criminal discard operation. I spent a lot of time ironing out the proverbial wrinkles with teams from the Home Office before and after the legislation was passed so I'm very used to your processes.'

Anthony noted the return volley and grinned to himself. 'It sounds to me that the Home Office were getting ahead of themselves.'

'It was always going to happen eventually, public opinion was too strong for it not to. We set up a theoretical infrastructure, researched the available technology and after the referendum we were perfectly placed to deal with the backlog.'

'Backlog?' Anthony said.

'Yes, a lot of people don't know this but when Eye-for-Eye came into effect it back dated sentences by five years.'

'I didn't know that. Was it strictly legal? Surely once someone is sentenced that's it?'

'It was legal enough. Obviously there were loopholes to close and legal arguments to be fought but after the first appeal was lost it became precedent.' Masterton chuckled, almost nostalgically.

'Ok, and presumably you've stayed with the firm continuously?'

'Yes. Before this posting I was over-seeing the criminal discard process at Wandsworth.'

'Sorry to interrupt. Can you give me some orientation?' Anthony stopped walking and gestured at the various buildings.

'No problem. Obviously the block we've come from is admin on the first floor. The ground floor is our rec area. It's a hard job and these boys need to blow off a bit of steam sometimes. They are young lads after all and they have to do what young lads do.' Masterton grinned. 'The other two buildings parallel to that are the accommodation blocks. The ground floor of the far one is the armoury and the infirmary. The two old, brick blocks, where you came into the facility, is the business end of the operation.'

'Ok then. I guess that's where we should head.' Anthony replied. He tried to sound professional, aloof. It wouldn't do for this minion to hear any anticipation.

'I have to ask, are you fully aware of what it is you will be seeing in blocks A and B? It's not for the faint of heart, one feels a certain amount of...melancholy. I find it best not to think about things too much and I never speak to the Discards, it encourages a way of thinking that's not all together healthy.' He said sounding uncomfortable.

'Please Mr Masterton, you have nothing to fear, I am not some silly school girl who is going to swoon at seeing the sharp end of the operation. I know what to expect. Lead the way.' Anthony smiled. This bloody fool showed too much humanity for his liking. He wanted to speak to them, touch them. He wanted to look one directly in the eyes and watch confusion metamorphose to horror.

They chattered aimlessly as they strolled into the shadow of the building. The entrance hall was as grand as the exterior had promised. The high ceiling made their footsteps echo back at them as they stepped across the chessboard tiled floor. It felt like an old ecclesiastical building rather than a place built for the purpose of incarceration. The only clues to its intended purpose were the solid, barred doors that led away to other parts of the building.

Masterton's voice took on a hushed, reverential tone as if in deference to the old building. 'This is block A. The Discards are initially brought into the front on their arrival. We have a delivery that is expected any time now.' Masterton checked his watch. Just then a crowd of operatives, a mix of men and women who wore white doctor's coats, walked through the lobby laughing and joking. Masterton shot them a look and they fell silent. They walked out of the front door and stood waiting on the tarmac outside.

'Where is your staff recruited? What's the process?' Anthony asked, more to kill time than through a genuine interest.

'Our operatives are carefully selected for their specific physical and mental attributes from the general G4ITAS employment intake. Our recruitment team take all our candidates through a rigorous selection process; fitness assessment, psychometric testing, literacy and numeracy. There is a very special set of criteria for operatives at the DPCs. Those who fit the bill are separated from the general operatives at the end of their induction training.' Masterton said.

'Ok. Let's move on to the process itself. A coach arrives, what happens next?'

'As you can see, we use our more…presentable members of staff to greet the coaches. We tend to try and keep the armed guards and the uniforms to a minimum, it helps maintain a calm atmosphere. Subterfuge is paramount in order to achieve our goals with the minimum fuss and risk to our staff.'

Anthony grunted. This prissy caution seemed misplaced. It occurred to him that what had fired his imagination about this place was its unashamed functionality. It was an honest way of dealing with social problems that had arisen through a lack of honesty. Masterton's euphemistic, cautious approach offended his sense of propriety.

'They are then led into the reception room where they are given a brief speech. They're told that they are to be given low demand work assignments but that they need to have a medical check to ascertain where they will be sent. Treating them as humanely as possible cuts out the risk of…unrest, which is stressful for both the Discards and my staff. Each process can deal with a hundred units and we run three processes at once. That takes us about an hour to deal with. We try to keep waiting to a minimum for obvious reasons.'

The lobby started to vibrate with the low, unmistakable rumble of large engines. Outside the gates swung open and the coaches drove in and parked in front of the building. Through the doors Anthony could see the first coach was already unloading. The operatives were smiling and directing people towards the building. The doors burst open bringing sound and a fresh breeze. Suddenly there were people everywhere. Elderly males straightened their backs and cast a self-important eye over the building as if to say they had seen it all before, nothing in here would surprise them; old females straightened their coats and gripped their handbags as if they contained the pitiful scraps of life savings; worried, harassed mothers ushered unruly broods; males who looked like they wanted to cause trouble pushed their shoulders back and their chests out as they tried to hide the confusion that they were here with the old people and the disabled. This was the perfect place for watching people, Anthony was transfixed. Their confusion, their hopes and their fears; he was privy to information that these unfortunates weren't. He knew their fate, that deeply personal, hidden truth that each person faces in their darkest dreams and coldest fears; he knew and he wasn't telling.

Although the reception was only a place to pass through, the crowd was dispersing in as many ways as it could, despite the efforts of the operatives who were doing their best to shepherd them. A hundred hushed conversations reverberated from the vaulted ceiling and bounced back as one solid sound. Occasionally the babble was punctuated by orders barked by one of Masterton's staff who suddenly seemed to be having a tough time controlling their temper. Anthony had in no way warmed to Masterton, but he had to appreciate how difficult it was to organise this breed, they had enough trouble on the platform. Eventually the head of the crowd was ushered through a set of double doors and into a large auditorium. After that they all followed, seeing little more than the back in front of them. Eventually, after a lot of confusion and shouting, the auditorium filled up and the coaches left. Anthony stood watching them leave; there was a certain malevolent poetry in their departure. Masterton ushered him over to the closed auditorium doors. He rushed. He didn't want to miss anything.

They stood quietly at the back, waiting along with the rest. A low buzz filled the air as they whispered to one another. After a few long moments a smiling man walked confidently on to the stage. He exuded happiness and confidence from every pore. His game-show-host smile made Anthony want to kick him in the teeth.

'Good morning to you ladies and gentlemen, I do hope that your journey hasn't been too stressful for you. My name is Trevor and I work for the company that has been charged with re-assigning each of you. We believe that every person is intrinsically valuable to our society and everyone can play a role in returning us to the levels of comfort, health and economic vitality of twenty years ago.'

'BOLLOCKS!' A man's voice boomed powerfully from the crowd, Anthony scanned the room but he couldn't see the culprit. Trevor's happy face didn't falter.

'I understand your discontent, sir. If I were in your position I too would no doubt feel the same.' It was amazing, somehow Trevor managed to look grave and concerned while he still had that 'punch me' smile on his face. Anthony wasn't sure if he actually did want to punch him or just congratulate his extraordinary duplicity.

Trevor continued: 'Please do not make the mistake of judging us by our government's standards, we are a different entity. Here you will be treated with the respect that, as human beings, we feel you deserve.'

The room erupted in spontaneous applause. Anthony smiled. The thought occurred to him that they were being treated like people for the first time in a long time.

'Thank you, thank you.' Trevor beamed. 'Now if I may, I would like to explain our process to you...'

'He's amazing isn't he?' Whispered Masterton. 'It's a pleasure to watch him work.'

'Where did you find him?' Anthony replied. His voice was low and slightly awestruck.

'Acting school. He's off his rocker, he really believes that he's helping ease their way.'

'...after I have finished speaking, someone will come up here and read the names out of the first people to go for medical checks. This is the first part of getting you back to work – understanding what you can and can't do and what you need to be healthy. Once your name has been read out we need you to go quickly and quietly to the back of the room and follow the green arrows to the changing area. There you will find private cubicles, each with a medical gown for you to put on. You can leave your clothes on the shelf provided; they'll still be there once you are done.' Trevor chuckled. 'You'll go in your gowns, to the waiting area outside the doctors' office. We have a team of doctor's waiting to receive you so that you can be processed and moved to your new homes as quickly as possible. Some of you will be staying here at this camp but most of you will go to sites not far from here that are managed by our sister company. These are low intensity job roles that won't be too physically demanding on you. You'll each have your own modest room and three square meals a day. For that provision we expect up to five hours a day of work. You'll be asked to do tasks such as mending clothes, peeling nuts and folding sheets.'

'Peeling nuts?' Anthony sniggered behind his hand.

Masterton fixed him with a strange look. 'We found that if we tell the Discards a believable version of events they comply more easily with our commands.' Anthony straightened his face.

'Now, we can't answer each of your questions at present, I'm afraid there is simply too much to do. However you will have a chance to voice any concerns and ask whatever you want of your doctor when you are privately interviewed. I wish you all the best with your new assignments and a prosperous future for us all.' Another round of applause broke out. Anthony looked around the room stupefied.

'Shall we move on to the next part of the process?' Masterton whispered in his ear. Anthony nodded thoughtfully. They slipped out of the rear doors of the auditorium as the operatives started herding the first shuffling units.

Masterton spoke rapidly as they walked. 'Anthony, I think the best way for you to observe will be via a video link that we have set up to monitor the process. Each Discard's face is recorded by camera as they enter the consultation room. This video file is automatically saved on to our servers and attached to the file NASRA sends us. After the Discard has been fully processed the file is sent electronically to the point of disposal where a visual match is made with the cadaver presented, this prevents any...slip-ups.

'And have there been any "slip-ups" as you call them Mr Masterton?'

'Ah, well...um...the process was far from perfect at its inception. Human nature has a way of... rebelling against such things as this... It's never easy, you understand.' Masterton bumbled uncomfortably.

'Oh, I understand only too well.' Anthony smiled.

Masterton frowned as he continued. 'After verification we archive the files. We have stored the details of every Discard who has passed through these doors since they were opened two years ago.'

'If at all possible, Mr Masterton, I would like to be present while the process is implemented. I think it would give me a better overview of how this all works.'

Masterton fixed Anthony with that strange look again, one that bordered on revulsion. 'I'm sorry, Anthony, but I can't allow it. What happens here is carefully planned and balanced to provide as smooth a service as we can manage. Your presence could upset the Discards and create a panic. We have only had one panic to deal with and it ended very stressfully for all our staff. I don't want it to happen again.'

'What happened on that occasion?' Anthony asked. Masterton's eyes darted furtively left and right.

'Well...um...sometimes events such as these get out of our control...and...' He blustered.

Anthony saw his opportunity. 'Surely as the manager of this facility "out of control" shouldn't be a phrase which ever passes your lips?' He smiled. 'Does the agency know about you losing control?' He stopped walking, forcing Masterton to do the same. The short man puffed his chest out and straightened his back in a bid to look dignified. He tried to speak but Anthony wasn't prepared to let him. 'It seems to me that your process is far from perfect. You've now mentioned out of control events, slip-ups and human nature rebelling. How you haven't had more of these..."occurrences" is beyond me. Obviously this should go in my report...' He left the sentence open to inference.

'What do you want?' Masterton asked shortly.

Anthony smiled, pleasantly. 'Put me in the room. I want to see.'

'Why? Why do you want to?' Confusion creased Masterton's brow.

'That is my own business. Your job is to give me my wish or, believe me you jumped up little fuck, I will personally see to it that you're unemployed within a week.' Anthony stretched his shoulders out, he felt good for the first time today. 'How long would the savings last for? How long before your wife's breaking up batteries with a hammer while your daughter sclls her arse to keep you in tatty-water? Hm? And believe me mate; I'll be there to buy it.' He tipped a lubricious wink. Masterton blanched.

'You wouldn't...'

'I fucking would, Craigy, make no mistake.' Anthony replied softly. He stared into the man's eyes.

'Ok.' The older man looked away and shook his head slowly.

'Excellent!' Anthony smiled brightly. 'What do I have to do?'

Masterton told Anthony what was expected of him, he listened carefully, nodding every now and then to show he was paying attention. Studious as ever.

Chapter 18

Ky disappeared into the ground without a word. Joshua followed awkwardly, dragging the rock back behind him, shutting out the grey light. The effort made him sweat uncomfortably in his thick jacket.

'Just wait one moment.' Whispered Ky. They seemed to be in a passage that was little bigger than the hole they had crawled through. The air was stale and close; a hot poisonous ink. He could feel the weight of the rocks above bearing down. He had an almost ungovernable urge to claw at the walls, to push out and break through, stand tall. He concentrated on his breathing.

'Found it.' Ky finally whispered and turned the torch on. The sudden blue light made Joshua wince. Seeing the cramped space made his heart surge more, he felt light headed. The boy crawled away from him down the passage, he willed himself to follow. He focused on the bobbing light ahead and slowed his breathing. He knelt on a sharp stone, his knee screamed with agony. After ten feet, the passage turned and opened out, suddenly he found they were in a space where he could at least sit up and crouch on his feet.

The torch darted around as they got their bearings, illuminating one corner and then another before he had time to process the images. Joshua scrabbled in his own pack to find his torch. With both lights they could see they were in what looked like a small cave carved out of the gritstone. It was low, only about three feet high and about six feet square. The only feature was a slot at the top of the far wall which had been blocked up with rocks. A dirty sleeping bag and Ky's tattered backpack were slung in a corner. Ky rested against a wall and busied himself taking off his jacket.

'Do you want to go first?' Ky said indicating towards the blocked up hole and passing him some battered binoculars.

Joshua crawled over to it. 'Maybe turn the torch out.' One of the rocks bore a fresh scratch, an X. He picked at it, gingerly in case they all tumbled down. It came away easily, sprinkling dust that found motion in a breeze. It stung Joshua's eyes and tickled his throat. He stared at the patch of light, tears blurred his vision. He blinked a few times to clear his vision and put the binoculars to his eyes.

 The position they occupied was higher on this side than where they had entered. It was clear that they were nearly at the top of a steep, rocky escarpment. Below them was a steep drop before gritstone boulders tumbled away towards a valley formed by a rocky ridge to his right and one to his left, above which the sky was pink and orange. 'Which direction does the sun rise in?' He murmured aloud.

'East.' He noted the lack of sarcasm in his response. Mentally he mapped out the points of the compass; he was looking to the north.

The camp, silent and watchful, sat below looking up at the higher ground surrounding it on three sides. Swollen, arthritic knuckles of twisted gorse grew up to the rocks below them and choked the incline from ridge to ridge. It grew up to the high, chain link fences of the camp, broken only by trickles of path that wound through the jagged spikes and yellow flowers. An approach road of fresh tarmac came from behind the west ridge and snaked up to the large gates. Inside the perimeter ran another chain fence, this one older and orange with rust. Between the two, Joshua could make out several dogs prowling. To the east of the camp were three pristine, white rendered buildings that reminded Joshua of a hospital or care home. They were looked down upon from the west side by a pair of two storey, red brick buildings which glowered down on these new upstarts who lacked the size or presence to challenge their pre-eminence. Although it was still proud and solid, the old building's window sills were peeling leprous paint and the roofs were missing slates and even showing their skeletal battens in places. In contrast, the stark new additions were bright and unblemished. To the rear of the brick buildings, a newly added concrete chimney jutted rudely into the sky. Despite the early hour a heavy dark smoke billowed out. He could smell it even from where he was; acrid and bitter but with another, more subtle scent that caught in his throat. Dotted around the complex were out-buildings and storage sheds. Along the far fence was a low building with a large roller shutter door that suggested a vehicle garage. Tall, steel guard towers occupied two corners on opposite sides of the installation. On the covered platforms he could clearly make out two armed guards in the each of the towers. The watch towers loured over the site, a commanding presence that reminded Joshua of a prison.

As he watched a silver car bounced up the uneven road to the gate. It stopped and two guards dressed in camouflage uniforms, rather than the usual black garb, approached from a small guardhouse. The passenger spoke to one for a minute and handed them something, before getting out of the car leaving the driver alone. The guards began walking back to the gate, the passenger started to follow them but something seemed to catch his attention, he seemed to look straight up the valley at him, staring into the binoculars. Joshua instinctively ducked down. Ky looked at him quizzically. He peered back out of the hole, the man was now talking to the guards and paying the rocky hill no attention. He sat down and handed the binoculars to Ky.

'Go for it, see what you think.'

While Ky looked, he bundled up his jacket in a corner and lay down, using it as a pillow. By the faint light from the opening he could see that the rough walls were covered in scratches and strange hieroglyphs that looked so old that they could have formed naturally deep in the bowels of the earth, were it not for the initials and dates they spelled out.

'What do you make of it?'

'It doesn't look like a work camp. That Mackey hasn't got a clue.' Ky replied.

'Yeah that's what I thought. It looks more like a prison, but then Mackey said they're bringing the elderly here…It doesn't make sense.'

'It makes sense if they're not bringing people here to work.' Ky said quietly without looking away from the camp.

Joshua thought about it for a moment. 'Do you mean what I think you do?'

Ky sat back down and handed him the binoculars. 'The chimney and the building around it are brand new. That wasn't part of the original camp. Why would you build a massive chimney?'

'For a massive fire?' The hairs on Joshua's neck pricked his skin. He sat at the hole, watching the camp. There was little movement other than the smoke that continued to billow from the chimney. The smell began to make him feel quite nauseated. His legs started to cramp and he was just about to offer the binoculars to Ky when he saw something; two figures walked around the side of the main building. He focused the lenses quickly. As quickly as they'd appeared they disappeared into the front entrance. He carefully replaced the rock plunging them once more into darkness, refusing to believe what he had seen. He sat down heavily feeling like he was going to vomit. He was glad of the darkness.

'Alright?' Ky asked from within the inky black.

Joshua tried to speak but his mouth felt frozen. His lip trembled and he had to swallow several times before he could talk. 'No, I don't think I am. You were right; they're killing people. They're disposing of the surplus – those who aren't of use.' Something heavy and wet slithered in his stomach.

There was a pause. 'What makes you say that?'

'I've just seen a bloke I used to know; Craig Masterton. He worked for G4ITAS, on their criminal discard team. He's down there with someone from NASRA.'

'Do you know the other one?' Ky asked gently as if he already knew the answer.

'It's Anthony Thomas. Beth's brother, my best friend.' The words didn't sound like his own, as if some malevolent entity had hijacked his voice.

'Shit…I'm sorry. People have had their suspicions, Kane's mentioned it. I don't know that Stickles does, but then that crazy old bastard hasn't got a clue what's going on. He wanted you to come and see if you could shed any light on this place, Kane wanted me to come so I could…guide you. It's real Josh, that camp confirms it.'

'Maybe I'm wrong. I mean, there could be loads of reasons why Anthony would be here.'

Ky turned the torch on. 'What about Masterton? Josh it looks like a prison camp, there's a newly built furnace tacked on the side. They're not burning rubbish. Or are they?' His face twisted into a shocking smile.

Joshua shook his head; he chewed at a loose shred of skin by his finger nail. 'It's not true; if it was then I would have heard. Surely I'd have heard something? If it's true then…oh my God, my parents.'

Ky shuffled over and squeezed his shoulder. 'We don't know that Josh, we don't know what the criterion is. We don't even know for sure if they are.'

'But you said…'

'I know. Look, let's just do what we came to do, watch the camp and report back what we see when we get back to London.'

'But what if they are? What if my parents are down there? And Anthony... surely he...' The low ceiling seemed to have dropped, crushing the air out of the hole, squeezing and concentrating, suddenly he felt hot. An oily sheen greased Joshua's palms. His breathing grew shallow. The light grew, blotting out all else, burning into his skin. From a vast distance away he heard the rattling whine of his chest desperately sucking at the thin air. And then Ky was there, holding his arms, talking. Garbled words in a steady low torrent that seemed to push back the walls and support the ceiling, lower the temperature and invite air back into the hole. Eventually he could breathe again. He focused on the words Ky spoke, using them as a beacon to guide him back. The boy sat back down, unfazed.

'Are you ok?' He asked.

'Yeah.' Joshua replied quietly. 'I just...my parents and this place... It makes sense.' Tears flowed now making his face throb.

Ky watched him with interest as he calmed down again, eventually he spoke. 'It's funny how someone can come into your life and you didn't realise they were missing until they arrive.' He smiled softly. Not the twisted grimace that looked so out of place on his face but a soulful smile that lit up his eyes, he looked almost shy to have shared it.

Joshua suddenly thought of another smile. For a moment he could almost smell the light fragrance that accompanied her whenever she came into a room. His heart tripped just a little before stuttering on. 'Are you talking about Meditant?'

Meditant for me. Beth for you.' Ky shrugged.

Joshua blushed and returned the shrug. 'How old are you?'

'I'm thirteen and a half.'

'No offense, but you're unlike any other teenager I've ever met.'

'None taken. My life's not been like yours.' Ky replied.

'Where are your family? How did you end up alone?' He expected the boy to clam up at any moment but he seemed open, expansive in a way that Joshua hadn't seen him before, even with Kane.

'My family? I never knew them, I was brought up on the streets. I was passed from mother to mother. Different faces, same name. Some died, some were locked up but somehow my fate was always separate from theirs. When they came to harm I just drifted to the next Mum.'

'That must have been a tough way to grow up.' Joshua was genuinely shocked, no-one had given him any idea.

'Yes and no.' Ky replied in a matter of fact manner. 'If you've never known the comfort of a bed how can it be a problem if one is taken away from you? If you've never had a house why would you miss one? I never had a loved one I could lose; no-one ever had that power over me, not until…well.' He shrugged.

'Not until you found Meditant?'

'Not until Meditant found me.' He nodded with satisfaction.

Joshua felt like he was starting to see why Beth cared about him so much. 'Why do you dislike me?'

'I'm warming to you, I guess.' He smiled that smile again. 'It's because you seem lost, uncommitted. You see everything happening around you but you don't feel a part, you don't feel you can affect it. The truth is, Joshua, you can. Be present, be with the struggle; not living in the maze of your own insecurities and anger. When I met you I didn't like you because you seemed like any other wide-eyed tourist at his first protest, watching from the side lines. When I found out that you were from an estate I was a little disgusted that you had allowed yourself to suck on the corporate teat for your education. I suppose I do understand though, I think I have for a while.'

'If you have for a while then why were you still a little bastard?' Joshua grinned.

'Just for my own amusement really.' He replied. 'Get some sleep, we'll watch the camp in shifts, I'll go first.'

Within minutes Joshua was curled up in a ball asleep, defying the cold, hard floor. Ky watched his bundle gently rise and fall. He seemed hypnotised. Finally he nodded grimly as if satisfied by something and opened the viewing hole to look down the hill.

Chapter 19

A heavy clunk told him that they had reached their floor. They stepped out into a still corridor with a polished floor like a calm pond whose surface refused to ripple as they walked.

Anthony was dressed in a white coat that Masterton had found for him. He caught sight of himself in a glass window and giggled. 'Look at me, I'm a doctor!' He grinned at Masterton who looked away. Anthony shrugged and straightened his tie.

'It's the first group of the day so there can't be any upsets. We have to work in this environment, we're not just tourists.' Masterton said.

'Yeah, yeah.' Anthony's heart was racing with impatient excitement. They stopped outside door marked 'staffroom'.

'This is as far as I will come. Our operative will take you from here.' Masterton opened the door, blocking Anthony's sight with his body. Inside he could hear laughter and men talking, the smell of cigarettes drifted out making him want one badly. 'Lee, come here please,' he said into the room. The laughter died.

The man who came to the door shocked Anthony with his youth. He was tall and broad with a good looking face. He wore a doctor's jacket identical to his own. His intelligent brown eyes studied Anthony with a curiosity that he made no attempt to conceal.

'Our official observer is going to observe the first process of the day. Will you see to it that he gets everything he wants?' The acid in the man's voice was inconsequential. Masterton turned smartly and walked back the way they had come, the heels of his shoes clicking against the polished floor.

'So who the fuck are you then?' Lee asked conversationally.

Anthony smiled in return. He liked his directness. He instantly felt he could warm to this man; he reminded him slightly of Joshua. 'I'm from NASRA. I'm supposed to be here to observe but I just blackmailed your idiot of a governor so I could get up close and watch.'

Lee nodded his head as if he understood perfectly without needing to ask about his motives. 'Cool. Masterton's a fucking twat. If there's anything you can do to get him replaced I'm sure the lads would be over the moon.' He stuck out a surprisingly large hand to shake, Anthony almost didn't respond out of fear that his own would be crushed. 'My name's Lee Cross.'

'Nice to meet you, Lee.' Anthony replied as he tried not to wince at the pressure on his hand. 'Anthony Thomas.'

'I'm pleased to meet you.' Lee grinned widely as if he genuinely was. 'The goons are there already, we might as well go down now.'

They walked along the corridor, away from the staffroom, and turned a corner. The subdued rumble of many hushed conversations met them. Anthony could see ahead of him a long queue wearing thin paper gowns. Each wore a placard around their neck bearing a barcode. The queue snaked down a stairwell out of sight. It occurred to Anthony that he had no idea of what method could dispose of this many in an efficient manner. He felt perspiration moisten the skin around his lips. The hubbub died down as their presence was noticed, Anthony realised that the doctor's jacket gave them an air of authority. Scrawny necks craned to see them pass. Hunched shoulders straightened themselves. Eyes; hostile, pleading, curious, scared, bored. A spectrum of shades and colours levelled at them, expecting everything and nothing. He smiled and nodded as they walked past. None responded.

Something caught Anthony's eye, making him double take as he passed. Wavy hair, hazel eyes, her face a splash of colour against the bland background. His heart swelled with violent love and fear. He choked down his panic as he realised that it wasn't Tamsin. A shy looking female nervously studied him back. She smiled slightly and he felt that pulse in his trousers again. He looked down and saw a heavily pregnant belly. He smiled, he hoped, warmly. He quietened the panicked chatter in his head and didn't look at any more until they reached a door at the head of the queue.

*

Of course she was grateful that she'd been assigned to light duties. Who wouldn't be? The initial hopefulness of the early days of the Transport Scheme had died away like so many broken hopes before. Rumours swept through the estate, dark tales of sweat shops, toiling in the fields, dangerous mines under Sheffield; the old regimes of health and safety doctrine thrown out in the name of expansion and mortal fear of a return to economic contraction. But it gave her hope that those judging saw fit to take her condition into consideration.

She felt tired now, so achingly tired. The last two days had been long and hard. The rattling train journey, people shouting and fighting all through the night and then the awful selection process at Manchester Piccadilly and the coach journey here. She hoped it would be over soon, that someone would show her to a clean bed with crisp white sheets where she could rest and sleep. She closed her eyes and held her swollen belly beneath the crinkly paper gown.

Two doctors came striding confidently down the corridor. She watched them pass and wondered if one could just listen to her baby's heartbeat, just to let her know that he was ok. Of course she didn't doubt that it was a he. He'd be strong, like his father had been. The shorter, black doctor looked right at her and smiled. She felt something good, a gentleness emanating from him. Her faith was restored a little. Everything would be ok.

*

178

Lee closed the door behind them. The chatter resumed outside in the corridor. The room was a small, dimly lit limbo, featureless aside from the door they had come through and another at the far end. The far door opened flooding the room with a celestial, white light. A figure appeared, silhouetted; a large built man wearing sunglasses grunted an acknowledgement and withdrew, letting the door swing soundlessly shut.

'Ready?' Lee said. Anthony nodded. Questions and their answers seemed unnecessary. Lee took out his phone and dialled a number. He repeated his question at whoever answered and nodded, satisfied with the response. He opened an application on his phone and loud music started to play from unseen speakers in the ceiling. It was nondescript and annoyingly calming, some hideous compilation of contemporary pop songs played on the sickeningly soothing pan pipes. The door opened. The voices outside were silent now, save for a far off bawling to get in line, keep quiet, you'll be processed now, then you'll get a cup of tea.

The procession came. Lee wordlessly scanned each bar code and gestured towards the back of the room. He only had to do that a few times before the procession gained momentum and each lemming followed the last. Their faces remained blank as they filed by, marching on towards the heavy door at the back that swung open and shut, open and shut. A steady rhythm counting each heartbeat as it passed. Bright light escaping in staccato flashes like a lightning storm. The girl came into the room. He caught her eye and tried to smile. She held his gaze, smiling back. A tacit exchange. He felt something deep in his stomach, a feeling that he had very little compare to. He made a gesture at Lee; a tip of his head towards the swinging door. Lee nodded.

*

Her turn came. She followed the line through the door. Soothing music filled her, making her smile. The queue filed through the room where the taller doctor was scanning their hideous, dehumanising bar codes. There must be other doctors, further along. Hopefully she could ask them some questions in there. It seemed a strange set up, alien. But the last couple of days had taught her to just go where she was told. That's all anybody did really, wasn't it? You were born into one layer of a bloated onion and that's where you stayed. No amount of hard work could make you move up a layer, not really. There were stories of the few who made it, the genius', freaks of nature born to the wrong parents, the scholarships, the lucky promotions. They were the exception rather than the rule, though. You went where you were told.

The black doctor saw her and looked at her. She had feelings about people, always had. She could tell the type of person someone was just by the quality of their eyes. How they reflected light, how they reflected shadow. She saw in him a lost soul but a good one. She wanted to reach out to him, to embrace him and tell him that everything would be alright; he could cling to her if he needed to stop himself from sinking. He would help her; he would listen. He was the man who would hear her baby's heartbeat for the first time. He moved towards the back of the room. He must be coming to talk to her, he had to be. The big doctor scanned her barcode. She smiled at him, not minding that he shared in the reflected gratitude that she felt for his colleague. There was enough to go around.

*

His eyes adjusted to the scalding light. He could see now. See it all. He'd heard it as he came through the door into the tiny lift lobby. They really didn't have long to scream and the music in the other room made a very efficient job of drowning it out. There would have been a panic without it. He'd nearly been a part of it, grabbed as he came through the door. He'd scolded the meat-head and showed him his ID. Meat-head had grunted and grabbed the next, shoving it toward another meat-head who cable tied the wrists and shoved it into the hole where the lift doors had been removed. The girl came in. She flailed her head, looking for something. Confusion made her eyes wild. She found what she was looking for. She found him. The moment slowed to a lazy amble as every detail of her etched itself onto the grain of his mind. A light sheen of iridescent sweat on her brow gently reflected the harsh light from above. Her eyes were lively and aware, calling to him, imploring him. The horror left, draining away like a lanced infection. He knew her. He'd shared in the fleeting swansong of her pathetic but intrinsically beautiful existence. In that singular moment he loved again. They were as one. *I love her.* The thought resonated, growing with each echo. He loved this woman and all she was. He loved her every detail, the feeling was reciprocated, he knew it, it had to be. He drank in her fragile beauty, her exquisite terror. Her light nourished and cleansed the shadows that chilled him. It was a pure, honest love, one born of a shared, profound experience that was more personal, more intimate than any physical union he had ever had before. The paper gown ripped at the collar exposing alabaster skin to the swell of her breast. Her swollen belly protruded from under the gown. Her mouth opened to call out to him, to beg him to save her. Would she know his name? He wondered about the life inside her, its sex, its father. Did it feel her fear? Suddenly the moment was lost, fading away like all the infinite moments before it and the infinite moments that would follow.

*

The door opened. Light flooded her head, blinding her. Hands were everywhere, grabbing, pushing, shoving. She whipped her head around, looking for the doctor with the soulful eyes. Sharp pain in her wrists. Biting snakes cut flesh. Her hands bunched into claws. She saw him, watching. His eyes had softened still more; he looked at her with sadness and love. A shove winded her, she wheezed at the thin air as she fell forwards then down, down, down. She landed with a wet, painful crunch on the kicking, writhing mass of bodies, fighting to stay on the surface of the fetid, stinking water that filled the lift shaft. She slipped between thrusting arms into the water, pushing down those beneath her. Screams and cries filled the shaft. Echoing, deafening; the sounds of madness. Hands grabbing at her, pulling her down, pulling handfuls of flesh. Mindless grasping claws panicking, panicking. Kicks, punches, bites. Teeth, flesh, nails. The stink of blood and shit and fear filling her nose, her lungs, her body. Desperate to keep her mouth shut, to stop death from flooding in. Weight crushing down. More wet crunches. Bursting chest. The bitter, foulness filling her mouth, thick and gurgling. More crunches, more weight, more, more, more. The darkness. The silence.

*

He walked back out into the other room, quiet, dazed. The last of them had passed through leaving peace behind. The operatives walked out and removed their sunglasses. They bolted the door behind them and left. Lee nodded gravely at him and squeezed his shoulder. Words would have corrupted the sanctity of the moment, a moment shared not only with the girl but with the man. Their eyes met and Anthony had to blink back emotion. A kind look passed between them, the tender sharing of something far greater than either of them. It passed and they both cast their eyes down in shame. Thoughts of the girl, her peace filled his heart. *Thank you. Thank you, my love.*

Chapter 20

The coming dawn hung purple and heavy above London. Expectant clouds curled and rolled, waiting for their waters to break. Joshua's eyeballs itched. Every time he closed them, mauve patterns, shards of shattered glass, blossomed kaleidoscopically, hypnotising him, enticing him to sleep. Ky banged on the metal door again. It clanged loudly, sounding obscene in the early morning still. Finally they heard the distant shuffle of Stickles ascending the stairs.

The journey south had taken them all night. Mackey had come as arranged and they'd stomped back across the moor, barely speaking an exhausted word before he had shown them to the back of another lorry, this one headed to London.

The door swung open. Stickles wore a threadbare, blue dressing gown. His bloodshot eyes regarded them with a baleful glare. 'What the devil do you two think you're doing here unannounced?' He spat. 'Get in here now. Bloody fools.' He ushered them downstairs muttering and swearing. The warm air and heady stench of weed hit them like a warm blanket. No-one moved amongst the dark plants and the table where the guards had played cards an eon ago was empty. Stickles sat down in his chair and picked up a half smoked joint from an ashtray. He lit it and gestured impatiently for them to sit down. 'So are you two idiots going to tell me what you are doing here?'

'Stickles, we've got something to tell you…' Joshua began.

'Tell me? Tell me?' He laughed nastily. 'You can start by telling me who the fuck you think you fucking are…no-one shows up here unannounced. No-one. You can also fucking *tell* me why you couldn't fucking *tell* me by text?' He started coughing, a foul fog erupted from his lungs. He waved the joint in the air, neither of them took it. He tossed it in the ashtray, his skinny body contorted and heaved as he fought for breath.

'The place on Saddleworth, it's a death camp.' Ky said when Stickles had regained his composure.

He smiled and nodded. 'And, pray tell, what brings you to this outlandish conclusion?'

Joshua spoke. 'I saw people I knew, someone who worked for G4ITAS's executions division and… that was it.' He finished quickly. Ky shot him a look. Stickles didn't seem to notice.

'Hm… Interesting.' His voice sounded hollow, he looked at the floor for a moment. 'Your orders are to not say a thing about this to anyone. Am I clear?'

Joshua looked at Ky to see if he shared his shock. The boy's face was as impassive as ever. 'What the hell are you going to do about it?' Joshua flared up. 'They're killing the people they don't want. We've got an army, firepower…we've got to stop them.'

'Oh Joshua, have we turned into an idealist now?' Stickles laughed and lit the joint again. He took several deep pulls drawing smoke deep into his lungs and holding it before letting out a dense cloud. 'Rebuild have over-shot their mandate. Of course, the general public are okay with state sponsored slavery, decades of the media's demonization of the impoverished have seen to that. But the impression of civility must remain, once that's gone the public won't stand for it. They'll rally behind this cause, which will force the corporations to switch their allegiance and the day will be ours. We may not even have to fire a shot; a bloodless coup.'

'Then let's do that. We can get evidence, we can put it up on social media, make it go viral. We've got the ability to stop this quickly.' Joshua said.

'Neither of you will say a word of this to anyone, not even your beloved Kane. The guarantees that I have over you will see to your silence. Understand? Your designated proxy will suffer should lips get loose. Hm?'

'Will you talk to the committee? Can I come with you?' Joshua had barely heard him; his exhausted excitement was slipping into his words.

Ky made a gesture with his hand, quietening him. 'I think I see what's going on here. You're not going to do a thing, are you?' His grey eyes coldly regarded Stickles. A small, bitter smile toyed with the corners of his mouth.

'Very good, boy.' Stickles cried, jumping up and spilling the ashtray. He clapped his hands. 'An astute boy you are, I've always said. Now, tell me why? Hm? Why?' He leaned forward and tapped his fingers together.

'Because the committee knows already. You're waiting until the surplus population is dealt with before you make your move.' Ky's face was grave. Deep lines were etched into the purple shadows beneath eyes that were wise and old, too old; ageless.

Stickles' grin wavered but remained. 'How right you are, boy.' He said so softly Joshua barely heard him. 'We must let Rebuild do what must be done. Let them get their hands dirty.'

'What must be done?' Joshua shouted, getting to his feet. The old man's solemnity enraged him as much as his words. His muted tone gave them a dignity they didn't deserve. 'They need to be stopped, if we let them do it we're no better.'

'You're no better anyway.' Stickles jeered. 'You wring your hands now but how many deaths did you facilitate while you worked for the beast? Our little NASRA turncoat. As flawed as Rebuild are, their brutal policies are useful to the administration in waiting. You sit there and shake your head like this is my fault. This is the decision of a committee of your betters, you whelp.'

Ky stood to join him. He calmly settled the full intensity of his gaze on Stickles. 'If you don't act I will.' He said softly.

Stickles' face flushed crimson. He coughed loudly several times before he could force a contemptuous snort. 'You boy? And how do you intend to do that?'

Ky smiled a gentle, mild smile. 'With the army of street people that I recruited for you, Stickles. You fed them and armed them but their loyalty is to me.'

*

Out in the silent city a grey dawn had broken. Ky strode purposefully down the street, away from the brewery and the gas works, heading towards the main road. Joshua had to half trot to keep up, even though his legs were longer. 'What are we going to do? What are you going to do? What was all that back there with Stickles?' Joshua's exhaustion was twisting his comprehension; he felt like he was losing his place in a book.

'Keep up, Josh.' Ky replied. He had taken out his phone and put it to his ear. Joshua went to make an angry reply but a tinny voice on the other end cut him off. 'Kane? It's me. Stickles will be sending visitors to the house, you need to get out. Call Happy and have him send someone to Reading for Josh's sister.' He hung up and put the phone back in his pocket. 'We need to get a bus to the nearest tube. We should be able to catch one at the end of the road.'

'Tell me what's going on, now.' Joshua grabbed Ky's arm, stopping him walking. His frustration was peaking.

Ky whirled around, his face set stern. 'We've not got time for this. Stickles will be sending people to Kane's and to your sister's. We all need to get somewhere safe. Call Beth, we'll have to go to hers.' He seemed to see something in Joshua's face that made him soften.

'Kane's had his suspicions about the committee's motives for a while. When Stickles had me form a division from the street people we kept them separate. They're armed and housed away from the other Freetopia forces.'

Joshua could barely compute what he was saying. 'How many men are we talking about?'

Ky grinned. 'A hundred armed men. So far.'

Joshua returned his smile. 'How many men does Freetopia have?'

'Nationwide; thousands. Now let's stop fucking about, you need to call Beth.'

Joshua took out his phone and found Beth's number. He pressed call and waited. After a few rings her sleepy voice was in his ear. For a moment he was disarmed, words tried to come but they hung back, shy. 'Beth… It's me…Josh…Um…Ky and I, we're in trouble can we come to yours?'

As he spoke Ky's phone rang. He picked it up and listened before hanging up without uttering a word. His face had turned a sickly grey.

Beth replied to Josh. 'Of course, just come over as quickly as you can.'

'We need to go to Kane's now.' Ky interrupted.

Who was that? Joshua asked Ky, trying to fathom what was going on.

'A friend. We need to go NOW.' He practically screeched. Naked fear danced in his eyes. Joshua hung up the phone without saying goodbye.

The bus and train were painfully slow. They stared with sunken eyes at the early wave of hi-vis commuters who passed blank faced and bleary eyed through the transport system. When the train arrived they all scrabbled for a seat, cutting dirty looks at the snifflers, the loud headphones and the woman with solemn eyes who passed through the carriage holding out a filthy hat in a scabrous claw. Joshua gave her what little change he had.

They pushed their way out of the tube station, past the suits and skirts that were coming to take their turn in the capital's arteries. They walked towards Kane's house in silence. People passed them as they left for work, casting maybe a curious glance before their eyes glazed again and moved on. Joshua's body trembled. He could feel the adrenalin dripping into his blood drop by drop, pushing its way through his veins, forcing his pulse to race. He strode as savagely as Ky, his strong legs no longer tired, feasting on the distance between them and the house. By the time they were nearly outside Kane's, his heart was thumping viciously against his ribcage. Ky tapped his arm, drawing his attention to something. It took him a moment to realise that the front door was ajar.

Inside the house was still. Ky began to softly climb the stairs while Joshua pushed open the living room door. The sofas had been over-turned and a bookshelf lay over them propped up at an angle. Books and ornaments were scattered over the floor. Kane was lying in the middle of it all as if he were part of the mess. His arm was twisted unnaturally behind his back. Black blood matted the thin hair at the back of his head. Joshua knelt down next to him and listened carefully; he was still breathing. 'Mate, are you ok? Can you hear me?' Joshua's voice was clogged with tears. He tried to turn him over but he was too heavy and awkward. A dull voice insisted that he should call an ambulance but he knew he couldn't. He crouched down low so that Kane could see him. His eyes were open a crack, he tried to smile when he saw Joshua.

'Did they get the baby?' He gasped. Joshua was just about to reply, to tell some well-meaning lie, but he heard a happy gurgle. He turned to see Ky stood at the living room door holding Meditant.

'He was hidden upstairs in a cupboard.' Ky said. His face was ashen.

Joshua turned back to Kane. 'It's okay, he's fine.' Kane's eyes were closed. Joshua felt for a pulse but he was already gone.

Just then there was a noise at the front door. Joshua shot to his feet, his hands balled at his sides. Ky gently placed the baby on the sofa. The living room door pushed slowly open. Beth's frizzy hair and wide eyes looked around. 'Josh? What's going on? I was worried.' She walked in the room properly and gasped as she saw Kane.

Ky picked up the baby. His was face was pallid, his eyes set with leaden determination. 'We're going to war.'

Joshua nodded. 'I need to go to Reading. I need to find my sister.'

*

Beth's moped buzzed through Reading's still streets. Despite it being the middle of the day, or maybe it was because of the fact, this part of town felt dead. Apart from the absence of life the town seemed normal, caught mid-breath like a gargantuan Marie Celeste. He could almost imagine that it was two in the morning and some alignment of the heavenly bodies had created a sliver of day amongst the still night and that soon they would be plunged into darkness.

Yewtree Lane was the gateway to the Beechfield Towers estate. It was lined on both sides with terraced houses whose gardens had always been well kept when Joshua was a child. Every front door stood open, taunting him, asking him why he was only here now. Beth slowed down as they passed. He peered into stark hallways stripped of anything that could be of use. Carpets were gone, wood had been stripped to leave skeletal staircases and the walls bore scars where electric cables had once been. In the middle of the road was an enormous, stinking pile of rubbish. The smell made them both gag, a warm, sweet stench of corrupt food that wasn't wholly unpleasant as it first curled into the nostrils; a second later a taste like hot, sour vomit assailed his taste buds, making his stomach contract. Ever since local council services had been privatised into a thousand despotic mini corporations, Joshua had heard stories of people dumping their waste in the poorer areas of towns, but it had seemed impossible. A dark cloud of buzzing flies hovered despite the cool temperature. Black bags had split open, pecked apart by obese pigeons and predatory crows, spilling their viscera of rotting waste and fat, pale maggots. Shabby bundles of cloth pretended to be those who had once worn them. Thousands of useless items; discarded.

At the end of the street the two tower blocks struck shabbily up towards the sky, flanked by rows of garages. Every garage had been broken into and pulled apart so many times that the owners hadn't stored anything in them in since Joshua was a boy. Some had been used for dumping more rubbish and piles of stinking bags tumbled out of the open doors in a rancid avalanche. Everywhere was an unearthly stillness. Panic swelled inside Joshua's mind threatening to burst.

Beth stopped the moped and turned to him. Her green eyes were wide and shocked. 'I don't like this, where are all the people?'

'We need to find out.... I need to see.' He replied softly, staring up at the towers. High above them, one of the windows had been left open. A yellow net curtain billowed in a breeze they couldn't feel from the ground. It looked like a ghost desperate to escape the desolate building.

Joshua got off the moped, feeling sore after their two hour drive. He waited impatiently as Beth climbed off and rested it on its stand. They hurried towards the entrance to the first tower. The squalid, piss smelling entrance hall was as ill-lit as it had ever been and the out of order sign on the lift was nothing unusual. Graffiti adorned the walls in a faded montage. A laughing cartoon man wearing a suit and bowler hat held his anatomically impossible penis as he urinated on a grey-faced, shoeless child; a shark-like cartoon moped chased a shackled figure wearing the G4ITAS uniform; a grinning lower case b, the symbol for bancor, ate a sobbing pound symbol that wrung its hands. Written above the pictures in a hasty, artless scrawl: THIS CITY IS MY CAGE. THIS LIFE IS MY PRISON.

 'What happened to all the people?' Beth asked, bewildered. 'You don't think Stickles…'

'This isn't Stickles' work.' Joshua said slowly and deliberately as if each word was an effort of will.

They climbed the stairs. Joshua had to hold himself back and wait for Beth to catch up. He hated the thought of her alone in this vacuum. Eventually they got to Tamsin and Mario's floor. He pushed the door open, not expecting to find it locked. The flat had been left in a state of calm order, as though the looters who had stripped the houses on Yewtree Lane weren't brave enough to venture this high up. Joshua wondered if they were scared of heights. He giggled shrilly. Beth jumped and shot him a strange, concerned look. Not a thing was out of place, it was like they had stepped out for a moment to go to the shops. He wandered from room to room, dazed, weakly pushing open doors and staring intently at the shabby furniture within. Beth stood in the hallway, her fingers sunk into the thick frizz of her hair. Joshua walked into the front room and suddenly his legs gave way. He sank into the sofa, dropping into a sag made by someone, maybe his sister. He felt like his body had given up, the last few days had finally caught up with him without warning. He felt delirious, almost hysterical. Beth came in and crouched down in front of him. Black tears streaked her face. 'Josh, remember they can both work, they'll be alright.' She searched his face, her green eyes flickering from left to right as she looked for any sign of comfort.

Joshua smiled, he gently pushed her hair back from her forehead. 'I'm going to find them, Beth. I can get onto the estate where they are, I'm sure of it. I'm going to find them and get them out.'

*

Joshua scanned a bleary eye around the beer garden of JR Wetherbury's but no-one would meet his gaze. Beer garden; the phrase implied grass, flowers, shrubs. Not a concrete slab, spread with weather worn wooden tables and decorated with leftover Christmas lights. A deep, icy chill had set in with the evening. Despite how drunk he was, Joshua shivered.

The weekend approached, one more lousy day at the office for most people. Those who couldn't wait that long had emptied straight into the pub. Plastic princesses drinking cheap, pink plonk from plastic glasses, shivered as they chain smoked and pretended not to shiver. Suited Dave's, ties set to casual, disappeared to the toilets and came back sniffing and wide eyed, maybe with the faintest smudge of white powder caught in a fastidiously shaped goatee. A rant formed behind his creased forehead, something about snorting the blood of the slaves who were forced to make that shit, but even through the fug he realised how hypocritical that was. He wondered what Beth thought, if he was being boorish, annoying. He doubted she'd be at the bar buying more drinks if he was. But what if one of the Dave's saw her? She was beautiful, they'd be mad not to try. Could her head be turned that easily, by some chancing, Reading wide-boy?

On cue she appeared at the door, her face taut with concentration as she struggled to open it and not spill the two pints of lager that she carried. A Dave dashed to help her, flashing a shark-like grin. She smiled back, her face coming alive, glowing like a Chinese lantern. The words were lost in the low buzz of the garden. Joshua spat hate with his eyes. Beth said something and gestured with her head. Dave responded, this time she laughed, her rich, deep chuckle reaching him a splinter of a second later. *What did he say? How did he make her laugh? Was she telling him I'm just a friend?* She came away still smiling.

'What was that about?' Joshua tried his best to sound nonchalant. She sat down next to him, a warm current of air that smelt sweet and fresh crept into his nostrils. He drank deeply.

'Nothing, he was just trying his luck. I told him you were my boyfriend. That's not weird, is it? I mean, that would be weird but it's not awkward is it? It is now isn't it? I….Oh shut up Beth.' Her mocha cheeks darkened with the roses that bloomed there. Joshua laughed heartily for the first time that day. 'It's good to see you smile.'

'I feel guilty smiling. I'm pretty sure she's not.' Joshua took a sip of his pint. 'I've always had it easier than her haven't I? I got to go to school, university, get a good job. Even Dad loved me and hated her.'

'None of that was your fault.'

'She never complained, not once. She never tried to make me feel bad about any of it. I think she was genuinely happy that life went ok for me.' Joshua said.

'She idolised you. I was always so jealous.'

'Of what?'

'Her relationship with you. Anthony was always such a bastard to me. I would pretend that you were my brother too…Obviously I had to make up some elaborate story to explain our different ethnicity but you know what I mean.'

Joshua smiled.   'He loved, *loves*, you really. It's just his way.'

'It's funny that you instinctively use the past tense for him. In my head I do as well. It's almost like he's dead.'

'Come on, Beth, don't talk like that.'

'It is though. He just seemed to get further and further away as we got older. When he left it just seemed right that he did.'

 Joshua thought of his own last conversation with Anthony; he turned away from the part of himself that agreed with her. He stifled a yawn that snuck up on him.

'God, you must be shattered. How long has it been since you slept?'

'Not far off forty-eight hours. Everything seems surreal now, fake. It's like I'm watching a cartoon.' He giggled as he imagined everything really looking like a cartoon.

 A perplexed smile turned up her lips. 'Share, Baker? I think you're starting to lose it.'

'Nothing, just thinking about cartoons. We seem to be losing everyone don't we?' He smiled again, more sadly this time. 'First your mum and dad and now mine; Anthony, Tamsin. Who next?'

'God, not each other, I don't think I could bear it.' Beth said quickly then looked away uncomfortably and took a large drink of her pint. Joshua blinked twice; drunk, exhausted, surprised.

'Say that again.'

'Say what?' Beth's eyes scurried around the chilly garden, dancing from faces to vaporous clouds; willow-the-wisps that rose into the night. Joshua gently touched her chin with one finger, holding her head in place.

'Say that again.' He repeated.

Her eyes settled on his. 'I couldn't bear to lose you.' Her voice was tiny and fragile. Her jade eyes stretched wide. The ghost of black makeup scratched her eyelid, applied long ago across the vast day. Tiny specks of reflected fairy lights made her iris' shimmer and change with every imperceptible movement of her body as it trembled. He looked at her lips, usually spread so widely in a smile, now they almost pouted with concentration, or fear, or both. He hesitated, the moment was ripening, soon it would be too long, too anticipated; it would pass like so many other wasted moments before it. What if she turned away? What if he tried to kiss her and she turned her cheek? Her eyelids pulsed open a fraction more. A subtle cue, a subconscious hieroglyph, readable only to the initiated. But he was the initiated, he'd known her all of his life, there was no need to be shy, scared, nervous. This was the most natural thing that could ever be. He leaned forward, his eyes closing themselves. He passed into her aura, her warmth. He found her. He felt something tangible, a connection, a crackle of energy. But something was wrong, something in his head held him back. He pulled away, only very slightly. She opened her eyes and he his. He saw her vulnerability; he saw her wanting. The doubt vanished along with the shadows. He smiled. She responded. This time they kissed.

Chapter 21

Mario smiled weakly, a meaningless widening of the lips that excluded the eyes. Tamsin looked away. His face blended into the others that surrounded them on all sides babbling with excited trepidation. She rubbed her swollen belly, she felt ashamed at the quiet, but insistent, voice that whispered that they would be alright now, surely Transports would have access to some kind of basic medical care that Mario couldn't possibly afford. *He* could though. She pushed the thought away. *He* couldn't be relied on for anything.

'NEXT FOUR STEP FORWARD.' An angry plasty shouted. Tamsin didn't like the way this spotty teenager fingered the trigger of the rifle that he clung tightly to. She wanted to walk over and gently take his hand away, to whisper in his ear that it was ok, these were his people, not some alien species, no-one would hurt him. The queue shuffled forward, it would be their turn soon, although their turn for what she couldn't really say. Her feet ached, she had to stand for the whole four hour train journey from Reading to Manchester. No-one had offered their seat. She reminded herself that other people were tired too and she wasn't special just because she was pregnant. She wondered if this was how cattle felt before they were slaughtered, shoved from one place to another with no care; nothing to remind you that you were a you and not an It. Below the rippling surface of shoulders and chests, Mario reached for her hand, she pulled away.

Their turn came. They were ushered into a forlorn branch of Tie Rack that must have stood empty since Day X. A rude plasty shoved Mario towards one cubicle and her to another. Inside a tired looking man of Asian descent sat behind a desk. He yawned without bothering to cover his mouth. 'Good afternoon, my name is Raj Bueller. Papers.' Tamsin handed over the paperwork that REW Development had given them when they had burst in without ringing the door bell and evicted them.

'And the other, come on I haven't got all day.' Raj Bueller spat, flapping his hand. Tamsin meekly handed over the questionnaire that was given to her by another faceless plasty on the train.

'It says here you've got a man. Is that right?'

'That…that's right…Mario, he's next door.'

'I don't care where he is love, alright? Is he going to look after you and…that.' He pointed at her belly with distaste. The baby moved inside as if he felt uncomfortable under the scrutiny. Warmth spread through her.

'Yes of course he is. Do you have children?' She smiled sweetly.

Raj glared back at her. 'They'd pay good money for you at the whorehouse, love. Pregnant bitches are always at a premium. Limited edition, see, the punters would be lining up around the corner.'

Tamsin felt the blood drain from her face. Her head felt light and empty. 'Mr Bueller…'

Raj leant over the desk. 'Watch your fucking mouth. I can do that to you.' He grinned nastily and stamped her paperwork with a theatrical thump. He held on to it for a moment before pushing it back across the desk to her with a sly smile. On top he had slid a business card for a Madame Selina.

'When you've shit that thing out, get in touch with this woman, she can get you out. You'll have to find someone who'll make a call for you, phones aren't allowed on the Reset.'

'What's the Reset?'

'The Resettlement Estate.' He rolled his eyes and shook his head. Relief flooded through her as she realised that she wasn't going to the brothel. 'Look those places aren't nice, my advice is get rid of…that…and call Selina. She'll get you out and give you a job. I've got a mate who's away today but I reckon he'd like to meet you.' His eyes scuttled over her body making her want to turn away, instead she picked up her papers and stood up.

'I'll be staying where my man is. Thank you for your time, Mr Bueller.' She started to walk towards the back of the cubicle where he pointed.

'The doctor will want to…examine you.' He chuckled deeply.

Another cubicle. The doctor shook so much he could barely sign his name on her paperwork. 'Remove your clothes.' He mumbled in a quavering voice. His eyes darted around the cubicle and all over her body, but avoided her face.

Tamsin hugged her arms around her body. 'Why? I don't need to be examined.'

'Yes you do. I'm a doctor and I say you do. Shall I call the guard and get him to help?' He screeched, still refusing to look at her face.

She reluctantly started taking her clothes off. Exhaustion and shame got the better of her and heavy tears began to roll down her face. She stood shivering in her underwear, the doctor looked like he was going to order her to take off the rest, but he seemed to think better of it. He touched her body, running his trembling hands over her skin and cupping her buttocks and breasts while he panted noisily. Tamsin closed her eyes. Her chest rose and fell quickly as she tried not to sob.

'You can dress now.' The doctor said eventually. He adjusted his trousers, making no attempt to hide his erection. Tamsin hurriedly put her clothes on and left the cubicle.

She was ushered outside the station where a queue of busses waited. Mario was waiting by the first bus with his nice, comforting smile. She shrank away from his cloying presence, all she wanted was to be alone. When it was full the bus pulled out into the street, immediately a volley of horns blared and traffic swerved around them. Life bustled around them, vital and pulsing, but inside the bus a nervous stillness had descended. Tamsin looked beyond her husband, out at the city. Wherever they passed, people stopped and stared, some even pointed. She wondered how they knew of their shame.

After a short journey, the coach pulled up in front of a grand building with Doric columns which reached for a high balustrade carved with ornate cherubim whose stony eyes watched them impassively. A plasty climbed on the bus, he held a rifle slung casually low at his hip. His fair hair was shaved short and he had a snake tattoo coiled around his neck. 'Everyone off the bus.' He turned sharply and got back off.

 Confused heads turned to one another, whispering as if he had spoken in another language. Tamsin felt an urge to scream. Tentatively those at the front began to rise. The plasty got back on and screamed something unintelligible. He grabbed the first arm he found and threw its owner out through the door. Several plastys waited outside the bus like a pack of dogs, baying at them to get moving. People began to get off quickly and assemble on the pavement where they were screamed at some more. When the bus was empty Snake-neck did a quick count before they were harangued inside like sheep by a skilled dog.

Inside the foyer of the building men in suits milled around, examining the new arrivals with great interest. They pointed and loudly discussed their physical attributes as if they were cattle. Tamsin stared at the ground refusing to make eye contact. They were ushered on through the foyer and into a dank, windowless room. At the back several plastys waited, regarding the new arrivals with stony glares. Tamsin noticed that the walls were lined with benches like a school changing room.

Snake-neck strolled to the front of the room. He stood with his hands behind his back, watching them. 'You will remove your clothes and leave them on the bench. You will then make your way through the door at the far end of the room.'

The Transports all looked at one another in confusion. Tamsin felt sad for these people. She was realising what was happening, what they now were; or weren't.

'I ain't fucking doing that.' A high pitched voice squawked from the crowd. They looked from one to another to see who had dared speak. Tamsin felt a bubble of anger growing in her chest, she reminded herself not to join this protest. A short, slight woman wearing pink, hoop earrings swaggered forward without looking around. 'I'm not stripping off so you fuckers can perv on me. Fuck off.' Snake-neck nodded at a large plasty who grabbed her by the arm and dragged her away from the crowd. She emitted a piercing shriek of rage that reverberated around the small room, Tamsin cringed. The woman tore at the plasty's face with acrylic talons but he thrust her easily away and hit her in the forehead with the butt of his rifle. Her head rocked back and her eyes rolled drunkenly, a vicious, purple welt instantly appeared. He drew the rifle back and hit her again while she was still dazed, this time in the nose. Blood foamed in bubbles as she struggled to breathe. The plasty paused as if admiring his work. Then he hit her again and again until she fell to the floor, twitching and shaking silently.

Snake-neck smiled pleasantly as if everything was going as planned. 'This silly cow has just lowered her value. Anyone else?' He paused and raised his eyebrows as if he expected a response. 'No? Good. Take your clothes off. Now.'

The group did as instructed. Tamsin looked around at people reluctantly shedding their clothes. Most were thin and frail, like walking skeletons. Some of the children had the distended bellies of malnutrition. The plastys at the front of the room sniggered and pointed at an over-weight man who blushed purple as he tried to cover himself. Tears of shame rolled quickly down her cheeks as she started to undress, turning away from the front of the room. She removed her outer clothes and carefully folded them. The others' were strewn carelessly on the benches so she moved some along and made a neat pile of her own, fussing over getting them straight. A coarse laugh brought her back to herself and she realised that nearly everyone was gone, only Mario held back looking pale and vulnerable in his nakedness; he shifted his weight uncomfortably from foot to foot, his eyes darted towards the sniggering pack of men at the front of the room then back to her.

'Don't worry about her, mate. We'll see she's ok.' One of the plastys who had remained shouted over. His friends laughed raucously, the noise amplifying as it ricocheted around the empty room.

'Come on Tam.' Mario hissed quietly.

'Oi, skinny bloke. He said fuck off.' Said another more threateningly. Tamsin hurriedly took of her bra and knickers, the plastys cheered and wolf-whistled. Mario's face turned red, he moved his body in front of hers. This time the jeers had a more threatening tone. Snake-neck opened the door and looked at them with withering disgust.

'Stop fucking around and get in there.' He jabbed a thumb behind him. Mario tried to shield her body as they scurried awkwardly towards the door.

Beyond was a large, stark room, tiled from floor to ceiling with chipped and dirty white tiles. It smelt of mould and damp and sweat. At the far end a fire hose was laid out on the floor in front of the Transports. Tamsin tried her hardest to hide her body, she felt grotesque. She looked at the red painted concrete floor, trying to avoid eye contact with anyone else. When she did glance quickly around she realised that everyone, men and women, were doing the same. Why was it they should be ashamed in front of these men or each other? They all had the same bodies. She realised that it wasn't their flesh they were ashamed of, it was their debasement.

Snake-neck walked to the front of the room with the large plasty whose cuffs were still sodden with the blood of Angry Girl. He picked up the fire hose and twisted the nozzle. Water roared from the end spraying the crowd. People gasped with shock as the cold water hit them, forcefully pushing them around like rag-dolls. He did a few general passes, letting the water fall like rain before aiming the jet at each individual in turn. The plastys giggled and shouted between themselves, directing him to spray different people. Tamsin shivered, half wet. Her body was taut with expectation. Snake-neck shouted at someone to hold up Angry Girl who kept sinking to the floor. She sobbed weakly as the water picked at the crimson rents in her face. He spent longer on her, working the jet into her wounds. The water reached Tamsin, nearly knocking her off of her feet. The breath was torn from her throat, she tried to scream but every time she opened her mouth she choked and coughed. The freezing water stung her flesh with a thousand needle pricks, each droplet mixing with her blood to pump ice around her body. He aimed the jet directly at her belly; she turned away instinctively and cowered over to try and protect the baby. He moved on to the next. She felt beaten, bruised as if he had scrubbed her with his hands. She looked at her own trembling hands. Tiny scars picked up through life had turned a shocking purple. She shivered uncontrollably. Mario slipped an arm around her waist and pulled her to him. His body felt cold and repulsive. Eventually the water was shut off. The only sounds were muffled tears and the drip from shaking bodies. A chilly mist hung in the air.

Snake-neck barked. 'Go back through where you came from. You'll find a bundle of clothes. They're yours. Get dressed quickly.'

They silently marched back through to the changing room where neat bundles of green cloth had replaced their own clothes. Tamsin unfolded a bundle. It was a tunic and matching trousers that would have been far too large for a fully grown man. She turned to Mario and gestured to ask if his was smaller. He stared back at her not registering. His face was pallid and his eyes were already scared and watchful. She forced herself to speak. 'My clothes are huge, are yours any smaller?'

'No I'm sorry, mine are…'

'STOP FUCKING TALKING!' The large plasty screamed, silencing Mario.

The door to the corridor opened and a man wheeled in a trolley piled high with shiny black work boots. He had a shaved head and wore the same green clothes that they had been given. He looked at no-one, muttering only what was necessary to match people with their size. All eyes followed his defeated shuffle as he passed them by.

They were marched down a long, empty corridor. The only sound was the sterile creak of brand new rubber on the cold, polished floor. Each face Tamsin looked at bore the same shocked and subdued expression. An invisible miasma poisoned the air around this silent green parade. A voice rang out from the head of the line, it halted obediently as one. Mario, who was a place in front of Tamsin, turned to smile at her.

'ALL EYES TO THE FRONT!' A plasty screamed. Mario snapped his head firmly back. She was grateful.

They waited in silence. Every now and then people were grabbed, as groups or couples, and shoved up the corridor towards a door that Tamsin couldn't see although she knew it was there. Some were families with children, some had the close look of couples, reassuring hands grasped one another, tacit assurances of trust and love laid bare on frightened faces. Others were clearly strangers, bewildered and alone but clinging desperately to one another's hands as they were pushed along. Snake-neck grabbed Mario and dragged him out of the line. He said something to him and Mario pointed at Tamsin. He grabbed her by the shoulder and shoved them forwards. They walked together past pale faces and dark eyes that stared with fearful curiosity. Mario reached for Tamsin's hand, she took it gratefully. Her feet felt like her new boots were crammed with lead, her belly felt hot and heavy. The child inside her squirmed. For a second she could feel two heart beats, her own, strong and heavy and the child's, light and quick. The plasty who had beaten Angry Girl waited at a door, he grinned widely as they approached. 'Smile. It might go better.' He said to Tamsin in an oddly sad voice. Before she could respond the door opened and they were thrust into heat and light and the loud babbling of hundreds of voices.

They stood on a stage in a large room. Below them, looking up curiously, was a small audience of twenty or thirty people. Mostly cold faced men in sharp suits, a few women speckled the crowd but their faces were no warmer. Opposite them, on the other side of the room, was another stage with another man and woman dressed the same as them. The woman's eyes met Tamsin's for a moment before a disembodied voice rasped through a speaker making her jump.

'And now, ladies and gentlemen, we come to lot 15. One breeding pair. Bidding starts at three hundred bancor, do I hear three hundred? Three hundred from Mr Rowley of Wal-Tesc. Thank you, sir. Do I hear four hundred from Mr Snape of Uk Coal and Gas? You seem hungry today Mr Snape...' The crowd laughed politely.

Tamsin understood their fate within moments. It took just a few more to realise the importance of the auction. It would mean the difference between hard toil in a factory or on a farm, or the deep, dark, dangerous coal pits that were opening under the northern cities and empty towns as the older, more accessible, seams ran out.

'...Six fifty from Mr Snape, Mr Rowley any advances? Seven hundred from Mr Rowley, seven fifty Mr Snape, Eight hundred Mr Rowley, eight fifty Mr Snape, Mr Rowley? No more from Mr Rowley? Last chance and… Oh I hear nine hundred bancor from Ms Purdew at Veolia. Ms Purdew were you in the lavatory? Mr Snape? No? Last chance Mr Rowley? SOLD for nine hundred bancor for the pair to Ms Purdew of Veolia. Moving on…'

Arms grabbed at them and dragged them off the side of the stage. Voices were everywhere around them, somewhere in the crush Tasmsin lost Mario's hand. People grabbed at her, pushing her along. Snarling, uncaring voices barked orders that she didn't understand. She was pushed down by the shoulders and forced into a chair. Her arm was grabbed and held by a strong man wearing the green uniform that she despised already. The metallic snarl of a steel rattlesnake tore through the air, Tamsin whirled her head around to see what was happening but it was on her, biting her arm, poisoning her blood as it scarred her.

And then it was over, the hands let go and pushed her onwards. The crowd was still around her but less insistent. Behind she could hear the low sing-song of the auctioneer bantering with Mr Rowley and Mr Snape while he flirted with the unseen Ms Purdew. Tamsin looked at her arm, bruised and inflamed, blood mingled with ink. It was the familiar block pattern of a scanable QR code. She touched the pale skin higher up and started to cry.

Chapter 22

'TIME AT THE BAR PLEASE, GENTLEMEN!' The age old cry rang through the dingy pub eliciting grumbles and tuts. Anthony sullenly swirled the last foamy dregs of beer in his glass before drinking it down in one.

'Selina's tonight, Anthony?' Slurred Raj.

'Not tonight, mate. I've got to go to the office in the morning.'

'That's the third time this week, what's happened? Are you turning into a career man on us?' Paul said as he returned from the toilet. The pub was nearly empty. It seemed that few people wanted to be out on a cold, rainy Manchester evening. Only a handful of die-hard regulars with uniform red noses and purple thread veins were hunched over the bar of The Prince, leering at the scantily clad hag who flirted uncomfortably with every man who passed through the doors.

'Are you coming, Paul, or have you gone all gay n'all?' Raj said.

'Nah, I'm a bit tired tonight. Selina has had enough of my money this week already.'

'It's only Tuesday.' Raj replied.

'I know but I blew a load in there on Saturday night.' The three men erupted with laughter. 'I meant a load of money but I definitely blew my load.' Paul added. The words were lost, Raj was already staggering out of the door.

'That bloke, fucking hell. He spends more time in Selina's dirty beds than he does his own.' Paul laughed. 'Night cap at mine?'

'Not tonight, mate.' Anthony replied. Since the visit to DPC04 he had been drinking more than ever but by himself. Conversation crowded his thoughts, he could only relax when he was either alone or with one of Selina's girls.

They left the warmth of the pub and set out for the walk home. Paul lived in the same block as Anthony so they set off in the same direction. Anthony loved Manchester by night, the dregs and die-hards meandered from the road to the pavement and back again, the street girls walked up and down Bridge Street nervously plying their trade and patrols of plastys watched with less interest than they paid to their watches, willing their shift to end so they could join the rabble. The city twitched with vice and tapped its foot to a dark beat.

Anthony stopped in the doorway of a long empty shop and started to urinate. 'Does any of it ever bother you?' Paul asked.

'Does any of what bother me? Pissing in a doorway?' He replied.

'Y'know. The selections, all those people. I see their faces at night.' Paul craned his neck back to make a study of the dark clouds that rushed past the hiding moon.

'What's wrong with you? They're scum, useless. It's the solution to a problem.' Anthony replied as he shook himself and zipped up.

'A final solution?' Paul said seriously.

'That's a fucking good one.' Anthony cackled. The fine but pervasive rain that had drizzled all day increased its intensity making them both shudder.

'Don't you ever question it?' Paul persisted. Anthony stared at him now.

'No I don't. I believe in what we're doing. If I didn't I wouldn't do it. You need to be careful about who you talk to about this stuff, you saw the memo about the internal investigations, someone's leaking to

Freetopia. The IT boys from MI5 have been working their arses off to remove that material from the internet.'

'I'm not fucking Freetopia.' Paul snapped.

'I didn't think you were.' Anthony replied in a soft tone. The two men stared at each other for a moment, oblivious to the rain that fell on their faces, until Anthony burst into laughter. 'Fucking hell mate you're easy to wind up!' He slung an arm over Paul's shoulder. 'Come on, let's get back. Maybe I'll have that drink with you after all you bloody sympathiser!'

Paul grinned. 'Who are you calling a bloody sympathiser?' Giggling like children the two men staggered down Bridge Street. Seemingly, without a care in the world.

*

The man who invented Optrex should get a bloody award. Anthony thought as he sat down opposite Rick Benson. Indeed, Anthony's reliance on the simple eye drop solution had probably saved him from unemployment a thousand times. Rick peered into his face looking for signs of a hangover and seemed satisfied. Anthony had got used to this tacit interrogation and took no offence. His relative sobriety was a small price to pay for the opportunity that he and Rick Benson had been secretly thrashing out.

'How goes it, Anthony?'

'Very well Rick. Have you heard from Whitehall?'

'I have but before we continue I have a few questions that I'd like to ask you.'

'Anything at all.'

'It's about your sister. It's come to my attention that she's a journalist for the Vircorp News. Why have you never seen fit to share this information with NASRA?'

'I never saw that it had any bearing on my job role, Rick. My sister and I don't see an awful lot of each other, besides Vircorp are a pretty much 'party line' affair are they not?'

'This may be true, but if we are to put you in a senior role, such as you are being considered for, then we need to know that you are strictly only playing for one team, do you catch my drift? However the problem is deeper than that.'

'Really? Anthony leaned forward with interest. Sweat tickled his ribcage.

'Yes. It seems that she has been sighted with your former friend, Joshua Baker, who is still at large following his implication in the death of Miss Forester. Do you know anything about this?'

It took Anthony a second to process what Benson had told him. He quickly recovered his composure, pushing away that aching sense of loss. 'No, nothing at all. I haven't spoken to her in months.'

Benson frowned. 'Obviously if you speak to her don't mention this. MI5 would like a word with you and I would imagine with your sister. Will this be a problem?'

'Not at all, Rick, I'll do everything I can to help.' He smiled what he hoped was a winning, "trust me" kind of a smile. He couldn't let this affect matters, his upward trajectory couldn't be halted.

'Well, I appreciate your co-operation. I must say though, this is causing questions to be asked at high level. These decisions aren't just down to me. It's a question of loyalty Anthony. The agency likes to know that its senior executives are singing from the same hymn sheet, as it were.'

Anthony smiled. 'I understand, Rick. There is a small matter that may…help…with any concerns that there may be…' He sat back in his chair, leaving the words to hang in the air, inviting interest, spinning their own deal.

'I'm listening.'

'As you say, Rick; it's all a question of loyalty…and I may know of someone who might not be as loyal as the agency would prefer.' He replied innocently.

Rick waited, each man willing the other to fill the silence. Finally he relented. 'Of course your loyalty is almost beyond question.' He purred sarcastically. 'However that may not remain the case if I feel you're withholding information…of course if your loyalty is proved…'

Anthony nodded, showing he understood that was all the reassurance he would get or deserved. 'A colleague has told me things that I found...unsettling... Paul Rice, I think he might not be all he seems to be...'

'It's noted, Anthony.' Rick replied in a tone that said he was hoping for a higher value scalp than that but it would do. 'Anthony, I am happy to inform you that you are to be the new Home Office Liaison Officer to DPC04. You will vacate your flat on Monday morning to report for duty at DPC04 on Tuesday morning. As you know we have a backlog of what we call 'special units' that we have deemed to be of…strategic value. DPC04 don't have an awful lot of space to detain them so I'm afraid expedience is required. They are mostly Freetopia suspects or confirmed members, although we use the terminology loosely to describe anyone who is there to be...' he seemed to struggle for the right word.

'Questioned?'

'Yes...quite...Now you will have your own office, secretary and wet operative...'

'Wet operative?' Anthony raised his eyebrows. He knew what Benson was talking about, he just wanted to make him squirm.

'Wet operative. I don't think we need to spell it out, do we?' His steel blue eyes held Anthony's to a win.

'Ok. Is the wet operative up to speed on...technique?'

'He's not been chosen yet but he'll be issued with certain...guidelines and equipment.'

'If I may I'd like to make a suggestion. There's an operative by the name of Lee Cross who I met on my visit to DPC04. I want him.'

'Very well.' Benson nodded, giving his approval. 'Anthony, may I speak frankly?'

'Of course.'

'Nobody will be coming to check on your work, you *are* the auditor. Do whatever you see fit to acquire the information that is necessary. Working at the camp you will come to understand your quota better than I can from behind this desk.' Benson chuckled self-indulgently. 'This kind of...work...isn't within G4ITAS's remit you see, in fact your operative is sourced by them but actually paid by NASRA.'

'Oh really? And why is that?'

'Their legal team ruled that this area of business was...difficult...and so it was pushed back on NASRA to implement.'

'I understand fully.' Anthony replied, and he did. G4ITAS didn't want to get their hands dirtier than was necessary to turn a profit. Rick

Benson stood and offered his hand to Anthony in an elegant gesture of dismissal. They shook. He allowed himself a satisfied smile as he shut the door behind him. *Life is good.*

Chapter 23

Raj Bueller stared hard at the cup of murky coffee that sat steaming on the desk. Without his eyes moving he took his hipflask from his pocket and poured a couple of fingers into the mug, bringing the level almost to the top. He leant forward and slurped the excess so that his shaking hand could hold it without spilling any. One of the juniors looked around the curtain of his cubicle. He quickly put the hipflask back in his pocket. 'What do you want?' He snapped.

'Sorry, Mr Bueller. Just to let you know, the train's here.' He waited as if he had something more he wanted to say.

'Are you fucking watching me? What's your problem? Huh?' He could hear the slur in his own voice.

'No, Mr Bueller. I was just…well… wondering if you were going to be ok this morning? I'm sure that Petyr and I could process the first train if you wanted to…sleep a little?' His voice was seductive, friendly. It invited him to accept the owner into his confidence, to weave stories into a rope that was long enough to hang himself with.

'You'd fucking love that wouldn't you?' He spat. 'You and that other reptile fucker next door. I bet it was you who got rid my boys, wasn't it?' Paranoia was rising in his chest. He choked it back down. You couldn't give these reptiles an inch; they'd take you for everything that they could. It had been three months since Anthony had left without a word as to where he was going. Paul had followed six weeks later. He felt marooned among the crocodiles. But he wouldn't let them win. He breathed deeply and calmed himself. He smiled nicely at the boy. 'I'm ready whenever you are.' He backed away out of the cubicle as though he daren't turn his back on him. He could hear them talking next door. Talking about him, no doubt; he didn't care, it would take more than a couple of jumped up kids to get him out of the job.

He didn't need them to tell him the train was here, he was an old hand at this game now. He could hear them out there, babbling and chatting, excited and unruly. They did sound lively today, almost too much. He felt unsettled and nervous. He took a deep sip of coffee, telling himself that it would help.

The first one came, then another and another. He settled into the job, watching the faces pass him by. Judging, stamping. The familiarity of the hatred he felt for them eased his mind. He shouted 'next' and a pale teenaged boy came into the cubicle. His arms were scarred with puncture marks, his eyes were alert and restless. Before Raj could speak the boy cut him off. 'Where am I going? Where are you sending me?' He sat on the edge of his seat, twitching to an unheard beat.

Raj sat back and studied him. He waited as long as he could before replying. 'I'm not in charge of sending you anywhere. I simply determine how fit you are for work.'

'I can't go to the mines. Not the mines. You have to promise me.' He replied. His eyes brimmed with frightened tears.

'Like I said, mate. It's not up to…'

'I'M NOT GOING DOWN THERE IN THE FUCKING DARK AGAIN. I'M NOT, I'M NOT!' The boy screamed jumping to his feet. Raj nervously fumbled for the panic button on the underside of his desk but it was unnecessary, two large plastys tore through the curtain and grabbed the sobbing boy by his arms, ruthlessly shoving his face onto the desk.

'We'll deal with this one Mr Bueller. Out through the blue door?' One of the plastys grunted, heaving the boy upright. A thin trickle of red blood ran out of his nose, spreading as it reached his lips.

Raj was about to say yes but a voice cut him off. 'What are you doing to that boy? You take your hands off him.' An old lady, who was waiting to come in, held the curtain back with a battered walking stick. The door to the platform was open and Raj could see many pairs of eyes peering in, curious at the commotion.

'There's fuck all to see here. Fuck off.' He screeched and bounded around to the other side of the desk. 'Get this cunt out of here.' He shouted to the plastys, gesturing at the pale boy.

Outraged voices shouted in from the platform. In a rage he grabbed the old lady by an arm and dragged her into the cubicle. She lost her balance and screamed as she fell to the floor. Raj felt her shoulder pop with a wet click. Outside he heard shouts of anger and the door to the shop slamming shut but he blotted it all out; what happened on the platform was the plastys' problem. The old lady wouldn't calm down so he stamped her paperwork with a 'D' and sent her on her way still weeping in agony. He shouted 'next'. Silence. He got up and went out to the waiting room. It was empty apart from the two juniors who were by the window, peering out of one of the whitewash smears. One of them saw him and gestured furiously to come and look.

Outside, order had broken down into a melee of arms and legs and torsos that heaved and breathed as though it were one sentient creature pushing outwards, stretching its muscles. He saw a flash of black and he realised that there were plastys at the centre of the mass, a panicking nucleus that fought to regain control over the organism that tore it apart. One plasty nearby climbed up on to a bench and levelled his rifle at the crowd. 'IF YOU DON'T STOP NOW I WILL OPEN FIRE. I WILL OPEN FIRE.' Fear undermined his words making them the shrill plea of a frazzled mother. There was a short burst of sharp, metallic claps. Smoke and flame belched from his rifle. His face looked shocked as though he had never fired it before. Small red divots flew up from the back of the beast which came alive in rage, pushing forward and over the plasty who screamed as he was sucked down into the maelstrom. There were more claps from further away down the platform, the mob screamed and stampeded, running over their fallen as they surged towards the door to the shop. He ran through to the back and tried to open the door. The reptiles were long gone already; cowards. They'd run while he had been watching. Had they locked it? Was it all a conspiracy against him? His brain still screamed these questions as he pushed desperately against the door he should be pulling. There was a tinkling crash as the window in the shop gave way. He was sobbing by the time the mob washed over him and out of the door. A deluge that, once free, could not be contained.

Chapter 24

If passion had a scent then this was it. Not a perfumed, artificial interpretation of what love smelt like; this was the musk of last night's heat, flavoured by the shadows left from laughter and the trembling moans that had soaked the sheets and enveloped them as they slept and dreamt of one another. Joshua opened his eyes properly; cursing that sleep was banished for the day.

The attic room that Ky had assigned to him was tiny, little more than a dusty gap between the ceiling below and the rafters of the old town house in the once affluent area of Didsbury in Manchester. The only furniture he had been able to drag up from the floor below was a double bed and a small table. They filled the room leaving only a small space for his over-flowing holdall.

The rich had fled to the relative safety of the south after Day X. A lot of their former residences had been appropriated by various groups and trashed for years until the plastys had come and brought order. Some had returned with the coming of Rebuild but swathes of the northern cities still remained ghost towns.

Somewhere a few streets away, Manchester was awakening with a dawn chorus of horns and revving engines. A thunderous roar flew over-head making the building rattle and groan. He snuffled his face into Beth's frizzy hair, smelling hair product and stale heat. 'What the hell was that?' She mumbled. He could hear the sleepy smile in her voice; it made his chest feel weak.

'I think it was fighter jets. I heard last night that there had been an attack further north somewhere.'

Beth rolled over so that her nose was touching his. 'Don't care right now. Do we have to get out of bed today?'

'Technically I don't, but you've got to go back to London.'

A frown darkened Beth's face. 'So I can spend my week fabricating stories about how G4ITAS are winning the battles, hunting down the Freetopia rebels and defending our freedom, etcetera, etcetera? Don't make me leave you again, it's not fair. When are you going to come back?' She sat up and pulled the duvet up to her chin. Her bottom lip protruded in a theatrical pout.

'Moving around the country probably wouldn't be the best move right now. I've got both NASRA and Freetopia looking for me.'

'Can't I just stay with you then? I can help you and Ky out.' Her smile was darkened by her worried eyes.

'No, it's not safe for you here.'

'Which means that it isn't safe for you either, doesn't it?' She retorted quickly before looking down at the rumpled duvet. 'Can't we escape to the country? We could go to Cornwall or Devon. I used to love it down there when I was a kid.'

'I wish we could.' He replied. Every time they had this conversation it twisted his soul.

'We could grow our own food, become self-sufficient and live off the land. No-one would ever find us. We could have a family and grow old together away from all the bollocks that's happening everywhere else.'

'Nothing would make me happier but we can't.'

'Why not?'

Joshua laughed. 'For a start neither one of us has a clue about farming or animals.'

'So? We could learn.' Beth snapped sulkily. 'Don't be practical, let me dream.'

'I need to be here with Ky. We've got to try and do something.' A pleading tone that he didn't like had crept into his words.

'All either of you are going to do is get yourselves killed. It doesn't have to be your fight, Josh.' She looked away, out of the curtained window. He didn't respond. They lapsed into a tense silence that the city outside was happy to fill.

'What about leaving?' Beth said without looking back. 'What about leaving the country?'

'How can we? I've got to find my sister.' Joshua replied quietly. They both knew that there was little that he could do for Tamsin now, even if he found her, but the pretence made him feel better, it gave him purpose. She went to reply but seemed to think better of it, preferring silence to the alternative.

Eventually she lay back down next to him. She tenderly kissed his neck, once, twice, seeming to apologise tacitly. He leant his head down and found her lips with his, kissing her hard as his hands smoothed her kinked hair. He touched her naked body; slowly, firmly moving his hand along the soft, loose flesh at the side of her midriff until he felt the swell of her breasts. She shivered and pushed her body against his and forced him onto his back. Giggling they wrapped the duvet around them in a warm, protective cocoon and the rest of the world ceased to exist. Somewhere in that ether of senses, touching, kissing, moving, Joshua wondered if they used each other to blot out reality. He didn't know, he had nothing to compare it to. He'd never felt anything that came even close to this. She moved slowly against his body; her eyes shut in ecstasy, her black hair hanging stiffly at her shoulders. The familiar heat came into the pit of his stomach, gripping him with warm fingers that crept into his belly; clutching, taut. The moment approached, she gently bit his neck as her body became rigid. The explosion. He watched through an opaque pain as she cried out and bit her lip, her eyes still shut, her eyebrows arching; her full hips grinding his body in time with the thud of pounding hearts. She twitched herself limp and collapsed on his body, keeping him inside her. Her wet face told him she was crying. He kissed her shoulder and ran his finger down her spine making her shiver. 'I love you Josh.' She whispered as she buried her face into his neck.

'I love you too. I'm never going to be away from you.' He scrunched his eyes tight, trying to stop the tears that were building.

They lay in perfect tessellation, dozing in a warm bubble. Eventually Beth awoke and sat up properly. 'Skin up.' She muttered dozily. Joshua sat up, reached down for his box at the side of the bed and busied himself.

'Do you think we'll ever get bored of having this much sex?' Joshua asked as he lit the splif, his voice was strained by the smoke he inhaled. He passed it to Beth.

'I hope not. I guess as we get old and the kids come along...'

'Who do you think they'll look like?' He asked with a grin, it was the first time procreation had come up in conversation and he found himself surprisingly at ease with the idea.

'Me, hopefully.'

'Bitchy.' Joshua took back the splif, and closed his eyes. The far off opiate rhythm of the street perfectly complimented the soothing warmth of weed that clutched at his brain. The air in the room was thick and close and sluggishly filled his lungs.

'I love you, Josh.' Beth's soft voice brought him back to a pleasing reality.

'I love you too.' He replied and kissed her naked shoulder. His heart quickened as the duvet slipped down to reveal her chest.

'I *really* love you. I've felt what I thought was love before but nothing like this...like this complete hold that you have over me. I love your mind, your compassion, I'm obsessed with your body...I adore your soul, Joshua Baker, and I think I always have done. Anthony was always so...brutal, argumentative. I mean he was great and I loved him...love him.' She corrected herself. 'But you were always so...kind. How the hell did you two work as friends?'

Joshua took the last drag of the splif and regretfully stubbed it out in the ashtray on the bedside table. 'We're not that different really, or we weren't when we were younger.'

'I don't think he ever got over losing Mum and Dad.' Beth said. He couldn't bear the flash of pain that passed over her face, he wanted to gather her up in his arms and protect her. He wanted nothing to ever hurt her again.

'I don't think any of us did. I mean, obviously they were your parents...'

'Of course it affected you and Tamsin too...'

'It did. My dad was, is...was…an arsehole. I know I shouldn't speak ill of the dead...'

'You don't know that he is.'

'Yeah I do. ' Joshua felt a stab of guilt that he felt sadder talking about Beth's parents than he did his own. 'Something started growing inside of Anthony afterwards; his hatred of anyone who was poor, unemployed. He saw...*sees* them as parasites that won't help themselves. He directed all of his hate towards the people who did it without thinking about the wider picture. The blame spreads further than individuals; useless governments, the corrupt City, unaccountable business; all these things created the conditions where kids are desperate and angry enough to rob and kill people like your mum and dad.' Joshua realised that he had maybe gone too far, he studied Beth's face.

She gazed into space for what seemed like an epoch. 'I think you're right. A few years ago I never would've agreed but now I do. I'm not saying that people aren't responsible for their own actions but society as a whole is responsible for the circumstances which encourage people to act in a certain way. Where does it all end? She turned her head to half face him. He could see the faint trace of tear that had rolled down her cheek.

He was so struck by her intense vulnerability that his foggy brain lost the thread of conversation. He struggled for a moment, his head empty. He opened his mouth, unsure of what was going to come out. 'It ends with us. All we can ever know is our own existence; we have these fleeting chunks of time which are ours and no-one else's. Life's made up of them and at the end of it they are the only things that are important. Our impermanence is us; it's stamped on our faces in our wrinkles. But there's beauty in this temporary state; our fragility determines our fear of loss. Our impermanence is where true love exists; it's what *makes* it exist. You only know how much you love someone when you lose them. Life will never be as beautiful as it will be in the final second.' He was almost trembling as he finished his speech, still uncertain of where it had come from.

 Beth leaned down and softly kissed his lips, his heart sped up until it felt as if it might burst. He could feel her sweet, warm breath on his face. 'You've grown up.' Her sad smile was hard to read. 'The most beautiful thing about life is you, Joshua Baker. I adore you.' She kissed him quickly on the end of the nose. 'I'm getting up.'

He smiled to himself as he watched her climb out of bed naked. She pulled on some old clothes and climbed noisily down the stairs. He heard the bathroom door shut and lock. He pulled on some jogging bottoms and went downstairs to the kitchen to make them both a cup of tea.

The house was spread over four floors including the attic rooms which he and Ky occupied. As he reached the first floor landing he could hear the hive humming. A lot of the boys would be out on their daily missions. Some would be procuring food and other vitals, some recruiting from the hardiest of the street flotsam who had so far evaded the round-ups. There was a unit watching the camp on Saddleworth Moor, the local G4ITAS headquarters and other locations that he and Ky had decided were of strategic importance. So far there were nearly a hundred and fifty of them, stationed here and at other properties around Manchester.

He and Ky had arrived at the house a few days after Kane's death and the heart-breaking dash to find Tamsin. He had no idea how Ky knew about the place but it was certain that he had; he left nothing to chance. Over the next few days Ky's private army had cleared the rubbish, the rotten carpets; any trace of former occupants, legitimate or not. Now each room was a billet filled with bunk beds that they had stolen from a raid on a Wal-Tesc distribution centre. At the time the mission had amused Joshua, the army of freedom fighters liberating consumer goods from a global conglomerate. When he had seen Ky's vision coming to life piece by piece, theft by theft, it had left him stunned. The boy's ambition had been trapped; now it was free.

Ky was stood in the kitchen holding Meditant as if he was waiting for him. 'Have you heard?' He demanded immediately.

'Heard what?' He replied as he tickled the baby's chin who giggled and wriggled in Ky's arms.

'The Newcastle Reset has been captured by Freetopia. They issued a statement earlier.'

'Freetopia did? Through Vircorp? They're reporting it?'

'Through Vircorp.' Ky beamed happily. 'I couldn't believe it myself at first but they have. And there are videos all over the internet; the selections, the market where the Transports are sold. There's even some weird stuff that is supposed to be executions.'

'How come it's all surfaced now? Surely it must have been out there already?'

'Rebuild are losing their influence. Someone has decided that the tide has turned and they've got to go. Now all the information that has been supressed will magically appear on the news feeds and timelines and in the mainstream media. They're on their knees, Josh.' Ky's face was happy and animated.

'But what replaces them?' Joshua replied. Just then his mobile phone rang, making them both jump. 'I'm assuming that you've heard that the revolution has begun?' Stickles' voice rasped in his ear without greeting.

'That's bad news for you, surely?' Joshua snarled after pausing for a shocked moment. 'There are still undesirables to be culled.'

'Come, come Joshua. The best revolutions are those that start organically, through the will of the people. Freetopia are responding to the common call to arms.'

'And what were you responding to when you ordered Kane's murder?' Rage carried the words from his lips.

'Kane's death was a most unfortunate incident; a wrong doing that lies heavily on my heart.' Stickles' voice dripped with sorrow.

'Bollocks. You had him murdered to get at me and Ky.'

'Reason Joshua, use reason. Kane was one of my best operatives, you and the boy were yet to do anything wrong, all I wanted was to take the baby, to demonstrate that I could. Kane fought back and the thugs I sent proved over-zealous in their task. I had them dealt with. You have to believe me, I have nothing but regret for what they did. But this is the past. I believe that we can help one another, you and I.'

'What? How?'

'I need something delivered to the Sheffield reset where you will find your sister.'

For a moment he felt faint, he swayed as if the old man had somehow physically struck him. 'How will I get on there?' He turned his back on Ky who was frantically waving his arms and shaking his head.

'We have developed something that will help. I will send someone to see you, I'm in Manchester, co-ordinating our forces in the north. You may take Ms Thomas as well, if you wish.'

'How do you know she's with me?'

'My dear boy,' He chuckled, a rusty bone scratching chuckle that made Joshua's balls shrivel. 'I'm Stickles. I know everything.'

Chapter 25

Anthony was satisfied with a hard morning's work. He washed his hands and face in the small sink inside the bright interview room. The only window faced east meaning that the morning had been sweaty and close, the sun reflected off the white tiles filling the room with light and heat. Soon it would slip mercifully over the top of the building to allow a cooler, more measured afternoon session.

Lee was fussing over his tool trolley, cleaning a steel hook with a rag before arranging all his implements with precision. Knives, gouges, hammers, a surgical blow torch; he was an artist and these were his medium. His young face wrinkled with concentration making him look childlike. Anthony supposed in some ways he was, his views of the world were undeveloped and simplistic, his knowledge of the fairer sex was far below where his had been at the same age and yet there seemed to be power in his naivety, a brutal force uncomplicated by love's hangover. His quiet demeanour hid a talent for the work that was astounding. They had grown close in the time he had been here, their separation from the rest of the camp staff and the intensity of their work had fostered an understanding that he had only ever had with Joshua. Today he looked tired and withdrawn. 'Why don't you go for a fag?' His words sounded hollow in the stark room.

Lee looked surprised. 'Don't you want me to finish this job off first, Boss?' He asked, raising one eyebrow. The job writhed in the dentist's chair that dominated the centre of the room, moaning behind the bloody rag that hung out of his mouth.

'It'll still be here when you get back. Take five.' He wanted some time alone with this particular candidate.

'Ok, I'll be back in a minute.' He smiled gratefully as he pulled the door shut after him. Anthony dried his hands on a plush towel, noticing with distaste that he had still left a faint, pink smear on the pristine white cotton.

He felt his back sweating and imagined the wet mark it would leave on his shirt. He considered loosening his tie but instead he opened the window. He stood for a moment breathing in the sweet, fresh air. The wind must be blowing the other way, he thought as he noticed the absence of smoke. He could hear birds singing from the moor but other than that, and the muffled sobs behind him, his world was silent.

Did time really fly when you were having fun? The implications of this question occurred to Anthony. How long had he been here? Four months? Six? It was easy to fall into the routine of DPC04. He felt like his days merged into one malevolent vortex of contorted faces, lies and more lies. Every night he chased away the faces with whisky and weed. They would stay away until sleep came, then return to stalk his dreams.

'Just me and you, Paul, some special time, just for us. How are you doing there?' Paul Rice looked near to breaking point, he'd come to recognise the signs. They all came in like Billy Big Balls, giving it 'I ain't telling you nothing.' Sooner or later they all got to this place where nothing mattered anymore. That was the key, while they still cared about life they would protect whatever treasure they guarded with a ferocious obstinacy. If you could break them down, scour their souls to a point where exhaustion and pain over-ruled anything outside of this white, clinical hell, they'd sing. Oh how they'd sing. The bloody mess in the chair mumbled something. Anthony pulled out the rag; he gasped in air.

'Please, Tony…' He managed to gasp. His lips had swollen to two red, puffy slugs. His bleeding eyes were sunk deep behind purple cushions.

'How many times did I tell you not to call me Tony?' He asked, giggling as though they had shared a joke. He jammed his thumb into a weeping charred wound on Paul's leg. He screamed long and loud.

'Shh, for fuck's sake; I've got a headache.' Anthony said grumpily. He considered putting the rag back in but the screaming settled into small whimpers. 'Now, Paul, I feel like we've shared an experience this morning that is far more personal than double ending whores at Selina's.' Anthony smiled at the memory, he checked to see if Paul had appreciated his reminiscence. It appeared to have been wasted. 'I think you're missing out vital parts of information. You've done well and given us a few names but I think there's more.' His head remained hung. He seemed to study the scorch marks on his legs. Anthony thought that the only thing holding him up was the leather chest strap that held him in the dentist's chair. He considered using some more pressure on him but he'd had a full morning, he couldn't take much more. When they couldn't take anymore, further pressure could be counter-productive. It was all about using enough, but not too much. Anthony considered his options. Usually by now he would have been tempted to relent and let Lee administer a massive dose of barbiturates that would end his pain. He would be collected by the porters and Lee would fetch the next one while he went for lunch. He had more he needed to know though, and he had an idea that Paul knew more than he was letting on. He leaned in close enough to whisper into a ripped ear. Heat billowed from his skin and hair, a warm rush that stank of sweat, blood and shit.

'You've messed your pants haven't you? Dirty boy...tut tut.' He whispered. 'I've got a hunch about a couple of names that I'm going to run past you, if you've heard them I want you to nod. If you tell me the truth I'll get our friend to put you out of your misery. Would you like that?'

Paul let out a sob, a heart-rending outburst that had little to do with pain. It never ceased to amaze Anthony that they always seemed to cling to life, even when it was what constituted life within these walls. 'Lie to me and I'll *know*. I'll see to it that the last twenty-four hours of your life will be a living hell that I won't let you escape from. Ok?' You could use mind tricks on them as you would a small child. As far as he could tell it was a power thing. The pain, the feeling of helplessness, they leant him a certain gravitas that had found its way into his swagger. 'Now, think hard, have you heard the names Joshua Baker or Beth Thomas? Think. Quickly.'

Slowly and deliberately he nodded his head. He tried to say something but it caught in his throat. He nodded again.

'Ok, it's your lucky day.' Anthony said in a voice that didn't seem his own. He felt as if his body were moving without the direction of his mind. *Josh you stupid, sympathetic fool, what have you done?* His heart felt heavy as if his chest were encased in concrete. He loosened his tie, he needed to think about this. 'In a while our mutual friend is going to come back and you are not going to mention either of them. If you do I will see to it that you live and live. I won't let you die for a long time. Do you understand?'

'Anthony, please is there nothing you can do?' Paul managed to rasp without looking up.

'I can't save your sorry life if that's what you mean. All I can offer is an easy way out.'

Paul swallowed hard. 'Ok, I won't mention them.'

'Good lad. In return I'll make sure it doesn't go on for too much longer. Do we have an agreement?'

Paul nodded. Anthony wondered if now that his fate was promised he could accept it. They always hoped, right up to the end. It was pathetic really, to put faith in a hope, a chance. He stared out of the window. *What the hell am I going to do about Josh?*

He stood for a while, losing himself in nature's theatre and his own thoughts. Eventually Lee came back, his face was hot and flushed. 'Alright Boss? Are we done with this one now?' He asked as he put back on his white jacket. Anthony was just about to reply when Paul started to scream, incoherently at first but then the raging sobs formed into words: 'Joshua Baker Beth Thomas Joshua Baker Beth Thomas. He's looking for them tell Rick Benson at NASRA don't trust him tell your boss tell your boss.' A thin stream of bloodied drool dangled from his mouth. He looked at Anthony through purple-shadowed, victorious eyes and grinned displaying the remains of his shattered teeth.

Anthony shrugged and smashed his fist into the grin. He barely noticed the skin on his knuckles tear. 'I want you to cut off its eyelids and put the ants in them. Then gag it and take it back down to the holding cells. We'll bring it back up later and see if it's ready to die. I'm having lunch outside on the green, coming?' He shook his hand, trying to clear the pain.

'Yeah ok, boss. I'll meet you down there after I've dealt with this.' Lee got to work while Anthony let himself out. As he closed the door he heard the screams begin again and smiled.

*

The sun blazed proudly in the clear sky as if pleased with its achievement. The warm weather seemed to have appealed to many of the staff and the parched grass was covered with people eating sandwiches from the canteen. Anthony and Lee lay back after eating and soaked up the sun. There were only a handful of women who worked at the facility and they all gathered together, unmindful of the attention that they were getting. They mostly did administrative jobs but a couple were processing operatives. Masterton had once told him that it helped keep the units calm to see women among the staff.

'You know if rumour is to be believed most of those women have, at one time or another, had sex with most of the men.' Anthony said lazily.

'Really? And do you think that's got any truth to it?'

'I'm inclined to think that it's wishful thinking on most parts. Most of the cavemen here couldn't pull a fucking toilet chain. They'd never have sex if it wasn't for the club.'

'The club?' Lee said.

'Has no-one told you about the club yet?' Anthony rolled his eyes. 'Christ I thought it was common knowledge...'

'No they haven't.' A note of indignation had crept into Lee's voice. Anthony thought about playing with him for a while but the hot sun and fresh air had a tempering effect on him.

'It's something that a few of the processing boys have set up. When they get a reasonably fit girl she's taken down to the cellar. If you're a member you get free access. We call it the Club House.

'Doesn't Masterton know about this?' An excited smile had appeared on Lee's face.

'He'd never admit to it but personally I reckon he goes down there himself. He's a man; he understands that we've all got needs. I reckon he sees it as necessary. You know him, he's such a fucking company bloke he'd never openly allow it.' Anthony said.

'So what happens, are they kept there permanently?'

'Well, there are always at least seven or eight units down there if that's what you mean?'

'No I mean do they...stay? What happens to them?'

'Who gives a fuck? There are a few of the processing boys who play a little rough. Personally, I like to go and sample the new toys before those oafs break them.' On cue a thick necked processor, who Anthony thought was called Berry, pulled off his shirt to reveal a tattooed, muscled body and started kicking a ball in an ill-disguised attempt to illicit some attention from the group of women.

Anthony laughed and shook his head. 'Fucking muppet. That's what I mean, these cavemen G4ITAS hire to do the dirty work have no class. Fuck running around, trying to get women's attention. If you're doing it right they'll come to you. Anyway, where was I? Oh yeah, the boys tend to try and keep the stock fresh, they get worn out quickly here.' Anthony gestured at Berry who had been joined by several other operatives who had also stripped off. He noticed Lee had an itchy, excited look in his eyes.

'So, how do I join?'

'It's done by recommendation and paying a little sweetener. I'll have a word for you.'

'Thanks boss.' Lee replied enthusiastically. They lapsed into a lazy, sunshine silence until Lee broke it. 'So what do you make of the rumours?'

Anthony shrugged. 'Freetopia haven't got the muscle to achieve anywhere near what they shout about. It'll come to nothing.'

'People are talking about it developing into all out civil war.' Lee looked at the sky, shielding his eyes. These things all felt academic and far off, abstract ideas that had no bearing on the day to day specificity of their lives.

'Trust me, it'll come to nothing.' Anthony repeated. He had other, more pressing issues on his mind than Freetopia's petty struggle for existence.

A few of the groups on lawn had dispersed and were walking back towards the buildings. Anthony checked his watch, it was five to two, the third delivery would be here soon and Masterton didn't like there to be people outside when they arrived. He'd sent an email just last week saying that it looked unprofessional. He absent-mindedly studied the torn flap of skin on his knuckle.

'So what was that all about with the candidate?' Lee asked. His voice sounded idle but Anthony had known him long enough now to realise that nothing slipped by him.

'Nothing.' He replied. In this place there could be no such thing as a confident. That would be a weakness.

Chapter 26

Another conveyor belt, cheap ready-meals replaced by rust and grime. The temperature in the vast warehouse was savagely hot, although it was still the middle of the night. The sun had heated the tin roof and concrete walls throughout the day and now it radiated a furnace heat that slowed the breathing and made every hammer stroke an act of will. Across the city a hundred, large chimneys ceaselessly belched smoke and fumes into the sky; the price of England's industrial revival. Factories, warehouses, workshops and the mine, all roared at a midday pitch, filled with sufferers who counted their blessings that they weren't on the day shift.

Tamsin knew they were north somewhere. Newcastle, Leeds, Sheffield, Liverpool; she had heard of all these places but she had no point of reference to work out where they were. They had made the journey to here from Manchester in the dark and they had both slept intermittently. There was no-one to ask, not really. No-one ever spoke to them past the barked orders of the plastys who counted them off the estate in the morning and back on at night. On the Reset, authority clenched its fist around you as it held you at arm's length. A tyrannical silence reigned everywhere, even when they weren't watched. It felt like an imposition to talk to people, to extract what little energy they had left to waste on futile conversation about the weather. They barely even spoke to the family who they shared a room with, although that was no hardship. She secretly called them the Terrible Townsends. They were an ignorant pack from Oxford who stole food from them whenever they could and often used the entire fresh water ration before they had made it home in the morning. She guessed that the city had been hard hit after Day X, at the time there had been stories of towns and even cities in the north that had been all but abandoned. As the Industrial Revival had gotten underway these places were repopulated by corporations looking for cheap property. The result had been that in these places the character of the towns had died as the old buildings were torn down to make way for cheap industrial property that was designed to be derelict with a decade.

A grimy coating of sweat clung to Tamsin. Her back was soaked beneath where her baby clutched her in a makeshift sling. She worried that the heat that must be coming off her would be too much for him but there was nothing else she could do. She reminded herself that it could be worse, at changeover the day shift whispered rumours of people collapsing and the foreman bringing around paper cups of water although she wasn't sure if she believed that.

 Although the work was noisy and the building seemed to quiver with the screeching of machinery, despotic silence reigned in the metal reclamation plant. A piggy eyed supervisor by the name of Branscombe suspiciously watched the night shift for crimes such as talking or laughing or theft. The metals they recycled had some value on the Reset's black market where they could be traded for boot laces, bootleg vodka and everything in between. The price attached to indiscretions was unpredictable. Some of the foremen were violent and thought nothing of beating any of the greenbacks, as they referred to themselves and each other on the Resets. Some of the harder, more dangerous work placements were reserved for repeat offenders: the furnaces, the acid baths or the much feared mine.

In the centre of the city was a heavily guarded pithead, sitting atop a gaping chasm where a tower block had stood before engineers had toppled it to get at a previously untouchable coal seam. The warren of hot, black tunnels and narrow passages which spread like malignant capillaries below the city, was notorious for its foul air and hot and dangerous work. It seemed that everyone had a lurid tale of rock falls, explosions, rape and death in the black pits, although it was only ever second hand. There was social hierarchy even here. The farm operatives looked down on the manufacturing technicians who looked down on the waste processors. The black faced mineral extractors, who could never completely scrub away their marks of shame, were treated with suspicion and an ill understood fear. They were the subclass of the subclass – the very lowest of the lowest. Tamsin wondered why they were treated so, the only reason she could find was that people feared not them but what they represented. To engage was to admit that they existed beyond the dark whispers that mothers used to control unruly children and lovers feared in the early hours when honesty was no longer a luxury but a necessity.

Others punishments were more subtle. A person would think that they had got away with whatever indiscretion they had committed, only to find that their electronic ration card had been wiped when they went to collect their pittance from the Supplies Point. Tamsin would see at least one every day, standing shocked at the counter while they were heckled and shouted at to move by the hungry queue. Although the beggarly portions of milk powder often contained rat droppings and the weevily, black bread was either stale or mouldy and the cups of oats were more like dust, these offerings were all they could expect to eat for the day. When the human body is far along the path to malnutrition, as most of the Transports were, a day without food could be the start of a terrible downward spiral. The people behind the counter were powerless to help; they had the same sunken eyes and swollen bellies as everyone else. As if following his mother's thoughts Aaron mewled weakly through the makeshift dust mask she tied on him before she started her shift. Her heart ached at the pathetic noise but she shook her head. *No, you can't have any milk, I'm dry. You'll have to wait until we get home where I've saved you the last crumbs of milk powder and rat shit.* She felt like a bad mother, a half-woman, a failure unable to produce the sustenance her infant needed. Tears threatened but her dehydrated body wouldn't let them fall. She risked humming gently, so gently that no-one else could hear the faint melody that rose and fell deep within her chest. The baby did though and he settled. She wondered if he would cry more if hc had the energy.

Tamsin picked a computer casing from the belt and dumped it on the desk in front of her. Sighing, she picked up the small hammer which

236

would be counted back in at the end of the shift, and hit the catches with a practised blow, cracking open the case like a child with an Easter egg. Once the dusty innards were exposed she set about snipping away the valuable spider's legs of insulated copper and hacking at circuit boards with a blunt chisel. The wire would be burnt in a great furnace which vomited choking, black smoke into the yellow sky above the city. The charred copper would then be collected and sent elsewhere for reprocessing. Scrapped circuit boards were soaked in gigantic acid baths to separate the prized metals: gold, cadmium, lead and who knew what else. The poor souls who worked in the acid leaching rooms wore filthy rags on their hands which were stained yellow with pus from weeping sores.

Mario worked silently across the belt from her. He had withered since they had been transported six months ago. He had never been a healthy looking man but his pallid face and slight body had given way to anaemic, translucent skin and the outline of bones. His belly was swollen and distended, his arms frail and spindly. His eyes were the worst, the light that once she had loved had been replaced by a watchful, defeated dullness. He had started to wake in the night coughing heavily. He always apologised and went to the corner of the room, knowing that if the baby awoke there would be no milk to help him back to sleep and she would be weaker the next day from another sleepless night. So instead he would hack into a filthy rag, trying not to wake them. By chance, the previous week, Tamsin had found Mario's rag with blood in it. She checked daily and it was getting worse. Of course he hadn't told her, he wouldn't want her to worry. She wondered if he was dying, she thought that maybe he was but she only had the energy to worry about and care for the tiny heart that beat at her back.

Tamsin dumped the broken circuit boards in a tub next to her and swept scraps of cable into a bucket that would be emptied periodically. She wiped her brow with a grimy claw. The sweat ran in her eyes making them sting. Mario looked over at her and smiled, she forced herself to return it.

'NO SMILING ON MY BELT!' Branscombe bawled. Tamsin cursed herself and her husband for being stupid and giving him an excuse. He stomped over to where she sat, his fleshy face red and sweaty. Branscombe was a Transport like they were but owing to some vague description of relevant experience he was put in a supervisor's position and shown preferential treatment in terms of rations and accommodation. Tamsin found it hard to hate him for that alone, you did what you had to. He puffed and panted up to Tamsin's desk where she calmly pulled another computer off the belt and hacked at the casing. She paused quickly to adjust Aaron who had fidgeted against her back.

'If you and lover boy over there can't find a way to stop mooning over each other like a pair of horny teenagers then I'm going to have to find something else for you. Understand?' He jabbed a thumb in Mario's direction.

'Yes Mr Branscombe.' Tamsin said without looking up from her work.

This seemed to anger the fat, sweaty man. He leant in close and dropped his voice although his eyes kept flicking to Mario to make sure he could hear. 'Of course I could find other duties for you; something lighter perhaps. Maybe if you came with me into the changing room for ten minutes we could discuss it.' A drop of sweat dripped from his nose landing on the metal desk in front of Tamsin.

'I'm quite happy in my work, Mr Branscombe.'

'Tight cunt.' He spat on the desk missing his sweat droplet by a fraction. 'You could bring that stupid baby, I'll make it worth your while…'

'No thank you Mr Branscombe.'

He looked over at Mario who furiously hacked at an ancient laptop. His face was deathly pale apart from two red patches which glowed on his cheeks. 'It seems your slut can't be bought…not yet anyway.' He laughed nastily as he turned to walk away, fury roiled and churned in Tamsin's belly. *How dare you humiliate him…like I have.* It was rage with herself, through the prism of this petty man that made her put her foot out from under the desk catching Branscombe's as he walked away. He fell forward against the timid lady who sat in front of her, seeming to bounce off before falling and splitting his scalp on a metal trolley full of scrap. A nervous laugh went up from the belt, one brave voice even cheered. Tamsin put her hand to her mouth in horror. Bransombe got to his feet unsteadily, he held a hand to his head. Blood trickled through his fingers. His face was purple and his eyes bulged. 'Do you have any idea of what I can do to you and yours?' He whispered in a tremulous voice. A shaking hand pulled his radio from his belt. He didn't move his eyes from Tamsin's. 'I need guards to the reclamation shop floor. We have a greenback who wants to be discarded.' He winked before walking unsteadily away.

Chapter 27

Joshua and Beth slipped unnoticed into the human river that flowed sluggishly toward the south security gate of the sprawling Sheffield Reset. The street was enclosed on each side by terraces of houses. Armed guards watched from first-floor windows. The air was thick and furiously hot, the sun hiding behind low yellow cloud. Thousands of filthy, sweaty people, wearing the green uniform of the Transports, moved stiffly in an unnatural silence, following the pair of hunched shoulders in front of them. Joshua felt like a tourist.

He blinked rapidly, it felt like he had grit in his eyes. The thick contact lenses, supplied by Stickles in return for delivering the flash drive shoved in his sock, replaced their own individual iris patterns, or so they were told. He clutched a fist, trying not to think about the maddening itch on his arm where Stickles' man had tattooed his QR code.

'I'm not sure about this.' Beth said in a low voice. He snuck a look, her eyes were red but that only helped her to blend in. She wiped her forehead with the sleeve of her green tunic and blew upwards to cool her face.

'Trust me, it'll be fine. Stickles said they use these all the time to slip in and out of the estates.' He smiled what he hoped was a reassuring smile. 'Don't worry.' Joshua reached out and held her hand, unseen beneath the surface. She squeezed back and smiled in return.

'And Stickles is someone of unquestionable integrity?' She smirked without humour.

'What choice did we have? We're going to get Tamsin back. Otherwise I've dressed up like an idiot for nothing.' Joshua spread his arms and grinned widely. A woman caught his eye. Her cheeks were sunken making her look as though she had sucked her cheeks in disapproval. Her face was lined and tired. Lose skin hung below her jaw-line. Her eyes were empty. His smiled died on his lips. He looked further behind her then all around him at the broken souls who bunched together, pushing closer and closer as they slowly inched towards the gate. Each face was haggard. Thousands of pairs eyes, etched with unique, esoteric patterns, glazed with identical apathy. It was as though their souls were taken along with their dignity and pride. However, every now and then there would be a flicker. The surface of the green pond would ripple, indicating that somewhere in the murky depths something lived on. Waiting.

Ahead of them, at the front of the queue, Joshua caught sight of an elevated guardhouse that stood over a line of booths blocking the street. Either side a tall, green fence spread as far as he could see. This was the south security gate. An angry, disjointed voice barked from unseen speakers. 'WAIT. FOWARD TO BOOTH TWO. WAIT BEHIND THE LINE. BOOTH FOUR. WAIT. BOOTH FIVE, STEP OUT AND REPEAT THE PROCESS.' One plasty stood on a roof, high above the waters so he could see over the crowd that washed past him on both sides. His red, sweating face was screwed up to look mean but it barely masked the nervous flicker of his young eyes or the way he chewed his lip. He held his standard issue SA80 rifle snugly into his armpit. The knuckles that gripped it were white. He looked ready to fire on the crowd in an instant. Joshua wondered what training G4ITAS gave these kids. He doubted it covered the complexities of crowd control or humane restraint. He had an image of the kid raking the column with gunfire at the slightest provocation, tearing flesh and smashing bone while the Transports trudged onwards without looking up. He shuddered.

They were nearly at the head of the queue. The dense crowd behind them surged forward, eager to re-enter their vast cage where food and sleep waited. The people in front of them were directed by the booming voice into the booths that separated England from this other place. Beth squeezed Joshua's hand tightly. He looked at her and imagined her being taken away from him by these spotty guards. What would they do to her? They would assume that they were with Freetopia and they'd be instantly separated. Beth would possibly be able to wriggle out of it by getting them to double check her press credentials although it would cost her job. He wouldn't stand a chance. He tried to keep his face calm and push away the feeling that they might only have one more minute together. A minute. A minute could be lifetime; it could be his lifetime, all he had left. What would he regret if it was, he wondered? He certainly wouldn't regret having got involved with Freetopia and he wouldn't regret the manner of his death, he'd made his peace with the possibility.

'NEXT. WAIT BEHIND THE LINE. STEP FORWARD. NEXT.' The guard's voice sounded bored. Joshua leaned in close to Beth.

'I'll wait for you on the other side. I love you.' He said, almost in a whisper.

'I love you too.' She whispered in reply.

'NEXT, STEP FORWARD. YOU...YOU, WOMAN. I'M TALKING TO YOU.' Beth realised that the guard was talking to her. She turned and mumbled a meek apology and stepped through a black curtain into the second booth. The curtain swung shut behind her. It was as though she had been eaten.

'NEXT. YOU, FORWARD. BOOTH FOUR.' The voice spoke. Joshua stepped forward, trying to not let on that his legs trembled. He entered the booth and pulled the curtain shut behind him. Inside it was almost entirely black, only a small LED light provided the bare minimum of illumination. He could just about make out the strange apparatus that looked like a cut up motorcycle helmet with wires coming out of it. At the far end another curtain led to the outside world. The irony occurred to him that in fact it was incarceration that he was stepping into. They were fooling the system to break into prison. It was only a housing estate, but he knew, and everyone else in this miserable queue knew, what this place really was. He took a deep breath and faced the cold machine. A sign told him to place his chin on the cushion and stare at the camera. The machine whirred and a red light shone in his eyes. Time slowed to a languid pace as electrons shot around a micro-processor and a data base was scoured for a match between Joshua's fake eyes and those of the dead man whose body was hidden somewhere in the vast estate. The digital imprint of his irises was his bequest, his contribution to the cause. Joshua wondered who he was, how he had died. Something made a binging noise. An inhuman voice told him to step out through the far curtain and to have a pleasant evening.

A cold breeze washed the sweat from Joshua's face. His eyes darted wildly in an effort to find Beth but not draw attention to himself. He saw her waiting by a redundant bus stop. She chewed her lips and played with her hair as she scanned the crowd. She saw him and smiled with a joy she could barely conceal. He wanted to grab her, to bury his face in her frizzy hair and breathe her deep into his chest, to feel her fill him. He struggled to not rush to her, hunching his shoulders and shuffling like everyone else as he crossed the street. But the evening was brighter and his step felt light. It occurred to him that living was a privilege only really understood by those who had to deal with the probability of the alternative.

'Shall we walk?' He asked, trying not to beam. Beth nodded her response as they moved away. They walked, holding hands, in a comfortable silence. The only two happy hearts in a sad procession.

Before the housing estate had been commandeered and secured to become a Resettlement Estate, the area had been a notorious slum. The estate was away from the sprawling mass of warehouses and factories that had replaced the city centre. NASRA and the sponsor corporations had spent nothing on modernising or even fixing the housing stock, they had simply built a formidable fence around a vast warren of former social housing. Tower blocks loomed over the endless rows of maisonettes and mean little closes where the houses fell over one another. The roofs were repaired with sheets of rusted corrugated iron. Grey, weather bleached boards covered some windows, others were open to the elements. Foul tide marks on the lower walls showed where dirty water and human shit bubbled up into the streets from the poorly maintained sewers every time it rained.

They passed by a row of dilapidated shops that had been knocked through to make one large store. Above the front someone had daubed in white paint the words "Supplies Point." A long queue of people snaked out of the door, shuffling and jostling with subdued menace. Joshua checked his watch and wondered how many of them would make it to the counter before curfew. People leaving the store clutched their precious bags of food tightly, nervously eyeing the gangs of young men who hung around the exit watching them pass, sniffing for the weak.

The tide surged onwards. Ripples peeled away to their own shores, havens of relative safety in the tightly packed blocks of maisonettes. No space had been wasted when the estate had been built sometime in the middle of the last century. The area they were in, adjacent to the south gate, was made up of rows and rows of maisonettes in their own smaller estates. These closes were all named after composers from distant memory. Beethoven, Mozart, Wagner, Puccini: creators of beauty whose names seemed obscene in a place so devoid of anything possessing that quality. In the distance tower blocks scarred the sky; still part of the estate but newer, cheaper, meaner. They reached a junction in the main road, sign-posted Elgar Close. 'It's this one.' Joshua said.

From several different directions people with hunched shoulders filtered onto the estate within the estate, a long looming structure that housed too many souls. Men, women, children – no-one was spared the ignominy of drudge. They all marched across the scarred tarmac of the empty car park like lines of worker ants returning to the nest. A dark maw leading into a stairwell was swallowing all who approached it. One by one the human traffic disappeared into the depths. The dank stairwell echoed eerily with climbing footsteps and hushed, reverential conversation. Ancient graffiti and mould clung to the walls in equal measure. They climbed to the second floor and turned onto a long passageway. The crowd had thinned and Joshua felt he could breathe at last. The front doors to people's flats each had an individual spray painted code of numbers separated by a line.

'What do they mean?' Asked Beth quietly, leaning in close to Joshua so that she could be heard.

'When the estates were being prepared for the arrival of the Transports they were emptied building by building and searched. Partly for evidence of Freetopia cells, mostly it was to ensure no-one had slipped through the net. The top number is the date they were searched and the bottom number is the call sign of the unit that checked them.'

'Why did they need to do that? Surely they could just check the electoral role? Didn't they make it illegal not to register?' Beth said.

'NASRA like to do things properly.'

'Will the people we're seeing be home yet? They might still be walking.'

'I hope so.' Joshua replied simply. They stopped at a door that looked like all the others. A new piece of plywood covered a hole where glass had once been. Joshua checked around them. People bustled past, keen to get to their own doors, no-one paid them any attention. He rapped twice, after a few seconds a voice floated out to them. 'Who is it?'

'Richard Parkman and Melissa Trenton.' Joshua replied. After a few seconds the door swung open. With one last check around them they entered into a gloomy hallway.

The person who had opened the door had already turned their back to them. 'Shut it after you.' He mumbled as he opened another door at the far end, pale light grudgingly showed them the way.

In the kitchen, two men stood waiting, they grimly nodded their welcome. The taller man was in his early fifties, Joshua guessed. The shorter could have been anywhere between forty and sixty, his wrinkled skin was sallow and didn't seem to fit his frame properly, hanging off him like a child wearing his father's suit.

'I'm Joshua Baker.' He said, without holding out his hand. 'And this is Bethany Thomas.'

'We know who you are.' The shorter man said abruptly in a thick mancunian accent. 'You'll call me Dowell, it's not my name but it'll do.'

Joshua nodded. 'I was told that you'd help me find someone.'

'I imagine you were.' Dowell replied, seeming to study them. The taller man said nothing, his face seemed gentler, Joshua wished he would speak instead. He stared back at Dowell, refusing to break and babble something to fill the uncomfortable silence.

'The facts that you've asked for were gained at great risk to our operative. I'd like to know why you are looking for this particular family.'

'Stickles told me that you'd give me the information in return for the data I have for you.'

'Stickles is no superior of mine. I don't take orders, I execute suggestions. It's not his place to make deals.' Dowel said. 'Besides, the revolution is in the interest of the greater good, do you not think that you owe it to your people to provide whatever service you can without thought for your personal gain?'

'Your people killed my friend. I'm only here because I was told that you could help find my sister.' Joshua snapped as he moved forward. Beth grasped his arm firmly.

'What about all the other families Joshua Baker?' Dowell replied angrily. 'Are you going to ride in on a white horse and whisk them all away to safety? What right have you to protect your own when people are dying in their thousands each day?' His voice became soft, he looked away.

Beth flashed her eyes at Joshua. 'Have you lost people, Dowell?' She asked. There was a long silence, the tall man shuffled uncomfortably, he took out a cigarette and fumbled in his pocket for a lighter.

'Weren't no shining knight to help them out of trouble, Bethany Thomas.' Dowell looked back, his eyes shining. 'My wife and babies were discarded at DPC04 last April. She told them I'd left her. If I hadn't been here fighting we'd all be together.'

'Then you know how Josh feels.' Beth moved forward and placed her hand on Dowell's arm.

'You're too late. I'm very sorry Joshua. They were discarded just a few days ago at DPC04. Now, I believe you owe me a flashdrive.'

Joshua looked blankly at Dowell as if he hadn't understood him. Beth gripped his arm tightly, he could feel her trembling. He reached down to his sock and handed the memory stick over, numb action replacing cohesive movement. He felt confused and dizzy, his heart seemed to miss every other beat, pounding slowly in his ears as he tried to focus on what he was saying.

'…now, you can't say here tonight, it's too risky. There's a family over in Hardcastle block who're putting you up for the night. Number 546. The patrols will leave their HQ at eight on the dot and patrol all night. There's usually about four squads, two on foot and two in meat wagons. The vehicles they use are electric and they drive without lights. They can just appear around a corner and then that's it.' Dowell moved forward to tacitly usher them out.

Beth shook her head at him. 'Are you some kind of monster?'

'You need to get moving,' Dowell said, consulting his watch. 'It's twenty minutes until curfew.'

*

Back out on the main road. The streets were empty and silent save the last stragglers who had held on at the Supplies Point until the last possible moment. The sun had all but vanished and a chill breeze was setting in. Beth reached down and took his hand. They trembled together. 'What do we do if no-one answers at the place we're going to?' She said.

'I don't know.' Joshua replied. Lead covered his chest, strangling his heart. There was a sign for Hardcastle block. They left the main road and turned into a close that was identical to where they had been.

'Josh, I don't know what to say.' Tears clogged Beth's throat. He glanced at her then looked forward again. He couldn't speak; talking about it would make it true.

The block was completely deserted. From behind closed doors chinks of warm light and conversation escaped into the chill evening. The stairwell was nearly black as they climbed in silence to the third floor. Number 546 was halfway along an exposed passageway high above the car park below. Joshua wondered if the plastys were out yet, patrolling, hunting for people like them; interlopers in this dead place. He wondered where Tamsin's home had been. He knocked. Moments slowed as time played its treacherous game. They exchanged a glance, he saw his own terror reflected in Beth's eyes. There was the shuffling whisp of slippers on a hard floor. The door opened a crack, a timid looking woman with a tired face looked out.

'Yes?' She said warily.

'Richard Parkman and Melissa Trenton.' Joshua said. It occurred to him that if this woman didn't know what they were talking about they would be stuck out for the night, trapped on this estate. The woman smiled and moved to let them pass. He felt nothing.

The kitchen was a dimly lit, carbon copy of the last. Faded green linoleum covered the floor, peeling and puckering in the corners. The ceiling was yellow, stained by decades of grease and cigarettes. The woman ushered them in and started to fill the kettle.

'You two look like you could use a cup of tea. Gawd you look like death you do. You can call me Mrs Hampton.' She said in a South London accent, with her back to them.

'Thank you so much for putting us up for the night, Mrs Hampton.' Beth said. 'I hope it's not too much trouble.'

'Don't you worry about it love. The people gave me some extra rations on me swipe card. I'm sure you're very nice but I aint doing it out of the kindness of me heart.' She switched on the kettle and finally turned to face them. Deep lines were carved into her face and her brown hair was greying at the temples. Joshua was sure that long ago she had been pretty but work and worry had conspired against her.

'How long have you been up here, Mrs Hampton?' Joshua asked.

'Too long love. I hate it here. It don't do my Mick's back any favours. They have him down them mines all night, six nights a bloody week, it's no wonder he comes home half crippled...'

'He does a night shift? What about the curfew?' Beth said.

'Don't matter when it suits *them,* do it? Still, we was starving half to bloody death when we came up here. Gotta look at the bright side says Mick; bollocks says I.' The kettle clicked and Mrs Hampton filled the cups she had prepared.

'I'd offer sugar, dearies, but I aint got none. Didn't have any when I went in the shop yesterday, I swear these days they have less and less in that bloody place. Shop they call it, I remember when you paid *money* in a shop instead of getting paid by a swipe on these blessed ration cards. When we came here it all sounded perfect. No rent, no bills, everything taken care of for you. Didn't bloody tell us we'd be living in a prison did they? Check your eyes as you go to the factory in the morning, check them when you come home. I swear those little red things give you eye cancer. Here you go dear...' She stopped her diatribe to hand over the steaming cups of tea. 'I had to share the bag for the three of us.'

'It's lovely, thank you.' Beth said gratefully as she took a sip. 'I hadn't realised how cold I was out there.'

'It's got nippy alright. It'll be winter soon dearie, there'll be a frost soon enough.' She let out a loud cackle that made Joshua and Beth both jump. Josh found himself warming to this woman, tears threatened again.

'Do you have children?' Josh asked as he sipped his tea.

'Just the one, here...' Sorrow crumpled her face for a moment but she composed herself quickly. 'Be thankful for what you have says I. He's in his room playing.'

'How old is he?'

'He's ten. His sister is thirteen. We lost her when we came up. She was born with Down's you see. Lovely girl my Erin, always smiling, always laughing! Gawd, her laugh! She could light your face up soon as you walked through the door, bless her. Still, they say she went somewhere they could look after her. I'll see her again, I put in a letter to that NASRA, them what moved us. They'll get her back to us I'm sure.' She turned away and busied herself with nothing. Josh stared into his tea and held back the sting of tears that made his eyes throb. He looked at Beth but she looked away.

'Sorry dears, never mind me.' Mrs Hampton said turning back. 'I'll do dinner. Now alls I got is this powdered protein stuff. I'll mix it up and fry it with some spuds. That do you?' There was nothing Josh hated more than dried insect protein; it reminded him of being a child. However, he smiled politely.

'That would be lovely, Mrs Hampton, thank you.'

'Thank you.' Beth's voice sounded a million miles away. Josh tried to make eye contact but she stared out of the window at the black night. He reached over and held her hand. A knock on the door made them both jump.

'Ooh. I was hoping you'd get some food. Everything's always easier on a meal I always says.' Mrs Hampton turned back to them but she looked at the floor. Something heavy hit the front door making it rattle in its frame. A child squealed from another room, Mrs Hampton put her hands to her face. 'You look like ever such nice people. Those Freetopias, they told me that I could see my girl, my Erin, you see? I had no choice.'

Joshua stared at her dumbstruck. The front door burst with a shriek of torn wood. Beth jumped and grabbed his arm. 'Erin's dead, Mrs Hampton.' He spat. 'And I'm fucking glad.' The kitchen door slammed open.

Chapter 28

'ONE, TWO, THREE, DRINK!' For the umpteenth time glasses around the small, smoky bar were upended, drained and slammed theatrically back on the scarred tables. Anthony slurped back warm beer, easing its flow down his throat so that he didn't cough. Showing weakness here wouldn't do. Foamy trickles tickled his face and neck as they rolled down to stain the collar of his shirt. He couldn't remember the game they were playing anymore and he had no idea who had incurred the penalty. He didn't care. Tell-tale red threads clinging to the sides of even younger noses than his, said there were a lot of people here who didn't care. He wondered if they would if they had to do what he had to, in the morning.

Across the table from him Lee whispered something to a brassy, red-headed woman from admin whose voluminous chest was only equalled by her mouth. Sam, Sarah? Something like that; Samrah worked for him. She tried to look coy and innocent despite the fact that she had slept with more than half the men at the table, himself included. An uncomfortable, awkward fuck who had wanted cuddling afterwards, he'd laughed before stalking out of her room and back to the bar. How long ago was that? Days? Weeks? Months? What did it matter? The game played on. She giggled shyly and melted just a little more towards Lee who blushed and played nervously with his packet of cigarettes. Her type was obvious to anyone with a little experience, she could be shy and playful but her fluttering eyelashes couldn't mask the cold, empty windows behind them. Sex and the comforting endorphin release that followed it was the only way slags like her could feel wanted, needed. She whispered something in Lee's ear, he nearly spilt his pint. Anthony smiled, the boy wasn't very good at this. Samrah reached her hand under the table and Lee's eyes widened for a moment.

He had given up chasing the office women. It was too easy, they were too easy. There was no challenge. Anthony used to enjoy the sexual pursuit, ever since he and Josh had stalked parties at school trying to work out the odds of a particular girl letting one of them touch her up. All that had grown trite. Will she? Won't she? Do I have the stomach to be obsequious enough to the pretty girl so she'll let me bang her? Shall I take home the hideous one who'll make an effort to please? Or make do with the dull eyed professionals at Selina's whose moans were as cardboard as the walls. He'd moved on. Now, he was all about taking it as his right from those who fought to protect their last shred of dignity because that was the only thing they had left. Their men had been taken, maybe their kids too, although sometimes they were kept with the woman; some blokes liked options. Occasionally you got one that would submit and there was a certain pleasure in that dominance, but the real fun came when they fought tooth and nail for that scrap of honour that they thought they still owned.

Lee stumbled to his feet with a sly nod in Anthony's direction before he and Samrah lurched out of the bar. Anthony coolly sipped his pint. *She'll be back in twenty minutes looking for the next one while his little fellas are still dying on her thighs.* The thought aroused him more than slightly. It was time. He drained his glass and slammed it down. 'That's me done boys, I'm off to The Club House.' His statement was met with a roar of approval. 'Go on son; there's fresh meat; get in there lad; give it one from me;' a tempest of thundering, macho banality. Anthony stepped out into the cool evening air and thanked the gods that he was out of that polluted atmosphere where the caveman was king.

He let himself into the old main building using his own key. The dank staircase that descended to the Club House was accessed through a door in the boiler room, placed away from the main areas as if even this purpose built prison was ashamed of its dark secret. The walls oozed fresh tears from the aged stone that had been carved to allow passage. The tears fed a ubiquitous green slime that clung to the cold granite. Anthony was always reminded of a film he had once seen as a child about castles, it excited a deeply buried part of his imagination. Coming down the stairs was entering a different world where different rules applied. Down here you could be anyone you wanted to be, a hero, a warrior; a god. He picked his way carefully, not wanting to get the slime on his suit. The beer and whisky he had consumed made him sway a little. He'd have a line when he got there to straighten himself out a bit. The burrow of the Club House was brightly lit by LED lights that gave it a faintly blue unnatural look, an electric ambiance that he loved. Along both sides of the corridor were rusty iron doors flecked with flakes of paint. As Anthony understood it, once these cells had housed particularly sensitive or violent prisoners, he preferred their latter day usage.

Over a beer in the mess earlier, a meat head called Floyd had told him about one of the new arrivals. Early twenties, very pretty and, in Floyd's words, very accommodating, Anthony's curiosity had been aroused. He headed straight down the corridor to cell ten where Floyd had said she was. The Club House rules were very simple: you left your security pass hung on a hook outside the door, that way everyone avoided the unpleasant potential of walking in on someone else then having to look him in the eye the next day. Tonight was busy, nearly every door had one or two cards all bearing near identical mug shots that dangled in the breeze his passing created. One door had four hanging up; he stopped outside for a moment but heard only muffled laughter. Very little could be heard through the heavy iron doors, the occasional grunt or even more occasional whimper. They always complained. Anthony's heart skipped a little faster as he saw the door to cell ten had no pass hanging up. He smiled and let himself in unannounced.

The cells were identically sparse, cold, dank and musty. Unsealed dirt floors, crumbling brick walls, a cheap wooden bed of tacked together pallets and a stinking pot for effluence, Anthony had been in each one at various times. Their lack of individuality helped to make every night meld into one continuous loop. This one was sitting on the bed with her legs drawn up beneath the chin, wearing a tatty thin summer dress that might have once been a pale yellow, now it was grey. He'd seen it before hanging from other skeletal shoulders in other cells. Her head didn't move to look at him as he walked in. Some were like this, dead with breath still in their lungs. Usually this was a quality that annoyed him but tonight he felt a stirring. A wet gurgling noise issued from the lap, it took him a moment to realise she was nursing her offspring, hidden behind the protective shield of legs. Greasy, lank hair hung over her brow, further shielding the baby.

'What's its name?' Anthony asked, more to break the silence than from any desire to know the answer.

'Will you let him finish feeding before...' The reply was sepulchral, but there was a quality to the voice that stirred something, a memory perhaps. She...it...sounded like someone.

'Yeah, why not?' He felt magnanimous, a kindly benefactor. He took out a packet of cigarettes and lit one. He thought for a moment. 'Do you want one?'

'Not right now...maybe...after.'

Anthony crouched against the wall and took out his hip flask, he took a shot to try and banish the chill that seeped into him whenever he came down here. He went to screw the lid back on but thought for a second.

'Do you want some of this?' He proffered the flask. For the first time she looked up. Soft hazel eyes which he knew met his. He had stared into those eyes while he ran a finger down her naked, soft back. Those loving orbs had captivated his mind night after night while he struggled to keep pushing her away. He knew the shape of that jaw, the sad expression on her face that had always been there, the light smattering of freckles he had joyfully teased her about in another life. Shock clutched his mind with frozen fingers. He dropped the flask. The confusion in her eyes was unmistakable but there was something else; hope.

'Anthony? Oh my God, what are you..? How..? Have you come to..?' Realisation crossed Tamsin's face like a cloud across the sun. Crushing horror crept into those eyes he adored. 'Anthony, what are you doing in this place?' Shakily he got to his feet, his body acting without direction from its master. His dark face paled, his mouth flapped uselessly open and shut. His brain refused to accept what it was seeing. It didn't make sense, he couldn't process her presence. It shattered something, some illusion of insularity that carried him through this game. He stumbled out of the room slamming the door behind him. Outside, he ran down the corridor towards the stairs, his hands flailed at the air as if to scratch away a hallucination. He stopped at the bottom of the stairs, he could hear voices. Suddenly he realised that they might go to cell ten and he hurried back but hovered outside of the door, unable to go in. He had to do something; he couldn't be seen like this. A shaky hand grabbed for his hip flask and realised that it was still in the cell. Reluctantly he pushed open the door.

She still sat on the bed but now the baby was beside her and she sat expectantly with her back straight staring accusingly at him. The hip flask was in her hand and she took a deep draft, grimacing as she did. 'Are you going to tell me what you're doing here? Or did you come back to show me like all the others?' Tamsin spat the words as though they tasted as bitter as they sounded.

'Tam...I...' He started but there was nothing to follow.

Her face softened slightly. 'Come and sit down. You look like you need some of this.'

Anthony obediently crossed and sat down on the hard bed in a daze. He took the hip flask and drank. The burning did little to soften the hard thoughts that glittered like steel knives at the edge of his thoughts.

'Has anyone...hurt you?' the words sounded hollow but it was all he could think to say.

Tamsin made a bitter noise deep in her throat. 'No, they've all been really nice. Really nice. Do you want to hear about just how nice they've been to me? Three of them were just fucking lovely earlier.' She angrily pulled her hair back to expose an ear that swelled pregnant with blood, her cheek was stained yellow, traces of blood remained in her blond hair.

Anthony looked away, the floor seemed fitting. He studied the hard packed dirt intently. *Why did they never seal the floor in here? Does water ever seep up through from the moors? Does it absorb blood well?* He shuddered and pushed the malevolent thought away but as it went others took its place. Why was it so hard to think of things happening to Tamsin? His mind whispered conspiratorially. *The things that I've done to other girls; sisters, mothers, daughters...What makes her so special? If it's happened to her it could happen to Beth and if she's involved with Freetopia it probably will.* He violently shot to his feet, his contorted face the embodiment of the pain and confusion he felt.

'Where's Mario?' Anthony asked.

Tamsin's face stayed impassive but her delicate jaw tensed slightly. 'We were separated when we got here. Is he...?' The rest of the words eluded her. They weren't necessary. Anthony nodded and stared at the floor.

It took Tamsin a moment to speak. The cool air hung heavy with expectation. Finally she broke their fast. 'Anthony, there's something I need to tell you. You have to help.'

He wrinkled his brow, struggling to take in the information he already had. 'What? What is it?'

Tamsin picked up the baby and meekly held him out to him. He sleepily rubbed his eye with a bunched fist. 'It's him. Anthony, this is Aaron. He's your son.'

Chapter 29

Retreating clouds, inner fog creeping back from whence it came. He was aware of his mouth first. His tongue, like a lizard's skin, rasped as it searched around his mouth for any drop of moisture; bitten ulcers, raw ragged skin in neat, identical rows in the middle of both cheeks; the sharp sting of stale vomit hurt the roof of his mouth when he breathed.

Tremors, rumbles, a rhythmic jolting. The *chicataca, chicataca* of a train hurtling through the long moments. Joshua struggled to open his eyes but when he did all was still black. A wave of panic rose in him gathering momentum. His stomach churned and roiled like the angry sea, retreating before terror crashed on the shore. He thrashed his head this way and that, unable to free himself from the heavy hessian sack. He tried to move his hands to drag away the fabric that clung hotly to his face but tight, cold bracelets held them behind his back. He attempted to roll over and sit up on the hard floor but he was too weak. The wave ebbed away. *Concentrate. Breathe in, breathe out; breathe in, breathe out.* Hot, hairy air. Moisture, sweat, gathered on his face. He counted breaths and laid still, letting reality wash coldly over him.

The drugs that had rendered him unconscious snarled their hangover. He tried to swallow but his only reward was a stale, dry click. He began to be aware of voices. He realised that they had been there all along, part of the darkness.

'What? Fuck off mate, do you actually think that Tession is ever going to leave QPR? He's won six consecutive league titles, that's more than Man U did, even in their best days.' The harsh rasp of an angry, opinionated brummie. 'and...and, that goalie, what's his name...Handerstrom. You've got less of a chance of scoring against him than this cunt has of living.' Laughter erupted. Joshua tried to count the people rather than dwell on their words.

'We pulled the short straw here lads, didn't we? Eh?' The excitable voice of a cockney. High pitched, young. 'I wouldn't have minded looking after the other one. She's a bit fat but better than this cunt. Asher reckoned they'd all had a go.'

More laughter. Joshua started counting breaths again. *It's not her, it's not her...* he clung to his mantra. The dark wave rose over him again threatening to break, he refused to let it. He lay still, he'd find out more that way. New voices. Heavy boots tramped past, a stray foot caught him on the chin making bright flashes appear in his eyes. Still he didn't move. Thunderous voices swapped insults, laughter. Too many noises to distinguish one from another. The new voices left and the old ones resumed debates that had little consequence. *Where is Beth? Is she nearby? What was happening to her?* Bleak thoughts rose in his mind like bubbles of gas through a viscous, black tar. He pushed them away. *Will I ever see her again?* The thought resonated in his mind, its echo filling the void. The threat of tears made his eyes and nose ache. He longed to cry, to rid himself of the hot agony, but nothing came. He concentrated hard, trying to force them to come as if the act would exorcise the pain from his mind. He conjured up the last things he could remember. The estate, Mrs Hampton, his words to her. Shame made him shake his head as if denying they were his.

'I hear he's a brutal fucker.' Another voice, almost brummie, except this one didn't sound as nasal, almost lighter in tone. Joshua placed the accent as closer to Wolverhampton: a yamyam.

'Do you think that's why he's going up there? I mean, if they just wanted to question him DPC03's near Leeds, surely it would have been quicker to take him there?' The brummie.

'The high value ones always go to 04. That's where they get the questions answered. I hear the rest of them just tickle them a bit. Something Thomas his name is.' The yamyam.

'I wouldn't want to be in his fucking shoes that's for sure...'

'I wouldn't have minded a few hours ago. Did you see his bird? I thought it was fucking Christmas!'

'Christmas would have been having her here instead of that sack of shit in the corner. Those lucky fuckers.'

Then the tears came, scalding, impotent rage. But through them a realisation. *NASRA bloke, something Thomas.*

*

Anthony flung open the door letting it bang against the building. He filled his chest, the dark chill clutched at his heart taking his breath away. His body was sheathed in an icy sweat from which his damp clothes offered little protection. As the autumn was upon them the nights were turning brutally chilly though the days were still hot and oppressive. He was sure the weather hadn't been this mercurial when he was younger. He staggered away from the main building in a dazed stupor that wasn't solely from alcohol. He felt dizzy and sick. The thought of going back to his box room, to feel fenced in and trapped, filled him with horror. He stared at the door he had left through. *Would anyone else try going to her cell tonight?* A shudder convulsed his body.

At a fork in the path he stopped, left would take him to the dorm block; right, around the inside camp perimeter. He turned left and strode, shivering, up the gentle rise. Beyond the rusty fence, which was nearly invisible in the dark, the ground rose toward the watchful peak whose dark features were hidden from view. He wondered how much it knew, what it had seen. Had it seen him? Did it know what he was, what he had become? He absentmindedly wiped tears from his face, dimly registering that he was crying. It had been so long; he hadn't even at his parent's funeral. Tamsin had been there, holding Beth's hand, giving out those tacky 'order of service' booklets, like anyone wanted a souvenir from a funeral. She'd been there, she'd always been there. He remembered her as a child, her wide, trusting smile, her curly dark hair that you could lose a hand in. Sometimes he would like to just bounce her curls in his hand while she giggled. Another memory of her, when they were older, sneaking her into his parents' house. He remembered the duvet on his bed falling away as she sat up and pulled her hair back into a thick mane and fanned her face; her smooth, flawless body, the heat of the night and the heat between them. The passionate shame that stirred him so much and the taboo that he'd finally walked away from. She was like his sister. It would have torn them all apart, surely? Something clicked, a connection made. *Why were Josh and Beth seen together?* What that could mean and all of its implications unfurled like a black orchid.

But that feeling tonight. Her vulnerable, pretty face, wet with tears, bruised, flawed and the harsh confusion of her presence. A shaft of light in the endless night. Tenderness when he had gone looking for brutality. The baby who slept in her arms who he hadn't been able to hold. Too tiny, too fragile for this savage place. The path reached the fence and he turned to follow it around. Something moved in the watchtower, no doubt the guard had his eye on him, his high calibre rifle half to his armpit in an alert pose. Anthony wondered what he would do if he tried scaling the fence? After all, *he* wasn't a prisoner, though it was standard practise to sign out at the gate rather than climb the fences. Maybe he should try it, provide some target practise for the patrol boys. He shuddered as he wondered if the silhouette on the tower would visit the Club House when his shift ended. What would it matter if he did? After all he had made full use of the facilities tonight. He touched his pocket, the key to cell ten was safe.

How could you? A voice in his head spoke on a loop. It could have been his mother's or Beth's. He took a swig of his hip flask emptying it. He thought about flinging it callously to one side but he very slowly and deliberately screwed the cap back on and put it away. He thought about the man who had given it to him, what would he make of his actions tonight? Of the man who he had become? But she wanted me to, he told himself. It was an extension of the mantra that had echoed in the deserted corridors of his mind while he did what he had done. She'd come to him for comfort, that was what he had given her. He watched himself in his memory, watched for signs. She had wanted him, hadn't she? She had when she came to him a year ago hadn't she? Of course he'd given her cash, a thick roll of bancors, but that was to help, it hadn't been payment. Had it? Had he miss-read? Then and now? Had he just raped the only woman he had ever loved, then left her there to rot? 'What have I become?' He whispered out loud to the still night. It didn't reply. He wondered if the baby had noticed, if he questioned what this new, cold place was; when they were going to go home. He wondered if he was scared of the monster that had come to his room. What a savage twist of the knife it was that she had arrived here, tonight, when tomorrow he was taking delivery of their brother. What a reunion it was going to be, he thought bitterly.

Chapter 30

'It's been too long, brother.' Anthony said quietly as he closed the door to the bright interview room. A chill breeze from the open window made him shiver.

Joshua lay prone, strapped into the dentist's chair. He grinned from beneath his blindfold. 'I heard a rumour that I'd be seeing you. Are you going to take this thing off me?' He shook his head in an uncomfortable gesture.

'Of course, sorry.' Anthony hurried forwards and took the blindfold off. Their eyes locked and they both smiled. 'It's good to see you, mate. Sorry it's not under happier circumstances.'

'I'd like to say you look well but I'd be lying.' Joshua studied him with concern. He felt embarrassed and uncomfortable. He waited, submitting himself to the examination. He saw his face every morning, he knew how he looked. Eventually Joshua spoke again. 'This is pretty uncomfortable, can you loosen me up?'

'Sorry, sorry. Here, let me help.' Anthony said as he rushed forward. He freed Joshua's hands from the cuffs that were welded to the back of the chair and loosened the chest strap. He left his legs strapped in. He paused in front of his friend, waiting to check he was comfortable. Suddenly Joshua flung a punch from his side catching him off-guard. Anthony staggered backwards missing the full force but still catching a glancing blow on his chin. He fell noisily against the trolley of tools.

'What the fuck was that for?' He whined as he rubbed his jaw.

'Just in case I don't get a chance. After.'

'After fucking what?' Anthony turned away, hiding his hurt. He returned order to the shiny tools and turned back.

'You know...after.' Joshua looked away, down at the rope that bound his feet. Hurt anger spiked Anthony's chest. 'So that's what you think of me is it? That I'm going to torture my best friend? Cheers.'

'That's what I'm here for, isn't it?' Bitterness seasoned his words.

Anthony nodded his head deliberately. 'You're here to provide information. If you do, we can talk about what happens after.'

Joshua smiled bleakly. 'What happens after? You haven't thought this through at all have you? You're going to have to kill me or at the very least authorise my death. How are you feeling about that?'

'I can help. I can make it easy, I might even be able to get you out. Don't play silly fuckers Josh, you know what I'm supposed to do if you don't give me information.' Anthony snarled.

He laughed, unnaturally loudly. The sound echoed around the small room, amplifying his mocking. 'Fuck you. I'm going to make you do this.' His voice quivered very slightly. Someone who didn't know him wouldn't have noticed. But he knew Joshua, and he knew fear.

He tensely in front of the chair, Joshua's head turned to follow him. Dull anger flared once more, he felt warm and uncomfortable. He loosened his tie and undid the top button of his shirt. 'Do you know how hard this is for me? You need to take this seriously. My balls are on the line here. If you don't talk they're going to assume that I've taken it easy on you. I should be going hard just to prove where my loyalties lie.'

Joshua frowned. 'Where exactly do your loyalties lie?

He turned and stared out of the window. Now that Joshua was here he felt naked. 'They lie with the good of the country...'

'You're the only person who believes that this is all for the greater good. Those with real power understand. Your power is petty, small. You're given an elevated position so that you can be an effective tool. Those with the real power know that none of this ideological shit matters – what matters is money and profit because money and profit provide more power. Your parents would be as disgusted with you as I am, as Beth will be. She'll hate you for this Tony.'

Anthony lashed out, hitting Joshua a savage blow on the cheek bone that made his head roll back. 'You don't talk about my sister. You dragged her into this, it's your fault she's here. You betrayed my parents' memory.'

Joshua rubbed his cheek as he hung his head. 'Yes.' He said simply. 'Anthony, I love her.'

'You selfish bastard. What about us? What about our friendship?'

'I don't see what that's got to do with Beth. If anything it brings us closer. She's not just some shag, I'm in love with her.'

'AND I WAS IN FUCKING LOVE WITH...' He exploded but stopped himself. He couldn't know. He didn't deserve to know.

Joshua's looked up. His cheek was already swollen in an angry, purple knot. 'You

were in love with her? With Tamsin?'

Anthony's face stayed grave. 'It's none of your business.'

'Tony, there's something you need to know, about Tamsin.'

'DON'T FUCKING TALK TO ME ABOUT HER.' Anthony roared. He took a deep breath and tried to calm himself down. 'We've got some questions that we need answered. You get a certain amount of grace because of our history, but the fact remains that you worked for NASRA and you are implicated in the death of one of our operatives: Miss Forester. You need to give me something now or I'm going to have to call for Lee.' He didn't feel the need to qualify who Lee was or his function. He could barely look at the man who he had thought was his friend. 'So? What have you got for me?' He spat.

'Who's Miss Forester?' Joshua asked, bewildered.

'The NASRA agent who was following you last year. You killed one of our own Joshua.'

'I did nothing and you know that I didn't.' His shook his head sadly. 'I've got nothing

to tell you Anthony, nothing at all. I don't know who you are or what you're capable of anymore. You've got to do what you have to.'

Anthony walked around the room again, going behind the chair so that Joshua couldn't see him. This was a tactic that usually had the effect of disquieting the candidate. 'Just give me something, Josh. Something I can take to my superiors. They know we were friends, if I go easy on you I could end up in that chair myself.' He could hear his voice settling into the tone he always used with the candidates; a soothing, calm cadence that offered an alternative to the physical pressure that the candidate knew was coming.

'I would never want to cause anything bad to happen to you, but I can't tell you anything. I'm sorry.' Joshua said quietly.

Anthony lingered by the open window. He breathed deeply and slowly, deliberately filling his lungs with fresh air before slowly emptying them. 'Well aren't you the martyr? When did you grow some balls, Josh? You're worth nothing to your new family. If your Freetopia won their pathetic struggle they'd become as corrupt as this government or any that has gone before it. Power corrupts and it always will. There's no room for idealism in government.'

'I will tell you one thing and one thing only. I am not a member of Freetopia nor will I ever be. As for family, I thought you were it, Beth certainly is.'

Scarlet fury rose in his chest again like a malevolent geyser. He swiped Joshua viciously around the back of his head. 'You don't get to talk about my sister. You've betrayed our parent's memory so you've betrayed her. Do you think my father would appreciate you taking the side of the people who killed him?'

'Tony, your parents weren't killed by the people you blame. It was a small gang and they were created by the ideology that you seem to think you're defending.'

Anthony grew short of breath. A headache was developing at his temples, a worming, insidious, crawling pain that burrowed into his thoughts. His hands trembled and cold sweat greased his palms. He walked around the chair again and coldly noted that Joshua had gone, in his place was another candidate, faceless like the rest. Faceless, meaningless. The man in the chair stared intently at him, defiant, judging. That boiling fury again. His arm tensed to slap the insolence away, to replace it with contorted agony. He could do that, or he couldn't; he held the power. He took a controlled breath. Anger would give that choice away. He wasn't afraid to get his hands dirty and do what was necessary, but if he chose to, not because he had roared into it like a blinded lion. He needed space, air. He had to get out of this stuffy, poisonous atmosphere.

*

Anthony grabbed Joshua's arms and cuffed him again before leaving the room without another word. The tension ebbed slowly away. Although he felt that he hardly knew Anthony anymore, all the old mood indicators that friends learn to read over the years hadn't changed. It was strangely familiar hearing the deliberate way he formed his words and seeing the veins pulsing in his forehead; it was like seeing a poor movie adaptation of a favourite book. He realised that beneath his fear, and the sickening worry for Beth, he felt sadder than he had ever been before.

He felt faintly ridiculous strapped to the chair. He found that if he shifted his weight around and craned his neck he could just see out of the window. Soon that hurt his neck and he sank back into the chair. He thought of Beth, he saw them making love under the sloped ceiling of his room. It occurred to him that perfect moments can only ever be memories because perfection can only exist with the benefit of hindsight. *When was our perfect moment? Anthony's and mine?* When floundered that friendship that had burned so brightly and seemed to define them both? Just now when he had walked in the room? When he had left the London office? Or had it set in earlier, a creeping dry-rot undermining the stable foundations that their friendship had been built on. What was it built on anyway? Girls, drink and drugs? Toy cars and plastic soldiers? Had it ever been anything deeper than that?

Boredom made him crane his neck again. Voluptuous clouds bustled quickly across the crisp blue sky, driven by a wind too lofty to grace the dirt with its presence. He tried to find shapes, meanings: a natural ink-blot test. He studied the trolley of shiny steel tools. They looked satisfyingly clean and smooth. He wondered how cold they would feel, how invasive. *Or Persuasive?* How many lives had ended in burbling confessions in this very seat? How many ruptured vows not to speak a word? How many names screamed at the white, unmarked ceiling? He closed his eyes and tried to remember the prayers his mother had sometimes whispered to him when he was small.

The door quietly opened and then shut. He kept his eyes closed. 'Nothing's changed. I'm still not telling you anything.'

'I'd better get to work then.' An unfamiliar voice replied, startling him. He opened his eyes and found a young man staring curiously back at him. *He looks like a kid.* It was impossible to reconcile this youth with the mental image he had built of the man who would torture him.

'Lee, I presume?' Joshua asked with a calm he didn't feel.

'That's me.' He replied amiably. His young, almost effeminate face had an air of intelligent curiosity. Joshua could almost feel at ease with this person.

'Where's Anthony?'

'He stepped out. This is usually where I step in.'

'But we haven't finished talking…We're friends, we…' Fear twisted in his belly; a slithering wet knot that pulled tighter and tighter.

'Yeah, whatever. Bored. Now what have we here…' He turned away to the steel trolley muttering to himself. Joshua deliriously thought of his mother making tea and had to stifle a fit of the giggles that shook his chest and hurt his eyes.

'We're friends. I don't think you should do anything until he's back…' He heard himself babbling incoherently. High pitched whines to seemed to come from somewhere else. The man nodded dismissively like a nagged husband, occasionally making some placating noise of acquiescence. Far from the maddening twitter of his own voice Joshua shivered as he realised this man had heard it all before, it was just another day at the coal face. He turned back to face him.

'Let's just pop this on you shall we? It'll help.' Lee held up a strip of elastic attached to what looked like an over-sized dummy. He moved behind him. Joshua thrashed his head from side to side but Lee grabbed his hair and held it firmly while he shoved the mouthpiece home, stopping Joshua's chattering teeth. He spoke gently to him while he performed this operation; the friendly, comforting voice of a father to his upset child. Joshua could taste rubber and blood, like greasy copper, sliding down his throat and sticking, making him want to cough but the dummy was pushed too far back to allow him to swallow. Lee had turned back to the trolley. 'Hm, let's see. You can't have said much or the boss wouldn't have left in such a rush. You proper pissed him off! Let's make sure you can still sing sweetly for him when he gets back.' He turned back to Joshua holding a bottle of clear liquid and wearing goggles. 'You got to be careful with this stuff!' He said cheerfully.

Joshua felt as if his heart would burst, his eyes bulged. The bitter rubber in his throat made it itch maddeningly, his teeth sank into its pliable flesh, sliding comfortably into neat holes made by someone else. Somewhere he registered a dull heat that moved from his bladder to the jeans that a million years ago had lain tossed to one side on the floor of his bedroom. He tried to go there, to escape to that wonderful place of soft colour, warmth and love. Lee straddled him and grabbed his hair, wrenching it violently back. 'Ok mate, this won't take a sec. Come on.' He crooned gently. One finger poked at his eye until it dragged the eyelid open. He squeezed his other eye shut as if it would make up for the one that was open. The plastic spout of the bottle rushed at him, growing and growing until an unseen hand squeezed. The smell of clean hit him, his mother scrubbing their toilet, the floors at school, something about vomit in a bus on a trip somewhere. Fire roared through his head, a crimson sea roared and roiled, thundering in his mind. His scream and the bitten rubber dummy fused together.

From somewhere that same convivial voice spoke. 'You're doing so well. Now for the other one, that's a good boy.' Light, brief, fleeting. The rising on an inky wave. He drifted away, floating on the dark current; away, away, away. But then, from that place, too far away to describe, he heard a roar, a slap of flesh against flesh. The unbearable weight on his legs shifted. Then that smell. *Her.*

Chapter 31

Time can have a mercurial quality that eludes quantifying; its steady tick staggering on to a languid tock. Lee fell away from Joshua's lap looking like a fully grown baby falling from his father's knee. Beth stood frozen, shock shone brightly in the twin full moons of her eyes. Lee looked up from the floor, his face a vision of hurt confusion; the kicked dog who can't understand why its owner is less than pleased with its ragged, half dead offering. *How do I get out of this?* The question, one of self- preservation, whispered itself without conscious input. 'Lee' Anthony barked 'did I give you any orders to do this?'

'Well no… b-but…' He stammered from the floor.

'Well nothing, get out in the office.' He fixed Beth with a pleading glance that he hoped conveyed that this mess wasn't his fault. The granite of her tacit reply made him feel five years old.

Anthony violently slammed the door to the interview room shut as he stalked out into the office after Lee. 'How the fuck am I supposed to interrogate an unconscious candidate, huh? How am I supposed to threaten to hurt his woman when he can't even see her?' His voice rose in pitch until he was practically screaming. Lee cowered as if under a physical assault.

'Boss, I'm sorry. It's just that we usually…'

'Fuck usually. There is nothing *usual* about what we do here. Get out, I don't want to fucking see you. Bring me a fucking bag to put this piece of shit in when I'm done with it.' He prayed that Lee would forget that there was already a black, rubber body bag in the store cupboard. 'I have to do everything my fucking self!' He stomped back into the interrogation room and slammed the door behind him.

'The fucking keys, Tony, where are the keys?' Beth sobbed as he walked in. She stood at the trolley sweeping through the tools, too panicked to look properly. She had untied Joshua's legs but his hands remained cuffed to the back of the chair. Anthony searched desperately on the trolley himself, his trembling hands spilling shiny tools and bottles. He cut himself viciously on a scalpel but hardly noticed the sharp blade slice effortlessly into him. He found the small key and dashed to the back of the chair, dripping blood. Beth leapt at him like a tigress protecting her cub. 'You stay the hell away from him.' She snarled through gritted teeth.

'There's a sink…' he pointed at the door then strode quickly out through the office to make sure no-one was in the corridor outside. Satisfied that they were alone, he ran back and helped Beth drag Joshua's semi-conscious body to his feet. His face was pale, his lips were almost invisible, his eyelids were purple and inflamed, the acid Lee had used dribbled red tears down his face.

'If we can wash it out we might save his sight.' He said lamely, huffing under the effort to move him. 'Come on, Josh, wake up.' He slapped his face to try and stir him but his own head rocked back from the force of a hard punch to the jaw. A black and crimson kaleidoscope exploded in his eyes.

'I told you not to touch him.' Beth's face was contorted with fury. Anthony stood back, his jaw still smarting from the blow, and watched as Beth struggled to get Joshua to his feet. Tears rolled down her face, darkening as they crossed a heavy bruise on her cheek bone. Anthony was transfixed, the imperfection encapsulated everything, all that was wrong. His sister was hurt and he was complicit if only by association. *What would Mum say?* Joshua murmured something unintelligible and seemed to take some of his own weight. He half walked out of the room, guided by Beth's comforting arm and soft words. Anthony sank into the still warm chair. He put his hands over his face and realised that they were violently shaking. He stared at them, willing them to stop. Suddenly a noise escaped his throat, surprising him. His chest hitched and he couldn't breathe. Finally he covered his face with his arms and sobbed like a small child. He wept for Joshua, for Beth, his parents, Tamsin, but most of all he wept for himself.

Eventually he stood up and straightened his tie. He wiped the tears from his face and drank from a bottle of water. He busied himself straightening up the tools and bringing order to the interrogation room. He went outside and fetched the steel trolley that they used for disposing of candidates. He got two rubber body bags from the store cupboard and laid them out flat. He looked at his watch. Lee had been gone for ten minutes, he could only hope for another ten.

*

'I thought you needed a bag?' Lee said tentatively as he walked, unannounced, into the interrogation room. 'Things got out of hand did they?' He gestured towards the trolley that held a large bag on each of its shelves. 'You did the girl as well?'

'He wouldn't talk, so I made him.' Anthony said simply.

'Did you get anything?'

'Nothing that we've not heard elsewhere already.'

Lee nodded. It wasn't unusual for the intelligence assets that they interviewed to be entirely useless. 'Do you want me to get rid of these?' Lee gestured at the trolley.

'No I'll do it myself, I'm going down for a fag anyway. I'll drop these off at the incinerator on my way. Go and have some lunch, I'll come and meet you.'

Lee bowed his head obsequiously, seeming to sense he was still unpopular. He paused for a moment as if about to say something but he left without another word.

Anthony yawned, he felt overcome by weariness. His eyes felt hot and sore and his entire body seemed to sag and ache. He grabbed his hi-vis jacket and wheeled the trolley out through the office door and down the silent corridor. This area was always empty, and yet today it seemed to breathe. As he passed through he fancied the building sighed its disapproval of his treachery. He stopped at the end of the corridor and waited for the goods elevator to arrive. As he did he hummed nervously to himself and smiled; it didn't hurt to assume he was being watched.

Like any other working building, lunchtime meant a lull in personnel at DPC04. Anthony wheeled the trolley through the deserted, ground floor corridors that hours earlier had rung with the excited and confused cacophony of Transports looking forward to the new life they had been promised. The bag on the top shelf twitched almost imperceptibly, Anthony nervously looked around, checking he was alone. 'Keep still.' He hissed, hoping his sister could hear through the thick rubber. It occurred to him that he didn't know if they could breathe in there; they weren't designed for live goods. He wheeled through labyrinthine corridors, past doors to wings that weren't being used; past empty offices where filing cabinets stood open, gathering dust where there was once paper; past a soft toy, dropped in the corridor just that morning. A rabbit hand sewn from rags. Worn and loved. Discarded.

He turned a corner into the corridor where the boiler room was. He prayed the double doors to that hot, grimy place would be shut. The men who fed the fires with coal and a more macabre fuel weren't the sharpest, but even they might raise an eyebrow at him walking past with a loaded trolley and not dropping it off. Mercifully they were shut and he tried to rush past as quickly as he dared. Just as he reached the doors, one of them opened inwards and a skinny man wearing a high visibility jacket stepped out eyeballing him suspiciously. His mouth hung open in an expression that matched his glazed eyes. A thick, grey, paste clung to the corners of his mouth, Anthony stopped and smiled congenially but he found himself staring at the mystery gunk with wonderment. *What is that even made of?*

'Alright ee there boss. You want me to take that?' The man asked in a broad West Country accent. The door behind him stood open. For the first time Anthony saw the piles of units waiting for disposal. Naked piles of wet bodies filled the room almost to the ceiling, still smeared with the sludge they had died in and twisted at grotesque angles. The floor was awash with a foul liquid. They were at least ten deep but it was difficult to tell where one tangle of stiff limbs met another. Cold, accusing eyes met his. He struggled to look away, to not see the bony old man whose grey, withered skin hung off him like stiff leather; the young woman whose stiff arms were held at him, her face screwed up, defiant even of death; the young man whose head hung at an un-natural angle. Why was he discarded, couldn't he have worked? *Maybe it was because he'd bad mouthed the bloke on the platform?* Anthony's stomach clenched into an iron fist.

'Not these mate. These are…going to the lab for forensic analysis. We found traces of terrahydrochloride on their clothes and we think it might lead us to a rogue explosives manufacturer.' He heard himself babbling guiltily and stopped before he could go any further. He doubted there had ever been such a substance as terrahydrochloride but the idiot's eyes clouded more than they were already. He hoped he wouldn't realise that there wasn't a lab, or anything like one, on the site.

'Ah…I see…' He replied, clearly seeing very little at all. A sly shaft of sun peeked through the clouds. 'Sure you're not keeping thems ones for yourself boss? I knows we likes to sometimes…' Anthony's stomach turned. He saw a way out.

'Well I…' He pulled what he hoped was a bashful face. The idiot tipped him a deliberate, conspiratorial wink that looked more like he'd had a stroke than a signal that they had an accord.

'I gets ya sir. Have fun.' Anthony forced himself to wink back and smile before he moved on. *Fucking dregs.*

He turned another corner, further along beneath the building's dusty tangle of nerves and capillaries; he had reached the door he sought. This was the dangerous part, if he was caught now he had no doubt that before the week was out he would experience the whole operation from a different perspective. He pushed the trolley against the wall and looked nervously around him, there was no-one to be seen in either direction. He opened the heavy metal door and checked down the stairs to the Clubhouse. The basement was usually deserted at this time of day, lunch meant more to the men here than sex, but there was always the chance that someone might have come to release some mid-day tension. He retreated to the trolley. After one final check around, he bent down and un-zipped the bottom bag. Joshua was still and pale, his colour complimenting the crisp white bandages that Beth had carefully dressed around his eyes. Anthony's heart stuttered. *Is he breathing? Has he suffocated?* His chest fell and Anthony let out a synchronised breath, realising that he had held his in sympathy.

'Josh, let me get Beth out and we'll help you ok?' Joshua reached for the bandages but Anthony gently stayed his hand. 'Not now, mate, not now…I'm so sorry.' He stayed silent. Anthony stood up and unzipped the bag that held his sister; her eyes glowered malevolently at him from the dark.

'Where are we?' She snarled.

'The safest place you can be for now.' He replied. A whining contrite note that irritated him had crept into his voice. He could feel his puddle of guilt evaporating under the glare of her hatred. 'Come on, you need to move.' He snapped. He helped her to wriggle out of the bag, she blew air on to her sweaty forehead but otherwise she didn't make a sound. Together they helped Joshua to get out. Other than the stiff movement of his body he looked as lifeless as the bodies that waited to burn.

There was so much that Anthony wanted to say, he wanted to babble apologise, to shout at them for getting involved in this; he wanted to weep like a child and beg their forgiveness. 'Come on, follow me.' He snapped.

'We're back here?' Beth asked. The anger in her voice had melted away to fear. Anthony was reminded of her as a little girl, emotion welled up in his throat again; he crushed the rebellion.

He led them down into the dungeon. Joshua walked carefully between them. Beth leant down to whisper to him to step down each brick step. They reached the corridor. Anthony quickly scanned to see if there were passes hanging by the doors, two rooms had the tell-tale pendants swinging gently like ugly pendulums, marking seconds incongruent with perceived time. He ushered them quickly along until they reached the door marked ten. Anthony pulled out the ancient key that he had stolen from the estates office last night.

*

A lock screeched in protest. Tired tumblers groaned against each other, threatening to snap the aged key. A clunk, heavy and metallic. Beth's breath, warm and sweet at his shoulder. The door opened quietly, its hinges oiled and silent; respectfully solemn. A rush of air, cool, musty and damp. It smelt of cobwebs, dust and time, lots of time. The draft made him shiver, pain flared in his eyes. The flesh around them stung as it caught the gauze. 'Oh my…oh Tamsin.' Beth's voice was choked with emotion. Joshua reeled. The despair in Beth's voice, dripping from her words like stagnant water, knotted his stomach. He resisted the urge to claw at his bandages, to rip them off. He needed to see his sister.

'Tamsin? Are you there?' His voice sounded strange and disjointed, as if losing his sight had somehow changed what was inside him.

'Quick, get inside.' Anthony ushered them in. Joshua violently shrugged his urging hand from his shoulder. The door clanged shut behind them making him jump. He could hear a soft mewling, a baby.

'They told me you were dead. Is the baby here? Where are we?' He asked. A body pressed against his. A different smell, female, but not Beth. The chest he felt pressed against him rose and fell, hitching words stuck in a throat that tried to disgorge them.

'Josh, what did they do to you?' Tamsin's voice came from the darkness like a beacon.

A sob rose in his throat, his eyes burned. 'Tam, we thought you were… Is the baby here? I can hear it. Where's Mario?' The warm body that crushed his tensed then trembled as she wept. It was all the explanation he needed. He felt his legs going weak. He twisted his head around, trying to fix on something to anchor himself to, a point of reference to reign this giddiness. He was sinking, fading into the viscous darkness.

'Sit him down. He's going to go.' Anthony said from far away. Hands grabbed him from all sides. Too many hands. He tried to count them, they seemed everywhere. He was gently forced down onto a wooden surface covered only by a thin blanket of rough wool. Strength gradually came back to his legs as he swam back through the thick blackness to reality.

'Is he ok..'

'Water..'

'Tried to wash…'

'Permanent damage…'

'Your fault…'

'Looking for…'

'And then…'

'Where are we? What is this place? Anthony?' Silence; oppressive and heavy as the darkness. 'Anthony?' He repeated sharply. Fury and frustration underpinned his voice with a steel foundation.

'It's where…these are holding cells. I've got the key and I can keep you all locked in here but only for today.' Anthony's voice floated from behind Joshua, he whirled around to face its source. 'I need to leave you here, I'll get you out tonight. If anyone knocks on the door, if you hear any noise at all; stay quiet.' Anthony's voice broke on the last words. The girls murmured, the door, creaking and rheumatic, opened and clanged closed. The tired lock scraped and complained. Silence.

Chapter 32

'Hold your arms out, Josh.' Tamsin commanded from his side. He felt her lean behind him and disturb the sheets, while she did she cooed and crooned. A warm bundle wriggled into his open arms.

'Who's that, Aaron? Is it your Uncle Josh? He's come to take us away. He's smiling, I think he likes you.' Tamsin's voice rang with smile that made Joshua want to weep with relief.

'Where's Beth?' He asked. A touch of panic crept into his belly.

'It's ok, I'm here.' She came from nowhere, a ghost who laid her forehead against his and kissed him softly. She tasted stale but sweet and familiar.

'You two…?' Tamsain asked.

Joshua smiled and nodded and grabbed her hand. 'I thought I'd lost you. I thought I'd lost you both…' He fought against the hard sobs that waited in his throat to choke him. He swallowed and breathed deeply.

'It's ok. We're all together now. Tony's going to get us out of here.' Beth soothed.

'Will he come too?' Tamsin said. She moved in close to them. Her head touched theirs where they joined. Joshua felt Beth put an arm around her.

'I don't know. I don't know how involved he is with…this.' The poison in her voice was unmistakeable.

Joshua looked down at the still baby who he couldn't see. His fresh, new smell hung in Joshua's nose. The soft blanket he was wrapped in felt good against his hands. 'I don't think he'll come. I think he'll get us out, but he won't come.'

'Why not?' Tamsin's voice sounded sharp and panicked. 'Why would he want to stay here?'

How could he explain to her that Anthony would stay for the power that had been arbitrarily given to him? He was addicted and would never leave through choice. 'Tony's lost to us. All we can do is hope he can get us out without getting hurt himself.'

'Would they do that? Hurt him?' Beth asked.

'If they find him helping us he'll be treated as a traitor.' He leant towards Beth and rested his head on her shoulder. The hysteria he had been holding in suddenly clogged his throat, he tried to cough to free his chest but sobs tore through him. 'What did they do to you?' He tried to say but emotion distorted his words. Her frizzy hair tickled his forehead. 'What have they done to both of you?' This time he spoke clearly. The question hung in the air.

Frustration and impotent rage roared in Joshua's ears, pounding a drum in time with his heart. 'We're going to bring this whole thing down if it kills me.' He spat as he moved away from Beth's shoulder and gingerly touched the bandages that covered his eyes. He lapsed into silence.

'What will we do when we get out of here?' Tamsin said eventually. She sounded conversational as if her question had no more levity than what was on the television that night.

'We'll get to the nearest city and vanish for a while. There are people who will look after us.' Joshua replied. He thought about Ky and Meditant. He wondered if the two babies would get to be friends.

'Where would we go? France?' Tamsin asked. Her voice flickered with hopeful excitement.

Joshua smiled. 'Maybe, or maybe America. I guess it just depends on our luck really.'

This time Tamsin squealed like an over-joyed child. 'Ooh, America! Is it as nice as people say? I've heard that everyone has jobs there. There's loads of money and everything's really cheap. I could send Aaron to school and we can all be together…' She suddenly went quiet.

'What is it, Tam?' Beth said eventually.

'We won't all be together though, will we? Our parents are all gone, so are Mario and Anthony… he's never going to be the same as he was; none of us will be. Everything has changed, nothing can ever be right again.'

They sat in silence, allowing Tamsin's words the space to grow. Gingerly, Joshua put his hands to his eyes. Dull pain still flared but not as severe as it was earlier.

'Do you think we should try taking those off?' Beth asked. Her voice was gentle with concern. 'If you're able to…it's just that…tonight…'

'Yeah I know. If we're making our escape it would help if I could see.' Joshua took a deep breath. Fear pulsed in his chest. 'Do it. Take them off.' He said. There was some shuffling movement and he could feel Beth standing in front of him. He could smell her sweetness masking a stale undertone; delicate and light, not the sour unpleasantness that rose from him. Her gentle fingers tugged at the back of his head. He recoiled slightly with shock as her breast brushed his face. Her hands sprang away.

'Did I hurt you?' She said, her voice panicked.

'No, it's ok, you just surprised me.' Joshua smiled. Beth slowly unwrapped the bandage until only thick, gauze pads remained pressed on his eyes. She peeled the first one off; Joshua could feel the flesh of his eyelid sticking slightly to it.

'Keep them closed. Wait until I've done the other.' She eased the second off. The cool cellar air felt crisp and good against the stinging skin. 'Ok, now try and open them slowly.'

Joshua took a deep breath. He relaxed the muscles in his face. He realised they had almost frozen in place as he had consciously kept them scrunched shut. He tried to ease them open but nothing happened. Pain tore through his eyelids. He sharply drew breath.

'Hold on. I think they're stuck shut.' Tamsin said from his side. 'Tilt your head back.' Joshua did as he was told. He started as cool water was poured on his face.

'Ok, head forward.' Beth said. Cold tears rolled down his face. He eased his eyes open. They flashed with pain but he willed them to open more. He could see a dark, grey shape before him; it moved slightly. He reached his arm out and touched it. The soft skin of Beth's face shocked his hand. 'Can you see me?' She asked. The grey shaped quivered.

'Sort of.' He moved his head around. Another shape was at his side. 'Tam?' He reached out and touched her.

'Yeah, it's me.' She laughed delightedly. She reached around and held up a slightly lighter shape. 'Can you see Aaron?'

Joshua grinned. 'Kind of.' He turned back to Beth and eased his eyes open to their full extent. Colourful spring crept into his dark winter and his smile spread further. He could see the dark, frizzy shape of Beth's hair and her brown skin. Behind her the brick wall was a vibrant block of orange. However, focus and detail still eluded him. 'I can see you and I can see colours but everything's blurry.' They washed his eyes out with more water and his vision improved a little more.

'I think you need to lie down and rest them.' Beth whispered as she gently pulled his head into her chest. Joshua shut his eyes again, as he did he felt a pang of fear that the disfigured blur that he had just seen was the last he would ever see of her.

Tamsin moved from next to him and they both helped to put his legs up. An intractable exhaustion washed over him and he stifled a yawn as he lay down on the hard bed. The small, warm bundle of his nephew was gently nestled into the crook of his arm.

'You both need a sleep.' Tamsin said, her voice was soft and motherly. 'Tonight's going to be a big night. Get some rest.' Her voice trailed to a whisper that seemed to come from far away. Joshua was retreating into the comforting clouds. The baby at his side snuffled and wriggled as he got comfortable and then joined him.

*

The raucous, grating scrape of the rusty door lock woke Joshua up. Instinctively he opened his eyes and a sharp stinging tore through his face as though someone had blown powdered glass into them. His vision was still blurry but he could see that Beth and Tamsin were both standing. A dark figure walked in and quickly shut the door. The baby started to cry.

'Well?' Beth snapped.

'Well what?' Anthony replied.

'How are you getting us out of here? I don't want to spend another minute in this fucking cellar.' Beth's voice was shrill and angry but there was something deeper, more unhinged. He wondered again what had happened to her since they had been arrested.

'Are you coming with us?' He asked as he swung his legs around and sat up. He glared at the top of the shadow that had come in.

'You all need to stop squawking at me, let me speak.' Anthony snapped. 'In a minute I'm going to go and double check the coast is clear. When I come back, Josh and Beth are going to go up wearing these.' Joshua could clearly see the bright yellow high visibility jackets that he handed to Beth. 'Beth, do you remember the way up? It's simple, up the steps and out the door, turn right and keep walking. There'll be a fire escape on the left, push the bar and go outside. Hold hands or something so that you can lead Josh, if you see anyone they can't realise he's been hurt. From there you follow the path towards the fence, anyone who sees you will assume you work here. If you follow the fence you'll come to a dip, from there you should be shielded from the watch towers a bit. Cut the two fences with this.' He leant down to what looked like a bag and pulled something out.

'What is it?' He said.

'Bolt cutters. They'll get you through the fence but they won't do much against the dogs, you'll have to go quickly.'

'That's a lot to remember. Where will you be? Are you coming?' Joshua asked.

'Do you want me to write it down?' Anthony sneered. 'I'll be following with Tam. When you're out you'll need to get out of sight of the towers. Head away but keep going level. As the hill starts to climb you'll see a path which will take you over the bank to the left of the camp as you look up at the hill. Follow it down the other side to a track. Here.' He handed something to Beth. 'In the phonebook there's an entry for "driver". Call him and he'll come and find you.'

'Who's that?' Joshua asked warily. He doubted many of Anthony's friends would be disposed to help them.

'I've hired a driver, some kid I know. He'll drop us into Manchester. He can't be trusted so tell him nothing. Don't answer questions or make chit chat. He'll do the job because I'm paying him well for it and he won't get a penny until we get there. Tell him nothing but do exactly as he says.'

'So where will you two be?' Joshua said.

'We are going to walk straight out of the gate. That's why you two are taking the baby in this bag.' He held up a dark shape. Joshua could hear the grin in his voice. He really thought he was clever.

Beth took it from him. 'You'd better see if the coast is clear. Hadn't you?'

Anthony grunted something unintelligible and left quickly, shutting the door behind him. 'I don't trust him.' Beth said hurriedly. 'Something's not right.'

'It seems strange that he wants us to go separately. I mean, I trust you with Aaron but…' Tamsin paused. '…but I guess if he's got a plan we should stick to it. What do you think Josh?'

He thought for a second. He agreed with Beth, something didn't feel right, but Tamsin was right too. 'What choice do we really have?' Neither of them answered.

The door lock screeched it cacophonic warning. 'Ok, it's clear. You two go, we'll follow.' Anthony's voice floated from the dark shadow at the door. Joshua stood and Tamsin embraced him, holding him tightly to her.

'Take care out there Josh. Whatever happens, look after my baby. He's sleeping, hopefully he'll…' She couldn't finish, her voice was thick with tears. She placed the heavy hold-all in his hand and squeezed his fingers shut around the handles.

'Shh, I'm going to see you in a minute and we'll be free. Just remember America, ok?' Joshua fought with his own emotions. He felt his free hand taken.

'Come on. We've got to go.' Beth said pulling him away.

He hung back a moment. Anthony's dark figure was before him. 'Mate, good luck. I'm sorry.' His voice sounded contrite and suddenly clogged with emotion.

'We'll talk about it another time. See you on the other side, eh?' Joshua replied. Beth pulled his arm again. He let her guide him away.

Chapter 33

The corridor was musty and dank but it felt fresh after spending the day and half of the night in the cell.

'What time is it?' As Joshua spoke something hanging brushed his arm. He jumped and the weight in the hold-all shifted slightly. His heart stopped. *What would they do if the baby woke up?*

'It's ok, it's nothing.' Beth whispered. 'It's three am. Why?'

He made no reply. Time was obsolete here, an abstract concept that leant confusion to a blurred world. He couldn't explain that by knowing *when* they were he could somehow anchor himself to this fuzzy, stygian dream.

The sharp light of the corridor glowed in his hazy vision making the doors they passed seem to skulk in the shadows. Beth's bright yellow waist coat showed him the way. Shards of blue light shone from the reflective bands that encircled her figure.

'There are stairs now, let me take the baby.' She said. He handed her the bag. 'Step up. Good. And again.' She whispered. Joshua put a steadying hand out, recoiling at the feel of the wall. Beneath the slime the old bricks gave slightly at the pressure of his touch; they felt like rotted flesh. *If we don't make it someone could scrape that from my cold fingers and know we were here.*

The door at the top swung silently open. The shadowy corridor beyond left Joshua almost blind again, he filled chest with fresh, clean air. Beth stopped them in front of a door. 'Ok, this is it. We have to try and go steadily and not look suspicious. Ok?'

'Ok.' Joshua replied. 'Give me the bag.' Beth hesitated for a second before handing it over. The weight was reassuring, it gave him purpose, control of at least one element. The door swung open and hit the wall behind with a shocking clunk that stopped his breath in his throat. He expected the baby to start screaming and sirens to wail their response. Nothing. It felt as though a magical incantation lay over them like a protective blanket. They paused for a moment then stepped out.

Freezing, crisp air hit Joshua like a glorious wall. It seemed to crystallise in his nose making the fine hairs rigid and frail. He breathed a huge gasp of the sweet elixir. As he exhaled he marvelled that he could see it expand and grow away from him, curling tendrils that rose into the night, whisping in ethereal contrails across the perfect disc of the sinking moon. The grass twinkled with a billion crystals that reflected tiny shards of light. 'Why couldn't it have been a cloudy night?' Beth whispered as she shut the door behind them. Although she was right he couldn't agree – a night had never looked as beautiful. The moon drenched everything in silver rain. This cold, brutal night was theirs, even if it was all they had. He decided that if he had to die tonight it would be out here, far away from the damp tunnels below.

As they walked out of the shadow of the building Joshua turned to face it. The bright moon cast a favourable light making it no longer seem malevolent, only sad and broken. He turned away. The path before them glowed in the moonlight and they held hands as they casually ambled. The desire to run was strong, his legs were taut and he had to force himself to relax. He trembled and shook almost uncontrollably. 'Are you cold?' Beth asked in her normal voice. It sounded piercing in the still night.

'No, I'm ok.' He could feel himself tensing up, his stomach was in knots. He didn't want to have to explain that this was what adrenaline did to him. Suddenly he was very aware of his palms, coldly sweating against hers, he wanted to let go and wipe them on his jeans but a voice in his mind whispered that if he did the spell would be broken. He wondered if they themselves were the magic and it was only their unity that kept them safe. Hand in hand they followed the path along the line of the fence.

'Can you see the watch towers?' Joshua said quietly. 'I can't make them out.

'Yeah. I can see where the land rises, it's just ahead…shit…' Beth hissed. Joshua looked up the path and saw a bright yellow waistcoat coming towards them.

'Keep calm.' Joshua said. 'We could be anyone. Just smile and nod.'

As the floating jacket came closer it grew legs and arms that swung officiously, almost marching. It was the strident walk of an important man. Joshua waited until he could see the shadows of his eyes. He prayed the baby would stay sleeping. 'Good morning. A beautiful night.'

'Morning. Quick stroll before the early shift? I must say you're keen.' Clipped, almost military. British through and through in this post-Britain age. *A very British genocide.* The words reverberated around Joshua's head. A burst of giggles fermented and rose like bubbles in his chest. Before the sentence was out of his mouth the man was moving away.

As Anthony had promised the ground rose and dropped suddenly, so much so that shallow steps were cut into the path. Beth spoke. 'I can only see the top of one tower and I can't see the other at all. We need to do this part quickly. Ready?'

'Let's do it.' He replied. They both fumbled to rid themselves of the treacherous waistcoats. Joshua carefully opened the bag, in the shadows he could barely make out the baby's features. He gently placed a hand close to his cheek, he felt warm enough. He packed the bright jackets in next to him and slowly and carefully zipped it up again. Free of the vest Joshua felt invisible yet so much more visible. 'Let's go.' He muttered, hoping he sounded braver than he felt.

The short grass was hard, crystalline; savagely frozen as it could only be in the dead of night before dawn's warm breath gave respite. Shotgun pellets of frozen rabbit's droppings sprinkled the ground and they had to watch for holes concealed in the grass. They crunched warily away from the path. Fear fluttered between them. Both were aware that they had left more than a path; they had left relative safety. At the fence they crouched down low. Thick frost clung to the chainmail that encircled the camp, only in places did grim rust leer through. Beth took the cutters out of the bag. 'Thank goodness he's slept through this.' Beth said looking lovingly down at Aaron.

'Don't speak too soon.'

 They waited silently; looking, listening. They could hear nothing but the barely perceptible hum of the night. Quickly Beth cut a line of links. Ice fell in a miniature snow shower. 'Check again for dogs.' Joshua hissed as Beth pulled open a hole.

'I have, it's clear.' She crawled through first. He carefully pushed the bag through after her. She held the fence open for him.

'Don't worry about me. Take the baby off the floor he'll get cold.' He snapped. Beth grunted her acknowledgement and picked up the bag. She crossed to the other fence, put down the bag and started to cut the links. Where the ice had fallen the dark wire was nearly invisible and Joshua struggled to get through, his clothes snagged and the rusted wires dragged and tore at his skin. Eventually he dragged himself free. He nervously looked from left to right.

'Come on, Beth.' He picked up the bag, he hoped it wasn't too cold and the baby was ok, he daren't open it again to check.

'I'm trying, this one's harder than the inside fence, it's newer. Here, you do it. You're stronger than me. Put the bag down.' Joshua hesitated. 'We'll be caught before he freezes, come on.'

He put it gently down. The heavy bolt cutters were freezing to touch but their satisfying weight felt reassuring. Beth guided the jaws onto the steel links and Joshua snapped them with a grunt. It was slow and painstaking work. He could feel his heart thudding against his ribs, he fancied he could hear Aaron's too; losing pace, slowing, slowing; each tiny drumbeat farther from the last. A misty vapour rose from them, a treacherous haze that announced their presence to anyone who cared to step out of the warmth of their cozy room in the watchtower. He imagined their scent curling to the noses of sleeping dogs who balefully regarded the bitter night from the haven of a kennel, talking to them in sweat and fear.

Joshua cut the last link. 'Come on, you first.' He held the fence open and Beth crawled through, pushing the bag in front of her. Joshua climbed through then pulled the bent wires back into shape to try and hold off detection for as long as possible. He turned back and grinned at Beth. 'First hurdle.'

Chapter 34

The rocky hill before them remained dark, silently watching the coming drama. Wiry grass and delicate weeds shrouded in ice shattered under the weight of their tread cautious. From the outside, the camp looked deserted. Floodlights shone brightly, banishing shadow to beyond the fences. The red brick chimney of the main building jutted into the dark sky, proudly shunning the light and striking into the black above. Beth's eyes followed his. 'Can you see that?' She stopped walking. Vapour drifted up from her in plumes.

'See what?' Joshua asked panting. He could see very little through the light reflecting off of his breath.

'The heat haze. I thought that was what you were looking at. The fires are burning.'

'I wonder if they ever stop.' They waited a moment, his words hung between them like a spell. 'Come on, we need to move.'

They retreated away from the wire fence, picking carefully through the sharp knots of gorse. Ice crunched softly underfoot and he wondered if they'd be gone before their tracks were noticed. He could hear tinny music playing from the nearest guard tower. He imagined the guard with his shiny, black boots up on the desk, picking his nose as he thumbed through a magazine. *Did he use the cellar? Has he touched my sister? Or Beth?* She turned back. He thought he could see her smile. *Is that reassurance? Can she read my mind?* He made his pained grimace into a smile.

'I think I can see the path.' She whispered. He didn't reply. He could see nothing. Blindly he followed. He wondered where Anthony and Tamsin were, if they had made it out yet. Before them the ground rose towards the dark hill. The path led away through the twisted undergrowth.

The camp had been set out to use the topography of the plateau to its advantage. The guard room was level with the top of the bank that enclosed one side of the valley. They took a path that was carved into the side of it and climbed at a gentle pace leading away from the camp. The path was little more than a rabbit-run that at some point had been lined with stones that made them slip. It ran along the side of the steep bank, doubling back in a gradual zigzag. Thorns snagged on their clothes and silver grass and plants rubbed at their legs soaking them. Joshua did all he could to lift the bag high so that the baby didn't get damp but after a while his arms lacked the strength. He felt the bottom, it was cold and wet. He thought about taking the baby out, to warm him up inside his jacket but there he might get in the way. A thin, crooked voice in his head whispered. *If you're chased it's easier to drop a bag than a baby.* Revulsion rocked him; the voice sounded like Anthony's.

When they were near the top Joshua turned around to look into the guard room. A large, uniformed man sat watching them back.

Joshua froze. 'Can he see us?' He hissed.

Beth stopped and looked back. 'No, can't you see the flickering of the TV? Come on, we need to keep moving.'

They scrambled up the last part of the track quickly. From the top Joshua could see far off clouds that blushed in the presence of the coming dawn. Blurred puddles of ink seeped into one another on the moorland as it undulated into the glorious, unbroken distance. Below them, on the other side of the bank, hidden from the camp, frost clung to what looked like a dirt track that plummeted downhill.

'I see it, I see the car!' Hope made Beth's voice sparkle. He found himself grinning. They carefully scrambled along the path that took them down the other side of the bank. They quickly reached the bottom of the incline where a dark saloon car was waiting in silence.

'What if it's not him? Maybe we should try calling on the phone Anthony gave us?' Joshua asked as he suddenly realised how vulnerable they were.

'If it's not he'd have seen us by now anyway. Let's just hope.' Beth replied. They cautiously approached the car. The windows were fogged making it impossible to see in. Beth tapped on the window. Nothing.

She looked around at Joshua who shrugged. 'Try the door.'

She reluctantly reached down for the handle then jumped with shock as it opened with a metallic wrench.

'Who are you? Names.' A voice spat from within.

Joshua stepped forward. 'Josh and Beth.'

The door swung fully open. 'Get in, quickly.'

Joshua got in the front seat and put the hold all on his lap. He was desperate to get the baby out and warm him up but he was scared of what he might find when he did. The driver reached into the back to unlock the rear door. Now he was in Joshua could see that he was young, not much more than a teenager. A long puckered scar, poorly healed, rippled the skin on the left side of his face. He sat back in his chair and started the engine. It leapt to life with a roar that shattered the stillness of the night. *The guard in the tower must have heard that.* Beth got in behind him and shut the door.

'We're glad to see you. Much longer and we would've frozen.' She blurted gratefully as she blew on her hands.

'Yeah yeah. We need to go. The sun will be up soon and the noise will bring a patrol.' He put the car in gear and began to move.

'Hang on.' Joshua pulled up the handbrake. The car jerked to a stop. 'Aren't we supposed to be waiting for two more?' He rubbed moisture from his window and looked outside, hoping to see Anthony and Tamsin rushing towards them.

'No. Mr Thomas ordered me to wait here for you two and then get away quickly. We've got to go now.'

'No, there are two more. Anthony…Mr Thomas is coming as well.'

'Please, this has to be a mistake.' Beth's voice was panicked.

'There's no mistake. He said you would say this and he said to tell you he was sorry. Now we've got to go, Mr Thomas is the sort of bloke who tells you what he wants and you do it.' He put the car in gear and started to drive away. Storm clouds broke in Joshua's head. An inarticulate roar thundered from his mouth and he thrust out an arm, half punching, half pushing the boy's head against the side window. The engine stalled and the car juddered to a halt.

'I'm not leaving without my fucking sister.' The boy's arms flailed uselessly as if shock had made him forgot how to use them. He wrenched the boy's head back and smashed it against the window again. From somewhere behind a heavy, maroon veil, Beth grabbed at his arms. He let go, shoved his door open and got out, almost dropping the hold all.

'Get the fuck out, get the fuck out.' The boy screeched in a high pitched rage. Beth hurried to jump out. The saloon's engine fired and it roared off down the track leaving behind it a creeping silence.

'Josh? What are we going to do?' Beth's voice broke as she burst into tears.

'I don't know, I need to think.' Joshua's head swam. The baby surely wasn't going to last much longer. The treacherous sun whose coming promised at least warmth also meant patrols and the noise from the car would have been heard. In his fury he pictured himself marching into the camp and dragging Tamsin to safety. Even through his anger he knew that would only bring about death for them all.

'Why, Josh?' Beth crouched to the floor and covered her face with her hands. 'Why would Tony do this?'

'I don't know but we need to move.' He put a hand on her shoulder.

'Where to?' Beth wailed. 'Our only chance just drove away. Why did you do it? What if it was all part of the plan? What if Tony is waiting for us somewhere?' She took her hands away from her face and stared up at Joshua. 'What have you done?'

'He's not waiting for us.' Joshua snarled angrily. 'He doesn't care. All the things that he's done, they've killed him. The Anthony that we grew up with is dead, Beth.' He looked up at the lightening sky. He felt anger and frustration course through his veins but he took a deep breath and tried to calm himself. He leant down taking care not to let the bag drag on the floor. 'I'm sorry. I'm so sorry. I've messed up and got us into this. I love you.'

Beth struggled to her feet. 'No I'm sorry. I love you too. It's not your fault, none of this is. But what are we going to do? Shall we head to the main road and hope we can hitch a lift?'

'No. We'd be caught by the patrols before we got there.' Suddenly his face lit up. 'Why didn't I think of it before? I've got an idea. Come on.' He pulled Beth insistently by the hand, back towards the track that they had come down. He glanced at the sky. The purple clouds which had been far away were drawing closer, but not enough to stretch the gloom out for longer. He could only pray that on the other side of the bank there was still enough shadow to get to where they needed to.

'Where are we going?'

'Quick, there's no time to explain. You'll have to lead the way, go back up the bank but not towards the camp, head the other way, toward the hill.'

They set off back up the path, clawing their way unsteadily through the white grass and frozen undergrowth. The bag snagged on some sharp gorse, immediately it wriggled and shook and a high pitched wail came, weak and scared. 'Hold on.' Joshua said stopping abruptly. Hot air tore at his throat and spilled into the night, boiling sweat trickled down his back in icy slivers. He unzipped the hold all and gently took out the screaming baby. 'Shh, Aaron, it's ok.' He cooed as soothingly as he could.

'Josh, where are we going?' Beth's voice had become high pitched.

'There's a safe place. It's near here.' He opened his jacket and held Aaron close to him before zipping it back up. The baby screamed at his chest. 'Come on, keep going. Stop at the top.'

Just before the ridge Beth stopped so abruptly that Joshua nearly ran into her back. 'Crawl to the top. I'm going to need your eyes.' Joshua whispered before he realised that the screaming baby would give them away before the sound of his voice. They both dropped onto their fronts in the cold, wet grass and crawled towards the top. They peered over the ridge into the valley below. The dawn cautiously peered back at them from the other horizon, an enemy soldier watching them watching him from the safety of his own line. The sky before them glowed pink. Purple and magenta streaked the clouds in the distance making them dark and angry, their edges bleeding and stained. The no-man's land below them was awash with shadows that promised nothing but the most temporary of sanctuary. Rolls of barbed gorse guarded shell holes and hollows where they might hide. To the right of their position the sullen camp awaited their ignominious return. Aaron had settled down to quiet snuffles, his ebbing energy spent on his high octane performance. 'Where is this place?' Beth whispered.

Joshua indicated with his head. It's at the top of the hill opposite the camp.'

'Where you and Ky watched from?'

'Yeah. Can you see anyone? Any patrols? Maybe just small lights from torches?'

'No, nothing.' Beth said.

'Can you see any tracks that go in that direction?'

'There's something down on the valley floor. I can see a few different tracks.'

'Ok. Stay low going over the bank. Don't stand up until we get lower.' Joshua replied. They scrabbled down mud, ice and grass soaked them. At the bottom, a clearly marked white track ran towards the direction of the hill.

'Should we stick to the paths? What about patrols?' Beth said.

'We've got no choice, if we have to pick our way through this stuff we'll be here all day.' Joshua said indicating towards the undergrowth. He checked the horizon again. The sun, emboldened while their attention was elsewhere, had snuck further over the parapet. The world was a sea of shadow. It occurred to Joshua that they were probably better concealed than they would have been an hour ago. 'Come on.' He whispered.

The path led through a maze of white, spiked walls and twisted roots that stuck maliciously out of the cold ground. Thorns tore at their arms and clothes ripping cloth and skin with equal ease. The inky shadows blurred in Joshua's damaged eyes. He fixed on Beth's heaving back and adjusted the weight of the baby who let out a weak wail before settling back to an unhappy silence. The terrain became rockier underfoot and gently rose as they got closer to the hill. The thick, high gorse gave way to sparse heather whose touch was gentler but lacked the height to cover them well. Joshua shivered as a bitter breeze got up. His eyes watered bringing back the pain.

Suddenly a deep voice boomed at them from behind. 'Stop where you are!' They both jumped. Joshua nearly obeyed.

'Keep going.' He parted. 'It can't be much further.'

Behind them three sharp, metallic claps applauded their stoicism. The shrubs around them whistled and cracked. Beth started to run. He focused on her back and sped up, praying he wouldn't trip. The baby started to scream again. Behind them the claps became a round of applause. Dirt kicked up in divots, wood snapped and shattered. Joshua's back was tensed as he ran, squeezing the screaming baby. At any moment he expected to feel a sharp thud in his back. A small hole would penetrate and explode out of his chest, mercifully killing Aaron at the same time. Better to get it quickly, he thought. Better to die out here in the crisp, fresh air than tied to a chair, wriggling and screaming like a trapped pig.

'The path splits.' Beth sobbed. Panic and despair distorted her voice. 'One goes up hill, one goes down. Down has more cover.'

'No,' Joshua shouted in return, 'take the one that goes uphill, to the left.' Before the words had left his mouth their feet were skitting across the frozen junction. The shooting stopped. Men's voices shouted from behind them. Boots thumped on the hard ground. A whistle blew a high pitched scream. A single crack, sharp and crisp as the air itself. Joshua was punched hard in his right shoulder spinning him almost off his feet. The baby stopped crying abruptly. Somehow he stumbled on. His breath tortured his throat, his head pounded. He waited for the heavy hand that had punched him to drag him to the floor. His shoulder felt hot and wet.

They joined another path that snaked around the rear of the hill. The voices behind seemed so close that they could pounce on them at any moment. He knew that the baby was gone, that he should throw him, it, away. But he couldn't, it didn't matter if it slowed him down, nothing mattered now. This was the end game, the final scene. The outcome was ordained, details didn't matter. In front of him, above him, climbing up the steep track Beth shouted something that was almost lost on a breeze. It sounded like she had shouted Ky's name. The air whizzed around him in a burst, something hot clawed at his neck. It suddenly seemed like there were a hundred guns all firing at once, but from ahead of him instead of behind. He fell to the ground, his blurred vision started to fade. Hands all around him were dragging him to his feet. Soldiers, clad in camouflage jackets. Through the haze he thought he recognised a face. 'Ky?' He managed to croak.

'Yes mate, I'm here.' The boy's face had aged, become timeless. He gently led him to the gap in the rocks, the entrance to the shelter. Beth was waiting there sobbing. He smiled and put his hand on her hair. 'I need to leave you now. We're going to take the camp.' Ky said.

'Tamsin.'

'Of course. Don't worry.' Ky smiled again. Joshua managed a weak effort in response.

'Come on, Father. We need to move now.' A voice behind them said. Ky nodded, then he was gone.

Anthony stood with his head bowed as Joshua and Beth's footsteps echoed away to a memory, each step feeling like it would be the last before another, fainter than before. Even though he stared at the floor he could feel the weight of Tamsin's gaze. Her expectation hung in the air; the question that she dared not ask, that he had no answer to. Finally he looked up. Tamsin remained where she had been seated when they had left. Her hands were folded and pushed between her legs. Her shoulders were hunched against the gathering chill. She stared at him without blinking. 'It was a lie, wasn't it?'

Words snagged in his throat making it hard to breathe and impossible to talk. He opened his mouth but nothing came. He nodded.

'It's because they know I'm alive, isn't it? Somehow, you got signed whatever paperwork you needed to say that Josh and Beth are dead, but officially I'm still alive.' He nodded again. Tamsin smiled sadly at him and patted the bed next to her. 'Come and sit with me.'

Anthony did as he was told. Tears prickled his eyes. Even now he could still smell her sweetness, a natural undertone that usurped the decay that clung to all who passed through this terrible place. She took his hand in hers; it felt cold and clammy.

'How does it happen?' She asked, studying their joined hands. A small sob escaped her lips.

'It...it's bad. I can't let you... it has to be different. I brought...something...' Tears flowed freely down his face now. He produced a syringe, taken from his office upstairs. His hand trembled as he held it open. They both stared; he was fascinated how something so innocuous could be so potent a symbol.

'I don't want to. I want to go the same way that Mario did. I betrayed him, that's the least that I can do.' She began to sob harder.

Anthony slipped his arm around her shoulders. He held her that way for a moment, for a minute; for a period of time that evaded the banality of quantification. Their bodies fed off the shaking of the other. Eventually he was able to speak. 'Please Tam, it's horrible. I can't let you. Please.'

She sat upright and shook his arm away. 'If you have to. But first...' Anthony nodded, he understood. He leant forward and kissed her, long and deeply. He moved away. She smiled and bowed her head. 'I'm ready now. His hand trembled so much that he struggled to find her vein. Eventually he did.

*

He left the room ten minutes later. Tears streaked his face. His legs shook as each step carried him out of Hades. He knew that he needed to go and tell the dregs in the incinerator room that they had something to collect from cell ten but the thought of them with their dirty, foul hands all over her was too much. He wandered through the empty corridors that soon would be echoing with confused voices until he came to a door to the outside. Dimly he was aware that it was probably the one that Joshua and Beth had used not an hour ago.

The cold slapped his face as though it was disgusted with him. The moon had sunk now and the morning was kissed by the pink of the coming sunrise. The grass underfoot was already starting to thaw, the frost not yet deep enough to last beyond the dawn. He looked up into the dark grey sky; he could smell the smoke. He wondered if there would ever come a day when he didn't. He felt exhausted yet wired. He wondered if he'd ever sleep again.

Suddenly a piercing wail made him jump. He had never heard the alarm siren, even as a test, but the panic that it instilled needed no rehearsal. The metallic rattle of nearby gunfire nearly made him run back inside. He froze for a moment, his mind wildly trying to make sense of the noises. Reality hit him with a sledgehammer: this was the liberation he had sworn would never come. For a moment he saw Tamsin's face, peaceful and sleeping; losing colour and warmth by the second. He fell against the wall and cried out; the piercing wail of an injured animal. Another burst of gunfire, this time nearby, made him wipe his face and move. He could see the dorm blocks emptying, a lot of the scurrying people held guns; they all ran in the direction of the main gate. His mind worked quickly. He knew where he needed to go. The place where no-one else knew you could get out, assuming that Joshua and Beth had cut the fence as he'd told them. As he ran he fumbled for his phone and dialled Lee's number.

Chapter 36

The fast-approaching thunder awoke Joshua from a mauve labyrinth of crooked dreams. The hot, heavy air in the tent throbbed as the helicopter came in to land. The roar came with a monstrous updraft which threatened to pluck out the pegs holding the thick canvas on the sodden ground. Joshua imagined it rising like a bizarre, angular hot air balloon, leaving him and Beth exposed to the rest of the refugee camp.

Beth rolled over making the pallets they slept on creak. She frowned sleepily at him and put her hands over her ears. 'I hope those noisy bastards have brought something worthwhile with them.' She shouted to be heard over the din. Aaron was already whining unhappily from the cot at the end of the bed that he had made out of more pallets and the foam from an old car seat. As usual Meditant stayed calm and placid. Joshua hurried to get out of bed before Beth could. His feet sunk into the grass. The damp had seeped through the ground from the torrential spring rain showers of a few days ago, it felt refreshing and pleasing. He felt his way slowly along the side of the tent using the warm canvas as a guide to help him.

His close vision was improving daily but his far sight was still very blurry. He had been to see the camp doctor a few days ago. He was far from a priority for the ill-equipped, over-stretched medical centre, but the doctor had agreed to see him as the hostilities were growing less ferocious and the torrent of wounded fighters from both sides was easing to a steady flow. He had entered the dank, cramped tent through a dimly lit ward that stank of bleach and an under-lying stench like dusty potatoes and rotten newspaper. Low camp beds covered almost every inch of ground. They were pushed up close to one another with only narrow walkways between the rows. Each bed held a crumpled bundle shrouded in grey blankets, some hooked up to drips that hung on metal stands, some sitting up watching the rest with hollow eyes. A chorus of soft moans drifted through the tent, lulling others to their long sleep. A nurse saw him watching and angrily asked him what his business was. He explained and she begrudgingly showed him into a curtained off room. The doctor who studied his eyes looked through a lens that magnified his own. Joshua could see that it his lid was purple and swollen. 'When did you last get a day off?' He joked nervously to distract himself.

The doctor, an ageless man with a haggard face, snorted sarcastically. 'No point in days off. I'm stuck here like everyone else.' He switched off the bright lamp he had been using to get a better view. 'There is some heavy scarring on the cornea itself. You'll need reconstructive surgery to restore your vision properly. Obviously that isn't anything that we can do here…' His voice trailed off as if to highlight the point.

'Of course. Thank you for having a look.' He replied as he got to his feet and slipped his jacket back on. He hadn't been expecting a much more detailed prognosis but Beth had made the appointment. 'Are things quieter here now?' He asked.

'There are less fighting men coming in but we're taking more civilians every day. Lots of explosives wounds, IEDs used by the rebels mostly but we're increasingly seeing people suffering from acute malnutrition.' He replied. His irritable tone didn't sit with his willingness to offer information.

'Really? Malnutrition? But…?'

'People can't feed themselves without supermarkets and they're not open for business. Now if you don't mind I've got ward full to attend to.' He snapped. Joshua had taken the hint and left him to his business.

*

By the time he had climbed back into bed with the two children the helicopter had turned its obtrusive engines off. Aaron continued to cry in Joshua's arms, Meditant seemed to try to comfort his younger friend, placing a tiny hand on his shoulder. An excited babble from outside began to grow. Despite the early hour, the crowds had descended to see what had arrived. Now that the UN helicopter runs from across the Channel came almost daily, the desperate scuffles had abated.

The Farthingloe refugee camp had established itself just outside of Dover, from the scared throngs of people running for their lives from the fighting. The French, assisted by the UN, had established the camp and extracted promises from Rebuild not to attack it; ostensibly as a humanitarian gesture but in reality to stop the exodus of people who were leaving for the continent and alarming French voters. G4ITAS had stationed a platoon nearby whose only task was to shoot the UN helicopters out of the sky as they came across the Channel. The international community had been mortified at Rebuild's actions and that had contributed to the shift in the balance of power that people had been talking about for days. Whatever the case, the arrival of the helicopters was starting to become just another rhythm in the day at the camp, rather than the potential for a riot which it had been.

Aaron stopped crying quickly and contented himself with gurgling and playing with Meditant who giggled and gurgled back. Beth's breathing had settled back into soft rasps that told Joshua that she had fallen back to sleep. She seemed less tired now that the morning sickness had passed but he still thought she needed plenty of rest. The long winter at the camp had been especially hard on her. In the early days, when his eyes had still been bad, it had fallen to her to fight for their survival. She had to queue for hours in the freezing rain to fill their water carrier; fight through the crowds to get supplies when only one airdrop a week was making it through; tend to the baby and try her hardest to keep the wounds around his eyes from suppurating. He had been worse than useless in those early days. His eyes had become infected on the long march south from Manchester. Initially Ky's crew had looked after them but Rebuild had begun to fight back with growing intensity and the Freetopia forces had scattered under the crush of superior weaponry, training and discipline. Ky had come to an uncomfortable agreement with Stickles to join forces and the Manchester house had filled with guerrilla troops who had no time for a half-blinded burden. He, Beth and Aaron had set out for the south on foot, joining the travelling caravan of freed greenbacks, injured fighters and terrified civilians from all echelons of society. War had an egalitising effect, he mused.

The heat in the tent was in heady, somnolent cohorts with the chorus of heavy breathing from Beth and Aaron. Joshua soon found his own eyes growing heavy, the beige and green blurs ran together and became red as his scarred eyelids flicked and closed. The buzz and mumble of the crowd that had gathered near to the helicopter drifted away on a brooding sea, dipping and cresting as the hubbub approached a far off horizon where it would fall off the edge of a flat world. Joshua welcomed that retreat. At the camp there was always a voice, a scream, some noise somewhere. He craved those precious moments when sleep would take him away to a place that was peaceful, where he couldn't smell the constant stench of cooking food, piss and shit. Just as he reached that far off plane, the tone of the crowd changed, the voices became more urgent, people began calling out to friends, phones began to beep and ring. It sounded as though a million robotic birds were taking flight amid a tonedeaf dawn chorus. He shook himself awake and lie listening for a moment. The rumble of the crowd sounded different to the angry stirrings that had preceded the food riots, this had a different tone, something that he couldn't place.

As quietly and softly as he could, he slipped out the bed, gently pushing Aaron and Meditant into the curve created by Beth's foetal position. Aaron snuggled against the round protrusion of her belly, curled up with his cousin through the thin membrane of skin that separated them. He pulled on the same pair of muddy, tattered old boots that had crossed Saddleworth Moor and quietly stepped out into the bright morning. Parts of the camp had been washed away in the recent foul weather and families had lost what little they had left. These poor people, the homeless among the homeless had been taken in by other families around them who had shared what they had with them. He compared it to what would have happened before these people had been uprooted. Somehow their desperation made them closer, a community instead of a million separate souls. This morning he could barely see the scarred earth at his feet, the pathway between the rows of tents was thronged with people. He let himself be carried along with the crowd, trying to concentrate on the blue jacket in front of him.

'Are you ok, can you not see?' A voice to his left, a teenaged girl, spoke above the crowd's din.

'I'm ok...I just struggle a bit.' Joshua replied. He tried to smile, to show that he was ok.

'Then I'll help you.' The girl said resolutely. She held on to his arm in a death grip and uncomfortably muttered random directions to him in a kind of running commentary that he found himself bemused by. It wasn't long before they reached what was the hub of the refugee camp – the Fire Place. The Fire Place was at the centre of Farthingloe farm, near to where the farmhouse itself stood. Most nights, weather permitting, a huge fire was built and the refugees would gather around it, sitting on logs and camping chairs as closely as they could to the roaring flames. Groups would form and separate and absorb each other and disperse as the night wore on. They would share information about their daily lives and trials at the camp but mostly they talked about the war; each hopeful update giving Freetopia more men, more firepower, more virtue. People spoke in hushed, reverential tones about Stickles and Ky like they were Gods rather than the flawed men he knew them to be. He had even heard people referring to Ky by the bizarre nickname that he seemed to have acquired - The Father; said with the capital letters that made it seem all the more ridiculous. He doubted that people knew just how young Ky was but he didn't feel the need to correct them or to dilute the story in any way. These people needed their heroes. He was always silent about his own role and how he had gotten his injuries.

'Someone is at the window of the farmhouse. They're leaning out; they've got a megaphone.' The girl gasped, still clutching his arm tightly.

A stuttering whine of feedback screeched and a familiar voice rang out across the field. An incredulous smile spread across Joshua's face, defying his stomach which churned with rage as he remembered Kane. 'FARTHINGLOE FARM, I AM STICKLES.' His voice was all the more self-important and intrusive for being detached from any physical being he could see. The people roared with fierce adulation, he was carried several metres forward on a delirious wave that passed through the crowd. The girl let go of his arm as she jumped up and down next to him. Her eyes looked as though she might cry at any moment. Joshua strained to see but the horizon beyond the waves of bobbing heads was grey and blurred to him. He felt alone, an outsider in this ocean of worship. 'MY MEN HAVE WON THIS WAR. IT IS OVER. YOUR SAFETY IS GUARANTEED NOW BEYOND THE CONFINES OF THIS CAMP.' The roar that issued forth from this ragged audience was beyond joy. Many screamed their relief. People leant against one another for support. Some crouched down in the mud, their faces in their hands as they wept for lost friends, family, for their lost lives. Stickles' assault battered on filling the air until it was taut and loaded.

'IT WOULD BE DIFFICULT TO GET FOOD AND SUPPLIES TO YOU OUTSIDE OF THE CAMP, SO FOR NOW PLEASE STAY HERE WHERE WE CAN LOOK AFTER YOU. PLEASE BE ASSURED THAT WE ARE WORKING HARD TO GET YOU BACK TO YOUR HOMES AS SOON AS POSSIBLE.' At that the crowd roared so loudly that the sodden ground shook. Feet stomped throwing splashes of muddy water and flecks of dirt into the air. Joshua imagined the water being squeezed out of it by thousands of feet. 'AS WE ARE TRYING TO RESTORE ORDER WE NEED PEOPLE WITH EXPERIENCE. PLEASE WILL ANYONE WHO PREVIOUSLY WORKED FOR THE CIVIL SERVICE, PARTICULARLY NASRA, MAKE THEIR WAY TO THE

ADMINISTRATION TENT WHERE YOU WILL BE TAKEN AWAY TO HELP WITH THE INITIAL NORMALISATION PROCESS. FURTHER INFORMATION WILL FOLLOW. FREETOPIA THANK YOU FOR YOUR SUPPORT AS WE FORM AN INTERIM GOVERNMENT TO ADMINISTER THE COUNTRY BEFORE WE CAN SET UP DEMOCRATIC ELECTIONS.'

Joshua knew how those democratic elections would go. But what did it matter? The goodys had won. Hadn't they? He found himself cheering along with the girl who had helped him.

The crowd hung around, waiting for something else, maybe some kind of fanfare, something to mark such an auspicious occasion. Joshua thought that maybe they needed to be together, that happiness and relief of this magnitude could only be if it was shared with other humans. He was eager to get back to the tent, he needed to share this moment with Beth; he needed her with him. Although the Fire Place remained full, the camp's thoroughfares were thronged with people singing, dancing in the muddy puddles, hugging and kissing one another with joyful abandon. They respectfully cleared passage around him, his scarred face announcing his disability. People came up to him and hugged him spontaneously, screaming in his ear that it was over, they could return home. He shouted back happy words that he could hardly hear.

He pushed the flap door to the tent open, tentatively in case Beth and the children were still asleep.

'Where have you been?' Beth scolded. 'Have you heard the news?'

He was just about to answer, to say yes and to ask her how she knew but a voice beat him to it making him look behind him where its owner sat on a chair, holding Meditant on his lap. His smile turned into a beam as Ky rose to greet him. 'I thought you would show up to see your boy but I didn't think it would be this quickly.' Joshua said. They hugged tightly, holding on for a long time. Joshua's ravaged eyes filled with tears that he fancied cleansed and healed them.

'I missed you. I could have done with some help.' Ky replied. Joshua was surprised to hear that his voice was choked with emotion. 'Come on, let's sit down.' He gently tried to lead Joshua towards the camping chairs that they had set up as a kind of living area.

Joshua hung back and frowned slightly. 'I'm no invalid. I'm capable of standing up.'

'Yeah? Well I'm not, I'm bloody knackered.' Ky replied.

'Sorry, ignore me.' Joshua ran his hands over Ky's shoulders and squeezed him to him again. 'You've grown, you're a lot taller and where did all that stubble come from? Is this why they call you The Father now?' He smiled and led his friend by the arm to the chairs.

'Yeah…that nickname didn't come from me.' His cheeks coloured scarlet.

'You look older.' Beth said. She sat on the side of the bed with the boys.

'And you look…different.' Ky replied. 'When is he due?'

'What makes you think it's a he?' Beth sounded surprised.

'Just a hunch. He'll be a play mate for Aaron and Meditant.'

Joshua studied the muddy floor. 'Mate…we need to leave…' He said quietly, almost in shame.

'Go? Where are you going to?' Ky replied. He could hear the unmasked hurt in his voice.

'America. We've got money from Beth's family, we've been waiting for hostilities to die down enough that we can get out safely, and of course there was Med… You know he's welcome to come with us.'

'No.' He replied quickly. 'No, the fighting has stopped now, he can stay with me.'

'Ky, are you sure?' Beth said gently. 'I know it's over but Stickles can't be trusted to honour any agreements you've come to.'

'If he's going to be the interim President, he's going to have to learn to be trustworthy.' Ky replied curtly. 'Sorry…I just don't want you to go.' His voice softened.

'We know. It's ok.' Joshua said. He studied his friend's face.

Ky paused for a long moment. 'I have to leave here later this afternoon. Do you understand that you won't be allowed to leave the camp for the foreseeable future?'

'What?' Beth snapped. 'That's absurd. We came here for protection, why wouldn't they let us leave?'

'The infrastructure wouldn't be able to cope with it. Those people who are left out there are barely scraping a living. So many people have left for Europe of the States that some parts of the country are almost empty. There are camps like this up and down the country. Guys, if this is what you want then you need to go today while I can get you out. If you don't then there's no telling how long you'll be here… or what might happen.'

'What's that supposed to mean?' Joshua asked.

'Beth was right when she said that Stickles isn't to be trusted. He's already doing things that I'm not comfortable with.'

'Like what?' Joshua said.

Ky glanced around him, his pinched face was suspicious and watchful. He was reminded of the march at Speakers' Corner when they had first met. 'They're rounding up anyone who worked for NASRA or the rest of the Civil Service. '

'I heard that in his speech, he said it was to help get things working again.'

'That's what he's saying and it might be true. Like I say, I don't trust him. I saw the aftermath of some of the things he and his men did. They were as brutal as Rebuild were at times.'

They all fell silent for a long moment while the words hung potently in the air. Finally Joshua broke the silence. 'What about G4ITAS? Their guards have appeared around here. People thought that it meant Rebuild had won.'

'Don't get me started about that, Josh. In the space of a few days we've gone from fighting them to being allied to them.'

'What? How does that work?' Beth asked.

'Essentially G4ITAS were nothing but a dumb instrument; hired thugs. They were in the employ of the government. Now Freetopia have taken the reigns they are controlling the force they were fighting until Rebuild officially capitulated yesterday.'

'I don't understand.' Beth said. Her forehead creased in concentration and her bottom lip stuck out ever so slightly as if she were sulking; she looked how she had when she was a little girl. Joshua suddenly felt an immense amount of sadness for what was gone and could never be again.

'G4ITAS had nothing to do with Rebuild's ideology. Essentially they've done nothing wrong.' Joshua said, shaking his head and laughing bitterly.

Ky smiled. 'They also have a contract with the REW government as well. There's no way the country could afford to buy its way out of it.'

'But surely under the circumstances no sane corporation would take a shattered country to the International Courts?' Beth said.

'Money's money. They have a right to go about their business that is enshrined in international law.' Ky replied.

Joshua shook his head in dumbfounded wonder. 'Just tell me how I can get my family out of this broken country.' He said quietly.

*

Although it was a novelty to be in a car the motion made Joshua feel close to queasy. There was only one undamaged runway in the country that was long enough to take the kind of aircraft they were boarding. That was at Heathrow, and time was running out to get there.

'Ky, if we miss this will we get our money back?' Joshua asked nervously.

'I don't know.' He replied easily without looking back from the front passenger seat where Meditant sat on his lap. He hadn't let go of him yet. 'We'll make it, try not to worry.'

'That's easy for you to say, you've not just spent a small fortune on this.' Joshua said and sat back. Beth shifted Aaron around to free up a hand and squeezed his leg. The driver speeded up.

The rich, green landscape passed by as quickly as the scarred road would allow them to travel. The long winter was receding now and the trees were coming alive again. In the distance he could see a far off haze that speckled the sky like he was seeing the world through a bad television set. At first he thought it was his own vision, then he realised that it was blossoms taking flight in a stiff breeze. He smiled at the realisation that life went on, it repaired and regrew in its rhythms and patterns as it always had. He reminded himself that spring was now a lot earlier now than it used to be. The world wasn't impervious to man's influence however resilient it was.

They drove past a burnt out hulk of torn metal that curled like last year's dead leaves beside the road. The armoured vehicle's tyres had burnt away in the fire that had consumed it. There was a melted patch of tarmac, a guilty stain, where the vehicle had burnt before being dragged out of the way. But dragged by whom? The government? The rebels?

'The M25 has been closed for months so we're going to have to cut through London.' Ky said disturbing his thoughts.

'Have we got time?' Joshua frowned as he squinted to see the time on the car's dashboard.

'Relax, Josh, I said I'd get you there.' Ky turned around and smiled. Joshua felt like a child demanding to know if they were nearly there yet.

As they drove closer to London the landscape began to change rapidly. The green expanse between buildings began to close, houses crowded together to make lengthy, mean terraces where walls had been blasted through and windows smashed. Front doors hung open, comfort and sanctity defiled by the rough touch of looters. Scorched carcasses of tanks and armoured vehicles guarded the ruins they had created. They drove past what had once been three tower blocks, now only dust streaked stumps poked through the mountain of rubble that surrounded them. Further into the city whole streets had been all but destroyed.

Joshua imagined the rebels fleeing from office to office as fighter jets screamed low across the city dropping fire and death from their sleek bellies. He felt a pang of jealousy. Beth's hand squeezed his, annoyingly comforting. He felt like a half-man; a child who had spent the war hiding in the folds of his mother's skirt instead of fighting with his friends. He pulled his hand away. In the distance a once tall building was now a half-destroyed mangled mass of curled steel that still had chunks of concrete clinging to it like mud caught in hair; he realised it was what was left of the Shard.

'I can't believe the damage to the City.' Joshua said. 'I'm shocked that Rebuild would do that. I mean, I can believe that they would do that to people's houses but not the City. I would have thought that the banks wouldn't have let them.'

'They didn't really.' Ky replied. 'The damage to central London was done recently, in the last few weeks. It was one of the things that turned the tide in our favour. The corporations were losing their taste for war and Rebuild were becoming increasingly reckless; that's why they pulled the plug on them. They formed a board they called the Transitory Mediation Committee who decided that G4ITAS wouldn't fight on Rebuild's behalf anymore and that was that. The board decided to award governance to Freetopia until elections could be held.'

'Isn't that a bit perverse.' Beth said, clearly incredulous. 'It was the demands of the boards of those companies that caused Rebuild to start the Discard Program.'

'I agree.' Ky replied. He turned around and his grey eyes settled on them both. 'We have to have joint patrols of Freetopia troops and G4ITAS plastys because neither side really trusts the other. There are lads working alongside lads who they were trying to kill a week ago. It's madness.'

'And how do your boys fit in with all that?' Joshua asked quietly.

'They're your boys too, Josh.'

He smiled sadly. 'They were always your boys. So, what happens to you all now?'

'Freetopia will argue over the scraps of power that the corporations allow them. They'll be allowed to march around the place for a while, thinking they're in charge, until they have to be reined in. By then Freetopia will be embroiled in the political side of things, open to shirt-and-tie assaults on all sides. They'll bend over and take it like every government before them and every one that comes after.'

Joshua grinned widely. 'True enough. And what about you and *our* boys?'

'We'll slip away until we're needed again.' Ky replied. He smiled. It was as crooked and uncomfortable as it had ever been. 'And what of you two? What does the future hold?'

Joshua thought about it for a moment and took Beth's hand. Aaron placed his on theirs and gurgled as if pointing out how clever he was. 'Peace and family.' He said at last.

Chapter 37

Anthony stepped from the back of the mopaxi and handed the driver a wrinkled and grubby ten bancor note. The driver looked at it with nonchalant disgust before plunging back into the snarling, beeping mechanised river of Marsham Street. He scanned the crowd looking for Lee. Every face in the busy lunch time rush was familiar. The faces, they were always from the platform or the camp or Selina's. They were never from NASRA or life before.

Everyone over a certain pay grade who worked for NASRA had been arbitrarily rounded up and imprisoned, ironically, in the old Saddleworth Moor camp – most recently known as DPC04. The knowing crowd passed around him, hiding their attention and accusatory stares behind a smokescreen of apathy. *I'm not fooled.* He was public enemy number one. The Beast of Saddleworth, or so the lurid Vircorp News had christened him. It had only been a year now since the end of hostilities, but how could they not know?

Anthony moved away from the road. He leaned casually against the glass wall of the Home Office and lit a cigarette. From where he stood he could see a steady stream of people leaving the main entrance to go for their lunch. A fresh-faced crowd, most of them would have been at university recently, or they were poached from the business world. They were part of the re-branding of government, the future administration for a fairer, more open and prosperous time, or so the newspaper said. Entire departments had been sacked or imprisoned, the executions of the higher ranking executives were still taking place. As he watched the exodus he saw himself and Josh, laughing as they pushed through the crowds, eager to get to the pub. He smiled and took a drag of his cigarette. His eyes misted up slightly but it felt good, it felt human. He caught sight of a newspaper seller standing next to a box that advertised that day's edition. Hastily scrawled across the front were the words 'Exclusive: Inside the Death Camps by Beth Thomas.' Anthony smiled. *Mum and Dad would have been so proud.* He took a paper and dropped some coins into the man's out stretched hand and folded it for later examination. Assuming there was a later.

'So where's the place Mr…Boyle?' Lee said from behind him.

Anthony whirled around, instantly on his guard. He relaxed as he saw who it was. 'It's close by.' He snapped. 'I didn't want to get dropped directly outside.' Lee grimly nodded his understanding.

The busy streets still bothered Anthony. All it took was one face, one flicker of recognition and the dogs would be on him. The press knew his name but not his face. So far.

Masterton was the first one they found. Anthony had watched his execution a few weeks ago, broadcast live on a pay-per-view channel; it was worth every cent. They rounded a corner and the view across Lambeth Bridge lay in front of them. Sunlight reflected off the sluggish Thames lending a brightness that seemed almost hopeful to Anthony. They turned right onto Millbank passing by heavy doors, embossed with stars and patterns. An engraved plaque told them they had reached Thames House.

The letter had appeared under the bedroom door of the cheap bed-sit he and Lee were forced to share. He had stared at it for an eternity, too afraid to pick it up. Lee had still been asleep, but he had seen it appear, pushed gently from the other side. He'd heard the floor boards creak under unseen weight. Heard them settle as the shadow left again. Mr Thomas, emblazoned across the front of the envelope. His real name seemed to scream at him from the white paper; his guilt and shame written for all to see. Somehow just those two words whose presence was so woven into his life condemned him to the reality of who and what he was. Finally he had opened it with a sickly dread.

Dear Mr Thomas,

We would like to summon you and your associate to a meeting at Thames House on 6th February at 12.30. Your attendance is mandatory. Failure to attend will result in details of your exact whereabouts being passed to the Genocide Investigation Committee.

Yours Faithfully

Edward Durban

Lee had wanted to run, to try and make it to a cross channel ferry and disappear onto the continent. Anthony knew it would do them no good. They'd shown their hand, they would be watching, waiting for them to make a break for it. The Genocide Investigation Committee had recruited operatives from the Resets, from the estates that hadn't been cleared yet and from the streets. Freetopia still didn't trust G4ITAS to be impartial and men were needed from somewhere. The thirst of these young men for retribution made them dogged, obsessive, incorruptible and brutal. If their location had been passed to the GIC they would have been arrested by now. Someone still had a use for them. But who? NASRA were disbanded, as were MI5 who had resided at Thames House. He vaguely knew an Edward Durban but he was a low ranking civil servant. There was no choice, they had to go.

The grand, arched entrance of Thames House was like a gaping mouth. Blue panels set with flowers lined the archway lending it an oriental look that felt incongruous with the neo-classical building. Orderly crowds passing through the turnstiles just inside the doors paid them no attention. Smiling faces, temporarily freed from the burden of work; Suits, sick of the bureaucracy but marking time; bored security, same uniforms, same faces. Paper, meetings, performance charts, security bulletins, IT logins, coffee, air-con, sneezes. They all smelt corrupt, sour. They worked in the grave, a bubble of sensory deprivation where colour was grey, light was gloom and the senses were dulled by grinding monotony. Anthony wondered if he would ever walk out again or if he would be bundled out into waiting meat wagons under a hailstorm of flashing lights and shouting journalists. *I may never walk free in the daylight again. At least I walked free for a while.* It was more than could be said for these bored corpses. He shivered as he remembered seeing Masterton's lifeless form twitching at the end of a rope, surrounded by prison guards who leered for the cameras.

They left daylight outside. They joined the queue for the security check. Two large guards manned a metal detector, searching bags, asking questions. A smartly dressed man approached them as they waited. 'Mr Thomas? I'm Roberts I'll take you to Mr Durban.' He flinched on hearing his name spoken out loud. The guards watched as Anthony and Lee were ushered past the waiting line of people and stepped around the metal detector. A dozen pairs of eyes watched them, jealously. Who were they? High ranking officials, too important to be checked? Foreign dignitaries exempt under international law? *Those who come willingly to die?* Anthony shuddered, for the first time he doubted his wisdom in coming here.

 The corridors of Thames House were bustling with people. Trolleys passed them by carrying boxes of paper and dusty computers wrapped in clear plastic. 'Things seem busy here Mr Roberts.' Anthony's voice was collected but his heart thumped aggressively against his ribcage.

'Even a year on we still have masses of information to collate and destroy. As I'm sure you are aware MI5 no longer exists and so all traces of its existence are still being…removed.'

'Including the staff?' Anthony smiled wryly.

Roberts gazed back coolly. 'Including some of the staff. Obviously not all were implicated in the Discard Program so we've had to tread lightly. Here we are.'

Roberts showed Anthony and Lee into a large office that smelt of new leather. Books lined the walls from floor to ceiling, their spines uncreased. Stacked crates sat in a corner. Behind a large desk sat Edward Durban. Anthony had met Durban several times at the Home Office before moving north. He had found him an intelligent, if quiet man. Too quiet for his own good had always been Anthony's opinion. As he squirmed under the man's intense scrutiny it occurred that quietness could be the silk glove over an iron fist.

'Mr Thomas, Mr Cross. Sit down.' Durban gestured with one flabby hand.

'I'm pleased to see you again, Mr Durban. Although our presence here is hardly in keeping with the government's stated transparency… I'm pretty sure the press would have a field day if they knew we were here.'

Ed Durban raised his eyebrows and chuckled. He took off his glasses and shook his head in bemusement. 'If you are trying to threaten me I would remind you of your position. What is said in this office is beyond the hearing of the sharpened talons of the hypocritical press. The witch hunt is on, Mr Thomas, it takes a special man to weave his way through the minefield that the last few years have produced. If you think that I wouldn't pay VirCorp News the requisite ten bancor to see you dancing on the end of rope you are sorely mistaken.'

Anthony grinned. 'I'm in no position to make threats, I'm merely making conversation. But you've not told me your secret yet, Mr Durban. You've survived the minefield.'

'The secret is in covering one's own arse. Something that you seem to have managed quite well. Tell me, how is it that out of all the higher ranking NASRA officers deployed to the DPC's and sorting stations, you alone have managed to elude the GIC?'

'I covered my arse, Mr Durban.' Anthony replied without irony.

Durban chuckled indulgently. 'Yes Mr Thomas, I'm sure you did. I imagine you would like to know why the pair of you haven't been handed over to the dogs?'

'Well, yes. As you've pointed out, my colleagues, guilty or not, have all been arrested or executed. I guessed you'd catch up with us at some point but I wasn't expecting this.'

'Please do not confuse me with those uncultured dogs at the GIC; terrible fellows hell-bent on revenge. They have no understanding of government process and culpability. You didn't take the decision to start the Discard Programme did you? No of course you didn't. Look, Mr Thomas, no-one in the civil service wanted a witch hunt. The figure heads of this administration rolled into governance on a wave of public support; a populist armed coup. Is this any way for a civilised country to behave? The sacrificial lambs have been slaughtered to appease the public fervour for such events, now the dust is settling we need to move forward. It seems that the new government want to create a new agency, MI5 has been tarnished and the public won't accept its existence anymore. However we still have a need for a domestic intelligence service and we need people who are qualified to fill the open vacancies. Mr Thomas your interrogation methods proved to be most effective and they did not go unnoticed. We would like you to head up a division of the newly formed Home Intelligence Service – The HIS.'

'And what division might that be Mr Durban?'

'Why, interrogation, Mr Thomas. The need for effective dialogue with our enemies will never go away. The country needs people like you and Mr Cross.'

Anthony laughed heartily for the first time in months. It felt good. 'Allow me to get this straight Mr Durban. Our new government, whose mandate is based solely on their opposition of acts of violence, want an agency to protect their position. Does that about cover it?'

'Mr Thomas, I'm sure you understand that an unelected government who have inherited such problems as they have will soon find themselves in an untenable position unless they stay on top of the malcontents who think that they can do a better job.'

'Although strictly speaking they themselves are malcontents who thought that they could do a better job?' A wry grin spread across his face. He leant back in his chair and exchanged a glance with Lee.

'Even more reason for them to be wary. The only shadow that we should ever really fear should be our own.' Durban tried to look stern.

Anthony threw his head back and laughed. 'Ok, Mr Durban, count me in.'

THE END